PRAISE FOR BRAD MELTZER'S *NEW YORK TIMES* BESTSELLING NOVELS

THE INNER CIRCLE

"All of Brad's books are a fascinating read. He is a great storyteller who keeps all of us on the edge of our seats...His new book is sitting on my desk right now, but not for long." —President George H. W. Bush

"[Meltzer] is an architect. His structures are towering, intricate, elegant, and surprising—but always grounded in humanity and logic." —Joss Whedon

"No other writer spins a yarn with so many expertly crafted layers as Meltzer and *The Inner Circle* is probably his best ever. An extraordinary accomplishment not to be missed from the finest storyteller going today."

—*Providence Journal*

"Excellent...engaging...Meltzer expertly develops the story." —*Booklist*

"Fascinating." —*Publishers Weekly*

"Meltzer manages to make all this historical info fascinating...I heartily recommend this book, which I hope will be the strong start of a dynamite series."

—*Washington Independent Review of Books*

"After a fast-paced opening, Meltzer sets the stage for another roller-coaster ride." —*Florida Times-Union*

"When it comes to penning crisp, crackerjack conspiracy thrillers, there's no one better than Meltzer."

—*American Way*

THE BOOK OF LIES

"A stunning tour de force...already a great storyteller, Meltzer rises here to the level of great novelist as well."

—*Providence Journal*

"Faster than a speeding bullet...Readers don't have much time to focus on anything other than catching their breath...The payoff is a doozie, though getting there is half the fun."

—*New York Daily News*

"Part *The Da Vinci Code* and part *North by Northwest* and chock-full of plot twists...artfully blends fact and fiction...you won't be able to put it down."

—*Boston Herald*

"A hot novel."

—Liz Smith, *New York Post*

"Has all the elements of a heart-pounding contemporary thriller, including wild twists, a homicidal maniac, and a maddeningly tense quest...A novel that succeeds on several levels...And when Cal resolutely sees things through to the ultimate conclusion, the truth the book reveals is simply exquisite."

—*Miami Herald*

"Terrific...a stunning suspense novel."

—Lou Dobbs, CNN

"Meltzer's tale of intrigue and pathos in politics engrosses." —*Entertainment Weekly*

"Fast-paced, page-turning...a fascinating insider take on D.C. politics." —Associated Press

"Lots of action...Much more skillfully written—and far more plausible—than Dan Brown's tedious bestseller...Fluidly integrated historical fact and fiction...Fans of thrillers that reach far back into history will be, well...thrilled." —*Booklist*

THE ZERO GAME

"Terrifying...astounds...electric." —*Associated Press*

"Playing games comes naturally in Washington, D.C. Here Meltzer takes it to new heights."
—*New York Daily News*

"High-octane suspense...an excellent suspense novel... rewarding." —*Oklahoman*

"An exciting novel filled with insider information about the inner workings of Congress." —*Roanoke Times*

"Rip-roaring...nonstop action...relentless...a clever hook...readers will be left breathless."
—*Publishers Weekly*

"Unforgettable...explosive...a *must*-read!...Proves Meltzer is at the top of his game." —*Exclusive Magazine*

THE MILLIONAIRES

"A fast-paced thriller...with a playful sense of humor...
a classic chase."　　　　　*—Detroit Free Press*

"Hair-raising...well-written...Excellent."
　　　　　　　　　　　　　　—Tampa Tribune

"A giddy thriller...banking, cybertheft, and Disney
World in a fast-paced tale of financial adventure."
　　　　　　　　　　　　　　—Publishers Weekly

"Good fun...Meltzer, often called the Grisham of financial thrillers, has a knack for keeping a story moving
while still throwing in plenty of insider information."
　　　　　　　　　　　　　　—Booklist

"A wild financial thriller...a Mad Hatter ride leading to
the audience singing Brad Meltzer's praise for an enlightening, exciting, and entertaining story."
　　　　　　　　　　　　　　—Midwest Book Review

THE FIRST COUNSEL

"Deliciously hard-boiled prose...pedal-to-the-metal pacing all the way to the climax."　　*—Entertainment Weekly*

"Impressive...fast-paced and suspenseful throughout."
　　　　　　　　　　　　　　—People

"A book for which the phrase 'page-turner' was meant."
　　　　　　　　　　　　　　—Chicago Tribune

"Ups the ante for legal thrillers with its intricate plot and clever, complex characters. Most impressive is Meltzer's knowledge of every nook of the White House. With all its grand history and mystery, the mansion comes alive."

—*People*

"Curl up in front of the fire with [this] edge-of-your-seat thriller." —*Cosmopolitan*

DEAD EVEN

"Heart-stopping intensity." —*San Francisco Chronicle*

"A gem of a plot...So strong...breezes along in high gear. Highly recommended." —*Chicago Tribune*

"Terrific...reads like a Tracy-Hepburn movie...complete with cliffhangers at the end of every chapter and a truly scary ending." —*Newsday*

"Gets the blood pounding."
—*New York Times Book Review*

"Races along...deftly written...haunting."
—*Entertainment Weekly*

"An absolute page-turner." —*Detroit News*

THE TENTH JUSTICE

"Inventive...fresh...thoroughly enjoyable."
—*Washington Post Book World*

ALSO BY BRAD MELTZER

The INNER CIRCLE

BRAD MELTZER

GRAND CENTRAL
PUBLISHING

NEW YORK   BOSTON

Grand Central Publishing
Hachette Book Group
1290 Avenue of the Americas
New York, NY 10104

www.HachetteBookGroup.com

Grand Central Publishing is a division of Hachette Book Group, Inc.
The Grand Central Publishing name and logo are trademarks of Hachette Book Group, Inc.

The Hachette Speakers Bureau provides a wide range of authors for speaking events. To find out more, go to www.hachettespeakersbureau.com or call (866) 376-6591.

The publisher is not responsible for websites (or their content) that are not owned by the publisher.

Printed in the United States of America

Originally published in hardcover by Hachette Book Group
First international mass market edition: July 2011
First U.S. oversize mass market edition: October 2011
First U.S. mass market edition: April 2015

10 9 8 7 6 5 4 3 2 1
OPM

For Theo,
my son,
who came into my life
when I needed him most

ACKNOWLEDGMENTS

I know who's in my inner circle. Many of them are listed below—including you, treasured readers, who give me the support that still lets me do this. So thank you to the following: My first love and first lady, Cori, who pushes me, challenges me, fights me, but most important, believes in me. Since junior high. Jonas, Lila, and Theo are my greatest and most beautiful treasures, and they astonish me every single day. There is no greater love than the love I have for them. Jill Kneerim, the patron saint of agents, who remains my steadfast champion and dear friend; Hope Denekamp, Caroline Zimmerman, Ike Williams, and all our friends at the Kneerim & Williams Agency.

This is a book about history and friendship—and the profound power when you combine the two. But it's also about what we'll do for our families, so let me thank mine, beginning with my dad, who taught me how to fight, especially when it came to those I love most, and my sister Bari, who continues to teach me even more of the same. Also to Will, Bobby, Ami, Adam, and Gilda, for everything a family can be.

Here's a secret: As a writer, you can only be as good as the readers you share your first drafts with. So let me start with the reader whom I couldn't do this without: Noah Kuttler. For every page I write, Noah hears it first. He is ruthless, insightful—and never takes his eyes off the craft. He's the one I count on to make sure I'm being intellectually honest—and also to make sure I'm not being the middle-aged cliché that my body so wants to be. Ethan Kline has read and improved every early draft since I started writing; and Dale Flam, Matt Kuttler, Chris Weiss, and Judd Winick have saved me in more ways than they'll ever realize.

In a novel so steeped in our nation's history, I owe the following people tremendous thanks for sharing that history: First, President George H. W. Bush, who inspired so much of this during a cherished conversation I will never forget. And while we're on the subject, let me thank the man himself—George Washington—for being such a wild genius (you'll see what I mean inside). At the National Archives, which everyone should go visit, Susan Cooper, Matt Fulgham, Miriam Kleiman, and Trevor Plante were my masterminds and guides. They answered every insane question I threw at them, and the best part of this process has been the friendship that we've shared. Special thanks to Paul Brachfeld and his amazing team, including Kelly Maltagliati, Ross Weiland, and Mitchell Yockelson, who I admire so much; Lisa Monaco, Ben Powell, Brian White, and all my friends at the Department of Homeland Security's Red Cell program for helping push this idea even further;

White House doctor Connie Mariano and my pals at the Secret Service took me back inside my favorite white building; Debby Baptiste toured me through the underground storage caves; Steve Baron for the St. Elizabeths's details; my confidants Dean Alban, Arturo de Hoyos, Brent Morris, Tom Savini, and Mark Tabbert for their great historical insight; and the rest of my own inner circle, whom I bother for every book: Jo Ayn Glanzer, Mark Dimunation, Dr. Lee Benjamin, Dr. David Sandberg, Dr. Ronald K. Wright, Edna Farley, Jason Sherry, Marie Grunbeck, Brad Desnoyer, and Kim from L.A. More Archives research came from Juliette Arai, Judy Barnes, Greg Bradsher, Cynthia Fox, Brenda Kepley, John Laster, Sue McDonough, Connie Potter, Gary Stern, Eric VanSlander, Mike Waesche, Dave Wallace, Morgan Zinsmeister, and in memory of John E. Taylor; thanks to A. J. Jacobs and Michael Scheck for their idiosyncrasies. The books *George Washington, Spymaster* by Thomas B. Allen and *Washington's Spies* by Alexander Rose were vital to this process. Finally, Roberta Stevens, Anne Twomey, Kevin Wolkenfeld, Alison Coleman, Pat Finati, Phyllis Jones, Linda Perlstein, and the great people at Mount Vernon lent their expertise to so many different details; Ananda Breslof, Kim Echols, Steve Ferguson, and Pansy Narendorf lent themselves; and these friends on Facebook and Twitter lent even more personal character traits: Steven Bates, Beth Bryans, Denise Duncan, Scott Fogg, Abraham Medina, Hector Miray, Matthew Mizner, Lisa Shearman, and Jason Spencer; Rob Weisbach for the initial faith;

and of course, my family and friends, whose names, as usual, inhabit these pages.

I also want to thank everyone at Grand Central Publishing: David Young, Emi Battaglia, Jennifer Romanello, Evan Boorstyn, Chris Barba, Martha Otis, Karen Torres, Lizzy Kornblit, the nicest and hardest-working sales force in show business, Mari Okuda, Thomas Whatley, and all the kind friends there who have spent so much time and energy building what we've always built. I've said it before, and it never changes: They're the real reason this book is in your hands. Special love to Mitch Hoffman, who never stopped editing and is a true part of the family. Finally, let me thank Jamie Raab. Over the past two years, we've shared overwhelming losses and watched our lives change together. Through that time, I've realized she doesn't just edit me. She lends me her strength. For that, I owe her forever. Thank you, Jamie, for bringing me home, and most important, for your faith.

EXITUS ACTA PROBAT

George Washington

In 1989, during his final minutes in the White House, outgoing President Ronald Reagan scribbled a secret note—and, it was reported, a picture of a turkey. The note said, "Don't let the turkeys get you down." He then slipped the note into the Oval Office desk and left it for his successor, President George H. W. Bush.

In 1993, President Bush left a private note in the desk for Bill Clinton, who left a note for George W. Bush, who left one for Barack Obama.

But there were two things no one knew.

The tradition didn't start with Ronald Reagan. It started with George Washington.

And the picture Reagan drew? It most definitely was *not* a turkey.

PROLOGUE

He knew the room was designed to hold secrets.

Big secrets.

The briefcase from Watergate was opened in a room like this. Same with the first reports from 9/11.

He knew that this room—sometimes called the Tank or the Vault—held presidential secrets, national secrets, and *pine-box* secrets, as in, the kinds of secrets that came with coffins.

But as he stood in the back corner of the small, plain beige room, swaying in place and flicking the tip of his tongue against the back of his front teeth, the archivist with the scratched black reading glasses knew that the most vital thing in the room wasn't a classified file or a top-secret sheet of paper—it was the polished, rosy-cheeked man who sat alone at the single long table in the center of the room.

He knew not to talk to the rosy-cheeked man.

He knew not to bother him.

All he had to do was stand there and watch. Like a babysitter.

It was absurd, really.

But that was the job.

For nearly an hour now.

Babysitting the most powerful man in the world: the President of the United States.

Hence the secure room.

Yet for all the secrets that had been in this room, the archivist with the scratched black-framed reading glasses had no idea what he'd soon be asked to hide.

With a silent breath through his nose, the archivist stared at the back of the President, then glanced over at the blond Secret Service agent on his far right.

The visits here had been going on since President Orson Wallace was first elected. Clinton liked to jog. George W. Bush watched baseball games in the White House Residence. Obama played basketball. All Presidents find their own way to relax. More bookish than most, President Orson Wallace traveled the few blocks from the White House and came to the National Archives to, of all things, read.

He'd been doing it for months now. Sometimes he even brought his daughter or eight-year-old son. Sure, he could have every document delivered right to the Oval Office, but as every President knew, there was something about getting out of the house. And so the "reading visits" began. He started with letters that George Washington wrote to Benedict Arnold, moved to classified JFK memos, and on to today's current objects of fascination: Abraham Lincoln's handwritten Civil War notes. Back then, if there was a capital case during a court-martial, the vote of "life or death" would come straight to Lincoln's desk. The President would personally decide. So in the chaos of President Wallace's current life, there was apparently something reassuring about seeing the odd curves and shaky swirls in Lincoln's own handwriting.

And that, as Wallace scribbled a few personal notes on his legal pad, was a hell of a lot more calming than playing basketball.

"Four more minutes, sir," the blond Secret Service agent announced from the back corner, clearing his throat.

President Wallace nodded slightly, beginning to pack up, but never turning around. "Is Ronnie joining us or no?"

At that, the archivist with the scratched reading glasses stood up straight. His supervisor, Ronald Cobb, was one of President Wallace's oldest friends from law school. It was Cobb who usually managed the visits and selected which priceless files the President would read. But with his recent diagnosis of pancreatic cancer, Cobb wasn't going anywhere for a bit.

"Mr. Cobb's at a chemo appointment, sir," the archivist explained in a voice that seemed strained even to himself.

Again, President Wallace nodded without turning around, flipping his legal pad shut.

It was the quick motion of the legal pad that caught the archivist's eye. For a moment, as the pale yellow pages fanned forward, he could swear one of the brown, mottled Lincoln letters was tucked inside.

The archivist squinted, trying to see. But from the angle he was at, diagonally behind the left shoulder of the President, the Lincoln document was—

No.

This was the President of the United States. He'd never...

No, the archivist told himself.

No. Not a chance. No.

"Before we go, I just need to hit the little vice president's room," President Wallace said, using the joke that always got him easy laughs with donors. He stood from his seat and held his legal pad at his side.

According to current research, when faced with an awkward social situation, the average person will wait seventeen seconds before breaking the silence.

"Mr. President," the archivist called out without even hesitating. "I'm sorry, but—"

President Wallace turned slowly, showing off his calming gray eyes and flashing the warm, fatherly grin that had won him the governorship of Ohio as well as the White House. "Son, I just need to run to the restroom, and then we can—"

"It'll just take a second," the archivist promised.

The room was no bigger than a classroom. Before the archivist knew it, he was standing in front of Wallace, blocking the President's path to the door. The blond agent stepped forward. Wallace motioned him back.

"Tell me the crisis, son," the President asked, his grin still keeping everything calm.

"I just... urr..." the archivist stammered, slowly starting to sway. "I'm sure it was just an honest mistake, sir, but I think you may've accidentally...huhh...In your notepad." The archivist took a deep breath. "One of the Lincoln letters."

The President laughed and went to step around the archivist.

The archivist laughed back.

And stepped directly in front of the President. Again.

President Wallace's gray eyes slowly shrank into two black slits. He was far too savvy to lose his temper with a stranger, but that didn't mean it was easy to keep that grin on his face. "Victor, I need you to excuse us a moment."

"Sir..." the blond agent protested.

"Victor..." the President said. That's all it took.

With a click and a loud metal *crunk*, the metal door to the Vault opened and Victor joined the other three agents stationed in the corridor outside.

Staring at the archivist, the President squeezed his fist around the legal pad. "Son, I want you to be very careful about what your next words are."

The archivist craned his neck back, taking in the full height of the President, who was so close the archivist could see the golden eagle and the presidential seal on Wallace's cuff links. *We have a set of LBJ's cuff links in our collection*, the archivist reminded himself for no reason whatsoever. And as he looked up at the most powerful man on the planet—as he studied the leader of the free world—it took far less than seventeen seconds to give his answer.

"I'm sorry, Mr. President. But those Lincoln documents aren't yours."

For a moment, the President didn't move. Didn't blink. Like he was frozen in time.

There was a deep *thunk* from behind the archivist. The metal door to the room clicked open.

"I toldja, right, Mr. President?" a familiar midwestern voice called out as the door clanged into the wall. The archivist turned just in time to see his boss, Ronnie Cobb, hobble inside, faster than usual. "I told you he'd come through. No reason to bother with Beecher."

The President smiled—a real smile—at his old friend and put a hand on the archivist's shoulder. "Good for you," he announced.

"I-I don't understand," the archivist said, still focused on Cobb. "I thought your chemo..." He looked at Cobb, then the President, then back to Cobb, who was beaming like a new father. "What the heck's going on?"

"Didn't you ever see *Willy Wonka*?" Cobb asked as he limped a few steps closer. "The big prize goes to the one who tells the truth."

The archivist paused a moment, looking at the two men. "What're you talking about? Why'd you mention Beecher?"

"Relax—we've got something a lot better than a spooky chocolate factory," President Orson Wallace said as he closed the door to the Vault, once again keeping his Secret Service agents outside. "Welcome to the Culper Ring."

1

There are stories no one knows. Hidden stories.

I love those stories.

And since I work in the National Archives, I find those stories for a living. They're almost always about other people. Not today. Today, I'm finally in the story—a bit player in a story about...

"Clementine. Today's the day, right?" Orlando asks through the phone from his guardpost at the sign-in desk. "Good for you, brother. I'm proud of you."

"What's that supposed to mean?" I ask suspiciously.

"It means, *Good. I'm proud*," he says. "I know what you've been through, Beecher. And I know how hard it is to get back in the race."

Orlando thinks he knows me. And he does. For the past year of my life, I was engaged to be married. He knows what happened to Iris. And what it did to my life—or what's left of it.

"So Clementine's your first dip back in the pool, huh?" he asks.

"She's not a pool."

"Ooh, she's a hot tub?"

"Orlando. Please. Stop," I say, lifting the phone cord so it doesn't touch the two neat piles I allow on my desk, or the prize of my memorabilia collection: a brass perpetual calendar where the paper scrolls inside are permanently dialed to June 19. The calendar used to belong to Henry Kissinger. June 19 is supposedly the last day he used it, which is why I taped a note across the base of it that says, *Do Not Use/Do Not Change.*

"So whattya gonna say to her?"

"You mean, besides *Hello*?" I ask.

"That's it? *Hello*?" Orlando asks. "*Hello*'s what you say to your sister. I thought you wanted to impress her."

"I don't need to impress her."

"Beecher, you haven't seen this girl in what—fifteen years? You need to impress her."

I sit on this a moment. He knows I don't like surprises. Most archivists don't like surprises. That's why we work in the past. But as history teaches me every day, the best way to avoid being surprised is to be prepared.

"Just tell me when she's here," I say.

"Why, so you can come up with something more mundane than *Hello*?"

"Will you stop with the mundane. I'm exciting. I am. I go on adventures every day."

"No, you *read* about adventures every day. You put your nose in books every day. You're like Indiana Jones, but just the professor part."

"That doesn't make me mundane."

"Beecher, right now I know you're wearing your red-

and-blue Wednesday tie. And you wanna know why? Because it's *Wednesday*."

I look down at my red-and-blue tie. "Indiana Jones is still cool."

"No, Indiana Jones *was* cool. But only when he was out experiencing life. You need to get outta your head and outta your comfort zone."

"What happened to the earnest you're-so-proud-of-me speech?"

"I am proud—but it doesn't mean I don't see what you're doing with this girl, Beech. Yes, it's a horror what happened with Iris. And yes, I understand why it'd make you want to hide in your books. But now that you're finally trying to heal the scab, who do you pick? The safety-net high school girlfriend from fifteen years in your past. Does that sound like a man embracing his future?"

I shake my head. "She wasn't my girlfriend."

"In your head, I bet she was," Orlando shoots back. "The past may not hurt you, Beecher. But it won't challenge you either," he adds. "Oh, and do me a favor: When you run down here, don't try to do it in under two minutes. It's just another adventure in your brain."

Like I said, Orlando knows me. And he knows that when I ride the elevator, or drive to work, or even shower in the morning, I like to time myself—to find my personal best.

"Wednesday is always Wednesday. *Do Not Change.*" Orlando laughs as I stare at the note on the Kissinger calendar.

"Just tell me when she's here," I repeat.

"Why else you think I'm calling, Dr. Jones? Guess who just checked in?"

As he hangs up the phone, my heart flattens in my chest. But what shocks me the most is, it doesn't feel all that bad. I'm not sure it feels good. Maybe it's good. It's hard to tell after Iris. But it feels like someone clawed away a thick spiderweb from my memory, a spiderweb that I didn't even realize had settled there.

Of course, the memory's of her. Only she could do this to me.

Back in eighth grade, Clementine Kaye was my very first kiss. It was right after the bright red curtains opened and she won the Battle of the Bands (she was a band of one) with Joan Jett's "I Love Rock'n Roll." I was the short kid who worked the spotlights with the coffee-breath A/V teacher. I was also the very first person Clementine saw backstage, which was when she planted my first real wet one on me.

Think of your first kiss. And what it meant to you.

That's Clementine to me.

Speedwalking out into the hallway, I fight to play cool. I don't get sick—I've never been sick—but that feeling of flatness has spread through my whole chest. After my two older sisters were born—and all the chaos that came with them—my mother named me Beecher in hopes that my life would be as calm and serene as a beach. This is not that moment.

There's an elevator waiting with its doors wide open. I make a note. According to a Harvard psychologist, the reason we think that we always choose the slow line in the supermarket is because frustration is more emotionally charged, so the bad moments are more memorable. That's why we don't remember all the times we chose the fast line and zipped right through. But I like remembering those times. I *need* those times. And the moment I stop remembering those times, I need to go back to Wisconsin and leave D.C. "Remember this elevator next time you're on the slow line," I whisper to myself, searching for calm. It's a good trick.

But it doesn't help.

"Letsgo, letsgo..." I mutter as I hold the Door Close button with all my strength. I learned that one during my first week in the Archives: When you have a bigwig who you're taking around, hold the Door Close button and the elevator won't stop at any other floors.

We're supposed to only use it with bigwigs.

But as far as I'm concerned, in my personal universe, there's no one bigger than this girl—this woman...she's a woman now—who I haven't seen since her hippie, lounge-singer mom moved her family away in tenth grade and she forever left my life. In our religious Wisconsin town, most people were thrilled to see them go.

I was sixteen. I was crushed.

Today, I'm thirty. And (thanks to her finding me on Facebook) Clementine is just a few seconds away from being back.

As the elevator bounces to a halt, I glance at my digital watch. Two minutes, forty-two seconds. I take Orlando's advice and decide to go with a compliment. I'll

·tell her she looks good. *No. Don't focus on just her looks. You're not a shallow meathead. You can do better*, I decide as I take a deep breath. *You really turned out good*, I say to myself. That's nicer. Softer. A true compliment. *You really turned out good.*

But as the elevator doors part like our old bright red curtains, as I anxiously dart into the lobby, trying with every element of my being to look like I'm not darting at all, I search through the morning crowd of guests and researchers playing bumper cars in their winter coats as they line up to go through the metal detector at security.

For two months now, we've been chatting via email, but I haven't seen Clementine in nearly fifteen years. How do I even know what she...?

"Nice tie," Orlando calls from the sign-in desk. He points to the far right corner, by the lobby's Christmas tree, which is (Archives tradition) decorated with shredded paper. *"Look."*

Standing apart from the crowd, a woman with short dyed black hair—dyed even darker than Joan Jett—raises her chin, watching me as carefully as I watch her. Her eye makeup is thick, her skin is pale, and she's got silver rings on her pinkies and thumbs, making her appear far more New York than D.C. But what catches me off guard is that she looks...somehow...older than me. Like her ginger brown eyes have seen two lifetimes. But that's always been who she was. She may've been my first kiss, but I know I wasn't hers. She was the girl who dated the guys two grades above us. More experienced. More advanced.

The exact opposite of Iris.

"*Clemmi...*" I mouth, not saying a word.

"*Benjy...*" she mouths back, her cheeks rising in a smile as she uses the nickname my mom used to call me.

Synapses fire in my brain and I'm right back in church, when I first found out that Clementine had never met her dad (her mom was nineteen and never said who the boy was). My dad died when I was three years old.

Back then, when combined with the kiss, I thought that made Clementine Kaye my destiny—especially for the three-week period when she was home with mono and I was the one picked to bring her assignments home for her. I was going to be in her room—near her guitar and her bra (Me. Puberty.)—and the excitement was so overwhelming, as I knocked on her front door, right there, my nose began to bleed.

Really.

Clementine saw the whole thing—even helped me get the tissues that I rolled into the nerd plugs that I stuffed in my nostrils. I was the short kid. Easy pickings. But she never made fun—never laughed—never told the story of my nosebleed to anyone.

Today, I don't believe in destiny. But I do believe in history. That's what Orlando will never understand. There's nothing more powerful than history, which is the one thing I have with this woman.

"Lookatyou," she hums in a soulful but lilting voice that sounds like she's singing even when she's just talking. It's the same voice I remember from high school— just scratchier and more worn. For the past few years, she's been working at a small jazz radio station out in Virginia. I can see why. In just her opening note, a familiar tingly exhilaration crawls below my skin. A feeling like anything's possible.

A crush.

For the past year, I'd forgotten what it felt like.

"Beecher, you're so... You're handsome!"

My heart reinflates, nearly bursting a hole in my chest. Did she just—?

"You are, Beecher! You turned out great!"

My line. That's my line, I tell myself, already searching for a new one. *Pick something good. Something kind. And genuine. This is your chance. Give her something so perfect, she'll dream about it.*

"So... er... Clemmi," I finally say, rolling back and forth from my big toes to my heels as I notice her nose piercing, a sparkling silver stud that winks right at me. "Wanna go see the Declaration of Independence?"

Kill me now.

She lowers her head, and I wait for her to laugh.

"I wish I could, but—" She reaches into her purse and pulls out a folded-up sheet of paper. Around her wrist, two vintage wooden bracelets click-clack together. I almost forgot. The real reason she came here.

"You sure you're okay doing this?" Clementine asks.

"Will you stop already," I tell her. "Mysteries are my specialty."

2

Seventeen years ago
Sagamore, Wisconsin

E veryone knows when there's a fight in the schoolyard.

No one has to say a word—it's telepathic. From
ancient to modern times, the human animal knows how to
find fighting. And seventh graders know how to find it
faster than anyone.

That's how it was on this day, after lunch, with everyone humming from their Hawaiian Punch and Oreo
cookies, when Vincent Paglinni stole Josh Wert's basketball.

In truth, the ball didn't belong to Josh Wert—it belonged to the school—but that wasn't why Paglinni took
it.

When it came to the tribes of seventh grade, Paglinni
came from a warrior tribe that was used to taking what
wasn't theirs. Josh Wert came from a chubby tribe and
was born different than most, with a genius IQ and the

kind of parents who told him never to hide it. Plus, he had a last name like *Wert*, which appeared in just that order— *W-E-R-T*—on the keyboard of every computer.

"Give it back!" Josh Wert insisted, not using his big brain and making the mistake of calling attention to what had happened.

Paglinni ignored the demand, refusing to even face him.

"I-I want my ball back!" Josh Wert added, sucking in his gut and trying so hard to stand strong.

By now, the tribe of seventh graders was starting to gather. They knew what was about to happen.

Beecher was one of those people. Like Wert, Beecher was also born with brains. At three, Beecher used to read the newspaper. Not just the comics or the sports scores. The *whole newspaper*, including the obituaries, which his mom let him read when his dad died. Beecher was barely four.

As he grew older, the obits became Beecher's favorite part of the newspaper, the very first thing he read every morning. Beecher was fascinated by the past, by lives that mattered so much to so many, but that—like his father—he'd never see. At home, Beecher's mom, who spent days managing the bakery in the supermarket, and afternoons driving the school bus for the high school, knew that made her son different. And special. But unlike Josh Wert, Beecher knew how to use those brains to steer clear of most schoolyard controversies.

"You want your basketball?" Paglinni asked as he finally turned to face Wert. He held the ball out in his open palm. "Why don't you come get it?"

This was the moment the tribe was waiting for: when chubby Josh Wert would find out exactly what kind of man he'd grow up to be.

Of course, Wert hesitated.

"Do you want the ball or not, fatface?"

Seventeen years from now, when Beecher was helping people at the National Archives, he'd still remember the fear on Josh Wert's round face—and the sweat that started to puddle in the chubby ledges that formed the tops of Wert's cheeks. Behind him, every person in the schoolyard—Andrew Goldberg with his freckled face, Randi Boxer with her perfect braids, Lee Rosenberg who always wore Lee jeans—they were all frozen in place, waiting.

No. That wasn't true.

There was one person moving through the crowd—a late arrival—slowly making her way to the front of the action and holding a jump rope that dangled down, scraping against the concrete.

Beecher knew who she was. The girl with the long black hair, and the three earrings, and the cool hipster black vest. In this part of Wisconsin, no one wore cool hipster vests. Except the new girl.

Clementine.

In truth, she really wasn't the *new* girl—Clementine had been born in Sagamore, and lived there until about a decade ago, when her mom moved them to Detroit to pursue her singing career. It was hard moving away. It was even harder moving home. But there was nothing more humbling than two weeks ago, when the pastor in

their church announced that everyone needed to give
a big *welcome back* to Clementine and her mom—
especially since there was no dad in their house. The pastor
was just trying to be helpful. But in that moment, he reminded everyone that Clementine was *that girl*: the one
with no father.

Beecher didn't see that at all. To Beecher, she was the
one *just like him*.

Maybe that's why Beecher did what he was about to
do.

Maybe he saw something he recognized.

Or maybe he saw something that was completely different.

"Do you want the ball back or not?" Paglinni added as
a thin smirk spread across his cheeks.

In the impromptu circle that had now formed around
the fight, every seventh grader tensed—some excited,
some scared—but none of them moving as they waited
for blood.

Clementine was the opposite—fidgety and unable to
stand still while picking at the strands of the jump rope
she was still clutching. As she shifted her weight from
one foot to the other, Beecher felt the energy radiating
off her. This girl was different from the rest. She wasn't
scared like everyone else.

She was pissed. And she was right. This wasn't fair…

"*Give him his ball back!*" a new voice shouted.

The crowd turned at once—and even Beecher seemed
surprised to find that he was the one who said it.

"What'd you say, Beech Ball!?" Paglinni challenged.

"I-I said…give him the ball back," Beecher said, amazed at how quickly adrenaline could create confidence. His heart pumped fast. His chest felt huge. He stole a quick glance at Clementine.

She shook her head, unimpressed. She knew how stupid this was.

"Or *what*…?" Paglinni asked, the basketball cocked on his hip. "What're you gonna *possibly* do?"

Beecher was in seventh grade. He didn't have an answer. But that didn't stop him from talking. "If you don't give Josh the ball back—"

Beecher didn't even see Paglinni's fist as he buried it in Beecher's eye. But he felt it, knocking him off his feet and onto his ass.

Like a panther, Paglinni was all over him, pouncing on Beecher's chest, pinning his arms back with his knees, and pounding down on his face.

Beecher looked to his right and saw the red plastic handle of the jump rope, sagging on the ground. A burst of white stars exploded in his eye. Then another. He'd never been punched before. It hurt more than he thought.

Within seconds, the tribe was screaming, roaring— *Pag! Pag! Pag! Pag!*—chanting along with the impact of each punch. There was a pop from Beecher's nose. The white stars in Beecher's eyes suddenly went black. He was about to pass out—

"Huuuhhh!"

Paglinni fell backward. All the weight came off Beecher's chest. Beecher could hear the basketball bouncing across the pavement. Fresh air reentered his lungs. But as Beecher struggled to sit up and catch his breath...as he fought to blink the world back into place...the first thing he spotted was...

Her.

Clementine pulled tight on the jump rope, which was wrapped around Paglinni's neck. She wasn't choking him, but she was tugging—hard—using the rope to yank Paglinni backward, off Beecher's chest.

"—*kill you! I'll kill you!*" Paglinni roared, fighting wildly to reach back and grab her.

"You tool—you think I still jump rope in seventh grade?" she challenged, tugging Paglinni back with an eerie calm and reminding Beecher that this wasn't just some impromptu act. It wasn't coincidence that Clementine had the jump rope. When she came here, she was prepared. She knew exactly what she was doing.

Still lying on his back, Beecher watched as Clementine let go of the rope. Paglinni was coughing now, down on his rear, but fighting to get up, his fist cocked back and ready to unleash.

Yet as Paglinni jumped to his feet, he could feel the crowd turn. Punching Beecher was one thing. Punching a girl was another. Even someone as dumb as Paglinni wasn't that dumb.

"You're a damn psycho, y'know that?" Paglinni growled at Clementine.

"Better than being a penis-less bully," she shot back, getting a few cheap laughs from the crowd—especially from Josh Wert, who was now holding tight to the basketball.

Enraged, Paglinni stormed off, bursting through the spectators, who parted fast to let him leave. And that was the very first moment that Clementine looked back to check on Beecher.

His nose was bloody. His eyes were already starting to swell. And from the taste of the blood, he knew that his lip was split. Still, he couldn't help but smile.

"I'm Beecher," he said, extending a handshake upward.

Standing above him, Clementine looked down and shook her head. "No. You're a moron," she said, clearly pissed.

But as the crowd dissipated and Clementine strode across the schoolyard, Beecher sat up and could swear that as he was watching Clementine walk away in the distance...as she glanced over her shoulder and took a final look at him...there was a small smile on her face.

He saw it.

Definitely a smile.

3

Thirty-two minutes later, as Clementine and I are waiting for the arrival of the documents she came looking for, I swipe my security card and hear the usual *thunk*. Shoving the bank vault of a door open, I make a sharp left into the cold and poorly lit stacks that fill the heart of the Archives. With each row of old files and logbooks we pass, a motion sensor light goes off, shining a small spotlight, one after the other, like synchronized divers in an old Esther Williams movie, that chases us wherever we go.

These days, I'm no longer the short kid. I'm blond, tall (though Clementine still may be a hair taller than me), and dressed in the blue lab coat that all of us archivists wear to protect us from the rotted leather that rubs off our oldest books when we touch them. I've also got far more to offer her than a nosebleed. But just to be near this woman who consumed my seventh through tenth grades...who I used to fantasize about getting my braces locked together with...

"Sorry to do this now. I hope you're not bored," I tell her.

"Why would I be bored? Who doesn't love a dungeon?" she says as we head deeper into the labyrinth of leather books and archival boxes. She's nearly in front of me, even though she's got no idea where she's going. Just like in junior high. Always prepared and completely fearless. "Besides, it's nice to see you, Beecher."

"Here...it's...*here*," I say as the light blinks on above us and I stop at a bookcase of rotted leather-bound logbooks that are packed haphazardly across the shelf. Some are spine out, others are stacked on top of each other. "It's just that we have a quota of people we have to help and—"

"Stop apologizing," Clementine offers. "I'm the one who barged in."

She says something else, but as I pull out the first few volumes and scan their gold-stamped spines, I'm quickly lost in the real treasure of this trip: the ancient browning pages of the volume marked *November 1779*. Carefully cradling the logbook with one hand, I use my free one to pull out the hidden metal insta-shelf that's built into each bookcase and creaks straight at us at chest height.

"So these are from the Revolutionary War?" she asks. "They're real?"

"All we have is real."

By *we*, I mean *here*—the National Archives, which serves as the storehouse for the most important documents of the U.S. government, from the original Declaration of Independence, to the Zapruder film, to reports on opportunities to capture bin Laden, to the anthrax formula and where the government stores the lethal spores, to the best clandestine files from the CIA, FBI, NSA, and every other acronym. As they told me when I first started as an archivist three years ago, the Archives is our nation's attic. A ten-billion-document scrapbook with nearly every vital file, record, and report that the government produces.

No question, that means this is a building full of secrets. Some big, some small. But every single day, I get to unearth another one.

Like right now.

"Howard...Howard...Howard," I whisper to myself, flipping one of the mottled brown pages and running my pointer finger down the alphabetical logbook, barely touching it.

Thirty-four minutes ago, as we put in the request for Clementine's documents, a puffy middle-aged woman wearing a paisley silk scarf as a cancer wig came into our research entrance looking for details about one of her relatives. She had his name. She had the fact he served in the Revolutionary War.

And she had me.

As an archivist, whether the question comes from a researcher, from a regular person, or from the White House itself, it's our job to find the answers that—

"Beecher," Clementine calls out. "Are you listening?"

"Wha?"

"Just now. I asked you three times and—" She stops herself, cocking her head so the piercing in her nose tips downward. But her smile—that same warm smile from seventh grade—is still perfectly in place. "You really get lost in this stuff, don't you?"

"That woman upstairs...I can't just ignore her."

Clementine stops, watching me carefully. "You really turned out to be one of the nice ones, didn't you, Beecher?"

I glance down at the logbook. My eyes spot—

"He was a musician," I blurt. I point to the thick rotted page, then yank a notepad from my lab coat and copy the information. "That's why he wasn't listed in the regular service records. Or even the pension records upstairs. A musician. George Howard was a musician during the Revolution."

"Y'mean he played 'Taps'?"

"No... 'Taps' wasn't invented until the Civil War. This guy played fife and drum, keeping the rhythm while the soldiers marched. And this entry shows the military pay he got for his service."

"That's...I don't even know if it's interesting—but how'd you even know to come down here? I mean, these books look like they haven't been opened in centuries."

"They haven't. But when I was here last month searching through some leftover ONI spy documents, I saw that we had these old accounting ledgers from the Treasury Department. And no matter what else the government may screw up, when they write a check and give money out, you better believe they keep pristine records."

I stand up straight, proud of the archeological find. But before I can celebrate—

"I need some ID," a calm voice calls out behind us, drawing out each syllable so it sounds like *Eye. Dee.*

We both turn to find a muscular, squat man coming around the far corner of the row. A light pops on above him as he heads our way. Outfitted in full black body armor and gripping a polished matching black rifle, he studies my ID, then looks at the red Visitor badge clipped to Clementine's shirt.

"Thanks," he calls out with a nod.

I almost forgot what day it was. When the President comes, so does the...

"Secret Service," Clementine whispers. She cocks a thin, excited eyebrow, tossing me the kind of devilish grin that makes me feel exactly how long I haven't felt this way.

But the truly sad part is just how wonderful the rush of insecurity feels—like rediscovering an old muscle you hadn't used since childhood. I've been emailing back and forth with Clementine for over two months now. But it's amazing how seeing your very first kiss can make you feel fourteen years old again. And what's more amazing is that until she showed up, I didn't even know I missed it.

When most people see an armed Secret Service agent, they pause a moment. Clementine picks up speed, heading to the end of the row and peeking around the corner to see where he's going. Forever fearless.

"So these guys protect the documents?" she asks as I catch up to her, leading her out of the stacks.

"Nah, they don't care about documents. They're just scouting in advance for *him*."

This is Washington, D.C. There's only one *him*.

The President of the United States.

"Wait...Wallace is *here*?" Clementine asks. "Can I meet him?"

"Oh for sure," I say, laughing. "We're like BFFs and textbuddies and...he totally cares about what one of his dozens of archivists thinks. In fact, I think his Valentine's card list goes: his wife, his kids, his chief of staff...then me."

She doesn't laugh, doesn't smile—she just stares at me with deep confidence in her ginger brown eyes. "I think one day, he *will* care about you," she says.

I freeze, feeling a blush spread across my face.

Across from me, Clementine pulls up the sleeve of her black sweater, and I notice a splotch of light scars across the outside of her elbow. They're not red or new—they're pale and whiter than her skin, which means they've been there a long time. But the way they zigzag out in every direction...whatever carved into her skin like that caused her real pain.

"Most people stare at my boobs," she says with a laugh, catching my gaze.

"I-I didn't mean—"

"Oh jeez—I'm sorry—I embarrassed you, didn't I?" she asks.

"No. Nonono. No."

She laughs again. "You know you're a horrible liar?"

"I know," I say, still staring at her scars.

"And you know you're still staring at my scars?"

"I know. I can't stop myself. If we were in a desert instead of in these dusty stacks, I'd bury myself right now."

"You really should just go for my boobs," she says. "At least you get a better view."

Instinctively, I look—and then just as quickly stare back at her scars. "It looks like a dog bite."

"Motorcycle crash. My fault. My elbow hyperextended and the bone broke through the skin."

"Sounds excruciating."

"It was ten years ago, Beecher," she says, confidently shrugging the entire world away as her eyes take hold and don't let go. She's staring just at me. "Only the good things matter after ten years."

Before I can agree, my phone vibrates in my pocket, loud enough that we both hear the buzz.

"That them?" Clementine blurts.

I shake my head. Caller ID says it's my sister, who lives with my mom back in Wisconsin. But at this time of the day, when the supermarket shifts change, I know who's really dialing: It's my mom, making her daily check-up-on-me call, which started the day after she heard about Iris. And while I know my mom never liked Iris, she has too much midwestern kindness in her to ever say it to me. The phone buzzes again.

I don't pick up. But by the time I look back at Clementine, all the confidence, all the conviction, all the fearlessness is gone—and I'm reminded that the real reason she came to the Archives wasn't to share old scars or see overmuscled Secret Service agents.

Last year, Clementine's mom died, but it wasn't until a few months back that Clementine called in sick to the radio station and went back home to clean out her mom's closet. There, she found an old datebook that her mother had saved from the year Clementine was born. Sure enough, on December 10, there were hand-drawn hearts and tiny balloons on the day of her birth, there was a cute smiley face drawn on the day she came home from the hospital, but what was most interesting to Clementine was when she flipped back in the datebook and saw the entry on March 18, which had a small sad face drawn in it, followed by the words *Nick enlists.*

From that, she finally had a name and a lead on her dad.

From me, thanks to our recent emails, she had the Archives.

From those, I had only one call to make: to our facility in St. Louis, where we store the more recent army enlistment records.

Ten minutes ago, Clementine was in front of me. But now, as I head for the metal door ahead of us, she starts falling behind, going surprisingly silent.

In life, there's the way you act when you know people are watching. And then there's the way you act when no one's watching, which, let's be honest, is the *real you.* That's what I see in Clementine right now: I spot it for just a half-second, in between breaths, just as I take the lead and she ducks behind me, thinking I can't see her. She's wrong. I see her. And feel her.

I feel her self-doubt. I feel the way she's unanchored.

And in the midst of that single breath, as her shoulders fall, and she looks down and slowly exhales so she won't explode, I spot that little dark terrified space that she reserves for just herself. It only exists for that single half-second, but in that half-second I know I'm seeing at least one part of the *real* Clementine. Not just some fantasized cool jazz DJ. Not just some ballsy girl who took on the bully in seventh grade. The grown her. The true her. The one who learned how to be afraid.

"I should go. I hate when I'm all woe-is-me-ish," she says, regaining her calm as I tug the metal door and we leave the stacks, squeezing back out into the pale blue hallway. She's trying to hide. I know what it's like to hide. I've been doing it for the past year of my life.

"*Don't go,*" I shoot back, quickly lowering my voice. "There's no—They said they'll have the results within the hour and...and...and...and we've got so much stuff to see here...if you want." I bite my lip to stop myself from talking. It doesn't help. "Listen, I didn't want to have to do this," I add. "But if you really want, we can take out the Louisiana Purchase and write '*Clementine Rulz!*' along the bottom."

She barely grins. "Already did it on the Constitution."

"Fine, you win," I say, stopping in the center of the hallway and leaning on the marble wainscoting. "You want to meet the President, I'll take you to meet the President."

She doesn't blink. "You don't know the President."

"Maybe. But I know what room he goes to when he does his reading visits."

"You do?"

"I do. Wanna see?"

She stands up straight and twists her forearm back and forth so her vintage bracelets slide from her wrist toward her elbow and her scars. "Is it far from here or—?"

"Actually, you're standing right in front of it."

I point over her shoulder, and she spins to find a metal door that's painted the same color as the pale blue hallway. Easy to miss, which is the whole point. The only thing that stands out is that the square glass window that looks into the room is blocked by some black fabric. Down by the doorknob, there's a round combination lock like you'd find on a safe.

"*That's it?*" Clementine asks. "Looks like my old gym locker."

I shake my head. "SCIFs are far safer than gym lockers."

"What'd you call it? A skiff?"

"SCIF—Sensitive Compartmented Information Facility," I explain, rapping the knuckle of my middle finger against the door and hearing the deep thud that lets you know just how thick it is. "C'mon, when you read a classified document, you think you just open it at your desk? People are watching from everywhere—through your windows, from listening and video devices—Big Brother doesn't just work for us anymore. So all around the government, we've got rooms built and certified by the CIA."

"Skiffs," she says.

"SCIFs. Walls with quarter-inch metal shielding,

floors with eight-inch metal plates to stop eavesdropping, no windows, copper foil in the corners to stop transmissions, bars over the vent shafts so Tom Cruise can't lower himself on his trapeze..."

"And you have one of these SCIFs here?"

"You kidding? Our legislative guys alone have *sixteen* of them. Every major building in D.C.—the White House, the Capitol, every Senate and House building— if you've got a bigshot in the building, we've got a SCIF in there too. And the biggest bigshots get them in their homes. Tiny little rooms for you to read the world's most vital secrets."

"Can we peek inside?" she asks, rapping her own knuckle against the door.

I force a laugh.

She doesn't laugh back. She's not trying to pry. She means it as an honest question.

"If you can't, no big deal," she adds.

"No, I *can*...I just..."

"Beecher, please don't make that stress face. I didn't mean to make you uncomfortable."

"No, I'm not uncomfortable."

"Let's go do the other stuff," she says, already walking away.

"Oh, just take the damn girl inside already," a deep voice echoes on our left. Up the hallway, an older black man with a caterpillar mustache heads our way carrying an oversized cup of coffee. Despite his age, he's still got the muscular build that first got him the job as one of our uniformed security guards. But one look at his dimpled chin and big-toothed smile, and it's clear that Orlando Williams is more pussycat than lion.

"This that girl you used to have a crush on? The one that's gonna mend that broken heart Iris left you?" Orlando shouts even though he's only a few steps away.

"Who's Iris?" Clementine asks.

Every office has a loudmouth. Orlando is ours—or more specifically, mine, ever since he found out that:

1. I was from his home state of Wisconsin, and
2. I was the only archivist willing to give his brother-in-law's boss a private tour of the Treasure Vault.

For better or worse, he's determined to return the favor.

"Just take her inside—I won't even put you in my floor report," he adds, tucking his clipboard under his armpit and taking a deep swig from his coffee cup.

"Orlando, I appreciate the kindness, but would you mind just—"

"*What?* I'm trynna help you here—show her your love of...adventure." Turning to Clementine, he says, "So he tell you about his wedding photographer days?"

"Orlando..." I warn.

"You were a wedding photographer?" Clementine asks.

"After college, I moved here hoping to take photos for the *Washington Post*. Instead, I spent three years doing weddings in Annapolis. It was fine," I tell her.

"Until he got the chance to help people directly and then he came here. Now he's *our* hero."

Clementine cocks a grin at Orlando. "I appreciate the unsubtle hype, but you do realize Beecher's doing just fine without it?"

Orlando cocks a grin right back. He likes her. Of course he does.

"Will you c'mon?" Orlando begs, focused just on her. "The President's not scheduled here until"—he looks at his watch—"ya got at least an hour, even more if he's late. Plus, the cart with his files isn't even in there yet. Who cares if she sees an empty room?"

I stare at the pale blue door and the combination lock, which of course I know by heart. No doubt, it'd be easy, but the rules say—

"Sweet Christmas, Beecher—*I'll* open the damn room for her!" Orlando calls out.

He heads for a call box and presses the silver intercom button. A small red indicator light blinks awake as a soft-spoken voice answers, "Security."

"Venkat, it's Orlando," he says, speaking close to the intercom. I recognize the name from our staff list. Venkat Khazei. Deputy chief of security. "I'm opening SCIF 12E1," Orlando says. "Just doing spot checks."

"Sounds good. Just remember: Moses is on his way, eh," Khazei replies through the intercom, using our own internal code name for the President.

"That's why I'm checking the room first," Orlando barks back.

The intercom goes quiet, then crackles once more. "Enjoy."

As Orlando strides back toward us, his toothy grin spreads even wider.

Under my shirt, I wear a thin leather necklace with an old house key on it. During high school, when I worked at Farris's secondhand bookshop, I found the key being used as a bookmark in some old dictionary. It's kooky, but that day was the same day I got accepted to Wisconsin, the first step in escaping my little town. The magic key stayed. I've been wearing it so long now, I barely even feel it. Except when I'm sweaty and it starts sticking to my chest. Like now.

"Beecher," Clementine whispers, "if this is skeeving you out, let's just skip the room and—"

"I'm fine. No skeeving at all," I tell her, knowing full well that Iris would've had me leave ten minutes ago.

"Here, hold this," Orlando says, offering me his cup of coffee so he can work on the combo lock.

"No food or drinks allowed in the SCIFs," I remind him, refusing to take it.

"Really, are those the rules, Beecher?" he shoots back. Before I can answer, he hands Clementine his coffee cup and gives a few quick spins to the lock.

With a click and a low *wunk*, the door pops open like the safe that it is.

Even Orlando is careful as he cranes his neck and glances inside, just in case someone's in there.

I do the same, already up on my tiptoes to peer over Orlando's shoulder and make sure we're all clear.

Clementine's different. She doesn't rush—she's not

overeager in the least bit—but with a quick, confident step she heads inside, totally unafraid. It's even sexier than telling me to stare at her breasts.

"Our own little Oval Office," Orlando adds, motioning palms-up like a flight attendant showing off the emergency rows. Yet unlike the Oval and its grand decor, the small windowless room is beige, beige, and more beige, centered around a wide oak table, a secure phone that sits on top, and two wooden library chairs.

When they first see it, most staffers blurt, *"That's it?"*

Clementine circles the desk, studying each beige wall like she's taking in a Picasso. "I like the poster," she finally says.

Behind me, stuck to the back of the metal door, is a poster featuring a steaming hot cup of coffee and a red-lettered warning:

A lot of information can spill over one of these.
Make sure that your conversation is secure to the last drop.

Yet as I read the words, my brain backflips to—

Crap. Orlando's coffee.

"No, *not on there*," I plead with Clementine just as she's about to take a seat and lower the open cup onto the President's desk. If it spills...

I reach to grab it; she jerks her hand to protect it. That's all it takes. The back of my hand brushes against the Styrofoam—the cup tips—and the light brown liquid splashes across the desk, racing to Clementine's side of the table.

A waterfall of coffee pours down, tap-dancing in a fine neat kick-line across the polished floor.

We need to get this clean before the President...

Clementine jumps back to avoid the mess, and her legs slam into her chair, sending the wooden seat toppling backward.

"Orlando, go get paper towels!" I yell, ripping off my blue lab coat to use it as a sponge.

The wooden chair hits the floor with a crack...

...followed by an odd, hollow *thump*.

I turn just in time to see the exposed bottom of the chair, where a square piece of wood pops out from the underside, falls to the floor—and reveals the shadow of an object hidden within.

From the table, coffee continues to drip down, slowing its kick-line across the linoleum.

My throat constricts.

And I get my first good look at what was clearly tucked inside the chair's little hiding spot and is now sitting on the floor, right in the path of the spreading puddle of coffee. It looks like a small file folder.

"Beech?" Orlando whispers behind me.

"Yeah?"

"Please tell me you had no idea that was in there."

"No idea. Swear to God."

He picks up the coffee cup and takes a final swig of whatever's left. As my magic key spot-welds to my chest, I know he's thinking the same thing I am:

If this was put here *for*, or even worse, *by* the President...

"Beech?" he repeats as the puddled coffee slowly seeps into the folder.

"Yeah?"

"We're dead."

"Yeah."

4

Running up the snowy front path, young Clementine Kaye bounced up the wooden staircase toward the small house with the dangling green shutter. She made sure her left foot was always the first one to touch the steps. Her mom told her most people lead with their *right* foot. "But hear me on this, Clemmi," Mom used to say, "what's the fun in being *most people*?"

Even now, at thirteen years old, Clementine knew the answer.

Reaching the front door, she didn't ring the doorbell that went *ding*, but never *dong*. She didn't need to ring the doorbell.

She was prepared. She had a key and let herself inside.

As the door swung open and the whiff of rosewater perfume washed over her, she didn't call out or ask if anybody was home. She knew no one would answer.

Her mom was still traveling—three shows in St. Louis—which meant she'd be gone until next week.

Clementine didn't even worry about getting help with homework, or what she'd eat for dinner. She'd grown accustomed to figuring things out. Plus, she knew how to cook. Maybe tonight she'd make her sausage stew.

In fact, as Clementine twisted out of her winter coat and let it drop to the linoleum floor, where it deflated and sagged like a body with no bones, she was all smiles. Giving quick chin-tickles to two of the three ginger cats her mom had brought back from various trips, Clementine was still moving quickly as she burst into the over-cluttered living room, turned on the CD player that teetered so precariously off the edge of the bookshelf, and inserted the disc labeled *Penny Maxwell's Greatest Hits.*

Penny wasn't just Clementine's favorite singer. Penny was Clementine's mother—who still had nearly three hundred copies of her *Greatest Hits* CD stacked in the closets, under the bed, and in the trunk and backseat of the car. It was yet another of Mom's brainstorms that brought more storm than brain. ("If you do a Greatest Hits *first*, it'll sell faster because people will think they're missing something.") Clementine didn't notice. For her, this was life.

Indeed, as the music began and the sly hook from the trumpet seized the air, Clementine closed her eyes, soaking in the familiar husky voice that'd been singing her to bed—with this same song, Billie Holiday's "God Bless the Child"—since she was a baby.

Mama may have, Papa may have
But God bless the child that's got her own

Clementine had no idea that her mom had changed the words so it was about a little girl. And had no idea that Billie Holiday had written the song after a particularly brutal argument with her own mother, over money—which is what *that's got his own* really refers to. But right there, as she stood there in the living room, swaying back and forth in the pretend dance she always did with her mom after school, thirteen-year-old Clementine Kaye wasn't sad about being alone…or having to cook dinner…or even having to fend for herself.

She was prepared. She was *always* prepared.

But more than prepared, she was just happy to hear her mom's voice.

5

I don't see what the big disaster is," Clementine says in the SCIF.

"Nonono—*don't touch it*!" Orlando yells as I reach for the small file folder.

"What? It's soaking wet," I argue, snatching it, now dripping, from the coffee puddle.

"We could've put it back," he says.

"It's soaking. Look. See the soaking?" I hold up the file so he can spot the drip-drip from the corner of the manila folder. "You think I can just shove this back under the chair like nothing happened? We need to report this."

"Lando, you there? Vault all clear?" a voice crackles through his walkie-talkie.

We all turn toward the upended wooden chair and the gaping hollow hiding spot underneath.

"Y-Yeah, perfect," Orlando reports back through his walkie.

"Good, because company's coming," the voice crackles back. "Service says ten minutes till departure."

From here, the White House is a ten-minute trip. But only three if you're coming by motorcade.

"We need to get out of here," I say, trying to sop up the coffee with my lab coat.

Orlando stays focused on the chair. On the side of it, just underneath the actual seat, there's a narrow slot—like a mail slot—cut into the piece of wood that connects the left front leg with the back leg. "D'you have any idea what this—?" He shakes his head, his toothy grin long gone. "You were right. We gotta report this."

"I take that back. Let's think about this."

"Beech, if someone's using this room as a dead drop..."

"You don't know that."

"A *dead drop*?" Clementine asks.

"Like a hiding spot," Orlando says.

Reading her confusion, I add, "It's a place where you leave something for another person, so you don't have to risk a face-to-face meeting. Like taping something below a mailbox, or in a hollowed-out tree, or..."

"...in a chair," Clementine says, quickly seeing the full picture. With the narrow mail slot underneath the seat, it'd be simple to slide an item into the chair seat, then take it out through the removable hollow bottom. "So if this SCIF is used only by President Wallace, and there's something hidden here for him..."

"Or *by* him," Orlando points out.

"Don't say that. We don't know that. We don't know *anything*," I insist.

"And you believe those words as they leave your lips? You really think this is all just some innocent *Three's Company* misunderstanding, Chrissy?" Orlando asks. "Or are you just worried that if I file an official report, your name will be permanently linked to whatever presidential bullcrap we just tripped into?"

On the corner of the file folder, a single drip of coffee builds to a pregnant swell, but never falls.

"We should open it and see what's inside," Clementine offers, far calmer than the two of us.

"No. Don't open it," I insist.

"What're you talking about?" Orlando asks.

"You ever seen a horror movie? There's that moment where they hear the noise in the woods and some dumbass says, *Let's go see what's making that noise!* And of course you know right there he's number one in the body count. Well…we're in the horror movie: At this exact moment, this little file folder is Pandora's box. And as long as we keep it shut—as long as we don't know what's inside the box—we can still walk away."

"Unless there's a real monster in the box," Orlando points out.

"Orlando…"

"Don't Orlando me. This is my *job*, Beecher."

"Yeah and two seconds ago you were telling me to put it back."

"It's still my job. I walk the halls, I check IDs—that's why it's called *Security*. Now I'm sorry if I find something in the President's reading room, but we did. And if he or anyone else is committing a crime or sneaking classified papers in or out of this building, you really think we should just walk away and pretend we didn't see it?"

I don't look up, but on my right, I can see the red-lettered warning poster on the back of the closed steel door. It doesn't bother me nearly as much as the disappointed expression on Clementine, who clearly doesn't deal well with weakness. The way her ginger eyes drill me, she has no idea which way I'm going to vote.

I wish she knew me better than that.

I toss the damp folder toward the desk. "Just remember, when the CIA grabs us in the middle of the night and puts the black Ziplocs over our heads, *this* is the moment where we could've avoided it." The folder hits the table with a *ptttt.*

Clementine doesn't say a word. But as she takes a half-step forward, she cocks her head, like she's seeing something brand-new on my face. I see the same on hers. I've known this girl since seventh grade. It's the first time I've ever seen her impressed.

"Beecher, it'll take two seconds, then we can leave," Orlando promises. "You'll never regret doing the right thing."

But as he peels open the folder, as he finally sees what's hidden inside, I can already tell he's wrong.

6

"Sweet Christmas," Orlando mutters.

"I don't get it. What is it?" Clementine asks, squeezing in next to me, though careful not to touch anything.

I have no such concern. From the pockets of my coffee-stained lab coat, I pull out the pair of cotton gloves all archivists carry, put them on, pick up the folder like it's live dynamite, and open it. Inside, it's not a top-secret memo, or the whereabouts of bin Laden, or a target list for our spy satellites.

"It's a book," Clementine says.

She's partly right. It has the *cover* of a book—cracked and mottled black leather with faded red triangles in each of the top and bottom corners. But the guts of it—almost all the interior pages—are ripped out. It's the same with the spine: torn away, revealing exposed, ancient glue and torn stitching. Without its insides, the whole book barely has the thickness of a clipboard.

I rub two gloved fingers across the cover. From the red rot (the aged, powdery residue that rubs off on my gloves), I'm guessing it dates back to at least the Civil War.

"*Entick's New Spelling Dictionary*," Orlando reads from the cover.

I check my watch. If we're lucky, Wallace still hasn't left the White House.

"Why would someone hide an old, torn-up dictionary for the President?" Clementine asks.

"Maybe *the President's* hiding it for someone else," Orlando offers. "Maybe when he's alone in the room, he puts it in the chair for someone to pick up later, and they still haven't picked it up yet."

"Or for all we know, this has nothing to do with the President, and this book has been hidden in that chair for years," I point out.

I swear, I can hear Orlando roll his eyes.

"What, like that's so crazy?" I ask.

"Beecher, y'remember when that sweaty researcher with the pug nose and the buggy eyes was coming in here and stealing our old maps?"

"Yeah."

"And when that looney-toon woman was nabbed for swiping those old Teddy Roosevelt letters because she thought she'd take better care of them than we were?"

"What's your point?"

"The point is, y'know how they both got away with their crimes for so long? They took a tiny penknife and sliced each page out of the bound collection, page by page so no one would notice, until almost nothing was left," he says, motioning with a thick finger at the old dictionary like he's Sherlock Holmes himself.

"And that's your grand theory? That Orson Wallace— the President of the United States, a man who can have any document brought *right to him at any moment*—is not only *stealing* from us, but stealing worthless dictionary pages?"

For the first time in the past five minutes, the office loudmouth is silent.

But not for long.

"The *real* point," Orlando finally says, "is that this book—this dictionary, whatever it is—is property of the Archives."

"We don't even know that! The spine's ripped off, so there's no record group number. And if you look for…" Flipping the front cover open, I search for the circular blue *National Archives* stamp that's in some of the older books in our collection. "Even the stamp's not—" I stop abruptly.

"What?" Orlando asks as I stare down at the inside cover. "You find something?"

Leaning both palms on the desk, I read the handwritten inscription for the second and third time.

Exitus
Acta
Probat

"*Exitus acta probat*?" Clementine reads aloud over my shoulder.

I nod, feeling the bad pain at the bridge of my nose. "Exitus acta probat. *The outcome justifies the deed.*"

"You know *Latin*?" Clementine asks.

"I didn't play Little League," I tell her.

"I don't understand," Orlando says. " 'The outcome justifies the deed.' Is that good or bad?"

"*Moses is in transit,*" Orlando's walkie-talkie screams through the room. They'll notify us again when he reaches the building.

I study the book as the pain gets worse. "I could be wrong," I begin, "but if I'm reading this right...I think this book belonged to George Washington."

7

"Wait whoa wait," Orlando says. "*George* George Washington? With the wooden teeth?"

"...and the cherry tree," I say, picking the book up and looking closely at the lettering. The paper is in such bad shape—deeply browned and rough to the touch—it's hard to tell if the ink is old or new.

Behind me, there's a jingle of keys. I spin just in time to see Orlando fighting with the small metal lockbox that's bolted to the wall in the back of the room. With a twist of his key, the box opens, revealing a stack of videotapes and a clunky top-loading VCR that could easily have been stolen straight from my grandmother's house. Our budgets are good, but they're not that good.

"What're you doing?" I ask.

"Sparing you a starring role," he says, ejecting one tape and stuffing a new one in. "Or would you prefer smiling at the camera while you hold the President's secret stash?"

I nearly forgot. Up in the corner there's a small video-camera that's been taping us since the moment we walked in. The only good news is, to maintain the security of each SCIF—and to keep outsiders from intercepting the video—each room is only wired internally, meaning there's no transmission in or out, meaning that tape—the one Orlando is pocketing—is the only proof that Clementine and I have even been in here.

"You sure that's smart?" I ask.

"It's smart," Clementine says, nodding confidently at Orlando. In all the panic, she's not panicking at all. She's watching...studying...taking it all in. It's no different than the jump rope all those years ago.

"Maybe you were right, though," I point out. "Maybe we should report this to Security."

"I *am* Security—I'm a *security guard*," Orlando says. "And I can tell you right now—*Absolutely. No question*—this right here shows a definite problem in our security."

"But by taking that videotape—"

"Beecher, I appreciate that you're a sweet guy. And I know you don't like assuming the worst about people, but let me give you a dose of real life for a moment: There are only two possibilities for what's happened here. Either Roman Numeral One: President Wallace doesn't know anything about this book, in which case we can all calm down and I'll start a proper investigation. Or Roman Numeral Two: Wallace *does know* about this book, in which case he's going to want this book back, in which case handing him a videotape with our faces on it is going to do nothing but make the President of the United States declare war...on us."

"Now you're being overdramatic."

"Overdramatic? What happened to the CIA grabbing us and putting the black Ziplocs over our heads?" Orlando challenges.

"That doesn't mean the President's declaring war."

"Really? I thought you knew your history."

"I do know my history."

"Then name me one person—Valerie Plame...Monica Lewinsky...I don't care who they are or how right they were—name me one person *ever* who went up against a sitting President and walked away the same way they walked in."

"Mark Felt," I tell him.

"Mark Felt?"

"Deep Throat. The guy who told the truth about Nixon."

"I know who he is, Beecher. But the only reason Mark Felt walked away was because *no one knew who he was!*" Orlando insists, waving the videotape in my face. "Don't you get it? As long as we have this video, we get to be Deep Throat and I get to do my investigation. We lose this video, and I promise you, if this book is something bad—and c'mon, you know it's something bad—we're gonna be racing head-on against a man who is so stupidly powerful, wherever he goes, they fly bags of his own blood with him. Trust me here. You wanted smart. This is us being smart."

"What about you?" I ask Orlando. "When you buzzed us in...when you called downstairs to that guy Khazei...Your name's already in the records."

"One disaster at a time. Besides, if we're lucky, this tape may even have who snuck in the book in the first place," he says as he tucks the videotape in the front waistband of his pants. "Now·tell me about the Latin: *Ex act probe it*?"

"*Exitus acta probat*. It's the motto on Washington's personal bookplate," I explain as he shuts the lockbox. "It's from his family's coat of arms—and on the inside cover of all of George Washington's books."

"And this is what it looked like?" Orlando asks, already heading for the door. "Three words scribbled on a page?"

"No…the coat of arms is a work of art: There's a picture of an eagle, two red-and-white stripes, plus three stars. But when Washington designed his coat of arms, he personally added the words *Exitus acta probat*," I say as Clementine motions me to follow Orlando and leave the room. We need to get out of here. But just as I move, my phone vibrates in my pocket. Caller ID reads *NPRC*, but it's the 314 St. Louis area code that reminds me why we're standing in this room in the first place.

Next to me, Clementine eyes the phone in my hand. She doesn't freak, doesn't tense up. But as her lips close tight, I get a second glimpse of the side of her she can't hide. The real Clementine. The scared Clementine. Twenty-nine years of not knowing who your father is? Whatever we stepped in with the President, it has to wait.

"Please tell me you've got good news," I say as I pick up.

"I can bring you information. *Good* and *bad* are the

subjective clothes you decide to dress it in," archivist Carrie Storch says without a hint of irony, reminding me that around here, the better you are with books, the worse you are with social skills.

"Carrie, did you find our guy or not?"

"Your girlfriend's father? In that year, in that county of Wisconsin, he was the only *Nicholas* to enlist on December 10th. Of course I found him."

"You did? That's fantastic!"

"Again, I leave the distinctions to you," she says, adding a short huff that I think counts as a laugh. Carrie never laughs.

"Carrie, what are you not saying?"

"I just bring you the information," she says. "But wait till you hear who the father is."

She says the words, pauses, then says them again, knowing I can't believe it.

The President of the United States should be here any minute. But right now, I wonder if that's the least of our problems.

"Clementine," I say, grabbing her hand and heading to the door, "we need to get you out of here."

8

They don't call them *mental patients* anymore.

Now they're called *consumers*.

Such a turd idea, orderly Rupert Baird thought as he pushed the juice cart down the pale sterile hallway. Almost as bad as when they started calling it KFC instead of Kentucky Fried Chicken. It was the same with the patients. If you're fried, you're fried.

Heh.

That was funny, Rupert thought.

But still a damn turd idea.

"Hey there, Jerome," he called out as he rolled the juice cart into Room 710. "I got apple and orange. What's your pick?"

Cross-legged on his bed, Jerome just sat there, refusing to look up from the newspaper advertising supplements, the only section of the paper he ever read.

"Apple or orange?" Rupert asked again.

No response.

"Any good coupons for Best Buy?" Rupert added.

No response. Same as ever.

Rupert knew not to take it personally—this *was* Ward 5 of the John Howard Pavilion, home to the NGIs. Not Guilty by reason of Insanity.

As he pivoted the juice cart into a three-point turn and headed for Room 711 across the hall, he knew that the next patient—no, the next *consumer*—would be far easier to deal with.

It wasn't always that way. When Patient 711 first arrived ten years ago, he wasn't allowed visitors, mail privileges, sharp objects, or shoelaces. And he certainly wasn't allowed the juice cart. In fact, according to Karyn Palumbo, who'd been here longer than anyone, during his second year on the ward, 711 was caught filing his middle fingernail to a razor point, hoping to carve a bloody cross into the neck of one of the girls from the salon school who used to come and give free haircuts.

Of course, they quickly called the Secret Service.

Whenever 711 was involved, they had to call the Secret Service.

That's what happens when a man tries to put a bullet into the President of the United States.

But after ten years of therapy and drugs—so much therapy and drugs—711 was a brand-new man. A better man.

A cured man, Rupert and most of the doctors thought.

"Hey there, Nico," Rupert called out as he entered the sparsely furnished room. There was a single bed, a wooden nightstand, and a painted dresser that held just Nico's Bible, his red glass rosary, and the newest Washington Redskins giveaway calendar.

"Apple or orange?" Rupert asked.

Nico looked up from the book he was reading, revealing his salt-and-pepper buzzed hair and his chocolate brown eyes, set close together. Ten years ago, in the middle of the President's visit to a NASCAR race, Nico nearly murdered the most powerful man in the world. The video was played time and again, still showing up every year on the anniversary.

As the screaming began, a swarm of Secret Service agents tore at Nico from behind, ripping the gun from his hands.

These days, though, Nico was smart.

He knew better than to talk of those times.

He knew he should've never let the world see him like that.

But the one thing that Nicholas "Nico" Hadrian didn't know back then, as he was tugged and clawed so viciously to the ground, was that he had a young daughter.

"C'mon, Nico—apple or orange?" Rupert called out.

Nico's lips parted, offering a warm smile. "Whatever you have more of," he replied. "You know I'm easy."

9

"Tell me what you're not telling me," Clementine demands as I reright the chair and finish my crude cleanup. Darting for the door, I've got the old dictionary in one hand and my coffee-stained coat in the other.

"Orlando, I have to—"

"Go. I need to rearm the alarm," he calls back, fiddling with the electronic keypad. "Just remember: zipped lips, right? Be Mark Felt. Not Lewinsky."

"That's fine, but if we look into this and it's actually bad..."

"...I'll be the first in line to hand them the stained dress," he says, patting the videotape in his waistband.

As he rearms the door, we're already running. Orlando's a big boy. He's fine by himself. Clementine's another story. She knows that last phone call was about her dad.

"They found him, didn't they?" she asks as we leave the SCIF behind and race up the hallway. In the distance, I hear the soft cry of police sirens wailing. Wallace's motorcade is close, and if this old dictionary really was put there for the President—if someone is somehow helping him grab it, or worse, steal it, or if there's something valuable hidden in it—the last thing we need is to be seen this close to the SCIF with—

"*Ding!*" the elevator rings as we turn the corner.

I pick up speed. No way anyone's fast enough to spot us.

"Beecher Benjamin White, you think I'm blind!? Step away from that girl right now...!"

Clementine freezes.

"...unless of course you plan on introducing me to her!" a young man with combed-back brown hair and a scruffy starter beard calls out, already laughing at his own lame joke. At twenty-nine years old, Dallas is a year younger than me and should be my junior. He's not.

"Dallas Gentry," he adds as if Clementine should recognize the name.

When it comes to archivists, everyone has their own specialty. Some are good with war records. Others are good with finding the obscure. But what Dallas is good at is getting his name in the newspaper. It peaked a few months back when he opened a dusty 1806 personnel folder from the War Department and found a handwritten, never-before-seen letter by Thomas Jefferson. Sure, it was dumb luck—but it was Dallas's luck, and the next day it was his name in the *Washington Post*, and Drudge, and on the lecture circuit at every university that now thinks he's the Indiana Jones of paper. To celebrate his rise, Dallas went full-on intellectual and started growing a beard (as if we need more intense bearded guys around here). The saddest part is, based on his recent promotion, it's actually working for him, which makes me wonder if he's the one staffing President Wallace today. But as I frantically fumble, trying to hide the dictionary under my coffee-soaked lab coat, this isn't the time to find out.

"Listen, we're kinda in a rush," I say, still not facing him.

Clementine shoots me a look that physically burns. At first I don't get it. She motions around the corner, back to the SCIF. Oh crap. Orlando's still in there. If Dallas waltzes in on him and then connects him to what's missing...

"I mean...no, we have plenty of time," I tell Dallas. "Boy, your beard looks cool."

Your beard looks cool? My God, when did I turn into Charlie Brown?

"Is that *buttered rum*?" Clementine jumps in, sniffing the air.

"You're close. Cherry rum," Dallas replies, clearly impressed as he turns toward her, staring at the piercing in her nose. It's not every day he sees someone who looks like her in D.C. "Where'd you learn your pipe smoke?"

"My boss at the radio station. He's been a pipe smoker for years," she explains.

"Wait, you started smoking a pipe?" I ask.

"Just for the irony," Dallas teases, keeping his grin on Clementine. He honestly isn't a jerk. He just comes off as one.

"Beecher, what happened to your coat?" a soft female

voice interrupts as Dallas reaches out to shake hands with Clementine.

Just behind Dallas, I spot archivist Rina Alban, a young straight-haired brunette with bright green reading glasses perched on her head, and triple knots on her shoes. In the world of mousy librarians, Rina is Mickey. She's ultra-quiet, ultra-smart, and ultra-introverted, except when you ask about her true love, the Baltimore Orioles. In addition, she looks oddly like the Mona Lisa (her eyes follow you also), and on most days she's just as talkative. But not today—not the way she's studying my bunched-up lab coat, like she can see the book that's underneath.

"Beecher, what *is* that?" Rina asks again.

"Coffee. I spilled my coffee," Clementine jumps in, restoring calm.

"Wait, you're the one he knows from high school, right?" Dallas asks, though I swear to God I never mentioned Clementine to Dallas. That's the problem with this place. Everyone's doing research.

"You really shouldn't have coffee up here," Rina points out, less quiet than usual. I know why.

Every month, the powers that be rank us archivists in order of how many people we've helped. From tourists who walk in, to the handwritten letters asking us to track down a dead relative, every response is counted and credited. Yes, it helps justify our jobs, but it also adds unnecessary competition, especially after this morning, when they told us Rina was, for the fifth month in a row, number two on the list.

"By the way, Beecher, congrats on the top spot again," Dallas says, trying to be nice.

"Top spot in what?" Clementine asks, peering down the hall and hoping to buy a few more seconds for Orlando.

"Being helpful. Don't you know that's what Beecher's best at?" Dallas asks. "He even answers the questions that get emailed though the National Archives website, which no one likes answering because when you email someone back, well, now you got a pen pal. It's true, you're walking with the nicest guy in the entire building—though maybe you can teach him how to help himself," Dallas adds, thinking he's again making nice.

Doesn't matter. By now, Orlando should be long gone from the SCIF. Nothing to worry about. But as Clementine steps between me and Rina, Rina isn't staring at me. Her eyes are on my coat.

"Clear the hallway," a deep baritone calls out. I turn just as two uniformed Secret Service agents exit from the nearby staircase. On my left, the lights above the elevator tell us it's back on the ground floor. The sirens are louder than ever. Here comes Moses.

Without a word, one of the agents motions to Dallas and Rina, who head back around the corner. Question answered. Rina and Dallas are the ones staffing Wallace in the SCIF.

I go to push the button for the elevator. The taller Secret Service agent shakes his head and points us to the staircase. Until the President's in place, that's the only way down.

"What happened to your coat?" the agent asks, pointing to the brown Rorschach blots.

"Coffee," I call back, trying to look relaxed as I head for the waiting stairs.

"Beecher, just say it," Clementine says as soon as we're out of sight. "Tell me!"

I shake my head, speedwalking us back through the musty stacks. I'm tempted to run, but as the motion sensor lights pop on above us, I'm reminded of the very best reason to stay calm. The sensors are the Archives' way of saving energy, but all they do is highlight us for the videocameras in the corner of each stack. And unlike the videotape Orlando swiped from the room, these beam right back to the Security Office.

"You sure this is right?" Clementine asks as we reach a section where the lights are already on. Like we've been here before.

"Of course it's right," I say, squinting at the record group locator numbers at the end of the row on our left. I pause a moment. A moment too long.

"You're lost, aren't you?"

"I'm not lost."

She studies me, strong as ever. "Beecher..."

"I'm not. Yes, I'm turned around a little. But I'm not lost," I insist.

"Listen, even if you are, it's okay," she says with no judgment in her voice. But as she looks away, she starts...chuckling.

"You're laughing?"

"I-I'm sorry," she says, shaking her head, unable to hide it. The worst part is, she's got a great laugh—a laugh from deep in her stomach, not one of those fake mouth ones. "It's just— All this running…and the videotape and the Secret Service…and everyone's got guns…This is the *President*, Beecher! What're we *doing*?" she asks, her laugh coming faster.

Before I know it, I'm chuckling with her. It starts slowly, with just a hiccup, then quickly starts to gallop. She's absolutely right. To be lost like this…what the hell *are* we doing?

My belly lurches, catapulting a gasp of a laugh that only makes her laugh harder. She bends forward, holding her side and shooting me another new look I've never seen before. It barely lasts a second—an appreciative grin that reveals a single dimple in her left cheek—

Poomp.

Half bent over, I look down and see that the dictionary that was hidden beneath my lab coat has slipped out, slapping against the stacks' 1950s linoleum floor.

Clementine stares down at the old book. Her laughter's gone.

Mine too. Reality's back. And so is her fear.

"Clemmi, listen to me—whatever we found in that room—whatever they're doing with this book—" She looks my way, her eyes wide. I take a deep breath. "I can fix this."

She nods, swaying just slightly. "You mean that, don't you?"

"I'm not sure. I think I do." I scan the empty stacks

and again study the record group numbers, determined to get us back on track. "Yeah. I do."

She studies me carefully, silence settling around us. Behind me, one of the motion sensor lights blinks off from inaction. I wait for the look she gave me before—the appreciative nod with the single dimple. It doesn't come. Instead, she stands up straight, turning her head, like she's studying me from a brand-new angle. She's no longer swaying. No longer moving. She's staring straight at me. I have no idea what she's seeing.

But I'll take it.

"My father's dead, isn't he?" she asks.

"What? No..."

"Beecher, you know who my dad is, don't you?"

"Let's just—"

"If you know..." Her eyes well with tears and, like that half-second when she thought I wasn't looking before, the girl who's always prepared... she's not prepared for this. *"...how could you not tell me?"*

She's right. Completely right. But to just blurt it here...

"Beecher..."

She doesn't say anything else. Just my name. But in those two stupid syllables, I hear everything in between. For twenty-nine years, Clementine Kaye has lived with empty spaces. And from what I know, she's lived with them better than me. In seventh grade, I remember being paralyzed when Mrs. Krupitsky had the class make Father's Day cards, thinking that's the day we always go to his grave. Next to me, young Clementine was already happily writing away, turning it into a Mother's Day card without even a second thought. But today, in those two syllables of my name, those empty spaces are back again, and I hear them loud and clear.

"Nico Hadrian," I blurt.

Her eyes jump back and forth, fighting to process. I wait for her to lean on the end of the metal shelves for support, but her body stays stiff. She's trying to will herself back to calm. It's not working. "N-Nico? Y'mean, like the guy who—"

"Him. Mm-hmm. Nico Hadrian." I nod, hoping to soften the blow. But there's no other way to say it. "The man who tried to shoot President—"

"But he's alive, right?"

"Yeah, sure—I mean, I think he's in a mental hospital…"

"But he's alive. My dad's alive." She reaches for the metal shelf on her left, but never grabs it. "It's—it's not what I expected, but I think—I think—I think—this is better than being dead, isn't it?—it's better," she insists, blinking over and over, brushing away the tears. "I was so scared he'd be dead." Her eyes stare straight ahead, like she can't even see I'm there. "I didn't think he'd be this, but—There are worse things in life, right?"

"Clementine, are you—?"

"There are worse things in life. He could've been dead; he could've been—" She cuts herself off, and slowly—right in front of me—it's like she's finally hearing her own words. Her jawbone shifts in her cheek. Her knees buckle. Before, she was unprepared. Now she's unraveling.

I grab her arm, tugging hard. Time to get her out of here. At the end of one of the stacks—the real end this time—I push a metal door open and the dusty old stacks on the ninth floor dump us into the polished office hallway on the third floor of the main building.

The sirens from the motorcade still scream through the hall. No doubt, the President is inside the Archives by now, probably already in the SCIF with Dallas and Rina. The sirens should be fading soon. But as we head down the final steps to the lobby, as I tuck the coat-covered book tight under my arm and tug Clementine along, the sirens keep wailing. By the time I wave my badge and hear the click that opens the heavy door, there are a half dozen armed Secret Service agents standing in the lobby. The sirens are louder than ever.

A blast of mean December air from outside nearly knocks over the lobby's Christmas tree as it sends its shredded paper decorations flying. On my right, I spy the source of the sudden wind tunnel: The automatic doors that lead out to Pennsylvania Avenue are wide open.

"*Step aside! Emergency!*" someone yells as a gleaming metal gurney comes blasting through the entrance, pushed by two impassive paramedics in dark blue long-sleeved shirts.

"What's going on?" I ask the nearest uniformed Secret Service guy. "Something happen with the President?"

He glances at my badge, making sure I'm staff. "You

think we'd be standing here if that were the case? We took him out of here six minutes ago. This is one of yours."

A strand of shredded paper kisses the side of my face, hooking around my ear. I don't feel it. I don't feel anything. "How do you mean, *one of ours*?"

"One of *them*," he clarifies, pointing with his nose at the Security guys who run the main check-in desk. "Apparently, some poor guy had a seizure—or heart attack—they found him on the floor of his office. I think they said his name was..."

"*Orlando!?*" a guard shouts from the check-in desk.

"*Orlando!?*" Clementine blurts behind me.

No. No no. He didn't just say—

The string of shredded paper slips off my ear, blowing into a small swirl at the center of the marble lobby. Clementine is silent behind me.

There's no way. I was just...he was just...

"Beecher," Clementine whispers behind me.

I'm already running, dragging her with me by her hand.

This isn't happening. Please tell me this isn't happening.

But it is.

10

M *ove! Move it! Move!"* I yell, running full speed up
the bright white basement hallway with the white-
and-gray checkerboard floor. The magic key
bounces against my chest as I fight my way through the insta-
crowd that's already forming outside Orlando's office.

I'm not a big person. Or strong. But I have two older
sisters. I know how to get what I want:

I lie.

"We're with them!" I shout as I point to the
paramedics who're barely fifty feet ahead, riding their
wake as they pull me and Clementine through the crowd.

Not a single Archives employee tries to stop me. Archivists aren't built for confrontation. They're built for obser-
vation, which explains why small groups of gawkers fill
the hall all the way to the front door of the Security Office.

I hear more whispers as I run: *Orlando...? Orlando...! Heard a seizure...Orlando...!*

"Don't assume the worst. He could be okay," Clementine says.

I refuse to argue as we squeeze into the large office

suite. Inside, it's quiet and looks like any other: a long rectangular layout spotted with cubicles and a few private offices. All the action is on our left, where I hear the squawks and crackles of far too many walkie-talkies. The paramedics have them. Security has them. And so does the small team of firefighters who arrived earlier and are now in a small circle at the center of the office, crouched on their knees like kids studying an anthill.

"They're still working on him," Clementine says.

That's good news. If they're working on him...

But they're not working. There're no frenzied movements. No CPR.

"On three," they call out, getting ready to lift the stretcher. "One...two..."

There's a metal howl as the stretcher's steel legs extend and pins and sockets bite into place. With a tug, the firefighters pull tight on the black Velcro straps that tighten around the white sheet...

Not just a sheet...under the sheet...

Orlando.

One of the firefighters takes a half-step back and we get a short but perfect view of Orlando's face. His skin is dry like a faded chalkboard. You don't need a medical degree to know when you're staring at a dead man.

"Beecher, take a breath," Clementine whispers behind me. "Don't pass out."

"I'm not going to pass out."

"You are. I can see you are."

"What do you want me to do? That's— We— This man's my friend!"

I crane my neck to look through the crowd, studying Orlando's profile. His head is tilted to the side—almost toward us—and the bottom right corner of his mouth sags slightly open and down, the way my mom looked when she had the complications with her heart surgery.

"He was just— We just saw him," Clementine whispers.

I try to focus on Orlando's eyes, which are closed and peaceful. But that bottom corner of his mouth, sagging open so slightly…

"I'm so sorry," Clementine offers.

A whiplash of pain stings my heart, my lungs—like every one of my organs is made of crushed glass. The shattered pieces cascade like sand down my chest, landing in my stomach.

Please tell me this wasn't because we were in that room… I say to myself.

"You heard them," Clementine says, reading me perfectly. "He had a heart attack…or a seizure."

I try to believe that. I really do. There's no reason to think otherwise. No reason at all. Except for that gnawing ache that's tunneling through my belly.

"What?" she whispers. "How could it not be a heart attack?"

"I'm not saying it's not, but…it's a hell of a coincidence, isn't it? I mean, think of the odds: Right after we find that hiding spot, Orlando just happens to—" I lower my voice, refusing to say it. But she hears it. When Orlando made that call through the intercom, he put himself on record. *He's* the only one listed as being in the SCIF, so if someone else went in that room after we left, if they went looking for—

Oh crap.

I look down at my bundled lab coat covered in coffee stains. It's squeezed by my armpit. But all I feel are the worn edges of what's hidden underneath.

The book. Of course. The stupid book. If that was left there for the President, and they thought Orlando took it—

"Beecher, get it out of your head," Clementine warns. "For anyone to find out he was even in there...no one's that fast."

I nod. She's right. She's absolutely right.

In fact, besides us, the only person who even knew Orlando was in there was—

"What an effin' nightmare, eh?" a soft-spoken voice asks.

I stand up straight as a burning sting of vomit springs up my throat. I know that voice. I heard it earlier. Through the intercom. When he buzzed us into the SCIF.

"Venkat Khazei," says a tall Indian man with low ears and thin black hair that's pressed in a military-combed side part. He knows I know who he is, and as he puts a cold hand on my shoulder, I notice that he's got the shiniest manicured fingernails I've ever seen. I also notice the equally shiny badge that's clipped to his waist. *Deputy Chief of Security—National Archives.*

And the only person who I'm absolutely sure knew that Orlando was in that SCIF and near that book.

"Beecher, right?" he asks, his sparkling fingers still on my shoulder. "You got a half moment to chat?"

11

What a horror—and especially with you two being so close, eh?" Khazei. asks, his accent polished, like a Yale professor. Across from us, a firewoman covers Orlando's face by pulling up the thin bedsheet that's neither crisp nor white. The sheet's been beaten and washed so many times, it's faded to the color of fog. Worst of all, it's not big enough to really cover him, so as he lies there on the stretcher, as the paramedics confer with the firefighters, Orlando's black work boots stick out from the bottom like he's in a magician's trick, about to float and levitate.

But there's no trick.

"Pardon?" I ask.

"I saw you run in with the paramedics…the concern you were wearing." Khazei stands calmly next to me, shoulder to shoulder, like any other person in the crowd. He's careful to keep his voice low, but he never steps back, never tries to draw me out or get me to talk somewhere private. I'm hoping that's good. Whatever he's fishing for, he still doesn't know exactly where he's supposed to be fishing. But that doesn't mean he's not hiding a hook.

"We're both from Wisconsin—he was always nice to me," I admit, never taking my eyes off the body, which sits right in front of Orlando's open cubicle. On the floor, there's a small pile of scattered papers and books fanned out at the foot of Orlando's desk. They could easily be the papers Orlando knocked over when he toppled from his chair. But to me, even as Khazei takes his manicured fingers off my shoulder, they can just as easily be the aftermath of someone doing a quick search through his belongings. But what would they be looking—?

Wait.

The video.

In the SCIF. Orlando grabbed that video so no one would know we were there. So no one would know what we grabbed. We. Including me. But if someone sees that video…If someone finds out I was in that room… Maybe that's why Orlando was—

No, you don't know that, I tell myself. I again try to believe it. But I'm not believing anything until I get some details. And until I'm sure that videotape is in my own hands.

"Do we even know what happened? Anyone see anything?" I ask.

Khazei pauses. He doesn't want to answer. Still, he knows he's not getting info until he gives some.

"Our receptionist said Orlando was being his usual self," he explains, "said he was humming 'Eye of the Tiger' when he walked in—*which is sadly typical*—then he headed back to his cube and then…" Khazei falls silent as we both study the covered body. It's the first time I notice that, across the room, mixed in with the still growing crowd, are two familiar faces—one with a crappy beard, the other with her green reading glasses and triple-knotted shoes.

Dallas and Rina.

Clementine coughs loudly from behind. I don't turn around. So far, Khazei hasn't even looked at her. He has no idea we're together. Considering who we just found out her dad is, that's probably for the better.

"Y'know he had sleep apnea, right? Always bitching about going to bed wearing one of those masks," Khazei explains.

I'm still studying Dallas and Rina, my fellow archivists. Unlike everyone else, who's pretty much standing behind us, the two of them are deep on the other side of the room, facing us from behind the cubicles. Like they've been here for a bit. Or are looking for something.

I continue to check each desk, searching for the videotape.

"One of the firefighters even said that if the stress gets high enough, you can trigger a seizure, but—" Khazei shakes his head. "When you spoke to Orlando earlier, he seem bothered or upset about anything?"

"No, he was—" I stop and look up at Khazei. He's not wearing a grin, but I feel it. Until this moment, I'd never mentioned that I'd spoken to Orlando earlier.

Dammit.

I'm smarter than that. I *need to be* smarter than that.

But the longer I stand here, the more I keep thinking that there's only one possible reason Orlando died. And right now, that reason is wrapped in my lab coat and clutched by my now soaking armpit.

"I'm just trying to talk with you, Beecher. Just be honest with me. Please."

He adds the *Please* to sound nice. But I'm done being suckered. Of the forty people rubbernecking around the office, I'm the one he's decided to chat with. That alone means one of two things: Either he's a hell of a good guesser, or he's got something else he's not saying.

I replay the past half hour in my head, scouring for details. But the only one I keep coming back to is Orlando's Roman Numeral Two: If this book does belong to the President, and the President finds out we have it, he's going to declare war on...

On us. That's how Orlando put it.

But there is no *us.* Not anymore.

Orlando's dead. And that means that whatever's really happening here—whether it's the President or Khazei or someone else that's playing puppetmaster—the only one left to declare war on...

Is me.

A single bead of sweat rolls down the back of my neck.

Across the way, Dallas and Rina continue to stand there, still facing us from the far end of the room. Dallas grips the top of a nearby cubicle. Rina's right behind him. Sure, they saw us in the hallway—just outside the elevator—but that doesn't tell them I was in the SCIF, or, more important, that I'm the one who actually has the book. In fact, the more I think about it, there's only one way anyone could've known we were in there.

My brain again flips back to the video.

"Beecher, you understand what I'm saying?" Khazei asks.

When Orlando grabbed that videotape, he told us it was the best way to keep us safe—that as long as no one knew we were in there, we could still be Mark Felt. But if that tape is out there...if someone already has their hands on it...they'd have proof we were in the room and found the book, which means they'd already be aiming their missiles at—

"Were you with him all afternoon?" Khazei asks. "What time did you leave him?"

"Excuse me?"

"I'm just reacting to *your* words, Beecher. You said you were with Orlando. But if you want, take a look at your calendar...at your datebook...whatever you keep it in. My only concern is getting an accurate timeline."

I nod at his swell of helpfulness. "Yeah...no...I'll look at my calendar."

"I appreciate that. Especially because..." He pauses a moment, making sure I see his smile. "...well, you know how people get."

"How people get *about what*?"

"About things they don't really know about that they think they know about," he says, his voice as kind as ever. "So if I were wearing your shoes, Beecher, the last thing I'd want is to suddenly be known as the last person to be alone with the security guard who mysteriously just dropped dead. I mean, unless of course it was just a heart attack."

On the back of my neck, my single drop of sweat swells into a tidal wave as I start to see the new reality I'm now sitting in. Until this moment, I thought the worst thing that could come from that videotape was that it made me look like a book thief. But the way the picture's suddenly been repainted, that's nothing compared to making me look like a murderer.

"Make way, people! Coming through!" the paramedics call out, shoving the stretcher and slowly rolling Orlando's body back toward the reception desk.

The crowd does the full Red Sea part, clearing a path.

But as we all squeeze together, I once again eye Orlando's cubicle, searching his messy desk, scanning the papers fanned across the floor, and scouring the office for—

There.

I didn't look for it before—didn't know it was that important—back in the corner, just outside his cubicle. Right where Dallas and Rina were first standing.

There's a black rolling cart, like you see in every A/V department, with a small TV on top. But I'm far more interested in what's underneath.

I push forward, trying to fight through the crowd as it squeezes back, bleeding into other cubicles to make way for the stretcher.

"*Easy!*" a middle-aged woman in full security uniform snaps, shoving me back with a shoulder.

It's just the shove I need. On the lower shelf of the A/V cart sits an ancient bulky VCR. Like the one upstairs, it's a top-loader. Unlike the one upstairs, the basket that holds the tape is standing at full attention, already ejected.

And empty.

No. It can't be empty! If someone has it...I bite down hard, swallowing the thought. Don't assume the worst. Maybe Orlando hid it. Maybe it's still—

I feel another shove from in front of me. It nearly knocks me on my ass.

"*Move, people! Show some respect!*" one of the paramedics shouts.

With a final swell, the crowd packs extra-tight, then exhales and loosens its grip, dissipating as the stretcher leaves the room. Within seconds, there are coworkers everywhere, whispering, talking, the gossip already starting to spread.

Fighting for calm, I search for Dallas and Rina. They're gone. I turn around, looking for Khazei. He's gone too.

But I hear him loud and clear.

Of all the people in this room, he came straight to me. And while I still don't know if Khazei's threatening me for the book, or just investigating the loss of an employee, based on the intensity of his questions, one thing is clear: The book...the video...the President...even Orlando...There are multiple rings on this bull's-eye— and right now, every one of those rings is tightening around my neck.

12

It was late when Dr. Stewart Palmiotti's phone began to ring. It was late, and he was comfortable. And as he lay there, toasty under his overpriced down comforter and protected from the December cold, he was perfectly happy to feel himself slowly swallowed by his current dream, a piano dream involving old childhood Italian songs and the pretty girl with the bad teeth who he always sees at the supermarket deli counter.

But the phone was ringing.

"Don't pick it up." That's what his ex would've said.

That's why she was his ex.

This wasn't just some random call. From the ring—high-pitched, double chirp—this was the drop phone. The phone that could go secure with the flip of a switch. The phone with the gold presidential seal on the receiver. The phone that was installed in his house two years ago. By the White House Communications Agency. And the Secret Service.

The drop phone was about to ring again, but as

Palmiotti knew, only a schmuck lets the drop phone ring twice.

"Dr. Palmiotti," he answered, sitting up in bed and looking out at the late-night snow that had already blanketed his street in Bethesda, Maryland.

"Please hold for the President," the White House operator said.

"Of course," he replied, feeling that familiar tightening in his chest.

"Everything okay?" whispered Palmiotti's... *girl-friend*? *Girlfriend* wasn't the right word. *Girlfriend* made them sound like they were teenagers.

Palmiotti wasn't a teenager. He was forty-eight. Lydia was forty-seven. Lost her husband to... she called it cancer of the soul. Meaning he was screwing the overweight girl from the dry cleaners.

It took Lydia two years before she would date. She was happy now. So was Palmiotti. He was happy and warm and ready to dream.

And then his phone rang.

Palmiotti didn't like being on call. He had given it up years ago. But that's part of the job of being personal physician—and one of the oldest friends—of the most powerful man in the world.

"Stewie, that you?" President Orson Wallace asked.

By the time they entered their freshman year at the University of Michigan, Palmiotti and Wallace had called each other by first names, last names, nicknames, and most every good curse word they could find. But it wasn't until Inauguration three years ago that Palmiotti started calling his friend *sir*.

"Right here, sir," Palmiotti replied. "You okay? What's wrong?"

The President doesn't have to choose his physician. Most simply go to the White House Medical Unit. But a few, like George H. W. Bush, who appointed a dear family friend, understand that sometimes the best medicine is simply having someone to talk to. Especially someone who knows you well.

"I'm fine," Wallace replied.

"If you're fine, don't wake me up in the middle of the night."

"Wait. You got Lydia sleeping there, don't you?"

At that, Palmiotti paused.

"Don't lie to me, Stewie." The President laughed. "I got satellites. I can see you right now. Look out your window and—"

"Orson, this a doctor call or a friend call?"

This time, Wallace was the one who was silent. "I just...I think I did something to my back. It's bothering the hell outta me."

Palmiotti nodded. His predecessors had warned him as much. Most calls from the Oval would be stress-related. "You want me to come over and take a look?"

"Nah. No. That's silly. It can wait till tomorrow."

"You sure?"

"Yeah—absolutely," the President of the United States said. "Tomorrow's just fine."

13

The archivist was patient.

Of course he was patient.

Impatient people would never stand for this—would never take a job where half your day was spent alone with ancient government paperwork, poring through memos and speeches and long-forgotten hand-written letters, treasure-hunting for that one minute detail that a researcher was so desperately looking for.

No, impatient people didn't become archivists.

And without question, this archivist—with the scratched black reading glasses—was plenty patient.

Patient enough to stay quiet all day.

Patient enough to let the ambulances fade and the EMTs and the firefighters and the Secret Service leave.

Patient enough to go about his job, helping a few tourists in the second-floor research room, then answering a few letters and emails that came in through the Archives website.

And even patient enough to drive home, cook his spaghetti with turkey meat sauce, and spend the last hour before bed noodling with a double acrostic word puzzle in *Games* magazine. Just like any other night.

That's how they taught him to do it.

But when all was quiet. When the street was dark. When he was sure that anyone watching would've long ago become bored and left, he finally reached into his briefcase and pulled out the true treasure from today's hunt.

According to Benjamin Franklin, "He that can have patience, can have what he will."

The archivist had something far more valuable than that.

He had a videotape.

The one Orlando was carrying when—

He put the thought out of his head as he slid the tape into his old VCR. Right now, the danger was that it was all coming undone... everything was at risk.

Hitting rewind, he leaned in close as the picture slowly bloomed onto his TV. The angle looked down from the top corner of the SCIF, no different than any security camera. Sure enough, there was Orlando, rushing around as—

Wait.

There.

In the corner. By the door. A shadow flickered. Then another.

Realizing he hadn't gone back far enough, the archivist again hit rewind.

The shadow—No. Not a shadow.

A person. Two people.

His eyes narrowed.

Now it made far more sense. That's why they couldn't find the book.

Orlando wasn't alone in the SCIF. There were two other people with him.

One of them a girl. And the other? The one with the bunched-up lab coat and the messy blond hair?

The archivist knew him. Instantly.

Beecher.

Beecher had what the Culper Ring wanted.

14

My phone starts screaming at 7:02 the next morning. I don't pick it up. It's just a signal—the morning wake-up call from my ride to work, telling me I now have twenty-four minutes until he arrives. But as the phone stops ringing, my alarm clock goes off. Just in case the wake-up phone call doesn't do its trick.

I have two sisters, one of them living in the D.C. area, which is why, instead of waking to the sound of a buzzer, my alarm clock blinks awake with a robotic male voice that announces, "...Thirty percent chance of snow. Twenty-one degrees. Partly overcast until the afternoon."

It's the official government weather forecast from NOAA—the National Oceanic and Atmospheric Administration—where my sister Lesley's been working for the past year and a half, studying tides and weather and sometimes getting to write the copy that the robotic voice announces. And yes, I know there's not much "writing" when it comes to saying it's "partly overcast until the afternoon." And yes, I'd rather wake up to music or even a buzzing alarm. But it's my sister. Lesley wrote that. Of course I support her.

As Robotman tells me about the rest of the forecast, I kick off the sheets and lower my head. My mom used to make us say a prayer every morning. I lasted until junior high, but even then, she taught me that I shouldn't start the day without being thankful for something. Anything. Just to remind you of your place in the world.

Closing my eyes, I think about…huuh…I try to tell myself it's good that Orlando's at least at peace. And I'm glad I got to know him. But when it comes to what I'm thankful for, no matter how much I think of Orlando…

I can't help but picture that look when Clementine first arrived yesterday—that self-assured warmth that she wears as coolly and comfortably as her thumb rings and nose piercing. But what's far more memorable is that fragile, terrified look she didn't want me to see as she ducked behind me in the stacks. It wasn't because she was shy. Or embarrassed. She was *protecting* me from that look. Sparing me the heartache that comes with whatever she thinks her life has become.

I help people every day. And of course, I try to tell myself that's all I'm doing right now—that I'm just trying to be a good friend, and that none of this has anything to do with my own needs, or what happened with Iris, or the fact that this is the very first morning in a year when I woke up and didn't eye the small bottle of Iris's perfume that I still haven't been able to throw out. I even tell myself how pathetically obvious it is to fill the holes of my own life with some old, imagined crush. But the truth is, the biggest threat to Clementine's well-being isn't from who her father is. It's from the fact that, like me, she's on that videotape from when we were in the SCIF.

The tape's still gone. But even without an autopsy, I know that's why Orlando died. It's a short list for who's next.

From there, I don't waste time getting ready. Four and a half minutes in the shower. Seven minutes for shaving, toothbrushing, and the rest.

"*Ping*," my computer announces from the downstairs kitchen table where I keep my laptop that keeps track of all the morning eBay bids. My townhouse isn't big. It isn't expensive. And it's in Rockville, Maryland, instead of in D.C.

But it's mine. The first big thing I bought after nearly a hundred weddings, plus two years of working my eBay side business and saving my government salary. My second big purchase was the engagement ring. I've been making up for it ever since.

In fact, as I head downstairs, on the beige-carpeted second-to-last step, there's a neat stack of a dozen postcards. Each card has a different black-and-white photo of the Statue of Liberty from 1901 to 1903. On the step below that, there's another stack—this one with black-and-white photos of baseball stadiums in the early 1900s. And there're more piles throughout the kitchen: across the counter (photos of old German zeppelins), on the microwave (photos of steam-engine trains), on top of the fridge (separate piles for dogs, cats, and tons of old automobiles), and even filling the seat of the bright orange

1960s lounge chair that I got at the Georgetown flea market and use as a head chair (each pile a different exhibit from the 1901 Pan-Am Expo in Buffalo, New York, including a big pile for the camel parade).

To anyone else, it's clutter. To me, it's how the world used to communicate: through postcards.

Back in the early 1900s, when you bought a new car, or new dress, or had a new baby, you took a picture, sent it to Kodak, and they'd send you back six black-and-white "real photo postcards," which you'd then send to family and friends. At the time, collecting those real photo cards was the number one hobby in America. Number one. But once World War I began, since the best printing was done in Germany, production halted—and a new company called the American Greeting Card Company filled the void, offering cheaper cards that Americans didn't like as much.

Of course, the final nail hit the coffin in the form of the telephone. Why send a card when you could just call up and tell them the news? But today, those real photo postcards are among the most collected items on eBay, as I learned when I sold a photo from a 1912 Stanford football game for a whopping $2.35.

To my mom, the cards are yet another example of my obsession with the past. To my sisters, who know me far better, they're the distraction that's only grown in size since Iris left. They may be right—but that doesn't mean distractions don't have benefits. The cards have oddly helped me settle back into my groove and find my sea legs—so much so that when an old friend like Clementine emails after fifteen years and asks how you're doing, instead of thinking about what's wrong with your life, you take a chance, hit the reply button, and say, "So glad you got in touch." That's even more valuable than the newest bids on eBay.

The problem is, by the time I reposition the piles on the kitchen table and pour my morning bowl of raisin bran, there's only one thing I really want to see on the computer. I start every morning with the obituaries. Mostly, I read about strangers. Today, at washington-post.com, I put in Orlando's name. His obit's not in there yet.

I put in the word *Archives*. Nothing there either. Not even a little blurb in the Metro section. I know what it means. If they thought it was foul play—even if it was suspicious and the cops were looking into it—there'd be ink on this. But as I swallow a spoonful of raisin bran, it looks like there's no current police investigation.

The worst part is, I don't know if that's good or bad.

Maybe it *was* just a heart attack, I tell myself, still hearing Khazei's words. For all I know, the only bogey-men are the ones in my imagination.

There's only one problem with the theory.

I look down at the vintage soft brown leather briefcase that's leaning against the leg of the table. The briefcase used to belong to my dad. He died when he was twenty-six. He never had a chance to use it. Today, it holds my keys, my journal that I keep all my eBay sales in, and the beaten old dictionary that sticks out from the back pouch.

Forget the videotape and Khazei and everything else.

The book. It still comes back to George Washington's book.

There's a reason that book just happened to be in that room, which just happened to be used by the leader of the free world. And until I find out what it is—

There's a quick double tap of a car horn, honking from outside.

"Coming!" I call out even though he can't hear me.

Grabbing my briefcase and winter coat, I head for the door, speedwalking through the living room, which is decorated with a used art deco black leather sofa that sits right below three side-by-side framed photo postcards from the 1920s, each of them with a different view of an old firemen's parade as it marched down the main street where I grew up in Wisconsin. The prints are the prize of my collection—and a daily reminder that if I mess it up here, that's exactly where I'm going back to.

Outside, the car honks again.

"I got it!" I shout, reaching for the door. But as I give it a tug, I see it's already open—just a bit—like I forgot to close it all the way last night. The thing is, I always close it all the way.

Standing in the doorway, I look back toward the living room, through to the kitchen. Both rooms are empty. Bits of dust turn silent cartwheels through the air. I recheck my briefcase. The George Washington book is still there. I tell myself I'm being paranoid. But as I leave, I pull hard to close the door—twice—and dart into the cold, which freezes my still damp hair.

Waiting for me idling in the street is a powder blue

1966 convertible Mustang that clears its throat and lets out the kind of hacking cough that comes with lung cancer. The car's old, but in perfect shape. Just like the driver inside, whose head is bobbing to the country music.

"C'mon, old boy...y'know I hate this neighborhood!" Tot shouts even though the windows are closed. At seventy-two years old, he's not rolling them down manually.

Racing for his car, I notice a thin man with a plaid green scarf walking his dog—a brown dachshund—on the opposite side of the street. I know most everyone on the block. Must be someone new. I can't think about it now.

Tot is far more than just my ride. He's the one who trained me on the job. And encouraged me to buy the house. And the only—truly *only*—one who doesn't bust my chops about Iris, but will always listen when I talk about whatever new set of old postcards I uncovered at the flea market. He's my friend. My real friend.

But he's also an archivist—since the very last days of LBJ's administration, which makes him the oldest, most senior, most resourceful researcher I've ever met. So as I hop in his car, open my briefcase, and hand him the tattered copy of George Washington's dictionary, he's also my best hope of figuring out whether this damn book could possibly be worth killing for.

15

There were faster ways for Dr. Stewart Palmiotti to get to work. As the President's doctor, he had a prime parking spot on West Exec. Not a far one either. Up close. Closer even than the spot reserved for Minnie. And Minnie was the President's sister.

From there, it was just a short walk through the West Wing. There was no need to take the long way around and walk past the Oval. But after that call last night…Palmiotti had been White House doctor for over three years. He'd been Wallace's dearest friend for over three decades.

Palmiotti wasn't some twentysomething novice. Rather than getting close, where he'd be spotted by the morning swirl of staffers and secretaries, he strolled casually past the Roosevelt Room, which had a clear view of the Oval Office's front door. Even back when he was governor, Wallace was always at his desk by at least 7 a.m. Even the day after he buried his mom.

Palmiotti glanced at his watch: 7:27. He looked over

at the Oval. There were no suit-and-tie agents standing guard outside the door. The President still wasn't in.

No reason to panic just yet.

From there, Palmiotti picked up the pace and made his way back outside, eyeing his own breath as he rushed down the West Colonnade and past the Rose Garden, whose snow had been melted away by the gardening staff. With a sharp left through the French doors, he stepped onto the long red-and-gold-trimmed carpet of the Ground Floor Corridor.

"He's still up there, huh?" he called out to Agent Mitchel, the uniformed Secret Service agent who was posted outside the private elevator on the left of the corridor.

Mitchel nodded, but the mere fact that the agent was there told Palmiotti that the President was still upstairs in the Family Residence.

"He's gonna be in a mood, isn't he?" Mitchel asked as Dr. Palmiotti headed to his own office, the White House Medical Unit, which sat directly across the hall from the elevator. Most staffers thought the Medical Unit was poor real estate, too far from the Oval. But as any doctor knew, the real action always happened at home.

"Depends," Palmiotti lied, well aware that from the phone call last night that something must've happened. "We know where he is?"

For a moment, the agent stood there.

"C'mon, I'm just trying to figure out what kind of day we're gonna have," Palmiotti added.

He wasn't stupid. After three years, he knew the Service protocol by now. To maintain some level of privacy, there were no agents or cameras allowed in the Residence. But to maintain some level of safety, the Service wired the floors of nearly every room up there. They did the same in the Oval: Weight-sensitive pressure pads under the carpets let them know exactly where President Wallace was at all times.

"Workout Room," Mitchel finally said, referring to the small room on the third floor installed by President Clinton.

Palmiotti rolled his eyes. The only time Wallace worked out was when he had something that needed working out.

"This from what happened last night?" the agent asked.

"Sorry?"

"I saw the call log. President called you at three in the morning?"

"No, that was nothing," Palmiotti said. "Same as always—just pulled his back again."

"Yeah, always his back," the agent said. "Though if that's the case, you really think he should be working out right now?"

This time, Palmiotti was the one who stood there. The Secret Service wasn't stupid either.

"Oh, by the by—Minnie's been looking for you," the agent added, referring to the President's sister.

Nodding politely, Dr. Stewart Palmiotti glanced down at his watch: 7:36. A new Wallace record.

"This something we should worry about, Doc?" the agent asked.

"No," Palmiotti replied, staring up at the red light above the elevator, waiting for it to light up … waiting for the President of the United States to come downstairs and tell him what the hell was going on. "I'm sure he's just running late."

16

*E*ntick's Dictionary?" Tot says, reading the embossed gold letters on the cover of the book as we weave through the morning traffic on Rockville Pike.

"Ever hear of it?" I ask, lowering the radio, which is pumping with his usual playlist—old country music by Willie Nelson, Buck Owens, and at this particular moment, Kenny Rogers.

"Don't you touch *The Gambler*," he threatens, slapping my hand away. He quickly turns back to the book. "Looks like it's…or at least what's left of it is…" He's blind in his right eye, so he has to turn his head completely toward me to see the book's torn-away spine and the missing interior pages. It's the same when he drives (which, legally, he can)—always with his head turned a quarter-way toward the passenger seat so he can get a better view of the road.

Most people think Tot looks like Merlin—complete with the scary white beard and the frizzy white hair that he brushes back—but he's far more of a Colonel Sanders,

especially with the gray checked jacket and the bolo tie
that he wears every day. He thinks the bolo tie makes him
look modern. It does. If you're in Scottsdale, Arizona,
and it's 1992.

"...I'm guessing pre-nineteenth-century—let's say
about..." Tot rolls his tongue in his cheek, already loving
the puzzle. Even his blind eye is twinkling. The only
thing that gets him more excited is flirting with the sixty-
year-old woman who runs the salad bar in the cafeteria.
But at seventy-two years old, Aristotle "Tot" Westman
could have worse weaknesses. "I'd say 1774."

"Close—1775," I tell him. "You're losing your
touch."

"Sure I am. That means you guessed...what?...Civil
War?"

I sit there, silent.

"Look at the threading," he says, running his finger
down the exposed spine and the mess of exposed thread.
"By the nineteenth century, it was all case binding—all
machine production—two boards and a spine, then glued
to the pages. What you have here is...this is art. Hand-
stitched. Or *was* hand-stitched before someone gutted it.
Is it one of ours?"

"That's what I'm trying to figure out."

"You haven't looked it up? Seen if it's in the system?"

"I need to. I will. It's just— Yesterday was—" I take
a breath. "Yesterday sucked."

"Not just for you. You see the paper this morning?"
he asks as he pulls a folded-up copy of the *Washington
Times* from where it's wedged next to his seat along with

a copy of the *Washington Post* and the *Baltimore Sun*. "Apparently one of our guards had a seizure or something."

He tosses the paper in my lap. I quickly scan the story. It's small. Buried on page two of the Metro section. Doesn't mention me. Doesn't mention foul play. Doesn't even mention Orlando by name ("The victim's name is being withheld until family can be notified").

"This wasn't in the *Post*," I say.

"Of course it wasn't in the *Post*. You read only one paper and you're only getting half the actual news— whatever biased side you happen to subscribe to. Can you imagine, though?" Tot asks, his voice perfectly steady. "Guy drops dead right in our building—right as President Wallace is about to arrive—and right as you're walking around the building with the daughter of Nico Hadrian, the very guy who tried to assassinate Wallace's predecessor."

I sit up straight as the traffic slows and a swarm of red brake lights flash their ruby smile our way. The only person who knew about Nico was the woman I called in our St. Louis records center. Carrie—

"Don't even feign the faux-shock, Beecher. You really think Carrie could find enlistment records—from Nowhere, Wisconsin—*from over twenty years ago* without calling for help?"

I shouldn't be surprised. When John Kerry ran for President and they needed to prove that he earned those Purple Hearts, they came to Tot. It was the same when they were searching for George W. Bush's National

Guard records. And the same with John McCain's military file. On my first day of work, a coworker asked Tot if he knew where to find the unit records for a particular company in the Spanish-American War. Tot gave them the record group, stack, row, compartment, and shelf number. From memory. On the anniversary of his fortieth year here, they asked him the secret of his longevity. He said, "When I first arrived, I started to open these boxes to see what's inside. I've been fascinated ever since."

"Honestly, though, Beecher—why didn't you just call me in the first place?" Tot asks. "If you need help..."

"I need help, Tot," I insist. "Major help. I need the kind of help that comes with a side order of help."

His face still cocked toward me, he holds the steering wheel of the old Mustang with two crooked fingers. The car was his dream car when he was young, his midlife crisis car when he turned fifty, and his supposed retirement present when he finally hit sixty-five. But it was always out of reach, always for another day—until three years ago when his wife of fifty-one years died from a ruptured brain aneurism. It was the same week I started at the Archives. He had nothing back then. But he somehow found me—and I found... When I used to work at the bookshop, Mr. Farris told me we're all raised by many fathers in our lives. Right now, I pray he's right.

"Tell me the story, Beecher. The real story."

It takes me the rest of the ride to do just that, and as we follow rush-hour traffic to his usual shortcut through Rock Creek Park, I give him everything from showing Clementine around the building, to Orlando offering to let us in the SCIF, to spilling the coffee and finding the book hidden below the chair.

He never interrupts. Forever an archivist, he knows the value of collecting information first. By the time we turn onto Constitution Avenue, I hit the big finale with the parts about Orlando's death, the suddenly missing videotape, and every other detail I can think of, from Dallas's lurking, to Khazei's passive-aggressive threat to make me look like the murderer. But as the powder blue Mustang growls and claws through D.C.'s slushy streets, Tot's only reaction is:

"You shouldn't've told me any of this."

"What?"

"You need to be smart, Beecher. And you're not being smart."

"What're you talking about? I *am* being smart. I'm getting help."

"That's fine. But look at the full picture you're now in the middle of: Of everything that's happened, there's only one detail—just one—that can't be argued with."

"Besides that I'm screwed?"

"The book, Beecher. Where'd you find that book?" he asks, pointing to the dictionary.

"In the chair."

"Yes! It was hidden in the chair. Y'understand what I'm saying? You may not know if it was hidden *by* the President, or *for* the President, or by or for his Secret Service agents or some other party we don't even know of— but the act of *hiding* and *finding* something, that's a two-party agreement. One hider and one finder. So to hide the book in that SCIF... to even get in that room..."

"You think it's someone from our staff," I say.

"Maybe from our staff... maybe from Security... but it's gotta be someone in our building," Tot says as we stop at a red light. "I mean, if you're hiding something, would you ever pick a room unless you had the key?"

Up ahead, the Washington Monument is on my right. But I'm far more focused on my left, at the wide green lawn that leads back, back, back to the beautiful mansion with the wide, curved balcony. The White House. From here, it looks miniature, but you can already see the specks of tourists lingering and snapping photos at the black metal gates.

"Beecher, don't think what you're thinking."

I stay silent, eyes still on the home of Orson Wallace.

"That's not who you're fighting, Beecher. This isn't you against the President of the United States."

"You don't know that."

"Sure I do. If it were, the paramedics would be carrying *you* under the sheet by now."

I shake my head. "That's only because they don't know I have their book."

For the first time, Tot's silent.

As we turn onto Pennsylvania Avenue, as he pulls past our building—a huge neoclassical granite archives that fills over two city blocks on our right—I ignore the fifty-foot-high columns and instead stare at the two smaller limestone statues that flank the front doors. There are four statues in total, representing the Future, the Past,

Heritage, and Guardianship. Tot knows better than I do which is which, but there's no mistaking the carved old man holding a scroll and a closed book on the right. Engraved at the base it says, "Study the Past."

I open the Washington dictionary and again read the words. *Exitus acta probat.*

"Think about it, Tot, of all the people in the building yesterday, I can account for everyone being where they were—Orlando…Dallas…Rina…even Khazei—everyone except for President Wallace, who just happened to pick the exact day, at the exact time of death, to stop by for his visit."

"Actually, he's not the only one."

"What're you talking about?"

He looks my way, turning far enough that I can see his good eye. "Tell me about the girl."

"Who?"

"The girl. The high school crush you're all gushy about."

"Clemmi?"

"*Clemmi?* No, no, no, don't do pet names. You barely know this girl two days."

"I've known her since seventh grade," I say as I reach to change the radio station.

"What're you doing?" Tot challenges.

"Huh?"

"Don't change my station. What'd I tell you about messing with *The Gambler*?"

"I know, and you know I love *The Gambler*, but— Can't we just…?" I twist the dial, searching for music. "I just want to hear something new—like maybe—do you know which stations play rap or even…Joan Jett?"

He pumps the brakes, nearly putting me through the windshield. "Beecher, don't you dare hit menopause in my car."

"What're you talking about?"

He raises his voice, trying to sound like me. *"I need something new. Where do they keep the rap music?"* Returning to normal, he adds, "This girl's been back in your life barely forty-eight hours, and what—suddenly you don't want to eat your raisin bran, or listen to the same boring old music anymore? Don't be such a cliché, Beecher. You have a good life. You moved past Iris…you were in a real groove."

"I *was* in a groove. But that's the problem with a groove—if you don't change it up, it quickly becomes a hole."

"Yeah, except for the fact you're already in a hole—one that can swallow you. You gotta admit it's odd, Beecher. The daughter of Lee Harvey Oswald walks back into your life—"

"Her dad's not Oswald."

"No, he's Nico Hadrian, who tried to assassinate a U.S. President. And she walks back into your life on the same day that another President just happens to be visiting our offices? Girl's got a pretty uncanny sense of timing, no?"

"Tot, she didn't even know who her dad was until we told her! How could she possibly be plotting against me?"

With a sharp right onto 7th Street, Tot makes another quick right toward the underground side entrance of the building, which is blocked by a bright yellow metal antiram barrier that rises from the concrete. Tot rides the brakes, giving the barrier time to lower. When it doesn't, the car bucks to a halt.

On our left, I finally see why Tot's so quiet. An armed security guard steps out of the nearby guardhouse, his puffed black winter coat hiding everything but his face and his unusually white front teeth. Ever since 9/11, when we became obsessed with terrorists stealing the Declaration of Independence, our building has limited the underground parking spots to a grand total of seven. Seven. Our boss—the Archivist of the United States—gets one. His deputy gets another. Two are for deliveries of new records. Two are for VIPs. And one is for Tot, a favor from a friend in Security who used to control such things during the Bush era.

As the guard with the white teeth approaches, Tot nods hello, which is always enough to get us in. But instead of waving us through and lowering the barrier…

The guard raises his hand, palm straight at us. We're not going anywhere.

17

Morning, morning," the duty nurse sang as Dr. Palmiotti stepped into the cramped reception area of the White House Medical Unit. As usual, her dyed black hair was pulled back in a tight military braid that was starting to fray from her bad night's sleep. Behind her, in the area between the bathroom and treatment room, she'd already tucked away the fold-down bed. The White House doctor arrived first thing in the morning, but the duty nurse had been there all night.

"Good night's sleep?" Palmiotti asked, amused to notice how the morning small talk sounded like a one-night stand.

"I tell my mom I sleep less than a hundred feet from the President. Vertically," duty nurse Kayre Morrison replied, pointing up at the ceiling.

Palmiotti didn't even hear the joke. He was peeking over his shoulder, back into the hallway. The red light above the elevator was still off. Still no sign of President Wallace.

"By the way, Minnie wants to see you," the nurse said. "She's waiting for you now. In your office."

"Are you—? Kayre, you're killing me. I mean it. You're striking me dead."

"She's the President's sister," the nurse whisper-hissed. "I can't kick her out."

Palmiotti shook his head as he trudged to his private office in the back of the suite. Typical duty nurse. And typical Minnie.

"Heeey!" he called out, painting on a big smile as he threw the door open. "How's my favorite girl?"

Across from his desk, sitting on the tan leather sofa, was a stumpy forty-two-year-old woman with a thick block of a body. She was dressed in her usual unconstructed dress, this one navy blue, plus her mother's long dangly silver earrings from the early eighties, which was about the time Palmiotti first got to know Jessamine "Minnie" Wallace.

"Okay, Minnie, what's it this time?"

Minnie lifted her chin, revealing a stout, squatty neck and a grin that—ever since her stroke—rose on only one side.

"Can't I just be here to say hello?" she asked with the slight lisp (another lingering side effect from the stroke) that made the word *just* sound like *juss*.

"Aren't you supposed to be doing physical therapy right now?"

"Already did it," Minnie promised.

Palmiotti stood there, studying her on the sofa as her thumb tapped against the bright pink cane that she still needed to walk. The handle of the cane was shaped and painted like the head of a flamingo. That was the problem with being the sister of the President—you wind up spending your life finding other ways to stand out. "You didn't do your therapy again, did you?"

"Sure I did."

"Minnie...Show me your hands," Palmiotti challenged.

Minnie half-smiled, pretending not to hear him. "I meant to ask, you still seeing Gabriel for lunch today?" she said, referring to the President's scheduler.

"Please don't do that," he begged.

"Do what?"

"What's it now? Reception in the Oval? Having the President speak at your annual convention?"

"It's a Caregivers' Conference—for the top scientists who study brain injuries," she explained, referring to the cause that she now spent so much time pushing for. "My brother already said he'd come, but when I spoke to Gabriel—"

"Listen, you know that if Gabriel tells you no, it's *no*," he said. But as he reached for the best way to track down the President—the earpiece and Secret Service radio that sat on his desk—there was a sudden burst of voices behind him. Over his shoulder, out in the Ground Floor Corridor, he saw a phalanx of staffers—the President's personal aide, his chief of staff, the press secretary, and an older black speechwriter—slowly gathering near the President's private elevator. Palmiotti had watched it for three years now. Forget the radio. The personal aide always got the call first from the valet who laid out Wallace's suits.

Sure enough, the red light above the elevator blinked on with a *ping*. Agent Mitchel whispered something into the microphone at his wrist, and two new Secret Service agents appeared from nowhere. Thirty seconds after that, President Orson Wallace, in fresh suit and tie, stepped out to start the day. For a second, the President glanced around the hallway rather than focusing on the swarm of staff.

The doctor shook his head.

Not every President is a great speaker. Not every President is a great thinker. But in the modern era, every single President is a master of one thing: eye contact. Bill Clinton was so good at it, when he was drinking lemonade while you were talking to him, he'd stare at you through the bottom of his glass just to maintain that lock on you. Wallace was no different. So when he stepped off the elevator and glanced around instead of locking on his aides...

...that's when Palmiotti knew that whatever happened last night, it was worse than he thought.

"*Just gimme a minute,*" the President mimed as he patted his personal aide on the shoulder and sidestepped through the small crowd—straight toward Palmiotti's side of the corridor.

Of course, the staffers started to follow.

Yet as the President entered the reception area of the Medical Unit, half the throng—the speechwriter and the press secretary, as well as the Secret Service—stopped at the door and waited in the hallway, well aware that their access didn't include a private visit to the President's doctor.

"*Dr. Palmiotti…!*" the duty nurse murmured in full panic. The only times the President had come this way were when it was officially on the schedule.

"I see him," Palmiotti called back from his office.

"Where you hiding him? You know he's dating again? He tell you he was dating?" the President teased the nurse, flashing his bright whites and still trying to charm. It was good enough to fool the nurse. Good enough to fool the two trailing staffers. But never good enough to fool the friend who used to get suckered trading his Double Stuf Oreos for Wallace's Nilla Wafers in fifth grade.

As the two men made eye contact, Palmiotti could feel the typhoon coming. He had seen that look on the President's face only three times before: once when he was President, once when he was governor, and once from the night they didn't talk about anymore.

The President paused at the threshold of Palmiotti's private office, which was when Palmiotti spotted the hardcover book the President was carrying.

Palmiotti cocked an eyebrow. *We're not alone*, he said with a glance.

Wallace dipped his neck into the office, spotting his sister, who raised her flamingo cane, saluting him with the beak.

Definitely not ideal.

The President didn't care. He stepped into Palmiotti's

office, which was decorated with the same medical school diplomas that had covered his first office back in Ohio. Back when everything was so much simpler.

"Mr. President..." Wallace's personal aide said, standing with the chief of staff at the threshold.

In any White House, the smart staffers get invited to *walk* with the President. But the smartest staffers—and the ones who get the farthest—are the ones who know when to *walk away*.

"...we'll be right out here," the aide announced, thumbing himself back to the reception area.

"Stewie was just examining my hands," Minnie announced, reaching forward from the couch and extending her open palms to Palmiotti.

"Wonderful," Wallace muttered, not even looking at his sister as he closed the door to Palmiotti's office. There were bigger problems to deal with.

"So I take it your back's still hurting you?" Palmiotti asked.

Orson Wallace studied his friend. The President's eye contact was spectacular. Better than Clinton's. Better than W's. Better than Obama's. "Like you wouldn't believe," the leader of the free world said, carefully pronouncing every syllable. "Think you can help with it?"

"We'll see," Palmiotti said. "First I need you to tell me where it hurts."

18

This is bad, isn't it?" I ask.

"Relax," Tot whispers, rolling down his window as a snakebite of cold attacks from outside. He's trying to keep me calm, but with his right hand he tugs at his pile of newspapers, using them to cover George Washington's dictionary.

"Sorry, fellas," the guard says, his breath puffing with each syllable. "IDs, please."

"C'mon, Morris," Tot says, pumping his overgrown eyebrows. "You telling me you don't recognize—"

"Don't bust my hump, Tot. Those are the rules. ID."

Tot lowers his eyebrows and reaches for his ID. He's not amused. Neither is the guard, who leans in a bit too deeply through the open window. His eyes scan the entire car. Like he's searching for something.

Circling around toward the trunk, he slides a long metal pole with a mirror on the end of it under the car. Bomb search. They haven't done a bomb search since we hosted the German president nearly a year ago.

"You got what you need?" Tot asks, his hand still on

the newspapers. The story on top is the one about Orlando.

"Yeah. All set," the guard says, glancing back at the guardhouse. Doesn't take James Bond to see what he's staring at: the flat, compact security camera that's pointed right at us. No question, someone's watching.

There's a deafening metal shriek as the antiram barrier bites down into the ground, clearing our path. Tot pulls the car forward, his face again mostly turned to me. His blind eye is useless, but I can still read the expression. *Don't say a word.*

I follow the request from the parking lot all the way to the elevators. Inside, as we ride up in silence, Tot opens up the folded newspapers, but it's clear he's really reading what's tucked inside—*Entick's Dictionary*. I watch him study the swirls and loops of the handwritten inscription. *Exitus acta probat.*

"See that?" I ask. "That's George Washing—"

He shoots me another look to keep me quiet. This time, I wait until we reach our offices on the fourth floor.

The sign next to the door reads *Room 404*, but around here it's called Old Military because we specialize in records from the Revolutionary and Civil wars.

"Anyone home...?" I call out, opening the door, already knowing the answer. The lights in the long suite are off. On my left, a metal wipe-off board has two columns—one IN, one OUT—and holds a half dozen magnets with our headshot photos attached to each one. Sure, it's ridiculously kindergarten. But with all of us always running to the stacks for research, it works. And right now, everyone's in the OUT column. That's all we need.

Knowing the privacy won't last, I rush toward my cubicle in the very back. Tot does his best to rush toward his in the very front.

"Don't you wanna see if the book is in our collection?" I call out as I pull out my key to open the lock on the middle drawer of my desk. To my surprise, it's already open. I think about it a moment, flipping on my computer. With everything going on, I could've easily forgotten to lock it last night. But as my mind tumbles back to the front door of my house...

"You do your magic tricks, I'll do mine," Tot says as I hear the *gnnn* of a metal drawer opening. Tot's cube is a big one, holding a wall of six tall file cabinets, stacks upon stacks of books (mostly about his specialty, Abraham Lincoln), and a wide window that overlooks Pennsylvania Avenue and the Navy Memorial.

My cube is a tiny one, filled with a desk, computer, and a corkboard that's covered with the best typos we've been able to find throughout history, including a 1631 Bible that has the words "Thou *shalt* commit adultery," plus the first edition of a *Washington Post* gossip column from 1915 that was supposed to say President Woodrow Wilson "spent the evening entertaining Mrs. Galt," a widow who he was courting, but instead said, "the President spent the evening *entering* Mrs. Galt." You don't get this job without having some pack rat in you. But with ten billion pages in our collection, you also don't get it without being part scavenger.

As my computer boots up, I grab the keyboard, all set to dig. In my pocket, my cell phone starts to ring. I know who it is. Right on time.

"Hey, Mom," I answer without even having to look. Ever since her heart surgery, I've asked my mother to call me every morning—just so I know she's okay. But as I put the phone to my ear, instead of my mom, I get...

"She's fine," my sister Sharon tells me. "Just tired."

I have two sisters. Sharon's the older one—and the one who, even when she went to the local community college, never stopped living with my mom. We used to call it Sharon's weakness. Now it's our whole family's strength. She looks like my mom. She sounds like my mom. And these days, she spends most of her life dealing with all the health issues of my mom.

Every two weeks, I send part of my check home. But Sharon's the one who gives her time.

"Ask her if she's going to Jumbo's," I say, using my mom's preferred lunch spot as my favorite code. If my mom's eating lunch there, I know she's feeling well.

"She is," Sharon answers. "And she wants to know where you're going Friday night," she adds, throwing my mom's favorite code right back. She doesn't care where I'm going, or even *if* I'm going. She wants to know: *Do I have a date?* and more important, *Will I ever get over Iris?*

"Will you please tell her I'm fine?" I plead.

"Beecher, how's your seventy-year-old friend?"

"And you're the one to talk? Besides, you've never even met Tot."

"I'm sure he's lovely—but I'm telling you, from experience: If you don't change the way you're living, that's gonna be *you* one day. Old and lovely and all by yourself. Listen to me on this. Don't hide in those Archives, Beecher. Live that life."

"Is this me arguing with you, or arguing with Mom?"

Before she can answer, I glance to my right. There's a solid red light on my desk phone. Voicemail message.

"I think I got you something, old boy," Tot calls out from his cubicle.

"Shar, I gotta go. Kiss Mom for me." As I hang up my cell, I'm already dialing into voicemail, putting in my PIN code.

While waiting for the message to play, I dial up caller ID on the keypad, study the little screen of my phone, and scroll down until I see the name of the person who left the last message.

Williams, Orlando.

My heart stops.

I read it again. Orlando.

My computer blinks awake. Tot yells something in the distance.

"*Message one was received at…4:58 p.m.…yesterday.*"

And in my ear, through the phone, I hear a familiar baritone voice—Orlando's voice—and the final words of a dead man.

19

On a scale of one to ten," Dr. Palmiotti asked, "would you say the pain is...?"

"It's a four," the President said.

"Just a four?"

"It *used to be* a four. Now it's an eight," Wallace said, pacing along the far left side of the doctor's office and glancing out the wide window with the stunning view of the White House Rose Garden. "Approaching a nine."

"A nine for what?" his sister Minnie asked, already concerned. The doctor was talking to the President, but it was Minnie, as she stood across from Palmiotti, who was being examined.

She held her right palm wide open as he poked each of her fingers with a sterilized pin, testing to see her reaction. Whenever she missed therapy for too long, sharp pains would recede and feel simply dull. "What's wrong with him?" she asked, motioning to her brother.

"Nothing's wrong," Palmiotti promised.

"If he's sick..."

"I'm not sick. Just some stupid back problems," the President insisted. "And a really crappy night's sleep."

"Listen to me, I know they won't say this on the front page of the paper, but you need to hear it, O: I have faith in you. Stewie has faith in you. Your wife and kids have faith in you. And millions of people out there do too. You know that, right?"

The President turned, looking at his sister, absorbing her words.

Palmiotti knew how much Minnie loved her brother. And how much Wallace loved her back. But that didn't mean it was always best for him to have her around. By now, most of America had heard the story: How Minnie was born with the genetic disease known as Turner syndrome. How it affected only females, leaving them with a missing X chromosome. How 98 percent of people die from Turner syndrome, but Minnie lived—and she lived without any of the heart or kidney or cognitive problems that go along with it. In fact, the only thing that Minnie Wallace got from Turner syndrome was that she was—like a few of its victims—manly.

Broad chest. Low hairline. Short neck. With one X chromosome, she looked like Moe from the Three Stooges. Perez Hilton said if she were one of the Seven Dwarfs, she'd be Stumpy. Or Fatty. Or Dumpy. When it first got posted, the President tried to let it roll off. He issued a statement saying that the comment made him Grumpy. But Palmiotti knew the truth. Nothing hits harder than when someone hits home. For the President...for Minnie...the last time Palmiotti saw pain like that was the night of the accident that caused her stroke.

The worst part was, he saw the makings of a similar pain right now—and from the strained look on the President's face, despite the little pep talk from his sister, that pain was just starting to swell.

"Minnie, go do your therapy," Palmiotti ordered.

"I can do it right here. You have the squeeze balls—"

"Mimo, you're not listening," the President interrupted. "I need to see my doctor. By myself."

Minnie cocked her head. She knew that tone. Grabbing her flamingo cane, she started heading for the door.

"Before I go…" she quickly added, "if you could speak at our Caregivers' Conference—"

"Minnie…"

"Okay. Fine. Gabriel. I'll talk to Gabriel," she said. "But just promise me—all these back problems—you're sure you're okay?"

"Look at me," Wallace said, flashing the insta-smile that won him 54 percent of the popular vote. "Look where I live…look at this life…what could I possibly be upset about?"

With her limp, it took Minnie nearly a minute to leave the office.

The President didn't start speaking until she was gone.

20

*B*eecher, it's me..." Orlando says in the message, his deep voice showing just a crack of flat Wisconsin accent.

My legs go numb, then my chest.

"Beecher, lookit this!" Tot yells behind me, though I swear to God, it sounds like he's talking underwater.

"Tot, gimme one sec," I call back.

My Lord. How can—? Orlando. That's... Orlando...

"You need to see this, though," Tot insists, shuffling toward me with a thick stack of paper held by a binder clip.

Still gripping the phone, I lean forward in my chair, lurching for the keypad and pounding the 3 button. *This isn't... focus!... start over... just focus...*

Beep.

"*Beecher, it's me,*" Orlando begins again. He pauses a moment.

"Y'ever see this?" Tot interrupts, waving the pages.

"Tot, please... can it wait?"

I hit the 3 button again to buy some time. The phone's

not near my ear, but I still hear Orlando's opening. *"Beecher, it's me."*

"You want to know if that was George Washington's dictionary or not?" Tot asks. "Just listen: When George Washington died, Mount Vernon made a list of every single item in his possession—every candlestick, every fork, every piece of art on his walls…"

I hit 3 again. *"Beecher, it's me."*

"…and of course, every one of GW's books," Tot says, tossing me the copy of *Entick's Dictionary*. It hits my desk with a dead thud.

"Okay…I get it, Tot."

"The more you rush me, Beecher, the slower I'm gonna talk."

"Okay, I'm sorry, just…*please*." I press 3 again. *"Beecher, it's me."*

"The point is," Tot continues, "the only way to find out if this is really GW's book is to first find out if he even owned a copy."

I hit 3 again. "And?"

"According to this, he had one." He points to the list. *One copy. Entick's Dictionary.* "Though if this is even the same copy, that still doesn't explain how it found its way here."

"Or even *if* it found its way here," I say. "For all we know, this isn't even part of our collection."

"Actually, that's easy enough to find out." Stepping toward my computer, Tot shoos me from my seat. "C'mon…Up!…Old man needs to sit," he says as I hop aside, stretching the phone cord to its limits. He's already

clicking at the keyboard. Perfect. I turn my attention back
to the phone...

"Beecher, it's me," Orlando begins again. He pauses
a moment. *"Crap, I don't have your cell phone."* He
pauses again, then his voice picks up speed. *"I need you
to call me. What you did..."*

What I did?

"Just call me," he finishes.

I hit the button and replay it again.

"Crap, I don't have your cell phone."

He pauses after that. Is that panic? Is he panicking? Is
he sick?

"Crap, I don't have your cell phone."

I listen closely, but I was wrong before. His voice
isn't picking up speed. It's fast, but no faster than usual.

"I need you to call me. What you did..."

There it is. The only moment his voice strains. Just
slightly on the word *did.* I hit the rewind button again.

"What you did..."

He means finding the dictionary.

"What you did..."

There's definitely an emphasis on the last word.

"What you did..."

It's just three syllables. Three dumb words. It's no different than looking at a photo of a happy, grinning child
and then being told he died in a brutal car accident. No
matter what you want to see, all you see is...it's not just
loss or sadness. To hear these words...uttered by this—
this—this—ghost...

"What you did..."

All I hear is blame.

"*Just call me*," Orlando finally says at 4:58 p.m. yesterday.

As his voice fades, I feel my body churn, straining for its own equilibrium. It doesn't come. I'm squeezing the phone so hard, streams of sweat run from my fist down the inside of my wrist, seeping into my watchband.

It's not until I look down that I spot Tot arching his head toward me, studying me with his good eye. If he heard...

He stares right at me.

Of course he heard.

I wait for him to judge, to warn, to say that I need to get rid of Orlando's message.

"You're not alone in this, Beecher."

"Actually, I kinda am," I say as I hear a beep on the other line. I look down at caller ID, which reads *Security*. I don't pick up. The last thing I need right now is Khazei quizzing me again about Orlando's death. Instead, I forward Orlando's message to my cell and delete it from voicemail.

Tot shakes his head. "I'm telling you, you're not alone. You need to hear that."

"That's fine—and I appreciate when someone says something nice to me, Tot, but... I'm just... I don't think I can do this."

"Do what?"

"*This*. Any of this. Tracking old books that're hidden for Presidents... playing Spy versus Spy... getting guilt and spooky messages from dead people..."

"Guilt? What're you talking about?"

"Didn't you hear Orlando's message? When he said, *What you did . . .*—heart attack or murder—he might as well have added . . . *when you caused my death.*"

"You really think Orlando was calling you for some bitter scolding?"

"What else am I supposed to think?"

At his jawbone, just below his ear, Tot twirls a few stray hairs of his wizard beard between his thumb and pointer-finger while eyeing the gutted copy of *Entick's Dictionary.* "Maybe he was amazed you found it. Maybe he just realized the consequences: *What you did . . .*" He lowers his voice to sound like Orlando: *". . . you just uncovered something no one knew existed. President Wallace was . . . God knows what he was up to, but you found it, Beecher. You're a hero."*

"A hero? For what? For spilling coffee? For trying to impress a girl from high school in the hopes of forgetting about my fiancée? I mean it, Tot. I woke up this morning with my feet sweating! Name one hero who has sweaty feet!"

I wait for him to answer—for him to pull some historian nonsense and tell me that Teddy Roosevelt was known for his sweaty feet, but instead Tot just sits there, still twirling his beard.

My phone again starts to ring. Like before, caller ID reads *Security.* Like before, I don't pick it up.

Nodding his approval, Tot takes a deep breath through his nose. "Beecher, y'know what the best part of this job is? For me, it's this sheet of paper," he says, picking up a random sheet of paper from my desk and flapping it back and forth. "On any given day, this sheet is just another sheet in our collection, right? But then, one day—9/11 happens—and suddenly this sheet of paper becomes *the most vital document in the U.S. government*." He tosses the paper back to my desk. "That's what we're here to witness, Beecher. We witness it and we protect it. We're the caretakers of those sheets of paper that'll someday define the writing of history."

"Tot, I think you're being a little dramatic about paper."

"You're not listening. It's not just with paper. It also happens with *people*."

At the far end of the office, the front door opens and there's a quiet metallic *clunk* on our magnet board. Like a periscope rising from a submarine, I peer above the cubicles and spot my fellow archivist Rina, who offers a surprisingly warm Mona Lisa smile considering how pissed she was yesterday at coming in number two in our internal rankings.

"You okay?" Rina asks me.

"Huh?"

"Yesterday—I saw you downstairs. With Orlando. You were friends, no?"

"Yeah…no…I'm okay. Thanks," I tell her as she heads toward her own cube.

Lowering periscope, I turn back to Tot. "Rina," I whisper, quickly adding, "So in this analogy, *I'm* the sheet of paper?"

"You've been here a few years now, Beecher—you

should know history isn't just something that's written. It's a selection process. It chooses moments, and events, and yes, people—and it hands them a situation they should never be able to overcome. It happens to millions of us every single day. But the only ones we read about are the ones who face that situation, and fight that situation, and find out who they really are."

"And now *you're* the one not listening, Tot. I know who I am. I fought for this life. And I spent two full years taking 140,000 photographs of overpriced wedding cakes, and grooms who think they can dance, just to make sure that I didn't have to go back to Wisconsin and say that life outside my mother's house was just too tough for me. I got further than my father, and his father, and every rotten classmate who used to aim for my head in dodgeball even though they knew headshots didn't count. But whatever history supposedly handed me...whatever we did find in the SCIF...I don't know what it is...I don't know where to start...I don't even know what I'm supposed to be looking for!"

Once again shaking his head, Tot turns back to my computer and hits the enter key. Onscreen, I see the Archives' history for *Entick's Dictionary*. Yes, we have a copy. Yes, it's in this building. And according to this, it's currently...

"*Signed out*," I blurt, reading from the screen.

It's the first good news I've had all day. Every day at the Archives, hundreds of people come to do research. To make it easier, once you register as a researcher, you can fill up two carts and keep them on hold, stored in our research room, for three days. And from what it says here, *Entick's Dictionary* is currently on hold for a researcher named...Tot clicks to the next screen.

"*Dustin Gyrich*," we both whisper as my phone rings for the third time. For the third time, I ignore *Security*.

"This guy Gyrich from us?" I ask as I pull open my top drawer and start flipping through our staff list. A...B...C...G...H...I...No one named Gyrich.

"I don't think he's a pro either," Tot adds, referring to the professional researchers people can hire by the hour.

Across the office, the door again swings open. "Beecher, you here!?" a familiar voice shouts.

Even without raising periscope, I smell the pipe smoke on Dallas. On most days, he ignores me. Today, his footsteps head right for me.

"Beecher?" he adds, sounding almost concerned. "You there or not?"

"Yeah...right here," I say, stepping out from my cube.

"Dammit, then why didn't you say something!? Security's worried— After Orlando— Don't *do that*!" he scolds, all his concern already faded in anger. "Next time someone calls your sorry ass, pick up the damn ph—"

Dallas cuts himself off, stopping midstep as he reaches my cube. He's not looking at me anymore. He's looking at what's behind me. I spin around, worried he sees the dictionary. But the dictionary's already gone— tucked away by the person still sitting at my desk.

"Hey, Tot," Dallas offers, scratching at his starter beard. "Didn't realize you were there."

Tot doesn't say a word. He just stares at Dallas, unblinking. It's nothing personal. When he turned seventy, Tot decided there were ten rules for living a happy life. The only one he's shared with me thus far is that, as an archivist, he won't make friends with anyone who says FDR knew about the impending attack on Pearl Harbor, since there's not a single sheet of paper in our building to back up that claim. I know another of his rules has something to do with white cotton panties and the keys to a great sex life (I made him stop talking because—just the thought of it made me want to be blind). And from what I can tell, there's a third rule that enshrines a venomous hatred for bullies—especially those who curse at Tot's friends.

The best part is watching Dallas take a half-step back. Even the most stubborn of cubs knows when the big cat's around.

"I was just saying…" Dallas stutters, "…I was telling Beecher I was worried about—"

"How'd you know someone was calling him?" Tot challenges.

"Pardon?"

"When you came in," Tot says. "You said Security was calling. How'd you know they were calling?"

"I-I was there," Dallas says.

"In the Security Office?"

"No…at sign-in…with the detectors," he says, referring to the check-in desk on the Penn Avenue side of the building. "They have a visitor for Beecher who's pretty insistent that she see him…"

"*She?*" I ask.

"Your friend. From yesterday. The one with the nose pierce…"

Tot shoots me a look. He's already called her the daughter of Lee Harvey Oswald. The last thing he wants is me bringing her in again.

"Clementine's downstairs right now?" I ask.

"Why do you think they keep calling you?" Dallas says. "They saw you check in at the garage, but when you didn't answer your phone—"

I glance at Tot, who doesn't need help putting the rest together. The only way to get Clementine into this building is if I personally go down and sign her in. And while the last thing I need right now is to put myself higher on the suspect list because I'm helping out the daughter of a killer, the less time I let her spend with Security, the safer I'm gonna be.

"*Tot…*" I say with a glance as I run for the door.

Go. I have it, he replies with a nod. It's never taken me more than three minutes and twenty-two seconds to get to the sign-in desk. And while I need to get Clementine, priority number one is still finding out who Dustin Gyrich is and why, on the same day the President was set to arrive here, Gyrich requested this old dictionary.

"I'm old and hate small talk," Tot tells Dallas as he turns back to my computer. "You need to leave right now."

As Dallas heads back to his desk, I pick up speed and make a sharp left toward the office door. But as I pull it open and bound into the hallway, I nearly smash into the chest of the tall man. And his shiny Security badge.

"Beecher, you know the one thing that really ticks me off?" Deputy Security Chief Venkat Khazei asks as I crane my neck up to see him. "When people here—people sitting right at their desks—don't return my calls."

He puts a hand on my shoulder, but all I can think is that he's the only other person in the entire building who knew Orlando was in that SCIF.

"Is there something I can help you with?" I ask.

"That's generous of you, Beecher," Khazei says. "I thought you'd never ask."

21

"You tell me what's easier," Khazei offers, trying hard to keep it nice. "We can talk out here, or at your desk, or—"

"Out here's fine," I blurt, determined to keep him far from the book.

"Where you headed anyway?"

"Wha?"

"You were running, Beecher. You almost smashed into me. Just wondering where you're headed."

"Stacks," I say with a nod, realizing that while Khazei was calling for info, it was the front-desk security guys who were calling about Clementine. "Just pulling a record from the stacks."

He looks down at my empty hands. "Where's the pull slip?"

Now he thinks he's being smart.

"Right here," I say, pointing to the side of my head and being smart right back. But the way his broad eyebrows knot together, Khazei doesn't like me being smart right back.

"Y'know…" he says, smoothing his thinning black hair to the side, "you were also running yesterday when you found out about Orlando."

"He's my friend. I shouldn't run when I hear my friend's dead?"

"I'm just saying…for a place that gets the gold medal for slow and quiet, you're rushing around a lot lately."

He watches me carefully, letting the silence of the empty hallway sink in. But all I'm really focused on is the thought of Clementine still waiting for me downstairs.

"You said you had a question, Mr. Khazei."

"No, I said I had something I was hoping you could help me with," he corrects, scratching his chin with the back of his hand. "I'm just wondering if you were able to look at your calendar…for when you were with Orlando."

"I looked, but I can't really nail it down. I saw him in the hallway. Maybe about a half hour before he…y'know…"

Khazei nods, but doesn't otherwise react. "Anything else you might've thought of? Anything that might be helpful as we look into his death?"

"I thought the paramedics said it was a seizure—that he had sleep apnea."

"They did. That's why they're paramedics, not coroners," Khazei says. "Now. Again. Anything at all—anything Orlando might've said, anything he did—that you think we should know about?"

I don't pause. "Nothing that I can think of," I tell him.

"I thought you said you guys were close."

"I said he was *nice to me*. We're both from Wisconsin, and he was always nice."

"And that's it?" Khazei asks.

"Why's that so hard for you to believe?"

"I don't know," Khazei replies, calmer than ever. "I guess...if he's just some nice guy from Wisconsin, well...why's he making you the very last person he calls before he dies?"

Over his shoulder, the elevator dings, bringing the morning's arrival of fellow employees. Khazei smiles, as if he's in control of that too.

"It's the twenty-first century, Beecher. You really think we wouldn't take the time to check the outgoing calls on Orlando's phone?"

It's the second time he's caught me in one of his lame little mental traps. I swear right now, he's not getting me for a third.

"Maybe it's better if we continue this conversation someplace a bit more private," Khazei suggests, motioning to the metal door that leads to the stacks. This time of the morning, there are already too many employees filling the hallway. "You said you needed to grab a file, right?" Khazei adds. "I'll walk with you."

Until yesterday, when he buzzed Orlando into the SCIF, I'd barely heard of Venkat Khazei. But if my gut is right, and he *is* doing more than just simply investigating Orlando's murder—if he really is after the book, or trying to make me look like a murderer as a way of getting it—the last thing I need is to be walking alone with him in the most remote section of our building.

"Actually, I'm okay talking out here," I say as the crowd disappears into its offices and, like a high school after a late bell, the hallway slowly drains back to its regular morning silence.

Khazei nods, pretending he's not annoyed. But as I wait for the final door to close in the hallway, I notice, through the front door to my own office, a thin pointed shadow, like a scarecrow, on the opposite side of the translucent glass. From its opaque outline, it could be any of our archivists—Tot, Dallas, Rina—but after swaying there for an instant, the scarecrow backs off. Like it knows I see it listening.

"So what was it that Orlando said in his last message?" Khazei challenges.

From his tone alone, I can tell it's his third trap. If he had the technology to know that I got Orlando's final message, it's just as easy for him to've already listened to that message. He's just testing to see if I'll be honest.

"Orlando just...he said he didn't have my cell phone and that I should call him back."

"Call him back about *what*?"

"Probably about what I did with some old blank letterhead I found from the Senate Judiciary Committee. It got sent over by mistake so I took one of the sheets—it was just a joke—and wrote a letter to Orlando saying he was being deported. Just dumb office stuff."

It's a good enough excuse delivered with good enough calm. I even used the words *what I did* to evoke the one unexplainable moment in Orlando's message. *What you did...*

But Khazei just stands there with his starched military posture, like a giant exclamation point. I glance back at my office. The shadow of the scarecrow is still there.

"Were you in SCIF 12E1 yesterday?" Khazei finally blurts.

"E-Excuse me?"

"It's a simple question. It requires a simple answer. Were you *in* or anywhere *near* that Vault at any point in time yesterday?"

I take a deep breath, trying hard not to look like I'm taking a deep breath. I don't know much about Khazei, but from what I can tell of our two conversations together, he hasn't asked a single question he doesn't already know the answer to, or at least have a hunch on. And considering that Dallas and Rina and at least one Secret Service agent saw me around the corner from that room...and that the videotape is still unaccounted for..."12E1..." I say. "That's the one the President does his reading in, right?"

"Beecher, at this moment, I am your friend. But if you want to make me an enemy..."

"Yeah, no...I definitely walked by the room. That's where I saw Orlando. I was giving a tour."

"But you're telling me you didn't go inside it?"

This is the moment where I can tell him the truth. I can tell him I went inside. I can tell him I didn't do it. But as I stare at Khazei, who's still the unmoving exclamation point, all he's going to hear is that I was the last person alone with Orlando before he died. And once he hears that... once he can confirm that I had actual access to the book...

I shake my head. "No. Never went inside it."

He tightens his stare.

"What?" I ask. "If you don't believe me, go check the tape. All those rooms are wired for video, aren't they?"

It's a risky bluff, but right now, I need to know what's going on. Sure, Khazei could've been the one who snatched that video from Orlando's VCR. But if he planned on using it to make me the murderer, we wouldn't even be having this conversation. So either Khazei has the tape and all he cares about is the book, or he doesn't have the tape and it's still out there.

"Amazingly, the tape is gone—someone took it from the SCIF," Khazei says flatly. "But thanks for the reminder. I need to tell the Service about that."

"The Service?"

"I know. But when Orlando's dead body showed up at the exact same time that President Wallace was entering the building... Apparently, the Secret Service doesn't like when bodies are that close to their protectee. So lucky us, they've offered to help with the investigation," he says, watching me more closely than ever. "What an opportunity, though. I'm guessing by the time they're done, they'll scan and alphabetize every atom, molecule— every speck of DNA—in the entire SCIF. God knows what you can find in there, right, Beecher?"

Just over his shoulder, there's a second *ding* as another elevator empties a group of employees into the wide hallway.

"Oh, and by the way," he adds as they fan out around us, "when you had your lab coat all bunched up yesterday—what was it stained with again? That was coffee, right?"

I nod and force a smile and—*Morning! Hey! Morning!*—wave hello to passing staffers.

"Enjoy your day," Khazei says, heading for the waiting elevator. "I'm sure we'll be talking again soon."

As the elevator doors swallow him whole, I take another peek at my own office door. The scarecrow's gone. At least I can finally catch my breath and—

No…

I run for the stairs. I almost forgot.

She's down there right now.

22

*H*old on…*not yet*…" the President said, holding up a single finger. Backlit by the morning sun, he studied the door to the doctor's office, which had already closed behind his sister.

Across from him, Palmiotti sat at his desk. Underneath the door, they could see the shadows of the staffers outside.

That's how it always was. Even in the most private parts of the White House, someone was always listening.

"So you were saying." Palmiotti motioned to the President. "About your back problem…"

"It hurts," Wallace insisted, still eyeing the shadows at the door. "And it's getting worse."

Palmiotti mulled on this. "Is it something I can take a look at personally?"

The President mulled too, once again staring out at the purposely melted snow of the Rose Garden. It took a ton of work to make something appear this undisturbed.

"Let me think on that," he said to Palmiotti. "Right now, we're probably better off sticking with the original treatment."

"Mr. President...?" one of the staffers called from the hallway. Time for him to go.

"Before you run," Palmiotti said. "Have you thought about surgery?"

The President shook his head. "Not with this. Not anymore."

"Mr. President...?" the staffer called again. Four uninterrupted minutes. For any President, that was a lifetime.

"I've got a country to run," Wallace said to his friend. "By the way, if you're looking for a good book..." He held up the hardcover copy of a book entitled *A Problem from Hell: America and the Age of Genocide* by Samantha Power. "Give it a look—it won the Pulitzer Prize," the President said, handing it to Palmiotti. Directly.

"You got it," the doctor said to his oldest friend as he glanced down at the hardcover book. *A Problem from Hell.* It sure was.

"Oh, and if you see Gabriel," Wallace called back as he headed for the door, "tell him to block out a quick drop-by in the schedule for Minnie's conference. But I'm not staying for photos."

"You're a sucker, y'know that?"

The President waved an absent goodbye, not saying a word. But his point was clear.

In Wallace's eyes, family came first.

It was a lesson not lost on Palmiotti, who knew exactly what was at risk if this current mess was what he thought. It'd be easy to walk away now. Probably smart too. The President's foot was clearly approaching the bear trap. But after everything Wallace had done for him... everything they'd done for each other...

Family came first.

"Oh, and Stewie, you need a haircut," the President added. "You look like dreck."

Dr. Stewart Palmiotti nodded.

A haircut. He was thinking the exact same thing.

23

T he girl."

"What girl?" asks the security guy with the round face and bushy eyebrows.

"The girl," I say. "There's supposed to be a girl."

He looks around the welcome area. The faded green rain mats and gray stone walls make it feel like a crypt. On the right, there's the metal detector and X-ray machine. But beyond a few more employees flashing their IDs, the only people I see are two other security guards.

"I don't see any," the guard says.

"Someone called me," I insist. "She was just here! Black hair. Nice eyes. She's really—"

"The pretty one," the guard by the X-ray calls out.

The eyebrows guard looks around.

"You don't know where she is, do you?" I ask.

"I think I—I signed her in. She was waiting right *there*," he says, motioning to one of the benches.

I'm not surprised. They may've given me and Tot the full once-over this morning, but for the most part, our security is at the same level as Orlando's top-loading VCR.

We don't even swipe our IDs to get in. Especially during the morning rush—I can see it right now—a lanky woman in a bulky winter coat waves her ID at the guard and walks right through.

"I swear—*right there*," he insists.

I glance at the sign-in sheet on the edge of the marble counter. Her signature is the exact same from high school. An effortless swirl. *Clementine Kaye.*

"Maybe someone already brought her in," the X-ray guard says.

"No one brought her in. I'm the one she was waiting—" No. Unless…No. Even Khazei's not that fast.

Pulling out my cell phone, I scroll to Clementine's number and hit send. The phone rings three times. Nothing but voicemail. But in the distance, I hear the ring of a cell phone.

"Clementine…?" I call out, following the sound. I head back past the guard desk and rush toward the Finding Aids room, where most visitors start their research. It would make sense. I kept her waiting long enough— maybe she came in here to look for more about her dad.

I hit send again. Like before, there's a faint ring. *Here.* For sure from here.

Hitting the brakes, I scan the mint green research room. I scan all four of the wide, book-covered desks. I scan the usual suspects: In the left corner, two elderly women are filling out paperwork. On my right, an old military vet is asking about some documents, a young grad student is skimming through genealogy reports, and—

There.

In the back. By the computers.

Staring at the screen, she leans forward in her chair, hugging the charcoal overcoat that fills her lap. Unlike yesterday, her short black hair has been divided into two ultra-hip pigtails like the kind you see on girls who make me feel just how old I've been feeling since she crashed back into my life and made me start searching for rap music instead of Kenny Rogers.

"Clemmi, what're you doing here?" I ask as I reach the back of the room.

She doesn't answer.

But as I get closer...as I see what she's looking at on-screen...something on YouTube...

There are videos in my family that, if you covered the entire screen except for one square inch, I'd still be able to identify the moment. There's the footage of me and my sisters, the two of them side by side on the vinyl couch in the hospital, holding baby me across their laps when I was first born. There's me at ten years old, dressed as Ronald Reagan for Halloween, complete with what my mom swore was a Ronald Reagan wig, but was really just some old Fred Flintstone hair. And there's the video of my dad—one of the only ones I have of him—in the local swimming pool, holding the two-year-old me so high above his head, then splashing me down and raising me up again.

But all those pale next to the scene that Clementine's staring at right now: of Nico Hadrian, dressed in a bright yellow NASCAR jumpsuit, as he's about to lift his gun and, without an ounce of expression on his face, calmly try to kill former President Leland Manning.

To most Americans, it's history. Like the first moon footage. Or JFK being shot. Every frame famous: the tips of the President's fingers blurring as he waves up at the crowd...his black windbreaker puffing up like a balloon...even the way he holds so tight to the First Lady's hand as they walk out on the track, and...

"Now you think I'm a nut," she says, still watching the screen.

"I don't think you're a nut."

"You actually should. I'm related to a nut...I'm sitting here, watching this old footage like a nut...and yes, it's only because you kept me waiting here that I put his name in Google, but still...this is really bordering on pathetic. I'm practically a cashew. Though watch when he steps out of the crowd: He totally looks like me."

Onscreen, the President and First Lady are flashing matching grins, their faces lit by the generous sun as they walk to their would-be slaughter.

"Okay, it is kinda nutty you're watching this," I tell her.

Her eyes roll toward me. "You're really chock full of charm, huh?"

"I thought it'd make you laugh. By the way, why'd you come here? I thought we agreed it was better to lay low until we—"

Standing up from her seat, she reaches into her purse, pulls out a small square present wrapped in what looks like the morning newspaper, and hands it to me.

"What's this?" I ask.

"What's it look like? It's a poorly wrapped present. Open it."

"I don't—" I look over my shoulder, totally confused. "You came here to give me a present?"

"What's wrong with a present?"

"I don't know...maybe because, between Orlando dying, and then finding your dad, I sorta threw your life in the woodchipper yesterday."

She regrabs the present, snatching it from my hands.

"Beecher, tell me something that upset you."

"What're you talking about?"

"In your life. Pick a moment. Pick something that hurt you...a pain that was so bad, you almost bit through your own cheek. Y'know...someone who really put you through the emotional wringer."

"Why would—?"

"Tell me who Iris is," Clementine says, reminding me that the people who know you the longest are the best at finding your weak spots.

"Why're you bringing up Iris?"

"I heard Orlando say her name yesterday—and within two seconds, you had the same pain on your face that you have now, like someone kicked your balls in. I know the feeling...y'know how many DJ jobs I've been fired from? So what happened to Iris? Is she dead?"

"She's not dead. She's an old girlfriend. We broke up."

"Okay, so she dumped you for another guy."

"That's not—"

"Beecher, I'm not trying to upset you...or pry," she says, meaning every word. "The point is, whatever it was—however Iris hurt you—you're over her now, right?"

"Absolutely," I insist. "Of course."

"Okay, you're not over her," she says as I stand there, surprised by the sudden lump that balloons in my throat and the familiar sting of self-doubt that Iris planted so deeply in my chest. "But you will be, Beecher. And that's what you did for me yesterday. For my whole life, I've wondered who my father might be. And now, thanks to you, I *know*. And yes, it's not the easiest answer. In fact, it may just be...it's kinda the *Guinness Book of World Records* crappiest answer of all time. But it's an *answer*," she says, handing the present back to me. "And I appreciate that."

Looking down at the present, I give a tug to one of the scotch-taped seams. As I tear the paper aside, I spot the turn buttons on what looks like the back of a picture frame. It's definitely a picture frame. But it's not until I flip it over that I see the actual picture inside.

It's a color photo of me in seventh grade, back when my mom used to shop for whatever Garanimals shirt I was wearing that day. But what I notice most is the other seventh grader standing next to me in the photo with the wide, surprisingly bucktoothed grin. Young Clementine.

The thing is, back then, we never had a photo of just the two of us.

"H-How'd you get this?" I ask.

"I made it. From our old class photo in Ms. Spicer's

class. You were standing on the left. I was on the right. I had to cut us out with an X-Acto knife since Tim Burton movies made me genuinely scared of scissors, but it still made our heads kinda octagonal-shaped, so sorry about that."

I look down at the frame, where both of us have our arms flat at our sides in standard class-photo positions. Our heads are definitely octagons.

"You don't like it?" she asks.

"No, I like it . . . I love it. I just . . . If you had scanned it in— I feel bad you had to ruin the actual photo."

"I didn't ruin anything," she insists. "I cut out the only two people I cared about in that class."

I look up at Clementine, then back down at the photo, which is choppy, poorly made, and completely unflattering.

But it's of us.

A smile grips my cheeks so hard, they actually hurt.

"By the way, don't think you get a pass on that Garanimals shirt," she tells me as the video continues to play onscreen behind her. Her back is to it, so she can't see it, but it's the part where Nico is about to step out of the crowd.

"Listen, I gotta run," she adds as a man with black buzzed hair, a big bulbous nose, and a bright yellow jumpsuit steps into the frame and raises his gun. My God—he *does* look like her. "They told me to come back in an hour," she says.

"Who did? What're you talking about?"

"The guards. At St. Elizabeths."

"Wait. As in *mental institution St. Elizabeths*?"

"Nico's there. Same place as John Hinckley—the one who shot Reagan. It's only ten minutes from here."

"Can we please rewind one second? You went to see Nico!?"

"I can't get in unless he approves me first. That's how they have to do it on his ward. I'm waiting to get approved."

"But he's—"

"I know who he is—but what'm I supposed to do, Beecher? Sit at home and do my nails? I've been waiting to meet this man for thirty years. How can I not—?"

Pop, pop, pop.

Onscreen, the gunshots are muffled. As Nico steps out of the crowd, his head's cocked just slightly—and he's almost...he's smiling.

Pop, pop, pop.

With her back still to the monitor, Clementine doesn't turn at the gunshots. But she does flinch, her body startled by each and every one.

"Shots fired! Shots fired!" the agents yell.

"Get down! Get back!"

"GOD GAVE POWER TO THE PROPHETS..." Nico shouts, his rumbling voice drowned out by all the screaming.

The camera jerks in every direction, panning past the fans in the stands. Spectators run in every direction. And by the time the camera fights its way back to focus, Nico is being pulled backward, lost in instant chaos as he's clawed to the ground by a swarm of Secret Service agents. In the background, two aides go down, the victims of stray bullets. One of them lies facedown holding his cheek. Luckily, the President and his wife get rushed into their limo and escape unharmed. It wasn't until later that Nico tracked them down and killed the First Lady.

In the corner of YouTube, I spot the viewcount on the bottom right: *14,727,216 views.*

It seems like a lot.

But in truth, fourteen million viewers are meaningless.

All that matters is this single one.

"Please don't look at me like that, Beecher. I can do this," she insists, even though I haven't said a word.

I don't care how strong she's pretending to be. I saw the way, even though she knew those gunshots were coming, she flinched at each pop. And the way, ever since Nico appeared onscreen, she still won't look at the monitor.

She knows what's waiting for her.

But she also knows there's no avoiding it.

"You're telling me if it were your dad, you wouldn't go see him now?" she asks.

I stay silent, thinking back to my first year at the Archives. My dad died at the age of twenty-six, in a stupid car accident on his way to enlist for the first Gulf War. He didn't get killed fighting for his country. He didn't die a hero. He didn't even die from friendly fire. Those people are given medals. But the grunts who aren't even grunts yet because they're driving to the recruiting office when some nutbag crashes into him on a bridge and kills everyone on impact? They die as nobodies. Their lives are half-lived. And during my first year here, I spent every single lunch hour going through old army records, trying to figure out which platoon he would've been in, and what kind of adventures he would've had if he'd made it to the enlistment office.

"If you want, I can go with you," I finally say.

"What?"

"To St. Elizabeths. I can go with you. Y'know...if you want."

I wait for her to smile. To say thanks. Instead, she shakes her head. "You can't."

"Sure I can."

"You don't understand."

"Actually..."

"I *know* your dad's dead, Benjy," she says, using the nickname only my mom uses. "You think I don't remember that? When we were little, you not having a father... You have any idea what that meant to me? How *not alone* that made me feel?"

The balloon in my throat expands, catching me off guard.

"But to have this chance right now..." She stares down at the old photo—the one of us—still refusing to face the video behind her. "My mom used to tell me that the best part of music—even as a DJ—was that when you go to a new city, you get to be a brand-new person," she adds. "And I chose Virginia because—all the pictures seemed to have horses in them. Horses are calming, y'know? But then to find out—of all the places I could've picked—I'm ten minutes from...from *him*," she says, thumbing back at the screen as Nico's video wraps up. "I'm not saying it's a sign—but I am saying...maybe some things are meant to be. Like reconnecting with you." Before I can say a word, she adds, "Besides, I want what's best for you, Beecher. And right now, bringing you to meet a delusional sociopath—even one who's been calmed down by medication—is not what your life needs at this moment. This is something I think I'm supposed to do myself."

"I understand."

"You *do*?" she asks.

"Don't you get it? I want what's best for you too."

She looks up at me and grins. "That homemade photograph really made you mushy, didn't it?" she asks.

"Hey, Beecher! *Phone!*" one of the staffers calls out from the desk behind us.

"Whoever it is, tell them—"

"It's Tot. Says not to let you give any lame excuses. Says it's important. He's on hold."

I shake my head, ready to ignore the call.

"He says don't ignore it!" the aide calls back. "On hold!"

"Just gimme one sec," I tell Clementine as I grab the phone at the circulation desk, which is just a few feet away.

"What're you doing with her?" Tot asks before I can even say hello.

"Pardon?"

"Clementine. You went down to buzz her in. That was twenty minutes ago."

I look over at Clementine, who's finally turned back to the computer screen, where YouTube has offered a variety of recommendations for the next video to click on. Even from here, I can see what she's looking at as bits of bright yellow jumpsuit peek out from each video option.

"Is this really that important, Tot?"

"You tell me. I found the cart for your guy Dustin Gyrich," he says, referring to the last person who requested a copy of *Entick's Dictionary*. "Now, do you want to hear his connection to the President or not?"

24

I'll call you when I'm done," Clementine says, stepping away from the computer and heading for the lobby. "I gotta go."

"Good. Let her," Tot says through the phone.

"Clemmi, just wait!" I call out as she pulls her coat on.

"Let her be," Tot says. "Whatever she's got going on, you've got enough disasters to deal with."

"What're you talking about?" I ask.

"I told you. Dustin Gyrich."

"So he's the last person to request the..." I look around, and I swear, in this wide mint green room, every person, from the old ladies to the young grad student, is looking directly at me.

"Yeah...to request the dictionary," Tot says in my ear. "That's the thing, though. At first I thought it was odd that he just happened to request the dictionary on the exact same day that President Wallace was here for his reading tour. But when I pulled the full record, well…Dustin Gyrich—whoever he is—has requested *Entick's Dictionary* fourteen different times, which isn't that unusual—"

"Get to the point, Tot."

"The point is, when I matched Gyrich's dates up with a calendar, guess who else happened to be visiting this very building on every one of those days? I'll give you a hint. It rhymes with *President*."

Across from me, Clementine buttons the top button on her coat and turns toward the main lobby to leave.

"Just wait," I whisper to her. "I'll only be a minute."

"You'll be way more than a minute," Tot says through the phone. "Unless you're no longer understanding the bad news I'm delivering."

"Thirty seconds," I promise Clementine.

She pauses a moment, like she really does want to wait. But as she did when the red curtain went up during the Battle of the Bands, Clementine stands there a moment, lifts her chin, and buries all her fears in whatever place she's come to keep them. The difference is, she's no longer facing testy tenth graders. She's facing her father. The destroyer.

"I'll be okay," she insists, even though I didn't ask her. Her eyes blink quicker than usual, just like when she flinched at those gunshots. Before I can argue, she's headed down the hallway, past the security desk, and through the automatic doors that take her outside into the cold. I look down at the homemade photograph of our younger selves. It's the second time in two days that I realize I'm seeing the soft side of her no one else knows.

The part she shares with no one. Ever since Iris . . . I forgot how good a simple crush can feel.

But it's not just the crush. There are some people in your life who bring back old memories. And there are others—your first kiss, your first love, your first sex—who, the moment you see them, bring a spark . . . and something far more potent. They bring back your old life and, with that, potential. And possibilities. And the feeling that if you were back in that time, life could be so very different from where you're stuck right now. That's the most tantalizing thing Clementine offers. I want my potential back.

"You hearing me, Beecher?" Tot shouts in my ear. "Over the past four months, every single time the President of the United States has come to this building, this guy Gyrich takes *this* copy of the dictionary—"

"Wait, wait, wait. I thought we weren't sure if the copy we found in the"—I lower my voice—"*in the SCIF* was the same one from our collection."

"And for the second time, are you hearing me? Where do you think I've been for the past half hour? I went down and pulled Gyrich's cart. He's got twelve items on hold here, but—what a coincidence—there's only eleven on the cart. So guess which one's missing? That's right—one copy of *Entick's Dictionary*."

"I don't know, does that really tell us that the Archives copy is the same as the beat-up one we have?" I ask, still watching through the glass of the automatic doors. Out by the curb, Clementine hails herself a cab. "The one we found doesn't have identifying information, or a stamp, or even most of its own pages," I say. "Would the Archives really keep something that beat-up and let it get checked out over and over again?"

"That's fine—and we can look into that," Tot agrees. "But it doesn't change the fact that fourteen weeks in a row, every time President Wallace comes here to visit—every single time—Gyrich requests the dictionary, puts it on hold, and makes sure it's out of general circulation. When it happens two times, that's dumb luck. Three times? That's a very weird fluke. But fourteen times in fourteen weeks?" His voice goes quiet. "That's a plan."

He's right. He's always right. But as I watch Clementine duck into her cab, there's a surprising new feeling tugging at my ribcage.

Since the moment I saw her yesterday, I've been looking at Clementine through the sparkly prism of exhilaration that comes with any old flame. But now, for the first time, I'm not just seeing what I want. I'm seeing what my friend needs.

The door to the taxi slams shut.

"Tot, I need to borrow your car."

"My car is nice. You're not taking it anywhere. And what're you talking about anyway?"

"I need to run an errand."

"No, you need to get up here so we can find this guy Gyrich and figure out what's really going on."

"And I will. Right after this errand."

I hear nothing but silence through the phone. "This is the part where you're being stupid again, Beecher. And inconsiderate, considering how much of my time you're wasting while you chase some girl."

"I'm not chasing a girl."

"So you're not going to St. Elizabeths?" he challenges.

I pause, thinking of the perfect lie. "Okay, fine. I'm going to St. Elizabeths. It's not far from here."

"Beecher..."

"You're forgetting, Tot. You're forgetting that there were three of us in that room. She was there with me—so if my life's at risk, her life's at risk too."

"You don't know that."

"I *absolutely* know that—and the last time we let someone who was in that room out of our sight, Orlando showed up dead. Besides, aren't you the one who said I should keep an eye on her...that it was too much of a coincidence that she showed up and all this went down? This is my chance to see what's really going on. And more important than any of that, she's about to step into what's probably the single roughest moment of her life. How do I let her do that alone?"

Once again, the phone goes silent. It's the last part that's getting to him. When Tot's wife died, he learned exactly what it feels like to face his worst moment by himself.

"That mean I can have the car?" I ask.

"Yes," he sighs. "Let's all be stupid."

Twenty-four minutes and fourteen seconds later, I twist the steering wheel of the powder blue 1966 Mustang into a sharp right and pull up to the small guardhouse that sits just inside the black metal gates.

"Welcome to St. Elizabeths," a guard with winter-grizzled lips says as he turns down the *Elliot in the Morning* show on his radio. Clearly, this guy's a genius. "Visitor or delivery?"

"Actually, a pickup," I tell him.

25

Every barber has one haircut he'll never forget.

For many, it's the first good one they give. Not the first *haircut* they give, but the first *good* one, where they realize just how much they can improve someone's looks with a few flicks of a scissors.

For others, it's at the end of their career, where they realize they don't have the steady hand that had served them for so long.

For a few, it's that moment when a particularly famous person sits down in their chair.

But for master barber Andre Laurent, a tall, hefty silver-haired black man with a just-as-silver mustache, the one that stayed with him was back in Ohio, back in the early eighties, when he was cutting the hair of that blond man with the odd cowlick, who always used to bring his eight-year-old son with him. In the midst of the cut, the door to the shop burst open and a young brunette with pointy breasts stormed in, nearly shattering the glass as the door slammed into the wall.

"You didn't tell me you were married!" she screamed

at the man with the cowlick. But all Laurent saw were the big ash-gray eyes of Cowlick's son, watching his dad and slowly, right there, trying to put it all together.

Back then, their small Ohio town would've feasted on gossip like that. Especially when the dad left his family behind a few years later. Especially as the ash-eyed boy grew older. Especially when he became the youngest state senator in Ohio history. Especially when he reached the governor's mansion. And even more especially when he made that run for the White House and nearly every reporter in the country came to Journey, Ohio, to see the small-town barbershop where Orson Wallace still got his hair cut on a biweekly basis.

To this day, Andre Laurent had never said a word. Like his father and grandfather—both barbers and both midwestern gentlemen—he never would.

"Mr. Laurent, I got a walk-in for you," the appointment girl with the squeaky voice called out from the front of the shop.

"Send him back," Laurent replied, brushing a few stray hairs from the barber chair's headrest.

For forty-three years, Laurent had barbered at the same place his father and grandfather learned their trade. It was called, obviously enough, Laurent's.

Three years ago, he had moved to Washington, D.C., taking a chair at a place called Wall's Barber Shop. He liked that Wall's still had its original stainless steel barber chairs. He liked that there was a working red, white, and blue barber pole outside. But he especially liked that, on 15th Street, it was walking distance from the White House.

"Shoeshine while we got you in the chair?" Shoeshine Gary called out to Laurent's client.

"*No*," the client said without looking at him.

When Barack Obama was first elected President, one of the very first things he said to the press was that if he could no longer go to his barber, his barber would have to come to him.

What a good idea, President Orson Wallace thought.

Finding a good barber was tough.

Finding someone you trust was even tougher.

That was the start of it. Once every two weeks, Laurent would trek to the White House to cut the President's hair. And sometimes, if there was a real emergency—especially over the past few weeks—the White House would come to him.

"What can I do to you?" Laurent asked as his client sat in the barber chair. "Shave or haircut?"

"How about both?" Dr. Stewart Palmiotti replied, leaning forward and tossing the fat hardcover book he was carrying onto the glass shelf that sat just below the mirror. "I think we're gonna need the extra time."

"As you wish," the President's barber said, reaching for a hot towel as the President's doctor tilted his head back.

Every barber has one haircut he'll never forget.

And some barbers have more than one.

26

The cobblestone Italian street was still damp from the overnight rain, and as the small, slender man stood there, he enjoyed the reflective view it created on Via Panisperna. *Like a whole different universe*, he thought, taking in the upside-down view of Sant'Agata dei Goti, the fifth-century church that now appeared—like magic—below his feet.

He'd been standing by the side door waiting for a while now, but he wasn't worried. In all their time coming here, she'd never stood him up. He knew she wouldn't start now. Not with what was about to happen.

"You look nervous," Lenore called out as she turned the corner and marched up the bumpy stone driveway.

"Not nervous," the man said. "Excited."

"You don't look excited. You look nervous."

The man smiled to himself, knowing better than to argue with Lenore, a woman well trained, from Princeton all the way up to the White House, in the fine art of arguing.

"If I weren't a little nervous, I'd be insane," the man said with a laugh.

Shoving hard on the carved wooden double doors, he pushed his way inside and winced as the hinges shrieked. But there was something instantly calming about being back here, especially that smell: the damp wood and the rosewater candles.

"The smell reminds you of your mother, doesn't it?" Lenore asked.

Ignoring the question—and the slamming doors behind him—the slender man headed straight for the source of the smell, the ancient iron rack filled with the white rose prayer candles.

"She had that smell on her when you were little," Lenore continued. *"When you went to church in Wisconsin."*

The man couldn't help but smile. In this world, there was nothing scarier than trusting someone. But there was also nothing more rewarding.

"They were good memories," he said as he picked up an unlit candle, dipped it into the flame, and whispered a silent prayer for his mother. Two years ago, for a prayer like this, he would've bobbed his head sixteen times before saying amen. He would've pulled out two eyelashes, setting them perpendicular in his palm until they formed a miniature cross. But today, as he looked up toward the intricate stained glass window...Nico Hadrian was better.

And so was former First Lady Lenore Manning.

Even though she'd been dead for two years now.

"Nico, let's go—they want you in the day room," the tall orderly with the sweet onion breath called out.

Peering over his shoulder, Nico looked across his

small bare room at St. Elizabeths Hospital. He looked past his single bed and the painted dresser that held his Bible and the Washington Redskins calendar. Italy was gone, and there was no one there except for Sweet Onion Breath.

"Please tell me you're not talking to no imaginary friends," the orderly pleaded. "You do, I gotta report it, Nico."

Nico cranked his small smile into a kind, wider one. He'd made the mistake of honesty once. He wouldn't make it again. "You know I don't do that anymore."

He was mostly right. After his escape and capture, when he was finally returned to St. Elizabeths, it took Nico four months before he stopped picking off his own fingernails, determined to punish himself for what he'd done. To be manipulated like that—to be so lost in the religious spirit—to kill in the name of God. By now, the doctors were thrilled with his progress. They gave him mail privileges, even access to the grounds. For the past two years, Nico had fought back to his own level of normalcy. Yes, he was better. But that didn't mean he was cured.

Turning toward the one window in his room, Nico watched calmly, patiently, as the single bed, wooden nightstand, and painted dresser were replaced by the ancient iron rack of white rose candles, and the wide shatterproof window turned back into the beautiful stained glass window of the church Sant'Agata dei Goti, the church dedicated to Saint Agatha, who never—even when the torturers severed her breast—ever renounced her faith.

"*You don't look nervous anymore*," the First Lady said.

"I think I'm excited. Yes. I'm very excited," Nico whispered to himself.

"C'mon, Nico—you have a visitor," the orderly called out as the church again faded and the hospital returned.

"No. I have more than just a visitor," Nico insisted as he headed for the day room. God always provided. "I have Clementine."

27

When I was in tenth grade, there was a kid in our class—Weird Warren—who used to be able to bend down his ear, and keep it down, so he'd look like an elf. Most of my classmates did their usual teasing, knighting him with the nickname. But Clementine—she said it so nicely I'll never forget it—she asked him if he could grant her three wishes.

Pounding the faded red button with the heel of his palm, the St. Elizabeths guard raises the gate arm, allowing me to drive past the guardhouse. I told him I was here to pick up records for the Archives. With my government ID, it was enough to send me toward the main security check-in and onto the property, a 350-acre piece of land that's encased by a ring of tall black metal gates.

As I head up the hospital's poorly plowed road and scan the parking lot that sits across from the main five-story brick building, Clementine's cab is long gone. She's inside, probably already with Nico. I have no idea what her three wishes would be today. But if I had the chance to get even two minutes with my dead dad, I know what at least one of my wishes would be.

As I kick open the car door in the parking lot, a blast of winter air stings my face, but before I get out I reach down and pull out the copy of *Entick's Dictionary* that's tucked underneath the driver's seat. Tot's idea. Based on this morning, Khazei isn't just asking questions anymore—he's circling for a kill. I still can't tell if what he really wants is the book or me, but either way, the last thing we need is to have this lying around the building. Still, that doesn't mean I can just leave it in the car.

For a moment, I think about hiding it in my briefcase, but if I do that, I risk security here rummaging through it. No. If this book is as important as we think it is—if Orlando really died for it—I need to keep it close.

Stepping outside and heading across to the building, I tuck the book under the back of my jacket and carefully slide it into the back of my slacks. It fits—with most of the pages gone, it's just the covers. I take a fast glance over my shoulder to make sure I'm alone. But as I look up, standing on one of the second-floor balconies is a pale bald man with no eyebrows.

I strain a smile, even as I pick up my pace.

He glares down. But his expression never changes. I don't think he even sees I'm here.

For a moment, I think about just waiting out here for her. But I don't slow down.

As I finally reach the front, the doorknob gives with

barely a twist. The cold has definitely eased up, but a pitiless chill climbs my spine. According to Clemmi, this is the mental hospital that holds not just Nico, but also John Hinckley, the man who shot Ronald Reagan. Why the hell's the front door unlocked?

I push the door inward, revealing a 1950s waiting room decorated in a pale drab green. Straight ahead, a thin guard who looks like David Bowie circa 1983 sits at an X-ray and metal detector also stolen from the same era.

"C'mon in—only about half our patients bite," a woman's voice calls out. She laughs a silly puffy laugh that's supposed to put me at ease. On my left, standing inside a thick glass booth, is a second guard—a female guard with a bad Dutch-boy haircut and great dimples.

"You must be Mr. White, correct?" She got my name from when I checked in at the guardhouse. "Relax, Mr. White. They keep the doors unlocked so that the patients feel they have more freedom. But not that much freedom," she says with the puffy laugh, pointing at a thick steel door that looks like a bank vault: the real door to get inside.

"Um…great," I blurt, not knowing what else to say.

"So how can we help you, Mr. White?" she asks as I realize she's one of those people who says your name over and over until you want to eat poison.

"Actually, it's Beecher. I'm here from the National Archives. Anyhow, we were thinking of doing an exhibit on the history of St. Elizabeths—when it was run by the government and founded to help the insane…then converted in the Civil War to help wounded soldiers…It's just a great part of American history—"

"Just tell me what time your appointment is and who it's with."

"That's the thing," I tell the woman behind the glass. "They told me to come over and that I should take a quick tour of the campus."

"That's fine, Beecher. I still need a name to call first."

"I think it was someone in Public Affairs."

"Was it Francine?"

"It might've been—it was definitely a woman," I bluff.

She lowers her chin, studying me through the fingerprint-covered glass.

"Something wrong?" I ask.

"You tell me, Beecher—you have no appointment and no contact name. Now you know the population we're trying to help here. So why don't you go back to the Archives and set up your meeting properly?"

"Can't you just call the—?"

"There is no call. No appointment, no call."

"But if you—"

"We're done. Good day," she insists, tightening both her jaw and her glare.

I blink once at her, then once at David Bowie. But as I turn to leave…

The steel door that leads upstairs opens with a *tunk*.

"—sure it's okay to go out here?" Clementine asks as she walks tentatively behind a man with salt-and-pepper buzzed hair and chocolate brown eyes that seem too close together. At first, the gray in his hair throws me off—but that bulbous nose and the arched thin eyebrows...God, he looks just like the video on YouTube.

Nico. And Clementine.

Heading right for me.

28

M r. Laurent, your next appointment's here," the girl called out from the front of Wall's Barber Shop, a long narrow shop that held seven barber chairs, all in a single row, with Shoeshine Gary up near the front door and local favorite James Davenport cutting hair in chair one.

Laurent glanced at her from the very last chair in the back, but never lost focus on his current—most vital—client.

"I should get back. It's late," Dr. Palmiotti said from the barber chair.

"Don't you go nowhere. Two more minutes," Laurent said, pressing the electric razor to the back of Dr. Palmiotti's neck. *Cleaning out the tater patch*—that's what Laurent's grandfather used to call cleaning the hair on the neck. The very last part of the job.

"So your brother…" Laurent added, well aware that Palmiotti didn't have a brother. "If he needs help, maybe you should get it for him?"

"I don't know," Palmiotti replied, his chin pressed down against his chest. "He's not that good with help."

Laurent nodded. That was always President Wallace's problem.

This close to the White House, nearly every business had at least a few hanging photographs of local politicians who'd helped them over time. Since 1967, Wall's Barber Shop had none. Zero. Not even the one from *Newsweek*, of Laurent cutting President Wallace's hair right before the Inauguration. According to the current owner, in the cutthroat world of politics, he didn't want to look like he was taking one side over the other. But to Laurent, the blank walls were the cold reminder that in Washington, D.C., when it all went sour, the only person you could really count on was yourself.

"Just be sure to say hello for me," Laurent said, finishing up on the doctor's neck. "Tell him he's in my prayers."

"He knows that. You know he knows that," Palmiotti said, trying hard to not look uncomfortable.

Laurent wasn't surprised. Like most doctors, Palmiotti always had a tough time with faith. Fortunately, he had an easy time with friendship.

With a tug at his own neck, the doctor unsnapped the red, white, and blue barber's apron and hopped out of the chair in such a rush, he didn't even stop to check his haircut in the mirror. "You're a magician, Laurent. See you soon!"

But as Palmiotti was paying the cashier, Laurent looked over and noticed the hardcover book with the bright red writing—*A Problem from Hell*—that was still sitting on the shelf below the mirror.

Palmiotti was at the cashier. There was still time to return it to him.

Instead, Laurent opened the drawer that held his spare scissors, slid the book inside, and didn't say a word.

As usual.

29

Y ou're anxious," Nico says to Clementine as he leads her past me and heads for the door that'll take them outside. Clementine nearly falls over when she sees me, but to her credit, she doesn't stop. Just shoots me a look to say, *What're you doing here?*

I turn back to the glass guard booth, pretending to sign in.

If I remember my history—and I always remember my history—when Nico took his shots at the President, he said it was because of some supposed ancient plan that the Founding Fathers and the Freemasons had hatched to take over the world.

Exactly.

He's crazy enough. He doesn't need to be more crazy by me confronting or riling him.

"There's no need to be nervous," Nico continues, reading Clementine's discomfort.

He shoves open the front door and steps out into the cold. As the door slams behind them, it's like a thunderclap in the silent room.

"Th-That was—You let him walk out the door!"

"…and he'll walk right back in after his visitor leaves," says the guard behind the glass. "Our goal is curing them, not punishing them. Nico earned his ground privileges just like anyone else."

"But he's—"

"He's been incident-free for years now—moved out of maximum security and into medium. Besides, this isn't a prison—it's a hospital. A hospital that's there to help him, not punish him. You gotta let a man walk outside," she explains. "And even so, we got guards—and a fence that's too high to hop. We see him. Every day, he does custodial work in the RMB Building, then feeds the cats there. By the way, Beecher, they still got that copy of the Magna Carta at the Archives? That stuff is cool."

"Yeah…of course," I say as I try to walk as casually as possible to the door.

The guard says something else, but I'm already outside, searching left and right, scanning the main road that runs across the property. In the distance, there's a guard walking the perimeter of the black metal gates that surround the hospital's snow-covered grounds. Ahead and down to the right, the concrete walkway looks like a squiggle from a black Magic Marker that slices through the snow. The plowed path is lined with trees and holds so many benches, it's clearly for strolling patients.

Nico's at least four steps in front of her, his left arm flat at his side, his right clutching a brown paper supermarket bag. He walks like Clementine used to: fearlessly forward as he follows the thin pedestrian path. Behind him, whatever confidence Clementine had—the woman who plowed just as fearlessly into the President's SCIF—that Clementine is once again gone. From the stutter in her steps...the way she hesitates, not sure whether she really wants to keep up...I don't care how far people come in life—or how much you prepare for this moment. You see your father, and you're instantly a child again.

As they step out onto the pathway, I stick by the entryway of the building, making sure there's at least half a football field between us. But as I take my first step out and my foot crunches against some thick chunks of snow salt, I swear on my life, Nico flinches.

He never turns. He doesn't glance over his shoulder to investigate. But I remember the news footage—how he has hearing and eyesight more acute than the rest of us. That's why the military first recruited him for sniper school.

I stop midstep.

Nico keeps going, marching his purposeful march, clutching the brown bag, and glancing just slightly to make sure the clearly uncomfortable Clementine is still behind him.

Leaving the entryway, I take it slow, always careful to use the nearby trees for cover. On my far left, the guard is still patrolling the gates. As I reach the beginning of the path, he spots them too.

It's not hard to see where he's leading her. The thin black path curves downhill toward another 1960s-era brick building. Throughout the wide campus, it's the only thing that's plowed. Even I get the message: This path is the one place patients are allowed to walk.

The farther they get, the more they shrink. I still can't tell if they're talking, but as they finally reach the front of the building, I'm all set to follow. To my surprise though, instead of going inside, Nico points Clementine to the wooden benches out front.

Taking the seat next to her, Nico puts the brown bag between them. Even from here, I can see Clementine scooch back, away from the bag. Whatever he's got in there...my brain can't help but imagine the worst.

That's when the cats start arriving.

A gray tabby races out of the building, followed by a chubby black one. Then two small matching orange kittens, followed by what must be their mom. There're half a dozen cats in total, all of them heading for the exact same spot: straight to the bench. Straight to Nico.

On my far left, the guard is still down by the perimeter fence, but he hasn't moved much. This is clearly Nico's routine. From the brown bag, Nico sprinkles the ground with whatever food he has inside. *Feeding the cats.* The woman behind the glass said it's one of his jobs. But the way Nico leans down to pet them—scratching tummies, necks, between ears, like he knows each of their soft spots—he isn't just feeding these cats.

He loves them.

And the way they rub against Nico, weaving infinity loops around his legs, they love him right back.

Sitting up straight and settling into his stiff, alien posture, Nico won't look at anything but the cats. I can't read lips, but I can read body language. Fidgeting next to him, Clementine looks even more awkward than he is, and from her hand movements—she scratches her wrist, then her neck, like there's something living beneath her own skin. Back at the Archives, she couldn't even look at Nico in the old assassination video. It's only worse here. No matter how ready she thought she was, she's not ready for this. Until...

He suddenly rises from his seat, standing erect.

The cats startle at the sudden movement, then settle back around his feet. Before Clementine can react, Nico looks at his watch and starts walking to the far side of the building. He's calm as ever. He makes a quick hand motion, asking Clementine to follow.

No, don't go with him—!

She pauses, searching around. She's definitely smarter than that. She needs to be—she knows who she's dealing with. But she can't help herself. A few cats trail him like the Pied Piper. A few others, including two tuxedo cats—black, with white bib and feet—start to groom themselves, then walk away, aloof. Clementine needs to decide which cat she'll be.

It doesn't take long. She's wondered about this man for nearly thirty years. She takes a few hesitant steps...then scratches the back of her neck...then follows.

Nico turns the corner and...

They're both gone.

I give them a moment to come back. Thirty seconds to see if they return.

Still gone.

There's no reason to break the emergency glass. Maybe he's just getting more cat food.

I search for the guard back by the fence. He's gone too.

I look around, but there's no one else. I can run back to the main building, but by the time I get there, God knows where Nico will be. More important, if something happened to Clemmi, it'd be my fault.

Tot called history a selection process that hands us situations we should never be able to overcome.

He's right. I can't overcome this. Nico's a trained monster. A killer. A destroyer.

I can't do this.

I can't.

But I have to try.

Running full speed, I race down the concrete path. With each step, my feet slap the pavement, splattering puddles of slush.

As I pass the front of the building, I spot the blur of my own profile in the reflection of the glass doors. The tuxedo cats are milling around, looking bored as they ignore me. I even see Nico's and Clementine's footsteps where the snow isn't melted yet. They can't be far.

At the corner of the building, I make a sharp left and...

Nothing.

A long alley of browning snow, a rusted Dumpster, and just beyond the Dumpster, an empty golf cart that—

Mrrow.

Cat. That's one of the cats.

I crane my neck.

There. In the back. The tabby one.

I'm already halfway there as its tail disappears around the back of the building. As I fly past the Dumpster—

Pfuump.

A thick forearm rams my neck, hitting like a baseball bat and clotheslining me so hard, my feet leave the ground.

Keeping his forearm at my throat, Nico shoves me backward by my neck until I crash—hard—onto the freezing concrete. The back of my head hits first, and a flash of bright stars blinds me on impact.

"What're you doing!? Are you crazy!?" Clementine shouts at Nico.

Her father smiles, heading toward me.

Before I can register anything, Nico's all over me.

30

Wasting no time, Nico climbs on my stomach, my chest, his baseball-bat forearm now pressing like a nightstick against my neck. His breath smells like cigarettes and old coins. I try to breathe, but he's...*huuuh*...*huuuh*...he's on my windpipe...I scream for the guards, but no one knows we're here.

"I heard you," he says, completely calm as his chocolate eyes rattle back and forth, picking apart my face. "In the entryway. I hear things better than you."

"G-Get off him!" Clementine shouts, racing out from where he shoved her behind the Dumpster. She plows toward him, ready to push him away.

"Do. *Not*," Nico says, whipping around and grabbing her wrist with one hand, while holding my throat with the other. I've never seen anything move so fast.

Clementine thrashes, fighting to get free. No. She's not fighting. She just wants him off her. Stumbling backward, her face goes gray and ashen like she's about to throw up. Back at the Archives, I remember what the *pop*,

pop, pop of the gunshots did to her. She could barely deal
with that. She certainly can't deal with this.

As she finally breaks free, Clementine falls on her ass.
It shifts Nico just enough that he lets go of my throat as
my lungs lurch for air.

"Huuuh…hgggh…"

He watches my face…studies my eyes as I look to
Clementine…

No. I shouldn't look at her.

Too late.

Glancing to his left, he studies Clementine, then turns
back to me.

"You know him," he says to Clementine, who's still
on her rear, crabwalking and scrambling to get away.
"You brought him here."

"I-I didn't," she insists. "I swear to—"

"God's name. Don't take it in vain," Nico warns, his
voice just a whisper.

I wait for her to say something, but from the panic in
her eyes…She can't. She's done. There's no reconnecting with this man. All she wants is out of here.

Nico turns, like a dog spotting a squirrel. His chest
rises and falls so quickly. He hears something.

"*Nico…?* " a sharp voice calls from the distance. We
can't see who it is, but the way Nico turns…Whoever's
coming…It's a guard.

Clementine crabwalks back even farther. With a leap,
Nico climbs to his feet and I get my first clear breath.

"*Nico, get yer ass outta there!*" a man shouts in a deep
southern accent.

I stumble to my feet just as a black guard with small shoulders turns the corner.

"What the hell you doing?" the guard asks.

Nico's eyes roll toward him, unafraid. "We were feeding the cats."

The guard shoots Nico a look that says, *Do I look stupid to you?* Then he shoots us a look that says, *Why'd you let him take you back there?*

"Public spaces only. You know that," the guard growls.

"We'll just be a minute," Nico says, gripping Clementine's shoulder as she rises to her feet.

"Nico, hands off her. You okay there, miss?" the guard asks.

"We're coming up front. To feed the cats," Nico replies. "The tabby still hasn't eaten."

"Nico, I am *not* in the mood for your freakiness right now. Shut your face," the guard says. "Miss, you okay or not?"

Clementine stiffens. I know she wants to run…to scream…to get away from here, but the last thing she needs is Nico freaking.

"We're coming to the front. To feed the cats," she repeats, her voice barely working.

Looking at all three of us, the guard studies us, especially Nico. "Public spaces. Everyone. Now!"

Nico doesn't move. But as Clementine takes off, he falls in behind her. Right next to me.

"You came here to protect her," Nico whispers to me. "To make sure she was okay."

I don't answer.

"You like her," Nico adds, calm as ever as we follow the guard out of the alley, toward the front of the building. "I see the way you study her. Is that why you brought a gun with you? To keep her safe?"

Clementine looks back at me. Just like Nico.

"A gun?" I ask. "I don't have a gun."

"I can see it," Nico says, never raising his voice. It's like he's part robot. "I can see it tucked under your jacket. In the back."

Patting myself around the waist, I quickly realize what he's talking about. The book. The dictionary. The way it props my jacket up in the back of my pants.

"No—okay—*look*, it's just— It's a book," I tell him, taking out the thin, gutted dictionary and showing it to him. "Just a book."

But as I hold it out between us, Nico freezes.

"You wanna feed your cats, feed 'em here," the guard calls out, pointing us back to the wooden benches in front of the building. No longer trusting Nico, the guard heads toward the building and stands in front of the doors, about fifty feet from us. This time, he's not letting us go far.

Clementine heads back toward the main path. She can't get out of here fast enough.

Still focused on the book, Nico's eyes squeeze into two angry slits. "Why do you have that?" he asks.

"Have what? The book?"

"Why do you have it!?" Nico growls. "Tell me why you brought it here."

"Just calm down," I say, glancing over at the guard.

Following my eye, Nico turns to the guard, then sits down on the bench, swallowing every bit of rising anger. However long he's been in here, he knows the consequences of losing his cool.

"Is this a test?" he asks. "Is that it? It's a test for me?"

"I don't know what you're talking about," I tell him, offering him a quick goodbye as I follow after Clementine. "I work in the Archives, and I found this book, so I—"

"*You* found the book?" Nico interrupts.

I freeze, confused.

Clementine keeps walking.

Nico's eyes go wide, his cheeks flushed with excitement. "Of course you found it. Of course," he says. "Why else would you be here?"

"Hold on. You *know* this book?" I challenge.

"Don't you see? That's why she found me," Nico says, motioning to his daughter.

Clementine stops, utterly confused—and for the first time, looks directly at Nico.

"And that's why *you* followed," Nico says, pointing to me. "God knows how I was misled. But God provides..."

"Nico, you're not making sense," I say.

"The book. To bring that book," Nico insists. "The Lord knows my belief is just in Him. I'm no longer fooled by ancient stories of devil worship or secret cults or—or—or— This isn't— This has nothing to do with me. It's not a test for *me*," Nico insists, his voice picking up speed. He points at my chest. "It's a test for *you*!"

I glance over my shoulder. To the guard, it just looks like we're talking.

"What kind of test?" Clementine asks, hesitantly walking toward us.

"This dictionary. *Entick's Dictionary*," Nico says, now locked just on me. "You work in the Archives. That's why you smell of wet books. Don't you know your history? This was the book George Washington used."

"Time out. You *do* know this book?" I ask again.

"It's the one Washington used. To test the loyalties."

"The loyalties of what?"

Stretching his long spider legs out, Nico creeps off the bench, stands up straight, and kicks his shoulders back. "What else?" he asks, eyeing the guard and smiling. "For the Culper Ring."

31

S ay again?" Clementine stutters.

"The Culper Ring," Nico says. "When George Washington was—" He cuts himself off, but this time doesn't look back at the guard. He looks at me. His eyes flick back and forth. "You of all people...You know who they are, don't you?"

"Me? Why should I know?" I ask.

He studies my face. Like he's looking for something no one else can see. "To work in the Archives...You know. I know you know."

This time I don't respond.

"Is he right? Beecher, please...say something," Clementine pleads, more unnerved than ever. "You know, don't you? You know what this Culper Ring is."

"Not what. *Who*," Nico says. "The strength was in the *who*. That's why they saved us," he explains. "Back during the Revolutionary War, the British were slaughtering us. Not just physically. Mentally too. War is mental."

War's not the only thing mental, I think to myself.

"If you know, please...why're you not saying anything?" Clementine asks, looking just at me and making me realize just how unsettling—and unlikely—all these coincidences are to her.

"*I don't know,*" I insist.

"You just said—"

"I've heard of them. I work in Old Military—of course I've heard of them—but all I know are the basics: They were George Washington's private spy group. He personally put the group together."

"You know why he brought them together," Nico challenges. "Why are you so fearful to show your knowledge? Is it her? Or are you uncomfortable around me?"

I again stay silent. Clementine knows *he's* the one I'm worried about. Indeed, my mind tracks back to the crazy Freemason/Founding Fathers conspiracy that caused Nico to shoot the President all those years ago. Nico was convinced Thomas Jefferson and the other Founders were trying to rule the world, and it was his job to save us.

The guy's got a PhD in crackpot history, so the last thing I need is to add another gallon of crazy to his tank. The problem is, like before, the *real* last thing I need is to rile him for no reason. "Okay, just listen," I say. "Back during the Revolution, George Washington was frustrated that our side couldn't keep a secret—our plans kept getting intercepted by the British, since they knew who all our military spies were," I continue, glancing back at the guard, who's watching us, but seems satisfied all is under control. "And that's when Washington decided to stop relying on the military, and instead put together this group of regular civilians..."

"That's the key part," Nico says. "The Culper Ring weren't soldiers. They were normal people—a group no one could possibly know—even Washington didn't know their names. That way they could never be infiltrated— no one, not even the commander in chief, knew who was in it. But this Ring—they were regular people," he adds, standing over me as his chocolate eyes drill into mine. "Just...just like us."

I scooch back on the bench, still wondering whether he's being extra crazy because of me, or he's just permanently extra crazy. Next to me, Clementine's just as worried. She's done asking questions.

"So these guys in the Culper Ring," I say to Nico, "I still don't understand what they have to do with *Entick's Dictionary*."

"Ask yourself," Nico says, pointing to me.

"Okay, this is just silly now," I shoot back. "I have no idea what the Culper Ring did with a dictionary."

"You know," Nico says. "Deep down, you should know."

"How could I possibly—? What the hell is going on?"

"Nico, please...he's telling the truth—he doesn't know what the book is for—we don't have a clue," Clementine says, locking eyes with her father. When Nico stares back, most people can't help but look away. She stays with him.

To Nico, it matters. Her glance is as mesmerizing as his own. He nods to himself slowly, then faster.

"The book—the dictionary—that's how George

Washington communicated with his Culper Ring," he finally says.

"Communicated *how*?" I ask. "There's nothing in the dictionary but empty pages."

Nico studies the guard, but not for long. "You can't see the wind, but we know it's there. Just like God. We know it's there. We feel it. Not everything can be seen so easily."

I flip the dictionary open and the only thing there is the handwritten inscription.

Exitus
Acta
Probat

The other pages—the few that haven't been torn out... "Everything's blank," I say.

"Of course they're blank," Nico replies, his chest rising and falling even faster. He doesn't care about the guard anymore. "This is George Washington you're trying to outsmart," he adds, now eyeing the dictionary. "He knew they'd be looking for it. That's why he always wrote it with his *medicine*."

"*Medicine?*"

"That was his code name for it," Nico says. "That's what he called his *invisible ink*."

32

Y ou don't believe me," Nico says, fine-tuning his gaze at me. "Of course you'd think like that."

"What're you talking about?" I ask. "You don't even know me."

"You're wrong. You're *very* wrong!" he growls, his chest pumping like wild.

"You got three minutes!" the guard calls out behind us, just to make sure we know he's watching. "Make them count."

Nico *psssts* at the two tuxedo cats, who continue to ignore him.

Clementine knows I'm not going anywhere. Not now. She stands there, still facing us. But she won't come closer. She's heard enough. She wants to go.

"*Tell me*," Nico says excitedly, sitting on his own hands as he returns to the bench. "When you found that book...for you to bring it here. You of all people..."

"Why do you keep saying that?" I scold.

"Benjy!" Clementine pleads.

"*Benjy?*" Nico asks, scanning my ID that hangs around my neck. "Is that your name?"

"My name's Beecher."

His eyes recheck my ID, which lists my full name in impossibly small type. He has no problem reading it. *White, Beecher Benjamin.* He starts to laugh. A strong, breathy laugh through his gritted teeth. "It couldn't be more perfect, could it?"

He's no longer excited; now he's absolutely giddy.

"Yesyesyes. This is it, isn't it?" he asks, his head turned fully to the left. Like he's talking to someone who's not there. "This is the proof…"

"Nico…" I say.

"…this proves it, right? Now we can…"

"Nico, if you need help, I can get help for you."

"You are," he snaps. "You're helping me. Can you not see that? To follow her here…to come see me…every life…all our lives are lived for a reason."

"Nico, you said it's a test for me," I say. "Tell me why it's a test for me."

Across from us, a gray tabby cat leaps up, landing delicately on the edge of an outdoor metal garbage can. There's not a single sound from the impact.

Nico still flinches.

"That's it, Nico! Time's up!" the guard shouts, quickly approaching. "Say goodbye…"

"How do you know this book?" I challenge. "What the heck is going on?"

"I have no idea what's going on," Nico replies, calmer than ever and still sitting on his hands. "I don't know who's using that dictionary, or what they have planned. But for you to be the one who found it...such a man of books...and the name *Benjamin*...like your predecessor—"

"Wait. My predecessor? Who's my predecessor?"

Nico pauses, again turning to his left. His lips don't move, but I see him nodding. I don't know who his imaginary friend is, but I know when someone's asking permission.

"We all have souls, Benjamin. And our souls have missions. Missions that we repeat, over and over, until we conquer them."

"Y'mean like *reincarnation*?" Clementine asks, earnestly trying to understand, though she still won't take a single step toward us.

"Nico! Let's go!" the guard yells. *"Now!"*

He barely notices.

"I can see who you are, Benjamin. I can see you just like the Indian chiefs who saw George Washington as a boy. They knew who he was. They knew he was chosen. Just as I knew when I saw *you*."

Oh, then that makes far more sense, I think to myself. "So now that we're all reincarnated, lemme guess—I'm George Washington?" I ask.

"No, no, no—not at all," Nico says. "You're the traitor."

"Nico, I'm taking mail privileges first, then the juice cart!" the guard threatens.

Nico pops from his seat and strolls toward the guard at the front of the building. But as he circles past us, he glances back over his shoulder, his voice barely a whisper. "All these years...haven't you seen the battles I've been chosen for? *I'm* George Washington," Nico insists, tapping a thumb at his own chest. "But you...I know you, boy. And I know how this ends. This is *your* test. *I'm* George Washington. And *you're* Benedict Arnold."

33

And now you know why they call it an *insane* asylum," I say, giving an angry yank to the steering wheel and tugging Tot's old Mustang into a sharp right out of the parking lot.

"Can we please just go?" Clementine begs.

"Benedict Arnold? He hears my middle name is *Benjamin* and suddenly I'm Benedict Arnold? He could've picked Benjamin Franklin or Benjamin Harrison. I'd even have accepted *Benjamin Kubelsky*."

"Who's Benjamin Kubelsky?"

"Jack Benny," I tell her as I pump the gas and our wheels kick spitballs of slush behind us. "But for your dad to look me in the face and say that I somehow have the soul of one of history's worst traitors—not to mention him trying to eat us..."

"Don't call him that."

"Wha?"

"*My dad,*" she pleads. "Please don't call him *my dad.*"

I turn at the words. As we follow the main road back

toward the front gate at St. Elizabeths, Clementine stares into her side mirror, watching the hospital fade behind us. The way her arms are crossed and her legs are curled on the seat so her body forms a backward S—to anyone else, she looks pissed. But I've seen this look before. It's the same one she had back in the Archives, when she didn't think I was looking. Over the past twenty-four hours, the real Clementine keeps showing her face, reminding me that pain isn't something she works through. It's something she hides.

In my mind, I was visiting a presidential assassin. For Clementine, it was the very first time she met her father.

"Y'know, in all the dreams where I get to see my dad again," I tell her, "the reunion always goes smoothly and perfectly."

"Me too," she says, barely able to get the words out.

I nod, already feeling like an insensitive tool. I should've realized what this visit did to her, but I was too busy being spooked out with this Culper Ring and Benedict Arnold hoo-hah.

"I'm sorry for surprising you like that," I tell her.

She waves me off. That's the least of her problems.

"So what'd he say?" I ask as I turn onto the poorly plowed streets of Martin Luther King Jr. Avenue. Clementine doesn't even blink at the gang-tagged storefronts and the two burned-out cars on our right. Craning her neck to look out the back window, she still can't take her eyes off the hospital. "When you first got there, did he seem—? Was he happy to see you?"

"Beecher, we can talk about anything you want—

even the Benedict Arnold stuff—but please...don't ask me about him."

"I hear you, Clemmi. I do. And I'm not trying to push, but for a moment, think of what just happened. I mean, no matter who he was, I would still saw my left arm off to have even thirty seconds with my father—"

"Beecher, please. Don't call him that," she begs. "Especially around him."

I pretend to stare straight ahead, focusing on the road. But the way those last words hang in the air...

Especially around *him*.

Clementine bends her knees, tightening her backward S and fighting to hold it together.

"You never told him, did you?" I ask.

She doesn't answer.

"He doesn't know he's your father?"

"I meant to. I was going to tell him," she finally says, still staring in the rearview. "But then..." She shakes her head. "Didja know he speaks to the dead First Lady? When we were there...that's who he was mumbling to. I read it in an article. I think he hides it from the nurses. They said he used to talk to his last victim as some desperate way to absolve himself."

I sit with that one, not sure how to respond. But there's still one piece that doesn't make sense. "If you didn't tell them you were a relative, how'd you even get in to see him?" I ask.

"Grad student. I told them I was writing a dissertation on complex psychosis," she explains.

"And they just let you in?"

"It's not up to the doctors. It's up to the patient. Don't forget, it's been a decade. Nico doesn't get too many visitors anymore. He okays whoever shows up."

"But to be that close and not tell him who you are..."

"You should be thanking me," she points out. "If I did, he probably would've called me Martha Washington."

"That's funny. I'm actually thinking about laughing at that."

"Of course you are. You're trying to get on my good side. Classic Benedict Arnold move."

I shake my head, amazed at just how much the joke burrows under my skin. "Clemmi...you know I'd never betray you."

She turns to me. A small appreciative grin lifts her cheeks. "Beecher, why're you doing this?"

"Doing what?"

"Besides these past few months of emails, I haven't spoken to you in fifteen years. You were cute in high school—in that quiet, smart, scared-of-me way—but we didn't stay much in touch. Plus at your office, you've got the head of security ready to pin you for murder. So why'd you come here? Why're you being so nice?"

Holding the wheel, I stare straight ahead, pretending to watch the road. "She was my fiancée."

"Huh?"

"Before. You asked before who Iris was, and I said she was my *girlfriend*. She was my fiancée. The one. We sent out invitations. The table seating was done. On one night with a few cheap margaritas, we even started picking baby names. And yes, there are worse things, but when it all fell apart, it felt like she strangled and killed my entire life. Everything was dead. Anyway, I figure after all the honesty you've shown me, you at least earned that back."

"So she *did* dump you for another guy?"

"Don't push. We're not being that honest yet," I say.

She stays with the rearview, her head slightly swaying back and forth, like she's whispering an imagined question to someone.

"I'm not a DJ," she finally blurts.

"What?"

"For the radio station—I'm not a DJ," Clementine says. "I sell ads. I'm just an ad sales rep. I-I thought you'd— I sell on-air ads for soft drinks, car dealerships, and in Virginia, we do a ton for places that help people addicted to chewing tobacco."

"But you told me—"

"I always wanted to be a DJ—I did it once for a few years at a community college's radio station. But for the past ten years, I'm just— I used to be a peacock; now I'm just a feather duster." Looking over at me, she adds, "I'm sorry for lying to you, Beecher. When we were first emailing, you said you had this perfect job at the National Archives, and when you asked me what I did, I wanted you to— I didn't want you to think I was a failure."

"Clementine, I'd never think—"

"And the lies just flowed, didn't they? Instead of an ad rep—shazam!—I was magically a DJ with the life I'd always dreamed for myself. And the worst part was how fast the bullshit came—flush with all the details, and all the old jazz we play, and…" She won't look at me. "I'm like *him*, aren't I? The imagined life…I'm a natural liar, Beecher. I am."

"Then I guess I shouldn't believe that either."

It's a good joke, but it doesn't help.

"I thought the worst part would be *seeing* Nico," she explains, "but the real worst part, now that I finally have—is how much of my life now sadly *makes sense*."

I'm all set to argue, but before I can say a word, my phone vibrates in my pocket. I can't ignore this one.

"Where are you?" Tot asks the moment I pick up.

"What's wrong? What happened?" I ask, knowing that tone and wondering if he found the videotape.

"Y'mean besides the fact that you're out fawning over some girl you barely know, who you're just stupidly smitten with?"

"That's not what's happening."

"Sure it's not. You've got a beautiful girl in a pristine automobile. It's not a guess, Beecher. It's science."

"Tot, can you please stop saying things that make me want to hang up on you?" I plead.

"Actually, no—especially when you hear this: Still no sign of the video, but I was able to track down your man Dustin Gyrich," he says, referring to the guy who checked out *Entick's Dictionary* every time President Wallace visited the Archives. "And, oof…it's a doozy, Beecher."

"What? He's got some kinda record?"

"Oh, he's definitely got a record," Tot explains. "I

started digging backwards through our pull slips, and from what I can tell...well..." Through the phone, I hear Tot roll his tongue inside his cheek. "Dustin Gyrich has been checking out books and pulling records for over a hundred and fifty years."

34

*T*hey didn't believe you, did they?" the dead First
Lady asked.

    Up on the third floor, standing near the edge of
the screened-in balcony, Nico watched the powder blue
Mustang squirm down the narrow paved road that led toward the guardhouse at the front gate.

"She's watching me. I can see her," Nico announced.

"Does that matter?" the First Lady asked.

"It means she'll be back again. I know she'll be back."

*"But what you said about the boy...about
Beecher...They never believe you."*

Turning to the First Lady, he asked, "Do *you* believe
me?"

*"Nico, you shot me with a bullet that sprayed my
brain across the front of my car's dashboard. You took
me away from my husband and children and grandchil-
dren. I want to hate you with everything I have left. But
this boy Beecher—he knows who he is. We all know who
we are, even if we won't admit it. So when he comes to
betray us—"*

"He may not betray us. That's his test. I have to give him his chance."

"A chance is fine. But if he fails, he better suffer the same punishment you gave me."

Nico nodded, turning back to the fading Mustang.

"What about the girl?" the First Lady added. *"You know who she is, don't you?"*

"Of course," Nico replied as the car finally turned the corner. "I may be crazy, but I'm not an idiot."

35

Pulling into Tot's parking spot in the basement of the Archives, I catch my breath and take a peek in the rearview. Morris the security guy thinks I don't see him as he peers down from the top of the ramp that leads outside. Like this morning, he did the full search, including the mirror sweep underneath the car. But he's not gonna find anything—including Clementine, who's no longer sitting next to me.

It was easy to drop her off half a block away. It'll be even easier to meet up inside the building. She knows where. Our Rotunda holds original copies of the Declaration of Independence, the U.S. Constitution, and the Bill of Rights. It also holds the best meeting spot for staffers to sneak their friends off the public tour and into their offices on the working side of the building—without ever having to put their names on the sign-in sheet.

It's bad enough I'm under Khazei's microscope. I'm not bringing Clementine—or her dad—there with me.

Of course, that doesn't mean I'm playing sacrificial lamb either. Beyond a good parking spot, there's one other thing waiting for me in the basement.

With the dictionary once again tucked into the back of my slacks, I throw the heavy car door open, climb outside, and stroll right under the eye of the security camera in the corner. It follows me all the way to the double doors that take me to the interior checkerboard floors of the building.

Within the Archives, most people think that basement offices—with no windows and no view—are the worst. But for one office in particular, the lack of sunlight is an absolute necessity.

There's no sign out front, no room number on the wall, and if you come at it from an angle, you can tell that the glass door, with its horizontal blinds pulled closed, is bulletproof. It needs to be. Forget the vaults upstairs. Here's where the real treasures are kept.

"Daniel, you in there?" I call out, knocking hard on the glass.

Underneath the door, it's clear the lights are off. I know his tricks.

"Daniel, I know you're there. I have something good for you."

Still no response.

"It's an old one too…"

Still nothing.

And then…

"*How old?*" a voice finally calls out.

"Let's go, Howard Hughes—open the door!" I shout.

There's a muffled click as the door swings wide, revealing Daniel "the Diamond" Boeckman, the handsomest man in the entire Archives, wearing a crisp white lab coat that I swear doesn't have a single crease, even in the tag. It's the same with his manicured nails, perfect tie, and immaculate brushed-back blond locks—there's not a thread, a hair, a molecule that's out of place. More importantly, he's one of the best talents we have in Preservation.

"Tell me your afternoon is free," I plead.

"Can't," he says. "I've got Dallas's original Thomas Jefferson letter that's going on display tomorrow."

Clementine's waiting. Time to go atomic.

I pull the dictionary from the back of my pants and hold it up in front of him. "Washington still beat Jefferson?" I challenge.

He studies the gutted dictionary. Ten years ago, a man in Rhode Island found an original music sheet of "The Star-Spangled Banner" folded up—and seemingly stuck—in an old family journal. Boeckman said it was a fake just by looking at the swirl in the handwriting. But that didn't stop him from calibrating the acidity of the paper, freeing the document from the journal, and even reassembling the individual ink flakes on the page, which proved the same. When it comes to document preservation, no one's tougher than the Diamond.

"The binding's gorgeous. Hand-threaded," he says, holding it in his open palm, like he's eyeing the Gutenberg Bible. "But that doesn't mean it belonged to GW."

"That's not what I'm after," I tell him. "You ever hear of Washington using invisible ink?"

He's about to hand the book back. He stops. "You think there's something in here?"

"You're the one with all the CSI chemicals. You find the answer, I'll owe you a monster one."

"All you archivists owe me monster ones. Without me, you'd be going to *Antiques Roadshow* to find out if half your stuff was real."

He's right. Fortunately, there's one thing the Diamond prefers even more than credit.

"How're things going with Rina?" I ask with a grin.

He doesn't grin back. There's not a person in the building who doesn't know about his crush on my #2 officemate.

"Beecher, you don't have half the testicles to make good on whatever inducement you're thinking of."

"That's true. But that doesn't mean I can't put in the good word for you."

With his free hand, he touches his perfect Windsor tie. And smiles. "You used to be one of the nice ones, Beecher. Now you're just like all the rest."

"Just look at the book. And the invisible ink," I tell him, tugging open the bulletproof door and leaving him the dictionary. "Rina sits right by me." I lower my voice. *"Oh, what's that, Rina? Oh, yes, isn't that Daniel Boeckman handsome?"*

"Tell her I'm sensitive," the Diamond calls back as I dart into the hallway. "She was upset yesterday— y'know, with the Orlando thing. *Sensitive* will serve me far better."

The bulletproof door slams with a boom, but what echoes are his words. *The Orlando thing.*

A man died. My friend. I still see him lying there—

his skin now chalkboard gray, the bottom corner of his mouth sagging open. It was yesterday! *The Orlando thing.* Like we're talking about someone who didn't refill the coffeepot.

The thought hits even harder as I follow the basement's white-and-gray checkerboard floor toward the elevators, just down from Orlando's office. But it's not until I turn the corner that the door to the Security Office opens and I spot...

My stomach lurches, like it's being squeezed in a slipknot.

Anyone but them.

36

I'm sorry for your loss. I'm sorry this happened. I'm just... I'm so sorry, I say to myself, practicing the words in my head. But as the tired African-American woman with the outdated clear plastic glasses and the faded red overcoat leaves the Security Office and heads toward me in the hallway, I can't muster a single syllable.

She doesn't notice I'm there. She's too focused on the person behind her—her son—who looks about my age as he carries a cardboard box, hugging it to his chest. He's got a deep dimple in his chin.

Just like his father.

I know them from the pictures on his desk: Orlando's wife and his oldest son. From the cardboard box, they came to clear out his desk.

As they trudge toward me at the elevators, it's like they're walking underwater while carrying a bag of bricks. But it's not the box that's weighing them down.

For a moment, the three of us just stand there in the silence of the hallway. Even now, his son offers up a we're-waiting-for-the-same-elevator smile.

I should say something.

I *need* to say something.

My brain slingshots to the very best advice someone gave me when they heard my dad was dead: Our fathers never leave us. Ever.

I could even say something about how nice Orlando was to everyone.

I can give them that one final memory.

But as the elevator rumbles, its doors slide open, and Orlando's wife and son step inside...

I just stand there in the hallway. Paralyzed.

They both stare at the floor, in no mood for eye contact.

The doors bite shut, consuming them whole.

And I'm still standing there, once again reminded that the only feeling more painful than *loss* is the feeling of *guilt*.

I reach for the elevator call button, but as my finger ignites the up arrow, I can't help but notice the sudden burst of voices coming from the open door of the Security Office. Following the sound, I lean back and take a fast peek into the wide room of cubicles, where small clusters of coworkers are talking—just whispering, gossiping.

It makes sense. With Orlando's wife and son gone, there's no need for whatever self-imposed silence the office had been carrying while his family went through his desk.

"You see them?" the receptionist asks me. "Just heartbreaking, right?"

She says something else, but I'm too busy looking at Orlando's cubicle on the left side of the office. All the photos…the holiday cards…the clutter of life…even his Wisconsin Badgers pencil cup…it's all gone. I search for his computer, but that's gone too (which probably means there's no chance the videotape is here either). I still need to check. With me and Clementine on it, that video holds our fate. But except for a few stray pens and a single pink photocopy that's push-pinned to the wall (the instructions for how to use voicemail), the only remaining proof that someone worked here is the big telephone, with the long cord and two blinking lights, that floats like an island at the center of the otherwise empty desk.

Orlando's desk phone.

According to Khazei, I'm the last person Orlando called. But that doesn't mean I'm the last one who *called him*.

I rush toward his desk—and just as quickly stop myself. This isn't the time, especially with half the staff still standing around and watching. But as I think about Orlando's wife and son…about everything I should've said to them just now…this is exactly the time. Forget the Culper Ring and the dictionary and all of Nico's ramblings. If I can find out what really happened to Orlando— I owe his family at least that much.

Sliding into his chair, I take a final glance around to see who's looking. But to my surprise, the only one watching is the person who just stepped into the office. I turn toward her just as she peeks inside. Rina.

I lock eyes with the Mona Lisa, but by the time the chair fully swivels around, she's already gone.

I saw her, though. I know she was there.

But right now, I need to stay focused on the current problem.

My fingers dive for the phone's keypad, tapping the button for caller ID. The first one reads *Security—ext. 75020*. Those're the guys from the front desk, probably wondering when Orlando was coming to do his shift. The next one's from someone in Exhibits. Then a call from *Westman, Aristotle—ext. 73041*.

Tot? Why's Tot calling him?

But as I scroll down to make sure I have it right, a brand-new name pops up. Then pops up again. It only gets worse.

Forget the slipknot around my stomach. My whole chest tightens like it's squeezed by a noose.

My fingers attack caller ID like a woodpecker. Of the last dozen calls made to Orlando…seven of them…eight of them…nine of them…my Lord, *ten of them*…

…are all from Rina.

I spin back toward reception.

"Get off me!" a woman's voice yells.

I know that voice. I've known it since junior high. It sure as hell ain't Rina.

By the time I see what's going on, sure enough, Rina's not there. But in her place—

"I said, get…*off*!" Clementine barks, fighting to get free.

Just behind her, Khazei grips her by the biceps. I almost forgot. I'm in *his* territory.

The deputy chief of security isn't letting go.

37

L *et go of me!"* Clementine insists, still fighting to free her arm from Khazei's grip.

He shoves her into the hallway, refusing to let go.

Khazei's no idiot. If he's bringing us out here, he's hoping to avoid a scene.

Too late.

"I didn't do anything!" Clementine adds, her feet slip-sliding along the checkerboard tile.

"Really? So waiting in the Rotunda—strolling there for nearly twenty minutes without taking a single look at the gasper documents," he shouts back, referring to the Constitution and the other documents that make tourists gasp. "You're telling me that you weren't waiting there for Beecher to sneak you over?"

"It's a public area! I can stroll there all I want!" she yells.

Khazei pulls her close, squeezing her arm even tighter. "You think I didn't look you up when you signed in this morning and last night? We've got cameras outside! I saw him drop you off on the damn corner!"

A puddle of sweat soaks the small of my back. The only reason I tried to sneak her in was so Clementine—and her dad—would avoid getting linked to everything with Orlando and the President. So much for that. Still, Clementine doesn't seem to care. She's got far more pressing problems to deal with.

"I swear to God, if you don't let go . . . !" she threatens, still thrashing to get free.

"Clemmi, calm down," I tell her.

"She can't, can she?" Khazei challenges. "Got too much family blood in her."

"*Get your hands off me!*" she explodes, the intensity catching me off guard. A flick of spit leaves her lips as she roars the words. Her eyes have volcanoes in them. This isn't anger. Or rage. This is her father.

Khazei doesn't care. He grips Clementine by the back of her neck, hoping it'll take the fight out of her.

He doesn't know her at all. And the way she continues to boil, her whole body shaking as she fights to break free of his grip, I start thinking that maybe I don't know her either.

She twists fast, trying to knee him in the nuts. He turns just in time to make sure she misses.

"Clemmi, please . . . It's enough," I beg.

"Stop fighting and I'll let you go," Khazei warns her.

"Get . . . off . . . me!" she snarls as a silver spit bubble forms at her lips.

"You hear what I said?" Khazei asks.

Clementine refuses to answer. Still trying to escape, she punches at his hands. Her body trembles. She's determined to break away. Khazei grits his teeth, pinching her neck even tighter.

"Let her go...!" I shout, shoving Khazei's shoulder.

"You listening?" he asks her again, like I'm not even there.

Her trembling gets worse. The spit bubble in her mouth slowly expands. She'll never give up. It has nothing to do with Khazei. Clementine just met her father for the first time in her life. She had to sit there and listen as he told us that our lives and our choices are predetermined. Then Khazei jumped in and basically accused her of the same.

Clementine looks over at me, her face flushed red. She's trying so hard to prove them wrong, to prove to the entire world—and especially to herself—who she really is. But as the volcanoes in her eyes are about to blow, that's exactly her problem. No matter how far we come, our parents are always in us.

"Eff. *You!*" she explodes, spinning hard and sending Khazei off balance, lost in his own momentum. Before he realizes what's happened, Clementine twists to the left and grabs the antenna of his walkie-talkie, yanking it from his belt and wielding it upside down, like a miniature baseball bat. It's not much of a weapon. It'll probably shatter on impact. But the way she's gripping it—the way she's eyeing his face—it's gonna leave a hell of a scar.

I rush forward, trying to leap between them.

"What in the holy hell you think you're doing?" a voice calls out behind us.

I spin around just as he turns the corner. Clementine lowers the walkie-talkie to her side. He's far down the hallway, but there's no mistaking the wispy white beard...the bolo tie...the one man who's been here longer than me and Khazei combined.

"Y'heard me," Tot says, honing in on me and re-adjusting the thick file he's got tucked under his arm. "Y'know how long I've been waiting, Beecher? You missed our meeting. Where the heck you been?"

I know it's an act. But I have no idea what I'm supposed to say.

"I...I..." I glance over at Khazei.

"He's been talking with me," Khazei says, his voice serene, making peace rather than war. He's definitely smarter than I thought. Khazei's been here a few years. Tot's outlasted eleven Presidents and every Archivist of the United States since LBJ. It's the first rule of office politics: Never pick a fight you can't win.

"So no problem then? They're free to go?" Tot challenges, lumping in Clementine and leaning in so Khazei gets a good look at his milky blind eye. "I mean, I thought I heard yelling, but I'm old and creaky," he adds. "Maybe I was just imagining it, eh?"

Khazei studies the old man. I can feel the anger rising off him. But as the two men share a far too long, far too intense look, I can't help but think that there's something else that's going unsaid in their little standoff.

Khazei puffs out his chest, all set to explode, and then...

He shakes his head, annoyed. "Just get them out of my face," he blurts, turning back to his office.

As Tot continues to hit him with the evil eye, I can't tell if I've underestimated the power of seniority, or the power of Tot. But either way, we're free to go.

"Clementine..." Tot calls out, pretending to know her.

"Yeah."

"Give the man his walkie-talkie back."

She hands it to Khazei. "Sorry. That's not who I usually am."

To my surprise, Khazei doesn't say a thing. He grabs the walkie, slotting it back into his belt.

I go to step around him, and he stabs me with a final dark glare. "I saw you sitting at Orlando's desk," he says. "Got something needling at your conscience?"

"Why should I? Everyone's saying it was a heart attack," I shoot back. "Unless you suddenly know something different."

"I know you were in that SCIF with him, Beecher. It's just a matter of time until that video proves it, and when that happens, guess who everyone'll be looking at?"

I tell myself that if it all comes out, I can point a finger at the President—but that's when Orlando's words replay louder than ever. No matter who you are or how right you are, no one walks away the same way from that battle.

"Beecher, if you help me with this, I promise you—I can help *you*."

It almost sounds like he's doing me a favor. But there's still plenty of threat in his voice. Before I take him up on anything, I need to know what's really going on.

"You want help? You should talk to Rina," I tell him. "Y'know she called Orlando ten times on the morning he died?"

He barely moves, once again making me wonder what he's really chasing: Orlando's killer, or the George Washington book?

Without a word, he turns back to his office. I race to catch up to Tot and Clementine, reaching them just as they turn the corner. Before I can say anything, Tot shoots me a look to stay quiet, then motions down to the real reason he came looking for me: the thick accordion file that's tucked under his arm. The flap says:

Gyrich, Dustin

The man who's been checking out documents for over a hundred and fifty years.

38

"How's my car?" Tot asks.

"How'd you get Khazei to back down like that?" I challenge.

"How's my car?"

"Tot…"

He refuses to turn around, shuffling as he leads us past dusty bookshelf after dusty bookshelf on the eighteenth floor of the stacks. He's not fast, but he knows where he's going. And right now, as the automatic lights flick on as we pass, he's got me and Clementine following. "Khazei doesn't want a fight," he explains. "He wants what you found in the SCIF."

"I agree, but…how do you know?"

"Why didn't he push back? If Orlando's death is really his top concern, why hasn't Khazei thrown you to the FBI, who're really in charge of this investigation…or even to the Secret Service, who by the way, have been picking apart the SCIF all morning and afternoon? You've got every acronym working quietly on this case, but for some reason, Khazei's not handing over the best pieces of dynamite, namely the two of you," Tot says as another spotlight flicks on. I search the corner of the ceiling. The stacks of the Archives are too vast to have cameras in every aisle. But near as I can tell, Tot has us weaving so perfectly, we haven't passed a single one. "Now tell me how my car is," he says.

"Your car's nice," Clementine offers, still trying to make up for the rage parade she just put on. "I'm Clementine, by the way."

For the second time, Tot doesn't look back. He doesn't answer either.

He wants nothing to do with Clementine. As he said this morning, he doesn't know her, doesn't trust her. But once she got grabbed by Khazei, he also knows he can't just chuck her aside. For better or worse, she was in that SCIF—she was there with Orlando—and that means her butt's in just as much of the fire as mine.

"Your car's fine," I add as we make a final sharp left. "Clemmi, this is Tot."

A spotlight blinks awake, and I'm hit with a blast of cold air from a nearby eye-level vent. Our documents are so fragile, the only way to preserve them is to keep the temperature dry and cool. That means intense air conditioning.

Tot hits the brakes at a wall of bookcases that're packed tight with dusty green archival boxes. At waist height, the bookcase is empty, except for a narrow wooden table that's tucked where the shelves should be. Years ago, the archivists actually had their offices in these dungeony stacks. Today, we all have cubicles. But that doesn't mean Tot didn't save a few private places for himself.

The spines of the boxes tell me we're in navy deck logs and muster rolls from the mid-1800s. But as Tot tosses the fat file folder on the desk, and a mushroom cloud of dust swirls upward, I know we're gonna be far more focused on...

"Dustin Gyrich," Tot announces.

"That's the guy you think did this, right?" Clementine asks. "The guy who's been checking out books for a hundred and fifty years. How's that even possible?"

"It's not," Tot says coldly. "That's why we're up here whispering about it."

"So every time President Wallace comes here on his reading visits," I add, "this man Gyrich requests a copy of *Entick's Dictionary*..."

"Just odd, right?" Tot asks. "I started sifting through the older pull slips...seeing how far back it went. The more pull slips I looked at, the more requests from Dustin Gyrich I found: from this administration, to the one before, and before...There were eleven requests during Obama's administration...three during George W. Bush's...five more during Clinton's and the previous Bush. And then I just started digging from there: Reagan, Carter, all the way back to LBJ...throughout the term of every President—except, oddly, Nixon—Dustin Gyrich came in and requested this dictionary. But the real break came when I tried to figure out if there were any other books that were pulled for him."

"Can't you just search by his last name?" Clementine asks.

"That's not how it works," I explain. "If it were today, yes, we've got a better computer system, but if you want to see who requested a particular document in the past, it's like the library card in the back of an old library book—you have to go card by card, checking all the names on it."

"And that's when I thought of *Don Quixote*," Tot says.

I cock my head, confused.

"Remember that list we looked at—from Mount Vernon—of all the books that were in George Washington's possession on the day he died? Well, in his entire library, guess what single book he had more copies of than any other?"

"Other than the Bible, I'd say: *Don Quixote*?" I ask.

"Uncanny guessing by you. And did you know that in 1861, during a U.S. Circuit Court case in Missouri—whose records we happen to keep since it's a federal trial—one of the parties presented into evidence all the personal property and baggage that was left behind by one of their passengers? Well, guess what book that passenger was carrying?"

"*Don Quixote*," I say for the second time.

"History's fun, isn't it?" Tot says. "That's now two books in our collection that were also in the collection of President Washington. Today, that copy is stored out in our Kansas City facility, but on April 14th, 1961, during the JFK administration, a man named D. Gyrich once again came in and—"

"Wait, what was that date again?" I interrupt.

"Ah, you're seeing it now, aren't you?"

"You said April 14th...?"

"Nineteen sixty-one," Tot says with a grin.

Clementine looks at each of us. She's lost.

"The Bay of Pigs," I tell her.

"Actually, a few days before the Bay of Pigs... but that's the tickle," Tot says, rolling his tongue inside his cheek. "Our dear friend D. Gyrich also came into the building and asked to see that same copy of *Don Quixote* on October 3, 1957, and on May 16, 1954, and on August 6, 1945."

My skin goes cold. It has nothing to do with the chill from the extreme air conditioning.

"What?" Clementine asks, reading my expression. "What happened on those dates?"

"October 3, 1957—that's the day before the Russians launched Sputnik, isn't it?" I ask.

"Exactly," Tot says. "And May 16, 1954?"

"The day before the *Brown v. Board of Education* decision was handed down. But that last one, I forget if it's—"

"It's the later one," Tot says, nodding over and over. "You got it now, don't you?"

I nod along with him. "But to be here the day before... to always be here the day before... You think he knew?"

"No one has timing that good," Tot says. "He *had* to know."

"Know *what*?" Clementine begs.

I look at her, feeling the icy cold crawl and settle into the gaps of my spine. Dustin Gyrich, whoever he is, was in here days before the Bay of Pigs…Sputnik…the *Brown* decision…and August 6, 1945…

"Hiroshima," I whisper. "He was here the day before Hiroshima."

"He was," Tot agrees. "And you'll never believe where he was before that."

39

O kay, here...go back another thirty years," Tot says. "Nineteen fifteen...two days before the *Lusitania* was attacked..."

"That's what brought us into World War I," I explain to Clementine, who's still confused.

"Then again in 1908, the week the Model T was introduced," Tot says, flipping through a stack of photocopies, his voice filled with newfound speed. "Some dates, nothing big happened. But I even found a visit two days before they changed the U.S. penny to the Abraham Lincoln design."

"How'd you even—?" I cut myself off. "That's impossible. He couldn't have come here."

"You're right," Tot says.

"Huh...*why?*" Clementine asks.

"We weren't open back then," I tell her. "The Archives was founded in 1934. Staff didn't start moving in until 1935."

"But lucky us, the Library of Congress has been making books available since 1800," Tot explains. "And when I called some of my friends there, well, considering that they're the largest library in the world, what a shocking surprise to hear that they had their own copies of *Don Quixote* as well."

"So even before the Archives opened..."

"...a Mr. D. Gyrich has been going in there and looking at old books that just happened to once be owned by General George Washington. Still, the real marvel is his timing: three days before the massacre at Wounded Knee...six days before the Battle of Gettysburg... They're still searching, but we found another all the way back to July 4th, 1826, when former Presidents Jefferson and Adams both died within hours of each other on Independence Day."

"He's like the evil Forrest Gump," I say.

"You say 'he' like he's one person—as if there's one guy who's been walking around since 1826," Tot counters. "No offense, but vampire stories are overdone."

"So you think it's more than one person."

"I have no idea what it is. But do I think there're a bunch of people who could be using that name throughout history for some unknown reason? We're in a building dedicated to housing and preserving the government's greatest secrets. So yes, Beecher, I very much believe that that kind of Easter Bunny can exist. The only question is—"

"They're communicating," Clementine blurts.

Tot and I turn. She's sitting at the dusty desk, flipping through Tot's stack of photocopies.

"They're talking to each other," she repeats. "They're

coming in here and they're using the books. That's how George Washington communicated with his group. It's like my d—" She cuts herself off. "Think of what Nico said."

"You spoke to Nico?" Tot asks me. "What'd he say? He knew something? What could he possibly know?"

Tot's questions come fast. They're all fair. But what catches me by surprise is the intensity in his voice.

"Beecher, tell me what he said."

"I will, but…can I ask you one thing first?"

"You said Nico—"

"Just one thing, Tot. Please," I insist, refusing to let him interrupt. "Yesterday…before Orlando was killed…" I take a deep breath, vomiting it all before I can change my mind. "When I was in Orlando's office earlier, on his caller ID…Why were you calling Orlando on the day he died?"

Clementine looks up from the paperwork. Tot freezes. And then, just as quickly, he smiles, his blind eye disappearing in a playful smirk.

"Good for you, Beecher. Good for you," he insists, doing the thing where he twirls his finger in his beard. "I told you to not trust anyone, and you're doing just that."

"Tot…"

"No, don't apologize. This is *good*, Beecher. Smart for *you* for asking that. This is *exactly* what you need to be doing."

I nod, appreciative of his appreciation, but…

"You never said why you were calling him," Clementine blurts.

Tot's finger slowly twirls out of his beard. "My ID," he says. "My Archives ID is about to expire, and they told me to call Orlando to get the paperwork for a new one."

"I thought the IG does all our investigations," I say, referring to the Inspector General's office.

"They do. But Orlando's the one who takes your photo. Go look. Across from his desk, there's one of those passport backgrounds that you pull up and stand in front of."

I look at Clementine, then at Tot. That's all I need. He just saved our asses from Khazei, and gave us his car, and did all this Dustin Gyrich research for no other reason than that he's my dearest friend.

"Beecher, if you don't want to talk about Nico, it's fine," he offers.

"Just listen," I tell him. "Do you know what the Culper Ring is?"

"Y'mean, as in George Washington's spy brigade?"

"So you've heard of them?"

"Beecher, I've been here since before Joe Kennedy had chest hair. Of course I've heard of—" He catches himself as it all sinks in. "Oh. So that's what Nico—"

"What?" I ask. "That's what Nico *what*?"

He thinks a moment, still working the details. "Beecher, do you have any idea what the Culper Ring actually did?" Tot finally asks.

"Just like you said: They were Washington's personal spy unit. That he used civilians to move information back and forth."

"Yeah, no—and that's right. They moved lots of information. Washington's top military spies kept getting caught by the British—his plans kept getting intercepted, he didn't know who to trust—so he turned to these civilians, these regular people, who wound up being unstoppable. But what the Culper Ring is really known for, and what they're treasured by history for, is—" He again stops. "Have you ever seen whose statue sits outside the original headquarters of the CIA?"

"Tot, I'm good, but I don't know this stuff like you do."

"Nathan Hale. You know him?"

"I only regret that I have but one life to lose for my country…"

"That's the one. One of Washington's earliest spies. And just to be clear, Hale never said that."

"What?"

"He never said it, Beecher. The *one life to lose for my country* part came from a play which was popular during Revolutionary times. But do you know why our leaders lied and said Hale was such a hero? Because they knew it was better for the country to have a martyr than an incompetent spy. That's all Hale was. A spy who got caught. He was hung by the British."

"And this is important because…?"

"It's important because when William Casey took over the CIA in the early eighties, it used to drive him crazy that there was a statue of Nathan Hale at headquarters. In his eyes, Nathan Hale was a spy who failed. Hale was captured. According to Casey, the statue in front of the CIA should've been of Robert Townsend."

"Who's Robert Townsend?" I ask.

"That's exactly the point! Townsend was one of the members of the Culper Ring. But have you ever heard his name? Ever seen him mentioned in a history book? No. And why? Because for two hundred years, we didn't even know Townsend *was part of* the Culper Ring. *For two hundred years, he kept his secret!* We only found out when someone did handwriting analysis on his old letters and they matched the ones to Washington. And that's the real Culper Ring legacy. Sure, they moved information, but what they did better than anyone was keep their own existence a secret. Think about it: You can't find them if you don't know they exist."

I look over at Clementine, who's still flipping through the photocopied pull slips. I'm not sure what unnerves me more: the way this is going, or that Nico's ramblings aren't sounding as crazy as they used to.

"So this Dustin Gyrich guy—you think he's part of…" As I say the words…as I think about Benedict Arnold…none of this makes sense. "You're saying this Culper Ring *still exists?*"

"Beecher, at this exact moment, the only question that seems logical is, why *wouldn't* they still exist? They were the best at what they did, right? They helped win a revolution. So you've got half a dozen men—"

"Hold on. That's all there were? Half a dozen?"

"I think it was six…maybe seven…it wasn't an army. It was Benjamin Tallmadge and Robert Townsend and I think George Washington's personal tailor…they were a small group with loyalty directly to Washington.

And if you're George Washington, and you're about to step into the Presidency, and you can't trust anyone, why would you suddenly disband the one group that actually did *right* by you?"

"See, but there's the problem," I point out. "To assume that this Ring—whatever it really is—to assume it lasted all the way to now...No offense, but these days, even the CIA can't keep their own spies' real names off the front page of the newspaper. No way could this town keep a secret that big for that long."

Tot looks at me with one of his Tot looks. "I know you have a security clearance, Beecher. Do you really think there aren't any secrets left in our government?"

"Okay, maybe there are still a few secrets. I'm just saying, over the course of two hundred years—with each new President and each new agenda—forget about even keeping the secret...how do we possibly know this group is still doing *right*?"

"I assume you're talking about what happened with Orlando?"

"Y'mean that part where Orlando suddenly shows up dead right after it looks like he's the one who has their book? Especially when *I'm* the one who has their book? Yeah, call me paranoid, but that's kinda the part I'm focusing on right now."

Tot runs his fingers down the metal ribbons of his bolo tie. He doesn't like the sarcasm, but he understands the pressure I'm under. Behind him, Clementine is flipping even faster through the photocopies. Like she's looking for something.

"Clemmi, you okay?" I call out.

"Yeah. Yeah, yeah," she insists without looking up.

"Beecher, I hear you," Tot continues. "And yes, over the course of two hundred years, who knows if this current Culper Ring has any relation to the original Culper Ring, but to assume that they've turned into the evil hand of history—"

"Did you not see that list?" I interrupt. "Hiroshima, Gettysburg, the Bay of Pigs—all we're missing is the grassy knoll and theater tickets with John Wilkes Booth!"

"That's fine, but to say that a single small group of men are at the cause of all those singular moments—that's just stupid to me, Beecher. Life isn't a bad summer movie. History's too big to be controlled by so few."

"I agree. And I'm not saying they're controlling it, but to be so close on all those dates...they've clearly got access to some major information."

"They're communicating," Clementine says again, still looking down. "That's what I said before. That's what Nico said: To send messages to his Culper Ring, Washington used to hide stuff directly in his books. So maybe today...they put info in a book, then someone picks up that book and reads the message."

"That's...yeah...can't it be that?" I say with a nod. "These guys have information—they sit close to the President, so they traffic in information—and in this case, in this book that was left in the SCIF, President Wallace has information."

"Or someone has information for President Wallace," Tot points out.

"Or that. That's fine," I say. "Either way, maybe this is how they share it."

"Okay—that's a theory—I can see that. But if it's really that earth-shattering, why not just bring it directly to the President?"

"Look at the results: Dustin Gyrich comes in here, then—kaboom—World War I. Another visit, then—kaboom—Hiroshima. This isn't small stuff. So for Gyrich to be back yesterday, there's clearly something big that—"

"Wait. Hold on. Say that again," Tot interrupts.

"Clearly something big?"

"Before that..."

"For Gyrich to be back yesterday?"

"We never checked, did we?" Tot asks.

"Checked what?"

"Gyrich's visit. We know the dictionary was on hold for him yesterday, but we never checked if Gyrich actually physically came into the building..."

I see where he's going. If Gyrich was here, if he checked in as a researcher and signed the log, we've got the possibility of having him on video, or at the very least fingerprints that can tell us who he really—

"Clemmi, c'mon..." I call out, already starting to run.

Clementine doesn't move. She's still flipping through the pull slips—the slips that every visitor has to fill out to look at a particular volume or box of documents—scanning each one like she's reading a prescription bottle.

"Clemmi!" I call again.

Nothing.

I dart to the desk and grab at the pile of photocopies. "C'mon, we can read this after—"

Her arm springs out, desperately clutching the pages. She's practically in tears. "Please, Beecher. I need to know."

Within seconds, she's back to scanning the documents.

Over her shoulder, I check the dates of the pull slips, trying to get context. *July 7, July 10, July 30*—all of them from ten years ago. What the hell happened in July ten y—?

Oh.

"You're looking for Nico, aren't you?" I ask.

She flips to another sheet.

At the NASCAR track. Ten years ago. That's when Nico took the shots at President—

"Please tell me they didn't know about that," I say.

She shakes her head, unable to look up at me. There's only so many punches this poor girl can take in one day. "They didn't," she says, her voice shaking as she nears the end of the pull slips.

"That's good, right? That's good."

"I-I-I guess," she says. "I don't even know if I was hoping for it or not...but if this Culper Ring knew about all those other parts of history...I...I dunno. I just thought they might—"

"Clemmi, it's okay," I tell her. "Only a fool wouldn't've checked. It's completely—"

"You don't have to say it's normal, Beecher. Searching to see if some secret two-hundred-year-old group knew about the day your father tried to murder the President... We're a little far from normal."

I know she's right, but before I can tell her, I feel the vibration of my phone in my pocket. Caller ID tells me it's the one call I've been waiting for. Extension 75343. The Preservation Lab downstairs.

"You ready for it, Beecher?" Daniel the Diamond asks before I can even say hello.

"You were able to read it?" I say.

"It's invisible ink, not the Rosetta Stone. Now you want to come down here and see what's written in this book or not?"

40

Andre Laurent hated hats.

He always hated them—even on a day like today, when the late afternoon winds were galloping down from the Capitol, barreling full force as they picked up speed in the wide canyon created by the buildings that lined Pennsylvania Avenue. Sure, a hat would keep him warm. But as Andre Laurent knew—as any barber knew—a hat did only one thing: ruin a good day's work.

Still, as Laurent leaned into the wind, fighting his way up the block toward the huge granite building, he never once thought about removing his red Washington Nationals baseball cap.

He knew its benefits, especially as he made a final sharp right, leaving the wind tunnel of Pennsylvania Avenue and heading under the awning that led to the automatic doors of the National Archives.

"Looks like Dorothy and Toto are flying around out there," the guard at the sign-in desk called out as Laurent pushed his way into the lobby, bringing a frosty swirl of cold air with him.

"It's not that bad," Laurent said.

He meant it. Compared to the permanent gray of Ohio, the winters in D.C. were easy. But as he approached the sign-in desk, Laurent couldn't help but think that was the only thing that was easier here.

Especially over the last few months.

"Research, or you got an appointment?" the guard asked.

"Research," Laurent said, noticing just how bushy the guard's eyebrows were. They definitely needed a trim, he thought, reaching for the ID Palmiotti had given him and carefully readjusting his baseball cap, which right now was the only thing protecting his face from the ceiling's security camera.

"And your name again?"

Laurent leaned against the sign-in desk, which was built like an airline counter—so tall it came up to his chest. He never liked coming here. But as they knew, the President couldn't get his hair cut every single day. "You don't recognize me by now? I'm here all the time," Laurent said as he held up the ID. "I'm Dustin Gyrich."

41

Y ou talk me up to Rina yet?" the Diamond asks.

"You're joking, right?" I shoot back. "How fast you think I am?"

"Plenty fast," he says, nodding a hello to Tot and taking a quick glance at Clementine. "Kinda like I was with this invisible ink problem you got."

He cocks both eyebrows, thinking he's hysterical. With a pivot, he spins toward the lab, inviting us inside.

"By the way, where's *she* from?" he adds, his back to us as he throws a thumb at Clementine.

"She's...er..." I reach over to Clementine and tuck the red Visitor ID badge that Tot got her inside the lapel of her jacket. "She works in Modern Military in College Park," I add, referring to our facility out in Maryland. "Her name's Lucy."

"*Lucy?*" Clementine mouths, making a face.

"Nice to meet you, Lucy," the Diamond says, his back still to us. "It's kooky though that a full-time employee would be wearing a visitor's badge."

I don't say a word as we pass a bank of map cabinets

and storage units. I shouldn't be surprised. He spends every day studying the tiniest of details.

"Listen, Daniel..." Tot begins.

"Tot, I don't care. I really don't," he insists. "Beecher, just make sure you put the word in with Rina. Fair trade?"

I nod. Fair trade.

"Okay, so on to your next nightmare," he says, leading us to a square lab table in back that's covered by an array of sky blue plastic developing trays, like you find in a darkroom. On the edge of the lab table is our copy of *Entick's Dictionary*. "How much you know about invisible ink?"

"I remember fifth-grade science fair: Someone writes it in lemon juice, then you heat the paper and voilà..."

As I flip the dictionary open, there's now a sheet of see-through archival tissue paper protecting each page. But except for where it says,

Exitus

Acta

Probat

...that front inside page is otherwise still blank.

"I thought you said you found the writing," Tot challenges, nearly as annoyed as I am.

"That's what I'm trying to tell you," the Diamond begs. "Whoever put this in here—they're not playing Little League. This is pro ball," he explains. "The best secret inks date back thousands of years, to China and Egypt—and by the eighteenth century, they were almost universally based on some organic liquid like leeks or limes or even urine. And like you said, a little heat would reveal the writing. But as George Washington understood, it's not much of a secret when every British soldier knows that all you have to do is wave a candle to see the magic appear."

"Get to the part about the pro ball," Tot tells him.

"That is the part," the Diamond insists. "Basic invisible inks require a heating process. You heat the paper, you crack the code. But to foil the British, Washington and his Culper Ring started playing with a *chemical* process."

"Wait... What was that?" Clementine asks.

"The chemical process?"

"No—before that," she says.

"She means the Culper Ring," I jump in. I know where she's going. She wants to know how much of Nico's ramblings were right. "So the Culper Ring were the ones who used this?"

"Of course," the Diamond says. "I assume you know what the Culper Ring is, yes?"

We all nod.

"Then you know the whole purpose of the Ring was to help Washington communicate his most vital secrets. In fact, invisible ink is just the start of it: The Culper Ring had their own codes and ciphers... they made sure no one used their real name... they would only write on the back of the fifteenth sheet of paper. That's why when William Casey took over the CIA—"

"We know the story. About the statue," I tell him. "They're the best spies ever. We got it."

"I don't think you do. As small a group as the Culpers were, they had a huge hand in winning the Revolution for us. And their best value came from the fact that all the vital documents were handwritten letters. So when Washington's orders kept getting intercepted over and over, he asked his Culper Ring to do something about it."

"Cue invisible ink."

"But not just any ink," the Diamond points out. "And this is the part that's brilliant. Instead of using heat, they would do the writing with a chemical that would disappear, which they called the *agent*. And then when you were ready to read it, you'd use a completely separate chemical, which they called the *reagent*."

"And that makes the writing reappear," Tot adds.

"Simple, right? *Agent* and *reagent*," the Diamond says. "As long as you keep the second chemical away from your enemy, they can never figure out what you're writing. So as you surmised, Washington and the Culper Ring would put their messages right into the first few pages of common books."

The Diamond points to the dictionary, and I can hear Nico's words in my head. *Not everything can be seen so easily.*

"They used books because no one would search for messages in there," Tot says.

"That was part of it. They also used books because they needed good-quality paper for the chemicals of the invisible ink to work best," the Diamond points out. "Back then, the paper that was in common pocket books like old pamphlets, almanacs..."

"...and dictionaries," Clementine says.

"...*and dictionaries*," the Diamond agrees, "was cheaper than good paper imported from England." Sliding on a pair of cotton gloves, he carefully reaches over and removes the dictionary from my grip, laying it face-open on the lab table.

"The one snag is, if you have a two-hundred-page dictionary, how're you supposed to know what page to apply the reappearing chemicals to?" he adds, flipping through the blank pages that are all slightly browned, but are basically indistinguishable from each other. "No surprise, the Culper Ring had a way around that one."

Tugging at the first piece of tissue paper, the Diamond once again reveals the book's handwritten inscription:

Exitus

Acta

Probat

"When it came to Washington's messages," he explains, "they knew to read between the lines."

I look at Tot, still lost.

"I'm not being metaphorical," the Diamond says. "That's where we get the phrase from. Do it: *Read between the lines*."

From the nearest developing tray, he pulls out a small square sponge no bigger than a matchbox. With a surgeon's touch, he gently dabs the wet sponge onto the page.

From the paper's textured fibers, faded light green letters rise, blooming into view and revealing the message that I'm now starting to think was intended for the President of the United States:

Exitus

FEBRUARY 16

Acta

26 YEARS IS A LONG TIME TO KEEP A SECRET

Probat

WRITE BACK: NC 38.548.19 OR WU 773.427

"Jiminy Crackers," Clementine whispers, her voice cracking. Her face is pale.

"Curiouser and curiouser, eh?" the Diamond asks, clearly excited.

The only one silent is Tot. I see the way he's looking at the message. He sees it too.

If these numbers are right...

We just jumped down a brand-new rabbit hole.

42

The guard at the sign-in desk studied the barber's ID, then looked back at Laurent.

This was the moment Laurent hated. If something were to go wrong, this is when it would happen.

The guard stood there, his cheeks just starting to puff.

Laurent tried to smile, but it felt like his whole body was flattening. Like the inside of his chest was now touching the inside of his back. He wasn't a spy. He wasn't made for this. In fact, the only reason he agreed to do it was... Dr. Palmiotti thought it was because the President of the United States asked personally. But it wasn't about the office.

It was about the man. A man Laurent knew since Wallace was a boy. A man who asked Laurent to move to Washington, and to whom Laurent made a promise. And while some people don't put high priority on such things in Washington, D.C.... back in Ohio, and in so many other places... there's something to be said about keeping your word.

"Here you go, Mr. Gyrich," the guard with the overgrown eyebrows announced, handing back the ID and waving the barber toward the X-ray machine.

As the conveyor belt began to whirl, Laurent filled a plastic bin with his keys, his cell phone, and of course the book he was carrying: *A Problem from Hell.*

It rolled through the machine without a hitch, and within seconds the barber was on his way. "Thanks again," he called to the guard.

"Anytime," the guard replied. "Welcome to the Archives. And happy hunting to you."

43

F *ebruary 16th,"* Clementine reads from the page. "Should we know that date?"

I shake my head at her. *Not here.*

"That's the date they found King Tut," the Diamond jumps in.

"Pardon?" I ask.

"How do you even know that?" Tot challenges.

"I looked it up. Before you got here," the Diamond explains, pointing down at the now revealed message on the front page of the dictionary:

Exitus

FEBRUARY 16

Acta

26 YEARS IS A LONG TIME TO KEEP A SECRET

Probat

WRITE BACK: NC 38.548.19 OR WU 773.427

"I couldn't find anything noteworthy on the twenty-six years ago part, but looking at just February 16th—that's the date the silver dollar became U.S. legal tender, and Howard Carter found Pharaoh Tutankhamen. Otherwise, it's pretty much a quiet day in history." Reading our reactions—and our silence—the Diamond adds, "Sorry. Didn't mean to pry."

"You're not prying. Not at all," Tot says, forcing a dash of thankfulness into his voice. "We just found this book mixed in with some old files from the early sixties, and we figured if someone scribbled in there, it might be fun to see what they were writing about."

The Diamond stares directly at Tot, unafraid of his blind eye.

"Do you have any idea how invisible ink works?" the Diamond asks.

"You just told us how it works," Tot shoots back.

"I did. I gave you a crash course. But if I gave you the full course, I'd also tell you that if the invisible ink sits for too long—if a few decades go by and we apply the reagent chemicals—that writing reappears in a color that's pale brown. Like a chestnut. Your writing here is pale green," he says, pointing down to the dictionary. "That's fresh ink—and by the brightness of the color, I'm wagering something that's been written in the last week or so."

Still pale as can be, Clementine looks at me. I look at Tot.

"Daniel, listen..." Tot begins.

"Nope. Not listening. Not butting in. I already told Beecher: I don't want your problems, and I don't want to be mixed up in whatever you're mixed up in. He needs my help, I'll give it to him. But don't treat me like an idiot, Tot. It makes you look pompous. And besides, it's insulting."

"I apologize," Tot says.

"Apology accepted," the Diamond replies as he hands me back the dictionary. "Though by the way, I can tell you right now: No way this book ever belonged to George Washington."

"But the motto..."

"*Exitus acta probat* never appeared as just three words on a page. Never. Not once in his collection. Trust me, I've verified over thirty books for Mount Vernon. Whenever Washington used the motto, it appeared with the full coat of arms, including the eagle, and the stripes, and the three stars. And even if that weren't the case, I also found *this*..."

He flips to the inside back cover of the dictionary. In the bottom right corner, the characters "2--" are written in light pencil. I didn't even notice it before.

"Is that another code?" Tot asks.

"The most important code of all," I say, remembering my time in Mr. Farris's store. "In used bookstores, that's the price."

"...or in some cases, what the bookseller paid for it," the Diamond adds, "so they know what to sell it for."

Tot rolls this one around in his head. "So rather than some rare George Washington edition, you think this book is worth about two bucks?"

"It's worth whatever someone will pay for it," the Diamond says. "But if I had to guess, sure, I'm betting this is a later edition that some counterfeiter doctored up to sell in some scam during the 1800s when Washington died. We see 'em all the time. Saw another one a few weeks back at a used bookstore in Virginia," the Diamond says. "So if I were you, I'd focus my energy on whatever book they want you to reply in."

"Pardon?" Clementine asks.

"You telling me those aren't library call numbers?" the Diamond challenges. "They wrote to you in this book, now you write back in another. Communicating through books. Someone's doing the Culper Ring proud."

I once again think of Nico as all three of us stare down at the last line of the message:

WRITE BACK: NC 38.548.19 OR WU 773.427

No question, they definitely look like library call numbers. "There's only one problem—" I begin.

"—and that is, we need to find those books right now," Tot interrupts, shooting me a long hard look. I take the hint.

But as we head for the door, I hear the song "Islands in the Stream." Kenny Rogers and Dolly Parton. Tot's phone.

"You've got Tot," he answers, flipping it open. He nods, then nods again. But he doesn't say a word. Even as he closes it.

"Daniel, thanks again for the help," Tot finally announces, motioning me and Clementine out into the hallway.

"Don't forget me and Rina," the Diamond calls as we leave.

The lab's bulletproof glass door slams shut with a cold clap, but all I hear is Tot's quiet huffing as he shuffles back toward the elevators.

"The book that's in those call numbers—you know which one it is, don't you?" Clementine asks.

Tot ignores her. So do I.

"Who was that on the phone?" I ask him.

"Matthew," Tot says.

"Who's Matthew?"

"The guard at the front desk. With the caterpillar eyebrows. I paid him twenty bucks to keep an eye out," Tot says as we all crowd into the waiting elevator. "Now if you move your heinie fast enough, we're about to get our chance to finally grab Dustin Gyrich."

44

*P*ing" the elevator sings in F-sharp as the doors slide open.

I race out first, darting into the hallway and heading straight toward the gray stone walls of the lobby. Behind me, Tot hobbles, trying to keep up. No surprise. He's got nearly fifty years on me. But what is a surprise is Clementine, who starts to run and quickly loses steam. Her face is pale white like an aged porcelain doll.

"You okay?" I ask.

"Go…If he's there…*Go!*" she insists.

I take the cue, picking up speed.

"He said he went into Finding Aids!" Tot calls out.

Pulling a sharp right, I cut into the mint green Finding Aids room, the same room I found Clementine in this morning, when she gave me the homemade photo of the two of us.

There's no one at the research tables. No one at the bookshelves. For visitors, the last pull from the stacks was done hours ago. It's too late. No one's here.

Except for the older black man in the dark wool pea

coat who's hunched in front of the small bank of computers.

"Sir, I'm checking IDs. Can I see your ID?" I call to the man.

He doesn't turn around.

"Sir...! Sir, I'm talking to you," I add, now on a mad dash toward him. I reach out to grab his shoulder.

"Beecher, don't—!" Tot shouts as he enters the room.

Too late. I tap the man hard—hard enough that he turns around and—he—

He's a she.

"I *know* you didn't just put your hands on me," the woman barks, twisting from her seat.

"Ma'am, I-I'm sorry...I thought you were...I'm just checking IDs," I tell her.

She flashes her badge, which says she's a researcher from the University of Maryland. But as I scan the rest of the room, there's no sign of...of...of anyone.

Including Dustin Gyrich.

It doesn't make sense. The guard saw him come here. For him to move that fast...It's like he knew we were coming. But the only ones who knew that were—

"Who's calling you?" Tot asks.

I spin around to see Tot standing next to Clementine. In her hand, her phone is vibrating.

She looks down to check the number. "It's my job— they probably want to know if I'm coming in tomorrow," she explains. "Why?"

"Why aren't you picking it up?" Tot pushes.

"Why're you using that tone with me?"

"Why aren't you picking it up?"

Clearly annoyed, and looking paler than ever, Clementine flips open her phone and holds it to her ear. She listens for a few seconds and then says, "I'll call you back, okay?" Reading Tot's reaction, she asks, "What?"

"I didn't say anything," Tot challenges, making sure she hears that challenge in his voice.

"Just say it," she pushes back.

He shakes his head.

"So now you don't believe me?" she asks, holding out the phone to him. "You wanna speak to them? Here—speak to them."

"Listen, everyone's had a long day," I jump in.

"And don't give me that evil eye stare you give everyone else," she says, still locked on Tot. He walks over to the main check-in desk. She follows right behind him. "Beecher's been in my life long before he's been in yours. I've been helping him since the moment this started—and what?—now you think I'm tipping off Gyrich or something?"

"Those are your words, not mine," Tot says.

"But they can just as easily be applied to *you*," Clementine shoots back. "Oh that's right—I almost forgot you got that magic phone call three minutes ago that sent us racing up here. What a perfect time for Gyrich to check in and say, 'All's clear.' I'm telling you now, you hurt my friend, and I'll make sure the world knows who you are."

I wait for Tot to explode, but instead, he stares down at a red three-ring binder that sits open on the main desk.

Of course. The binder...

"Beecher..." Tot says.

I fly to the desk.

"What?" Clementine asks. "What is it?"

Ignoring her, Tot flips back one page, then flips forward to the current one.

"Every day, this room is staffed by us—by archivists," I explain. "We're on call for an hour or two each day so when visitors come in, we can help them with their research. But more important, the supervisor who runs this room marks down the exact time each of us gets here, just so she knows who's staffing the room at any particular moment."

"And of the fifty archivists in this building, look who was the very last one who was in here today—according to this log, barely ten minutes ago," Tot says, stabbing his crooked finger at the last name on the sheet.

4:52 p.m.—Dallas Gentry.

My coworker. And officemate. And along with Rina, the one other person staffing President Wallace yesterday when he was arriving in the SCIF.

45

Six minutes ago

When he was cutting hair, Andre Laurent put no premium on speed.

His focus was accuracy. Precision. Giving the client exactly what he wanted. Or at the very least, convincing the client that whatever he gave them was exactly what they wanted.

But this was different.

As he entered the mint green Finding Aids room on the first floor of the Archives, Laurent didn't waste a single second.

Without question, today was very much about speed. Most of the time, the goal was to move slowly—to go to the upstairs research room, pull a cart full of documents and pamphlets and half a dozen other records, and then hide what they needed right in plain sight.

But if what it said in *A Problem from Hell* was true... if someone else had grabbed the dictionary...

He didn't even want to think about it.

A quick scan of the room told him he at least picked the right time. God bless government employees. This close to five, nearly all the staff was gone.

"Can we help you?" an older employee called out as she wheeled a rolling cart filled with small boxes toward the microfilm reading room on their far left.

"I'm actually okay," Laurent said, waving his thanks, but not moving until she was gone.

When she was out of sight, he cut past the main research desk and headed for the bookshelves that lined the walls of the room. Ignoring record group numbers, he started counting. The one...two...three...fourth—here—fourth bookshelf on the right. Like nearly every other shelf in the room, it was filled with old leather books—mostly brown and dark blue, but a few red ones as well—each volume dedicated to a different subject matter. On the top shelf was a row of black binders and some pamphlets. According to the spines, *Record Group 267*.

Laurent nodded. That's the one. Glancing over his shoulder, he double-checked that the supervisor was gone.

All clear.

Reaching to the top shelf, he used two fingers to tip back one of the thick black binders. As he removed it with one hand, he placed it squarely on top of the book he was carrying—*A Problem from Hell*—and then, in one easy motion, slid both books onto the top shelf and headed for the door.

The theory was so simple it was elegant. Archives

employees are concerned about visitors sneaking records out. But no one ever suspects someone sneaking something *in*.

There it sat. Just another book in the world's biggest archive.

Thirty seconds after that, Laurent was gone.

Thirty seconds after that, he was outside, using a crowd of departing employees to keep him out of the eye-space of security.

And thirty seconds after that, he was on his phone, dialing the number that by now he knew by heart.

As it began to ring, a beat-up Toyota whizzed by. On the back was a faded presidential bumper sticker: *Don't Blame Me—I Didn't Vote For Wallace*.

In the barber's ear, the phone stopped ringing. Someone picked up.

Laurent didn't say anything. He didn't have to.

Without a word, he shut the phone. Message sent.

Fourth bookcase. Top shelf. Fast as can be.

Just like the client wanted.

46

H e's gone," I say.

"Check his desk," Tot says.

I go cubicle to cubicle, passing my own in our office on the fourth floor, but I already know the answer.

When we first got here, I saw the metal wipe-off board and the little magnet heads with our pictures on them. There were two people in the IN column. Everyone else is OUT. Including the one archivist we came here to see: Dallas.

"No answer on his cell. Maybe he's downstairs," Tot says. "Or in the stacks."

"He's not," I say, heading back to the magnets in front. "You know how he is—he doesn't check out until the moment he's leaving. God forbid we shouldn't know that he's always working and—Hold on. Where's Clementine?"

Tot looks over his shoulder. The door that leads out to the hallway is still open.

"Clemmi?" I call out, craning my neck outside.

She's sitting down, cross-legged on the tiles. "Sorry, I'm just—It's been a long day."

"Y'think? Usually, when I meet my long-lost father, and get nabbed by Security, and find secret writings that may lead me to a murder, I'm way peppier than that."

Forcing a smile, she reaches up and grips the door-frame to help her stand. But as she climbs to her feet, her face—it's not just white anymore. It's green.

"You're really not okay, are you?"

"Will you stop? I'm fine," she insists, forcing another smile. But as she tucks a few stray strands of black hair behind her ear, I see the slight shake in her hand. I've had twenty years to romanticize Clementine's strength. It's the worst part of seeing old friends: when your rose-colored memories become undone by reality.

"We should get you home," I say, quickly realizing that, in all my excitement to see her, I have no idea where she lives. "Where in Virginia are you going? Is it far?"

"I can take the Metro."

"I'm sure you can. But where're you going?"

"By Winchester. Not far from Shenandoah University."

I look at Tot, who's already shaking his head. That's far. Real far. "You sure the Metro goes out there?" I ask.

"Metro, then commuter bus. Will you relax? I do it all the time."

I again look at Tot. He again shakes his head.

"Don't ask me to drive her," Tot says.

"I'm not asking you to drive her."

"And don't ask me for my car," he warns.

I don't say a word. Clementine's face is green; her hand still has the shakes. Tot may not like her. And he may not like how overprotective she's being. But even he can see it. She's not making it home by herself.

"I'm fine," she promises.

"Beecher..." Tot warns.

"It'll be good. You'll see."

"No. I won't see," Tot says. "I'm tired and I'm cranky, and thanks to your dictionary I got nothing done today. The last thing I need is a two-hour tour of Virginia. You take her home, you come back and pick me up."

"Right. Yes. You got it."

Within six minutes and nineteen seconds, Clementine and I are in the powder blue Mustang, pulling out of the Archives garage and plowing into the evening traffic.

I know Tot's worried. He's always worried. But when I think of what we've been through today...

How could it possibly get worse?

47

The archivist had to make one stop first.

With Beecher now gone, it wouldn't take long. Just a quick moment to duck back into Finding Aids and head for the one...two...three...fourth bookshelf on the right. The archivist glanced back, but knew no one was here. That's why they picked this room in the first place.

The President was always so focused on the SCIF. And that made sense. The SCIF was secure. The SCIF was perfect.

Until yesterday, when it wasn't.

Reaching for the top shelf, the archivist shoved aside the black binders and went right for the book. *A Problem from Hell*.

From a pocket, the archivist took out a small plastic bottle about the size of a shot glass with a triangular nipple on top. The nipple was actually a sponge. The archivist flipped to the copyright page of the book, turned over the small bottle, and let the liquid mixture that was inside the plastic bottle soak into the triangular sponge. With a quick few brushes, the archivist painted the page.

Within seconds, small green handwriting revealed itself.

The archivist read it fast, already knowing most of it. But at the end...

The archivist nodded. When it came to Beecher...and this woman Clementine...That's exactly what had to happen.

The words faded back to nothingness as the archivist slapped the book shut and headed through the lobby, out into the cold of Pennsylvania Avenue.

"*Taxi!*"

A black-and-yellow cab bucked to a stop.

"Where you going tonight?" an older cabbie with a round nose and thick bifocals asked, handing the archivist a laminated card as he slid inside.

"What's this?" the archivist said.

"My mission statement."

Sure enough, the laminated card said: *To take you to your destination in an environment that is most pleasing to you.* Underneath was a listing of all the local radio stations.

Only in D.C. Everyone's a damn overachiever.

"Just turn the corner up here," the archivist said. "I'm waiting for some friends—they're in a light blue Mustang."

"Y'mean like that one?" the cabbie asked, pointing through the windshield as the classic car, with Beecher and Clementine inside, climbed up the security ramp and made a sharp right into traffic.

"That's the one. Beautiful automobile, huh?"

"Y'want me to follow it? Like the movies?" the cabbie asked.

"You can stay back a bit. Even if you lose them," the archivist said, holding *A Problem from Hell* on the seat, "I already know where they're going."

48

You feeling any better?" I ask Clementine.

"Yeah."

"That doesn't sound better. That sounds like a yeah."

She sits with it a moment, staring into the mirror on her side of the car and eyeing the bright lights of the mob of cars behind us. Using the rearview, I do the same, making mental notes of who's behind us: a blue Acura, a few SUVs, a disproportionate number of hybrids, and the usual rush-hour taxis. Nothing out of the ordinary. It doesn't make me feel any better.

"Tot hates me," Clementine says.

"Why would you say that?"

"Y'mean besides the long glares and accusatory stares—or maybe when I answered my phone and he basically said, *Who're you talking to? I hate you?*"

"He's just worried about me."

"If he were worried, he'd be sitting in this car right now. He doesn't like me. He doesn't trust me."

"Well, *I* trust you."

As I tug the wheel into another right and follow the rush-hour traffic up Constitution Avenue, she doesn't respond.

"What, now I don't trust you?" I ask.

"Beecher, the fact you were there for me today—with Nico—I know how you feel. And I pray you know how I feel. In all these years...People aren't nice to me the way you're nice to me. But the only thing I don't understand: How come you never told me what you saw in those call numbers—y'know, in the book?"

She's talking about the invisible ink message:

Exitus

FEBRUARY 16

Acta

26 YEARS IS A LONG TIME TO KEEP A SECRET

Probat

WRITE BACK: NC 38.548.19 OR WU 773.427

"You know what those numbers mean, don't you?" she asks. "You know what books they are."

I shake my head.

"Beecher, you don't have to tell me. Honestly, you don't. But if I can help—"

"They're not books," I say.

Making a left and following the parade of cars as it edges toward I-395 and the signs for the 14th Street Bridge, I take another glance at the rearview. SUVs, hybrids, taxis—a few pushy drivers elbow their way in, but for the most part, everything's in the same place.

"Beecher, I was there. The guy in Preservation said—"

"The Diamond doesn't know what he—"

"Wait. What's the diamond?"

"Daniel. In Preservation. That's his nickname. *The Diamond*," I tell her. "And while he's clearly the expert on book construction and chemical reactions, he doesn't know squat about library science—because if he did, he'd know that neither of those is a call number."

She squints as if she's trying to reread the numbers from memory.

"NC 38.548.19 or WU 773.427," I repeat for her. "They *look* like library call numbers, right? But they're both missing their cutters." Reading her confusion, I explain, "In any call number, there're two sets of letters. The NC is the first set—the N tells us it's *Art*. All N books have to do with art. The C will tell you what *kind* of art—Renaissance, modern, et cetera. But before the last set of numbers—the 19—there's always another letter—the *cutter*. It cuts down the subject, telling you the author or title or some other subdivision so you can find it. Without that second letter, it's not a real call number."

"Maybe they left out the second letters on purpose."

"I thought so too. Then I saw the other listing: WU 773.427."

"And the W stands for...?"

"That's the problem. W doesn't stand for anything."

"What do you mean?"

"Years ago, every library had their own individual system. But to make things more uniform, when the world switched over to the Library of Congress system, every letter was assigned to a different subject. Q stood for *Science*. K stood for *Law*. But three letters—W, X, and Y—they never got assigned to anything."

"So if a book begins with an X—"

"Actually, Xs sometimes mean books that're held behind the main desk, maybe because they're racy or dirty—guess where *X-rated* comes from? But you get the picture. A book that starts WU . . . that's just not a book at all."

"Could it be something besides a book?"

"Ten bucks says that's what Tot's working on right now," I explain as I check in the rearview. The towering Archives building is long gone. "I know under the filing system for Government Publications, W is for the old War Department. But WU—it doesn't exist."

"So it can't be anything?"

"Anything can be anything. But whatever it is, it's not in the regular system, which means it could be in an older library that doesn't use the system, or a private one, or a—"

"What kind of private one? Like someone's personal library?" she asks.

I rub my thumbs in tiny circles on the steering wheel, digesting the thought. Huh. With all the running around for Dustin Gyrich, I hadn't thought about that.

"Y'think the President has his own private library at the White House?" she asks.

I stay silent.

"Beecher, y'hear what I said?"

I nod, but I'm quiet, my thumbs still making tiny circles.

"What's wrong? Why're you shutting down like that?" she asks. Before I can say anything, she knows the answer.

"You're worried you can't win this," she adds.

All I hear are Orlando's words from that first moment we found the book in the SCIF. *Name me one person ever who went up against a sitting President and walked away the same way they walked in.* "I *know* we can't win this. No one can win this. No one wins against a President."

"That's not true. As long as you have that book—and as long as he doesn't *know* you have that book—you have him, Beecher. You can use that to—"

I start breathing hard. My thumb-circles get faster.

"You okay?" she asks.

I stay silent.

"Beecher, what's wrong?"

Staring straight ahead, I motion outside. "Bridges. I don't like bridges."

She glances to her right as we're halfway up the incline. But it's not until the road peaks and we pass the glowing white columns along the back of the Jefferson Memorial that she spots the wide blackness of the Potomac River fanning out ahead of us. The 14th Street Bridge's wide road doesn't look like a bridge. But based on the shade of green that now matches my face with hers, she knows it feels like one.

"You're kidding, right?" she laughs.

I don't laugh back. "My father died on a bridge."

"And my father tried to kill the President. Top that."

"Please stop talking now. I'm trying not to throw up

by visualizing that I'm back in colonial times writing letters with a dipped-ink pen."

"That's fine, but have you even seen what you're missing? This view," she adds, pointing out her window, "you can see the entire back of the Jefferson Memorial."

"I've seen the view. We have the finest shots in the world in our photographic records. We have the early files from when the commission was first discussing it. We even have the original blueprints that—"

"Stop the car."

"Pardon?"

"You heard. Stop the car. *Trust me.*"

"Clemmi, I'm not—"

She grips the handle and kicks the car door open. Blasts of cold air create a vacuum that sucks our hair, and a stray napkin on the floor, to the right. The tires of the car *choom-choom-choom* across the plates in the bridge's roadbed.

I slam the brakes and an opera of horns finds quick harmony behind us. As I jerk the wheel and pull us along the shoulder of the bridge, the open door of the Mustang nearly scrapes against the concrete barrier.

"Are you mental!?" I shout as we buck to a stop. "This isn't some eighth grade—!"

"Don't do that."

"Huh?"

"Don't go to eighth grade…don't talk about something old…don't bring up old memories that have nothing to do with who we are now. *This* is all that matters! *Today,*" she says as the horns keep honking behind us.

"The cops are gonna be here in two seconds," I say, keeping my head down and staring at my crotch to avoid looking over the bridge. "You can't stop at national monuments."

"Sure you can. We just did. Now look up and tell me what you see."

"I can't."

"You can. Just try. I know you can."

"Clemmi..."

"Try, Beecher. Just try."

In the distance, I hear the sirens.

"Please," she adds as if she's pleading for my soul.

In no mood to face another set of law enforcement officers, and still hearing Orlando calling me Professor Indiana Jones, I raise my head and quickly glance to the right. It lasts a second. Maybe two. The wind's made a wreck of Clementine's hair, but over her shoulder I have a clear view of the bright white dome of the Jefferson Memorial. I pause, surprised to feel my heart quicken.

"How's it look?" she asks.

"Truthfully? Kinda horrible," I say, eyeing the curves of the marble stonework. "It's just the back. You can't see the good part with the statue."

"But it's *real*," she says, looking over at the memorial. "And at least you saw it for yourself. Not in a book. Not in some old record. You saw it here—*now*—in the freezing cold, from the side of a bridge, in a way that no tourists ever experience it."

My fists still clutch the steering wheel. I keep my head down, again refusing to look outside. But I am listening.

"That was the part I liked," I say.

"You sound surprised."

"I kinda am," I admit as my heart begins to gallop. "I'd never seen it from this angle."

Turning away from the Jefferson Memorial, Clementine glances my way—just a bit as she peers over her shoulder—and looks back at me. Our eyes lock. She won't let herself smile—she's still making her point. But I see the appreciation for the trust.

"She did dump me," I blurt.

"Excuse me?"

"My fiancée. Iris. You asked before. She did dump me."

"I figured," she says. "It's pretty obvious."

"But it wasn't for another guy."

"For another *girl*?" Clementine asks.

"I wish. Then I would've at least had a good story."

This is the part where she's supposed to ask, *What happened?* But she doesn't.

My head's still down. My hands still clutch the wheel. As I relive the moment, she sees the pain I'm in.

"Beecher, if you don't want to, you don't have to say it. It really doesn't matter."

"She dumped me for the worst reason of all," I say as the sirens continue to get closer. "For absolutely no reason at all."

"Beecher…"

I clench my teeth to keep it all in. "I mean, if she fell in love with someone else, or I did something wrong, or I let her down in some unforgivable way…That, I'd understand, right? But instead, she said…it wasn't *anything*. Not a single thing. It was just *me*. I was nice. I was kind. We just…she didn't see the connection anymore." I look up at Clementine, whose mouth is slightly open. "I think she just thought I was boring. And the cruelest part is, when someone says something mean about you, you know when they're right."

Watching me from the passenger seat, Clementine barely moves.

"Can I tell you something?" she finally offers. "Iris sounds like a real shitwad."

I laugh, almost choking on the joy it brings.

"And can I tell you something else, Beecher? I don't think you're in love with the past. I think you're scared of the future."

I lift my head, turning toward her in the seat next to me. When we were leaving St. Elizabeths, Clementine said that the hardest part of seeing Nico was that so much of her life suddenly made sense. And I know I'm overstating it, and being melodramatic, and rebounding something fierce just because we raised the specter of Iris—but ever since Clementine returned to my life…life doesn't make complete sense. But it definitely makes more sense than it used to.

I turn toward the passenger seat and lean in toward Clementine. She freezes. But she doesn't pull away. I lean even closer, moving slowly, my fingers brushing her cheek and touching the wisps of her short black hair. As my lips part against hers, I'm overcome by her taste, a mix of caramel and a pinch of peach from her lip gloss.

There are great kissers in this world.

I'm not one of them.

I'm not sure Clementine is one of them. But she's damn near close.

"You got better since Battle of the Bands," she whispers as she takes a quick breath.

"You remember that?"

"C'mon, Beecher...how could I forget my first kiss?" she asks, the last few syllables vibrating off my lips.

Within seconds, I'm no longer leaning toward her. She's leaning toward me.

I'm overwhelmed by her scent...by the way her short black hair skates against my cheek...by the way her hand tumbles down my chest and slides so close to everything I'm feeling in my pants.

Behind us, a flood of red lights pummels the back window. I barely heard the siren from the police car, which is now two cars behind us, trying to get us moving.

Taking a breath, I slowly pull away.

"Feeling any better?" she asks.

"Definitely better. Though also pretty terrified that we're still on this bridge."

She offers a quick laugh. But as she settles back in her seat, she knots her eyebrows, offering a brand-new look—a sad silent confession that I've never seen before. Like yet another new door has opened—I'm starting to realize she's got dozens of them—and I finally get to see what's inside. "We're all terrified," she says as we race ahead and leave the bridge behind. "That's how you know you're alive, Beecher. Welcome to the present."

* * *

"Please make next...left turn," the female GPS voice announces through my cell phone over an hour later. *"Destination is...straight ahead...on the left."*

"Clemmi, we're here," I call out as I hit the brakes at the red light, waiting to turn onto her narrow block. As I've done at every stop since the moment we left the highway, I check the rearview. No one in sight.

When we first arrived in the small city of Winchester, Virginia, a huge brick residence hall and an overabundance of kids with backpacks told me we were in a college town. But as with any college town, there's the *good part* of the college town, and the *bad part* of the college town. The closer we weaved toward Clementine's block, those students gave way to boarded-up row houses, far too many abandoned factories, and even a pawn shop. Let's be clear: The good part of town never gets the pawn shop.

"Clemmi, we're...I think we're here," I add as I turn onto the long dark block that's lined with a set of beat-up skinny row houses. Half the streetlights are busted. At the very last second, I also notice a taxi, its dim lights turning onto the block that we just left.

Two years ago, the Archives hosted a brown bag lunch for an author who was presenting a book about the effects of fear and its role in history. He said that when you go down a dark alley and you feel that tingling across the back of your neck, that's not just a bad feeling, that's a biological gift from God—the Gift of Fear, he called it.

He said when you ignore that gift—when you go down the dark alley and say, *Y'know, I'm sure it'll be okay*—that's when you find real pain.

Next to me, while I'm still replaying our kiss, Clementine is fast asleep in the passenger seat, exhausted from the long ride as her chin rests on her clavicle. It's late enough and quiet enough that when I listen closely, I can hear the rise and fall of her breathing. But as I squint to read house numbers and pass one home with a door off its hinges, and another with a spray-painted sign across the front that reads *PVC pipes only, no copper inside*, all I hear right now is God's biological gift telling me this is not where I want to be.

Behind us, a car turns onto the block, then changes its mind and disappears.

"*Destination*," the GPS voice announces. "*You have arrived.*"

Leaning forward, I double-check the house numbers: 355. This is it.

With a jerk of the wheel, I pull into the nearest open spot, right in front of a freestanding row house with a saggy old sofa on the front porch. I remember having a house like this. Back in college.

As I shift the car into park, my hand knocks into Clementine's purse, which sits between the bucket seats and opens its mouth at the impact. Inside, I spot the edge of a purple leather wallet, a ring of keys, and a single sheet of paper that makes me smile. Even with just the light from the lamppost, there's no missing what's on it—it's young me and Clementine, in a photocopied black-and-white version of the framed photo she gave me earlier today. She gave me the color one. But she kept a copy. For herself.

"Mary Mother of Christ! What you do to my girl?" a cigarette-stained voice calls from outside.

I jump at the noise, but as I scan the block, I don't see—

"*You!* You heard me!"

The sound takes me up the cracked brick steps, to the front door of Clementine's house. The screen door's shut, but thanks to the glow of the TV inside, I see the outline of an old woman with a bob of white hair.

"She said she'd call me back—she never called me back!" the woman shouts, shoving the screen door open and storming out into the cold wearing a faded pink sweatsuit. She hobbles down the stairs.

Right at us.

49

Clemmi, this would be a good time to get up…" I call out, shaking her awake. As I kick the car door open, the woman—in her late sixties, maybe seventies—is already halfway down the stairs. She's a thin and surprisingly tall woman whose sharp features and natural elegance are offset by the slight hunch that comes with age.

"And I'm freezing!" she yells. "Where the hell you been?"

"Nan, you need to get inside," Clementine pleads, snapping awake and racing from the car.

Nan. Nana. Grandmother. Clemmi's grandmother.

"Don't you tell me where to go!" the grandmother explodes, narrowing her glassy blue eyes, which seem to glow in the night. As she reaches the curb, she shoves a plastic bottle of pills at Clementine's chest. "With dinner! You know I take my medicine with dinner!" Turning to me, she warns, "Don't you think I'm talkin' 'bout drugs either! Rectal cancer. I got cancer in my rectum," she says, patting the side of her leg. I didn't notice it at first. The lump that's hidden inside her sweatpants. A colostomy bag.

"What kinda person leaves ya with no way to open your medicine?"

"Nan, I'm sorry…"

At first, I assume it's Clementine's way to soften Nan's outrage, but the way Clementine won't look her in the eye…She's terrified of this woman.

On our far left, at the very end of the block, there's a loud *clink-clink*. Like a beer bottle spinning on concrete. Clementine and her grandmother don't even notice. I tell myself it's a cat.

"Of course you're sorry," Nan growls, snatching the now open prescription vial from Clementine's hands. Again turning to me, she adds, "Who're *you* anyway? You the one who did this to her?"

"Did what?" I ask.

"Nan!" Clemmi pleads.

"Y'know what this chemo costs? Two hundred dollars a bottle—and that's *with insurance!*"

"Nan!"

Nan stops right there, locking back on Clemmi. "Did you just raise your voice at me?"

"Don't talk to him like that."

Clearly smoldering, Nan slides her jaw off-center, opens her mouth, and pops her jawbone like she's cocking a gun. It freaks the hell outta me. From the look on Clementine's face, I'm not the only one.

"I know you want me dead," Nan says.

"I don't want you dead," Clementine pleads, cutting

past her on the stairs. "If I wanted you dead, I would've never agreed to look after you."

"Look after me? *I'm not a cat!* This is *my* house! You live with *me!*"

At the end of the block, a car door slams. I squint, cursing how far it is. No way was that a cat.

"Um...Clemmi," I try to interrupt.

"I'm not fighting with you, Nan. Not tonight."

"Why? Because your boyfriend's here in his nice fresh suit? You're worried about him seeing the real you—the girl that lost her job at the radio station and is lucky to live with an old lady?"

Clementine freezes. Nan stands up straight, well aware of the damage.

"You didn't even tell him you lost your job, did you?" Nan asks almost as if she's enjoying herself. "Lemme guess—you're still trying to impress him."

"Will you stop?" Turning to me, Clementine adds, "I swear, I was gonna tell you—I just figured one lie at a time—"

"I absolutely understand," Nan interrupts. "A girl in your condition—"

"*Nan!*" Clemmi explodes, her voice echoing up the dark block. "Beecher, I'm sorry—I really am. She gets mean when it's late."

"Hold on, this is *Beecher?*" Nan asks. "This is the one you used to have the crush on? He's a nothing—look at him!"

"You know nothing about him!" Clementine threatens.

"I can see right now...!"

"No. You can't see anything. And y'know why?" Clementine growls, turning back and leaning in close on the staircase. "Because even on your very best day, you're not *half* the person he is. Not *even close*," she insists as Nan takes a small step backward, down to the lower step.

"Beecher, I'm sorry—I'll call you tomorrow," Clementine calls out as she tugs her grandmother by the arm. "Nan, let's go."

Anxious to disappear, Clementine races up the stairs. Her grandmother's about to follow, but at the last moment the old woman turns back to me, feeling my stare. "What? You being judgmental? Say it already."

"You're lucky you have her," I tell her.

Her jaw shifts off-center, and I again wait for the pop. The only thing that comes is her low whisper, each syllable puffing with a tiny blast of cold air. "Go lick yourself, Dudley Do-Right. If it wasn't for you knocking her up, she wouldn't even be in this mess."

A buzzing in my ears becomes deafening.

"Wh-What?"

"You think I'm blind *as well as* dumb? Would you really be coming back here if she didn't have you by the scrotum with this kid thing? I swear to Christ, they keep getting dumber."

"Nan! Come inside!" Clementine calls out.

With a final angry glare—a protective glare—the old woman makes her way back up the brick staircase, the colostomy bag swaying like a pendulum inside her pant leg.

For a moment, I just stand there.

Pregnant.

If it's true…it'd certainly explain why Clemmi was nauseous before—and more important, why now, of all moments, she suddenly started looking for her father.

Still, as it all sets in, as I realize where I am—alone…in the dark…with no one around—I need to get out of here.

Opening the door and sliding inside Tot's car, I notice a black leatherette glove in the passenger seat. The fingers are thin. Definitely Clementine's.

I look up the brick staircase. Both the screen door and the main door are shut. But I can still see the glow of the light inside.

I should leave her alone. She's had enough embarrassment for one night. But if I drop it off now…It'll only take a second. I can even make sure she's okay.

I elbow the car door open.

As I hop outside, a hard shove drills me from behind, knocking me face-forward to the pavement. I fight to stop the fall, but my arms—*zzzzppp, zzzzppp*—they're pinned…handcuffed…Whoever it is, he's strong. My arms are pinned behind my back.

Help! Someone help, I want to yell as my chin stabs the concrete and the wind's knocked out of me. A sharp knee digs into my back and long strong fingers stuff a smelly rag in my mouth. The smell…It's awful…Like burnt hair.

I try to spit out the rag, but the strong fingers grip my mouth and pinch my nose, making me take an even deeper breath.

Facedown on the pavement, I twist like a fish, trying to fight...to get free...to get a look at my attacker. A second knee stabs my back.

Dizziness sets in...

No, don't pass out!

I twist again and he shoves my face down, pinning my left cheek to the cold pavement, which now seems soft and warm. Like it's melting. The world seesaws and continues to tumble.

The very last thing I see, in the reflection of the Mustang's shiny hubcap, is an upside-down, funhouse-mirror view of my attacker.

50

I'm awake.

I was unconscious, now I'm awake.

It takes nothing to snap between the two. No time.

My eyes open, and I'm staring at bright yellow flowers. Sunflowers. My sister loves sunflowers.

I blink quickly, struggling to adjust to the light.

It's light. Is...is it daytime?

No, the curtains are closed. The light's in here.

There's the hum of central heating.

My brain's swirling. Is Clemmi...? Yeah...I remember...Clemmi's pregnant.

Nuhhh.

Clemmi's pregnant and my chin hurts. It hurts bad.

My shoulders are sore. A hard tug tells me why. My arms are still handcuffed behind my back.

But as I look down, what catches my eye is the chair I'm sitting in. It's got armrests. Upholstered fancy armrests. With nailheads.

I look back at the sunflowers. They sit in a fine Asian vase on a beautiful hand-carved coffee table.

In the Archives, I've read the top-secret reports of where the CIA brought all the terror suspects after 9/11. It wasn't a well-appointed room like this.

But even without the handcuffs, drugging, and kidnapping, I'm starting to think this is worse.

I glance around, trying to figure out how long I've been out. It looks dark through the closed curtains, but it could just as easily be early morning. I search the room for a clock. Nothing. In fact, the more I look around—at the little wastebasket, at the built-in library, where every leather-bound book is the exact same size—the whole room is so perfect, it makes me wonder if I'm in some kinda hotel, or...maybe this is someone's private SCIF...

On my left, I spot a framed black-and-white photograph of the White House covered with scaffolding and surrounded by dump trucks. It's from 1949, back when they were doing the construction that added the Truman Balcony.

Please tell me I'm not in the White House...

There's a flush of a toilet behind me.

I twist in my seat, frantically following the sound. Someone's in the bathroom. But what grabs my attention is the sliding mirrored door of the closet that sits next to it.

The closet's empty. No clothes...no shoes...not even a set of hangers.

It's the same all around.

No trash in the garbage. No photos on the walls...or the end tables...The chocolate brown leather sofa on my left has no give in any of the cushions. Like it's never been sat in.

What the hell is this place? Why aren't there any signs of life?

I try to fight free, but my head nearly caves in. Whatever they drugged me with...the dizziness...it's still taking its toll.

From the bathroom, there's a rush of water from the sink. Underneath the door, a shadow passes and...

Click.

I spin back as my weight jerks the chair into a half-spin. The bathroom door opens and my attacker reveals— That smell...Of cherry rum.

Cherry rum pipe smoke.

"Man, I really messed up your chin, didn't I?" Dallas asks, stepping forward, scratching at his little beard, and reminding me why he was always the most hated archivist in our office. "Sorry, Beech—we just needed to get you out of there. When I saw someone following—"

"What're you talking about? What the hell's going on?"

"I can explain."

"You damn well better explain!"

My brain flips back to yesterday. When they were taking Orlando's body out, I spotted Dallas with Rina, and they quickly ran for cover. Right now, though, he stands his ground, taking new pride in whatever it is he's up to.

"Remember when you first started at the Archives, Beecher?"

"Are you about to make a speech right now? Because if I get out of these handcuffs, I'm about to kill you."

"Listen to me," Dallas insists. "Remember that first night when you worked late, and visiting hours were over, and all the tourists were gone—and you made your way down to the Rotunda, just to stand in the darkness so you could have your own private viewing of the Declaration of Independence? Every employee in the building has that moment, Beecher. But as you stood there by yourself and you studied those fifty-six handwritten signatures that changed the entire world, remember that wondrous feeling where you dreamed what it would be like to be a part of history like that?" Dallas touches the gash on my chin. From the pain, I jerk my head up. He gets what he wants. I'm now looking him right in the eye. The smell of his pipe seeps off him. "This is your chance to add your signature, Beecher. History's calling you. All you have to do is help us."

"*Us?* Who's *us?*"

"The Culper Ring," Dallas says. "We're the Culper Ring. And with your help, we can catch the other one."

"The other *what?*"

"The ones who did this. The ones who killed Orlando. The other Culper Ring, of course."

51

It was cold and late—well past two in the morning—as Dr. Palmiotti stared at the drop phone that sat on his nightstand.

But as he lay there, wrapped in his down comforter, he knew he wasn't even close to sleep.

For a while, he tried his usual tricks: visualizing a walk in the wide green stretch of grass in the arboretum behind his college dorm. He didn't particularly like the outdoors. But he liked the idea of it. And he liked college. And usually, that was enough to do the trick.

Not tonight.

"Baby, you're gonna be exhausted tomorrow," Lydia said, rolling toward him as she faded back into her own slumber. "Stop worrying about him. If he needs you, he'll call."

He was still amazed to see her do things like that—to read him so clearly…to *feel* him being awake. He was lucky to have her. She understood him better in six months than his ex-wife did in nearly twenty years. And for a while, he thought about just that—in particular, about their night at the Four Seasons and the thing with the fishnet stockings she had done for his birthday— hoping it would be the key to his sleep.

But once again, the doctor's thoughts wandered back to his friend, and the message the President had written, and to this nightmare at the Archives—which of course took Palmiotti right back to his nightstand, to the phone with the gold presidential seal on the receiver.

If he needs you, he'll call.

It was good advice. But the one thing it failed to take into account was just how complex a President's needs were. In fact, it was those particular needs that caused the Ring to be created in the first place. Both Rings. And while it was bad enough that someone accidentally found the book, if the rest was true, if there was now a third party involved and the original Culper Ring was closing in…In med school, they used to call it CD. It had the same acronym in politics. Certain Death.

Palmiotti stuck his leg out from the comforter, trying to break his sweat. The drop phone would be ringing any minute.

But for the next hour and a half, nothing happened.

Palmiotti was tempted to call the medical unit. From there, the on-duty nurse could confirm that Wallace was upstairs. But Palmiotti knew he was upstairs. At this hour, where else would the President be?

By 4 a.m., the doctor was still tossing and twisting, eyeing the phone and waiting for it to ring. He knew his friend. He knew what had to be going through his head. He knew everything that was now at stake.

The phone *had* to ring.

But it never did. Not tonight.

And as Dr. Palmiotti stared up at his ceiling, both legs sticking out of his comforter, one hand holding Lydia, it was that merciless silence that worried him most of all.

52

"Why am I in handcuffs?"

"Beecher, did you hear a word I just said?" Dallas asks.

"Why am I in handcuffs!?"

"So you wouldn't do exactly what you're doing right now, namely throwing a fit rather than focusing on the big picture," Dallas shoots back. "Now. For the second time. Did you hear what I said?"

"There are two Culper Rings. I got it. But if you don't undo these cuffs…"

"Then what? You'll scream? Go. Scream. See what happens," he says, motioning at the barely lived-in room.

I take another glance around, still stuck in my seat. I'm not sure I believe there's really such a thing as a two-hundred-year-old secret spy unit. And even if I did, I'm not sure why they'd ever pick Dallas. But there's only one way to get answers. "Where are we anyway? What is this place?"

"I'm trying to tell you, Beecher. Now I know you don't like me. I know you've never liked me. But you need to understand two things: First, I want to get you out of here—the longer we keep you out of sight, the more suspicious it looks. Second, I'm on your side here. Okay? We're all on your side."

I'm about to unleash, but as my shoulders go numb, I stay locked on the priorities. "Undo the cuffs."

"And then you'll listen?"

"I can't feel my pinkies, Dallas. Undo the cuffs."

Squatting behind me, he pulls something from his pocket and there're two loud snaps. As the blood flushes back to my wrists, he tosses the set of clear plasticuffs into the no-longer-empty trash can.

"Here...take this," he says, reaching for the bookcase and handing me a square cocktail napkin. I didn't even notice it before—an entire shelf in the bookcase is filled with a high-end selection of rum, vodka, scotch, and the rest. Whatever this room is used for, it clearly requires a good drink.

He pulls a few cubes from a silver ice bucket and drops them in my napkin. "For your chin," he explains, looking surprised when I don't say thanks.

"At Clementine's...to be there," I say as I put the ice to my chin. "How long were you following?"

"I wasn't *following*. I was trying to talk to you—to get you alone. I mean, yesterday in Orlando's office...this morning when Tot chased me away. Have you really not noticed how often I've been showing up?"

"So you gas and cuff me? That's your solution? Send an email next time! Or wait...just call! It's a lot less headache!"

Shaking his head, Dallas takes a seat on the leather sofa. "You really don't understand how this works, do you? Face-to-face—that's the only reason it's lasted. The problem is, every time I get near you, you're running off with your little group, and no offense, but...your high school first kiss? That's who you're trusting your life to?"

"I'm not trusting my life to her."

"You *are*, Beecher. You don't think you are, but you are. What you found in that SCIF—that was a miracle that happened—a true gift from God that you stumbled upon." I watch him carefully as he says the words. He's the only person besides Tot and Clemmi to even guess how this all started, which brings a strange reassurance that makes me think he's telling the truth. "But I promise you this," Dallas continues, "if you don't start being careful—when they confirm you have it—they'll put you in the ground even faster than Orlando. That's not just hyperbole, Beecher. That's math."

The ice on my chin sends a waterslide of cold down my Adam's apple and into the neck of my shirt. I barely feel it. "You keep saying *they*. Is that who you saw following me?"

"I couldn't see who they were. I think they spotted me first."

"Y'mean the car that almost turned down the block?"

"That wasn't just a car. It was a taxi. A D.C. taxi. Out that far in Virginia. Real hell of a commute, don't you think—unless that's your only choice because someone borrowed your car."

Omigod. The Mustang. "Is Tot's car...!?"

"His car is fine. We had it driven here, then sent a text from your phone saying you'd pick him up tomorrow. He didn't reply. You see what I'm getting at?"

I know exactly what he's getting at. "You think it was Tot in that taxi."

"I have no idea who it was, but I do know this: There's no way the President is pulling this off without help from someone inside our building."

The napkin filled with ice sends a second waterslide down the inside of my wrist, to my elbow. Orlando said it. Clemmi said it. Even I said it. But to hear those words—*the President*—not the president of some useless company—*the President of the United States*. This isn't just confirmation that the message in that dictionary was meant for Orson Wallace. It's confirmation that when it comes to my life— I can't even think about it.

"Tell me what the Culper Ring really is," I demand.

"The true Culper Ring?"

"The one that did this. The one the President's in."

"The President's in both."

"Dallas, I'm officially about to leap over that coffee table and stuff my foot through your teeth."

"I'm not trying to be coy, Beecher. I swear to you, I'm not. But this is two hundred years of history we're talking about. If you want to understand what the Culper Rings are up to now, you first need to know where they originally came from."

53

Clementine knew it wasn't good for her.

That's why she waited until the house was quiet.

And why she locked the door to her room.

And then waited some more.

There were enough surprises tonight—most notably the kiss from Beecher. Clementine knew he'd try—eventually he'd try—but that didn't mean it didn't catch her off guard. Plus, the old woman had already done enough. She didn't need to be there for this too.

For comfort, Clementine whistled a quick "psst psst—here, Parky" at her chubby ginger cat, and as he always did, Parker slowly circled his way up the arms of the forest green futon to Clementine's lap, rubbing his head into her palms.

The cat's kindness was one of the few things Clementine could count on these days, and it was exactly that thought that brought the sudden swell of tears to her eyes.

It reminded her of when she first moved to Virginia

and ventured into the local Home Depot to buy a barbecue grill to celebrate the Fourth of July. Stopping one of the orange-overalled employees—a short man with chapped lips and greedy eyes—she asked, "Do I need to spend the few hundred bucks to buy a good grill, or would one of the fifty-dollar cheap grills do the job just as well?"

Licking his chapped lips, the employee said, "Let me explain it like this: I'm a car guy. I love cars. I love *all* cars. And I especially love my 1989 Camaro RS, which I recently spent over $3,000 on to put in a sunroof. Now. You ask yourself: Why would someone spend $3,000 to install a sunroof in some old car from 1989? You wanna know why? Because I'm a *car guy*. That's who I am. That's what I care about. So as you look at these grills, you need to ask yourself..." He took a deep breath and leaned in toward her. "Are you a grill gal?"

The man didn't need to say another word. Smiling to herself, Clementine grabbed a cheap fifty-dollar grill and marched toward the cash register. She wasn't a *grill gal*. Or a *car gal*, a *clothes gal*, or even a *shoe gal*.

She knew who she was. She was a *cat gal*.

No, it wasn't in that crazy-cat-lady way. And yes, there were plenty of people who love their cats and buy them cute plastic toys and high-end scratching posts. Pets can be the very best family members. But there were still only a few who annually throw their cat a real birthday party...or make appointments solely with *feline-only vets,* who only see cats as patients...or make sure that their cat's food and water bowls sit atop a wrought-iron base that keeps the bowls at cat-eye level so that their pet doesn't have to bend to drink.

Some people buy sunroofs. Some buy expensive grills. And some spend their money on a treasured pet. Clementine could even laugh at the insanity of it, but she was proud of being a cat gal—it was always her thing. Until she arrived at St. Elizabeths and saw her father so delicately and beautifully tending to all the cats there.

Just the sight of it made her feel like someone had hollowed out her body and stolen all her organs for themselves. Like her personal parts were no longer her own. It was the same feeling she had when she found out Nico was living so close to where she moved in Virginia. Or when he said that everything in life was already decided. Or when she read that he was almost her age when he had his first psychotic episode.

Of course she told herself none of that meant anything. Life was full of woo-woo coincidences.

But it was still her dad...her dad who lived near her...and looked so much like her...and somehow loved the exact same thing she loved so damn much. With everything else that she'd lost in life—the DJ jobs...the advertising jobs...even her mom—maybe in this moment, Clementine was due for a gain. Plus, it was still her dad. How could she not have some emotional connection?

And that was the one thing that Beecher—who lost his own father—understood better than anyone. Sure, seeing Nico was the hardest thing Clementine had ever done, but like any orphan, she wasn't tracking down her father to learn more about him. She was tracking him down to learn more about herself.

With the push of a button, Clementine's laptop hummed to life, and she sat back on the futon with Parker in her lap and the laptop by her side.

"I know, I know," she whispered to Parker.

It definitely wouldn't be good for her. And the worst part was, she knew the pain was only getting worse.

Of course, if she wanted, she could stop it. It'd be so easy to stop. All she had to do was shut the laptop. Slap it shut, go to sleep, and replay those moments of Beecher's reaffirming kiss.

Indeed, as her fingers flicked across the keyboard and she hit the enter key, all she had to do was close her eyes.

But the saddest truth of all? She didn't want to.

Onscreen, the video on YouTube slowly loaded and began to play. Clementine leaned toward the computer, wrapping her arms around Parker's body. She pulled the cat close—especially when the man with the big politician's grin stepped out onto the NASCAR track, his black windbreaker puffing up like a balloon.

On the far right of the screen, a man in a yellow jumpsuit entered the frame and raised his gun.

And as she had so many times before, Clementine felt her stomach fall as she watched her father try to murder the President.

54

"I know about the Culper Ring," I tell Dallas. "They were George Washington's civilian spy group. They hid messages...they stayed secret...and from what I can tell, they stuck around long enough to have a hand in Gettysburg, World War I, and even somehow Hiroshima."

"How'd you know that last part?" Dallas challenges.

"You think you're the only history nut in the building? We all have access to the same records. Once we found the name Dustin Gyrich—"

"Gyrich. Okay. Okay, you're further than we thought," he says, almost to himself. "But you're wrong about one thing, Beecher: From Gettysburg to Hiroshima to anything else, the Culper Ring has never *had a hand* in these events. You're missing the mission completely."

"But we're right about the rest, aren't we? The Culper Ring that George Washington started, it still exists."

Leaning forward on the leather sofa, Dallas uses his top two teeth to comb the few beard hairs below his bottom lip. He does the same thing when our boss scolds him for falling behind on the quota we have for answering researchers' letters and emails. It's also my first clue that while he's happy to answer some of my questions, he's not answering all of them.

"Beecher, do you know what the President of the United States needs more than anything else? And I don't just mean Orson Wallace. Any President, any era. Obama, the Bushes, Thomas Jefferson. What's the one thing they need more than anything else?"

"You mean, besides smart advice?"

"No. Smart advice is easy. You're the President. Every genius in the world is banging down your door. Try again."

"This is already a stupid game."

"Just try again."

"Privacy?"

"That's top three. You're Reagan. You're Obama. You have more power than anyone. What's even more vital than privacy?"

"Trust."

"Getting warmer."

"Someone who cares about you."

"Getting colder. Think back to George Washington. Why'd he say the Culper Ring helped him win the Revolutionary War?"

"They brought him the best information."

"*Information!* There. *Bull's-eye.* You see it now, right? That is the most, and I mean *the most*, vital thing that a President needs to do his job: reliable information. You understand that?"

"I'm not an idiot."

"Then understand this: Our bureaucracy is so vast, by the time a piece of information makes its way to the President's desk, it's like a chewed-over dog bone. It goes from the guy on the ground, up to a supervisor, up to an analyst, up to a chief of staff, up to a deputy secretary, then up to the real secretary, then through the true honchos who pick through it...and then, if it's lucky, there it is...dumped on your desk, Mr. President. And now you have to take that drool-covered piece of info and use it to make a military, or environmental, or financial decision that'll affect millions or maybe billions of lives. You ready to rely on that?"

"It's not that simple."

"It *is* that simple. It's always been that simple. And it is—still—the greatest problem facing every President: You're the one man in charge, and every day you're making life-and-death decisions based on the work of total strangers with unknown agendas. And that's why, when you're sitting there with all those above-top-secret reports about every problem in the world, you can't help but wonder: *What* don't *I know? What'd they leave* out *of these reports? And what're the motives and biases built into the info I'm getting?*"

"So the Culper Ring works for the President."

"No. The Culper Ring doesn't work for the President. It works for the *Presidency*. It serves the office, just as George Washington designed it—a built-in backstop to be used when it was needed most. Think about it, Beecher—before you drop the bomb on Hiroshima, wouldn't you want to be absolutely sure the Japanese weren't already about to surrender? Or before you went to slaughter your brother in Gettysburg, wouldn't you want to make sure you had the right general in place? Major General Meade was installed just four days before the fighting at Gettysburg began. Pretty good timing by Lincoln, eh?"

My mind swirls through the examples we found in the Archives—the Bay of Pigs...Sputnik...the *Lusitania*—each one its own critical moment in presidential history. It swirls even more when it reminds me that of all the theories we had, it's still Nico who was most correct. The President's definitely communicating through that dictionary. But it doesn't change the one thing I refuse to lose focus on:

"You said there were two," I tell Dallas. "Two Rings."

"And now you're seeing the problem," he says with a nod. "Every once in a while, there's kind of a...speed bump."

"Define speed bump."

"Beecher, I've already kept you here for too long. If they're watching—"

"Tell me about the second Ring, Dallas. Tell me, or I swear to you, I'll type up this crap and you'll be reading about it in the *Washington Post* tomorrow!"

"I know that's not true—that's not who you are. And if I didn't know that, we wouldn't even be having this conversation."

"Then have the damn conversation!"

Like before, he uses his teeth to comb at some stray

beard hairs. But unlike before, his head is cocked to the side, his eyes staring off. Like he's listening to something.

"What're you doing?" I challenge.

He doesn't answer. But as he turns his head, I spot— in his ear—there's something in his ear.

"Is that an earpiece? Are you—? Is someone listening to us right now!?" I shout as I start to search the room. No mirrors. No cameras in the corners.

"They said to calm down, Beecher. You already passed the test."

"What test? Who's *they*? How the hell're they seeing us!?"

I rush to the little minibar, shoving the bottles of alcohol aside. I pull the top off the ice bucket. No wires anywhere.

"It's on you, isn't it? You're wearing a camera!"

"Listen to me, Beecher—"

I hop over the coffee table, knocking the flowers to the floor. He leaps off the sofa and, like a lion tamer, grabs the armchair, trying to keep it between us.

"Will you listen to me!?" he says. "This isn't about you!"

"That's not true! This is *my life* you're screwing with!"

"You idiot! Your life's *already over*!"

I stop at the words.

His fingers dig into the back of the armchair.

"What'd you say?" I ask.

He doesn't answer.

"You said my life is over."

"We can protect you. We're protecting you right now." To prove the point, Dallas heads to the closed curtains and spreads them just a few feet apart, revealing a city block filled with parked cars, but empty of people and bathed in darkness. We're on the second floor of a brick townhouse, and though it takes me a moment, as I scan the restaurants across the street...that CVS.

"We're in Woodley Park," I say.

"We are. But we're also in the only residential house on a busy street where it's difficult to stop, making this building nearly impossible to observe without being observed. When it went up for sale, we were bidding against both the Israelis *and* the Palestinians."

"So this is...what?...some sorta safehouse?"

"You see that homeless guy across the street?" Dallas asks. "He'll be there until 4 a.m., at which point another 'homeless man' will clock in and take his place for a full eight-hour shift. Think about it, Beecher. There's a reason the FBI is the second biggest property renter in Washington, D.C. This is how you do it right."

I turn away as he lets the curtains shut. "You said my life is over."

• "Beecher, you have to understand. When you found what you found..."

"I don't even know what I found. Tell me what I found."

"You found proof. That dictionary— That's proof that they exist."

"That what exists? A second Culper Ring?"

Dallas shakes his head, double-checking that the curtains are shut tight. "Don't call them that. They don't deserve to be called that."

"That's what they are, though, aren't they?"

Dallas sits with this a moment. I can't tell if he's thinking, or listening to whatever's being whispered in his ear, but eventually he says, "Every dozen or so administrations, it happens. It has to happen, right? Every person who's sworn in as President has his own agenda, and some of these guys—I heard the first was Millard Fillmore, though I think if you look at Ulysses Grant, or probably Harding—"

"I don't care about the 1920s or Teapot Dome."

"What about Watergate? You care about that one?"

"Time out. You're telling me that this other Culper Ring—whatever you want to call them—that they're the ones who pulled off Watergate?"

"No. Richard Nixon pulled off Watergate. But to make it happen, well..." Dallas heads over to the framed photo of the White House under construction. "Imagine the Culper Ring—our group, the *true* Culper Ring—as this giant *outer ring* that circles and has been protecting the Presidency for over two hundred years," he says, using his pointer-finger to draw a huge circle around the entire photograph. "And then imagine a guy like Nixon, who rides into power, and looks at that big wide outer ring and says to himself, 'Huh. I should have something like that around *me*.' "

"Like an *inner* ring."

"Like an inner ring," Dallas agrees, drawing a miniature

little circle just around one of the White House windows. "Welcome to the speed bump. So he calls in a few friends that he knows he can trust—G. Gordon Liddy, Howard Hunt, and the rest of the crew—and voilà, Nixon has an inner ring that reports just to him. They call themselves the Plumbers. The rest, as they say, is you-know-what."

I stare at his imaginary circle around the White House window. At the Archives, we've got the original blueprints to the White House. Dallas didn't pick a random window. He picked the one on the second-floor Residence that I know President Wallace uses as his private office. "So you think—with the dictionary—you think that's what Wallace is doing right now? You think he's talking to his own personal Plumbers."

"You don't see the problem there?" Dallas asks.

"I guess I do, but...He's the President. Isn't he entitled to talk to whoever he wants, as secretively as he wants?"

"He absolutely is. But that doesn't mean he—or one of his group—is allowed to murder anyone they think is an accidental witness."

Orlando. Of course he's talking about Orlando. But for him to use that word. *Murder.*

"It wasn't a heart attack, was it?" I ask, though I already know the answer.

Once again, Dallas stays quiet. But unlike last time, he doesn't look away.

"Dallas, if you can confirm it, I need you to tell me," I demand. "I know the autopsy was today. If you have the results..."

"You don't need me to tell you anything," Dallas says with an emptiness in his voice that echoes like a battering ram against my chest. "They'll release the first round of tox reports in the next day or so, but you know what those results are. Just like you know nothing at this level is ever just an accident."

As the full weight of the battering ram hits, I nearly fall backward.

"Just remember, Beecher, when Nixon's Plumbers first started, they were on the side of the angels too, helping the White House protect classified documents." Like a woodpecker, Dallas taps his finger against the small window in the photo of the White House. "Absolute power doesn't corrupt absolutely—but it will make you do what you swore you'd never do, especially when you're trying to hold on to it."

I nod to myself, knowing he's right, but… "That still doesn't explain why you need me."

"You're joking, right? Haven't you seen the schedule?"

"What schedule?"

"Tomorrow. He's coming back for another reading visit." Eyeing the confusion on my face, Dallas explains, "The White House asked for you personally. You're his man, Beecher. When President Wallace comes back to the Archives tomorrow—when he's standing there inside that SCIF—they want you to be the one staffing him."

55

It was only six seconds.

Six seconds of film.

Six seconds on YouTube.

But for Clementine, who was still curled on her futon, still clutching her cat for strength, and whose tired eyes still stared at the laptop screen, they were the most important six seconds of the entire video.

At this point, she knew just where to put her mouse on the progress bar so the little gray circle would hop back to 1:05 of the video. At 1:02, Nico first raised his gun, which you actually see before you see him. At 1:03, as he took a half-step out from the crowd of NASCAR drivers, you could make out just the arm of his jumpsuit—the bright sun ricocheting off a wide patch of yellow. At 1:04, the full yellow jumpsuit was visible. He was moving now. But it wasn't until 1:05 that you got the first clear view of Nico's full face.

The view lasted six seconds.

Six seconds where Nico's head was turned right at the camera.

Six seconds where Nico was calm; he was actually smiling.

Six quiet seconds—before the shooting and the screaming and the mayhem—where Clementine's father didn't look like a monster. He looked confident. At ease. He looked happy. And no question—even she could see it as his lips parted to reveal his grin—their expression was exactly the same. It was the only lie Beecher had told her. But she knew the truth. She looked just like her father.

Pop, pop, pop, the gunshots hiccupped at 1:12.

But by then, Clementine had already clicked her mouse, sending the little gray circle back to before the chaos began.

She'd been at it for a while now, over and over, the same six seconds. She knew it wasn't healthy.

Hoping to switch gears, she reached for her phone and dialed Beecher's number. Even with the long trek back, he should be home by now.

But as she held the receiver to her ear, she heard a few rings, then voicemail. She dialed again. Voicemail again.

She didn't think much of it. Instead, to her own surprise, she found herself thinking about their kiss.

She knew Beecher had it in him.

But as she was learning, Beecher was still full of surprises.

He's probably just asleep, she thought as she clicked back, and the video started again, and she watched again to see just how much she wasn't like her father.

"I know—I promise," she told her cat. "This'll be the last one."

56

You should put the ice on your chin," Dallas says.

"I don't need ice," I say, even though I know I do. My chin's on fire. But it's nothing compared to what's coming. As I nudge the curtain open, I stare outside at a homeless man who's not a homeless man, from a residential townhouse that's not really a townhouse, and refuse to face my officemate, who I now understand is far more than just an officemate.

"Beecher, for Wallace to request you—it's a good thing."

"Yeah, that makes complete sense. In fact, it's absolutely obvious why locking me in an impenetrable bulletproof box with the most powerful man in the world—with no witnesses or anything to protect me—is just a perfect peach of an idea."

"We think he's going to make you an offer," he finally says.

"Who is? The President?"

"Why else would he ask for you, Beecher? You have something that was intended for him. So despite Orlando's death, and the FBI and Secret Service sniffing around the room, Wallace is coming right back to the scene of the crime, and he's asked for you to personally be there. Alone. In his SCIF. If we're lucky, when that door slams shut and those magnetic locks click, he'll start talking."

"Yeah, or he'll leave me just like Orlando."

Dallas shakes his head. "Be real. Presidents don't get dirt under their nails like that. They just give the orders. And sometimes, they don't even do that."

There's something in the way he says the words. "You don't think Wallace had a hand in this?" I ask.

"No, I think he *very much* had a hand in this, but what you keep forgetting is that what you found in that chair isn't just a book. It's a communication—and communications take two people."

"From the President to one of his Plumbers."

"But not just one of his Plumbers," Dallas corrects. "One of his Plumbers *who works in our building*. That's the key, Beecher. Whoever did this to Orlando...to be able to hide the book in that chair...to have access to the SCIF...it has to be someone on staff—or at the very least, someone with access to that room."

"To be honest, I thought it was *you*."

"*Me?*" Dallas asks. "Why would it possibly be me?"

"I don't know. When I saw you in the hallway...when you were with Rina. Then when Gyrich came back to the building, you were the last person in Finding Aids."

"First, I wasn't *with Rina*. We got off the elevator at

the same time. Second, I stopped in Finding Aids for two minutes—and only because I was trying to find you."

I see the way Dallas is looking at me. "You have someone else in mind."

"I do," he says. "But I need you to be honest with yourself, Beecher. Just how well do you really know Tot?"

57

N ope. No. No way," I insist. "Tot would never do that."

"You say that, but you're still ignoring the hard questions," Dallas says.

"What hard questions? *Is Tot a killer?* He's not."

"Then why's he always around? Why's he helping you so much? Why's he suddenly giving you his car, and dropping everything he's working on, and treating this..."

"...like it's a matter of life or death? Because *it is* a matter of life or death! My life! My death! Isn't that how a friend is supposed to react?"

"Be careful here. You sure he *is* your friend?"

"He *is* my friend!"

"Then how come—if he's the supposed master of all the Archives—he hasn't accepted a single promotion in nearly fifty years? You don't think that smells a little? Everyone else at his level goes up to bigger and better things, but Tot, for some unknown reason, stays tucked away in his little kingdom in the stacks."

"But isn't that why Tot *wouldn't* be in Wallace's

Plumbers? You said Wallace's group is all new. Tot's been here forever."

"Which is why it's such a perfect cover to be there for Wallace—just another face in the crowd."

"And why's that any different than what *you're* doing with the Culper Ring?"

"What *I'm* doing, Beecher, is reacting to an emergency by coming directly to you and telling you what's really going on. What Tot—"

"You don't know it's Tot. And even if it was, it doesn't make sense. If he's really out for my blood, why's he helping me so much?"

"Maybe to gain your trust…maybe to bring you closer so he has a better fall guy. I have no idea. But what I do know is that he *is* gaining your trust, and he *is* bringing you closer, and he was also the very last person to call Orlando before he died. So when someone like that loans you his car, you have to admit: That's a pretty good explanation for why you're suddenly being followed by a taxi."

I'm tempted to argue, or even to ask him how he knew that Tot called Orlando, but my brain's too busy replaying "Islands in the Stream." Tot's cell phone—and, just like Clemmi said, the call that sent us racing up to Finding Aids at the exact same moment that Dustin Gyrich snuck out of the building.

"You need to start asking the hard questions, Beecher—of Tot or anyone else. If they work in our building, you shouldn't be whispering to them."

He's right. He's definitely right. There's only one problem.

"That doesn't mean Tot was the one in the taxi," I tell him. "It could've been anyone. It could've been Rina."

"I don't think it was Rina."

"How can you—?"

"It's just my thought, okay? You don't think it's Tot. I don't think it's Rina," he insists, barely raising his voice but definitely raising his voice.

As he scratches the side of his starter beard, I make a mental note of the sore spot. "What about Khazei?" I ask.

"From Security?"

"He's the one who buzzed Orlando into the SCIF. And right now, he's also the one spending far too much of his time lurking wherever I seem to be."

Dallas thinks on this a moment. "Maybe."

"*Maybe?*" I shoot back. "You've got a two-hundred-year-old spy network talking in your ear, and that's the best they come up with? *Maybe?*"

Before he can respond, there's a loud backfire. Through the curtain, a puff of black smoke shows me the source: a city bus that's now pulling away from the bus stop across the street. But what gnaws at me is Dallas's reaction to it. His face is white. He squints into the darkness. And I quickly remember that buses in D.C. don't run after midnight. It's well past 1 a.m.

"Beecher, I think we need to go."

"Wait. Am I...? Who'd you see in that bus?"

He doesn't answer.

"Tell me what's with the bus, Dallas. You think someone's spying from that bus?"

He closes the shades, then checks again to make sure they stay closed. It's the first time I've seen him scared. "We'd also like to see the book."

"Wha?" I ask.

"The book. The dictionary," Dallas says. His tone is insistent. Like his life depends on it. "We need to know what was written in the dictionary."

He puts a hand on my shoulder, motioning me to the door.

I don't move. "Don't do that," I warn.

"Do what?"

"Rush me along, hoping I'll give it out of fear."

"You think I'd screw you like that?"

"No offense, but weren't you the one who just gave me that lecture about how every person in our building was already screwing me?"

He searches for calm, but I see him glance at the closed curtain. Time's running out. "What if I gave you a reason to trust us?"

"Depends how good the reason is."

"Is that okay?" he adds, though I realize he's no longer talking to me. He nods, reacting to what they're saying in his earpiece. Wasting no time, he heads for the closet and pulls something from his laptop bag, which was tucked just out of sight.

With a flick of his wrist, he whips it like a Frisbee straight at me.

I catch it as the plastic shell nicks my chest.

A videotape.

The orange sticker on the top reads: *12E1*.

That's the room...the SCIF...Is this...? This is the videotape that Orlando grabbed when we—

"How'd you get this?" I ask.

He shakes his head. "That's your get-out-of-jail-free card, Beecher. You know what would've happened if Wallace or one of his Plumbers had seen you on that tape?"

He doesn't have to say the words. I still hear Orlando: *If the President finds that videotape, he's going to declare war...on us.* The war's clearly started. Time to fight back.

From my back pocket, I pull out a folded sheet of paper and hand it to Dallas. He unfolds it, scanning the writing.

"This is a photocopy," he says. "Where's the original? Where's the book?"

This time, I'm the one shaking my head.

"You hid it in the Archives, didn't you?" he adds.

I still don't answer.

"Good. Well done. You're finally using your head," he says as he rereads the revealed note we found in the dictionary:

FEBRUARY 16

26 YEARS IS A LONG TIME TO KEEP A SECRET

WRITE BACK: NC 38.548.19 OR WU 773.427

"You know those aren't—"

"We know they're not call numbers," I agree. "But beyond that, we're stuck."

He stares at it for a few seconds more. "Unreal," he whispers to himself. "And the ink was green when you found it?"

"Bright green—new as can be," I tell him. "Whoever these Plumbers are, they like your formula."

He nods, definitely annoyed that there's someone else using their Culper Ring magic tricks. "How'd you know to look for the invisible ink?" Dallas asks. "Was that Tot?"

"It was someone else."

"Who?"

"Are you taking me to *your* leader?" I ask, pointing to his earpiece. "Then I'm not taking you to *mine*," I add, once again realizing just how valuable Nico's advice has been—and how I wouldn't even know about the invisible ink without him.

"So what do I do now?" I ask as he slides the photocopy into his briefcase. "How do I tell you what happens with the President? Do I just find you at work, or is there some secret number I should call?"

"Secret number?"

"Y'know, like if something goes wrong."

"This isn't Fight Club," Dallas says. From his back pocket, he pulls out his wallet, opens it up, and hands me a Band-Aid.

"What's this?"

"It's a Band-Aid."

"I can see it's a Band-Aid. But what is it? A transmitter? A microphone?"

"It's a Band-Aid," he repeats. "And if there's an

emergency—if you need help—you take that Band-Aid and you tape it to the back of your chair at work. Don't come running or calling…don't send emails…nothing that people can intercept. You tape that Band-Aid up, and you head for the restroom at the end of our hallway. I swear to you, you'll have help."

"But what you said before…about my life already being over."

"Beecher, you know history isn't written until it's written, so—"

"Can you please stop insulting me, Dallas. I know what happens when people take on sitting Presidents. Even if I survive this, I'm not surviving this, am I?"

He studies me, once again combing his beard with his teeth. "Beecher, remember that mad scientist convention the government had last year?"

"You're insulting me again. I hate locker room speeches."

"It's not a locker room speech. It's a fact. Last year, the army had a 'mad scientist' conference, bringing together the wildest thinkers to predict what the most dangerous threats will be in the year 2030. And y'know what they decided the number one threat was? *The destructive and disruptive capability of a small group.* That's what they're worried about most—not another country with a nuke—they're terrified of a small group with a committed goal. That's what we are, Beecher. That's what the Culper Ring has always been. Now I know you're worried about who you're going up against. But the Presidency will always be bigger than a single President. Do you hear that? Patriots founded this country, and patriots still protect it. So let me promise you one thing: I don't care if sixty-eight million people voted for him. Orson Wallace has never seen anything like us."

Dallas stands at the door, his hand on the top lock. He's not opening it until he's sure I get the point.

"That was actually a good locker room speech," I say.

"This is our business, Beecher. A fireman trains for the fire. This is our fire," he says, giving a sharp twist to the first of the three locks. "You help us find the Plumbers and we'll all find out who did this to Orlando."

"Can I ask one last question?"

"You already asked fifty questions—all you should be worrying about now is getting a good night's sleep and readying your best game face. You've got breakfast with the President of the United States."

As the door swings open, and we take a carpeted staircase down toward the back entrance of the building, I know he's only partly right. Before my breakfast date with the President, I've got one thing I need to do first.

58

Pulling into his parking lot, I give a double tap to the car horn and brace for the worst. It's nearly seven o'clock the next morning. Being late is the least of my problems.

As the door to his townhouse opens, even Tot's Merlin beard doesn't move. His herringbone overcoat is completely buttoned. He wants me to know he's been waiting. Uncomfortably.

"Get outta my car," he growls, limping angrily around the last few snow pucks on his front path.

"I'm sorry—I know I should've done that," I say as I scootch from the driver's to the passenger seat.

"No. *Out*," he says, pulling the driver's door open and thumbing me into the parking lot.

He won't even look at me as I climb past him.

"Tell me you didn't sleep with her," he says as he slides behind the wheel.

"I didn't." I take a breath. "Not that it's your business."

He looks up. His eyes are red. Like mine. He's been up late.

"Beecher..."

"I'm sorry—I shouldn't've snapped—"

"Stop talking, Beecher."

I do.

"Now listen to what I'm saying," Tot adds, holding the steering wheel like he's strangling it. "Girls like Clementine...they look nice—but they can also be as manipulative as a James Taylor song. Sure, they're calming and bring you to a good place—but at their core, the whole goal of the damn thing is to undo you."

"That's a horrible analogy."

His glance tightens.

"What happened to your face—to your chin?" he asks.

"Brick steps. Clementine has brick steps. I slipped and fell. On my face."

He watches me silently. "That's a tough neighborhood you were in. Y'sure nothing else—?"

"How'd you know that?"

"Pardon?"

"The neighborhood. How'd you know it was tough?"

"I looked it up," he says without a moment's hesitation. "What else was I supposed to do when I was sitting in my office, waiting for you?"

A gust of cold air sends a whirlwind of remnant snow swirling in front of Tot's car. I ignore it, my gaze locked on Tot.

"Thank you for at least filling up the car with gas," he adds.

I nod even though it wasn't me. I forgot about the gas. The Culper Ring clearly didn't. I'm still not sure I trust them, but if I'm keeping score, including the videotape, that's at least two I owe them. And regardless of what they expect in return—regardless of what was really hidden in that dictionary—one thing is clear: Getting to the bottom of the Culper Ring and their enemies—these so-called Plumbers—is the only way I'm getting to the bottom of Orlando and saving my own behind.

"You getting in the car, Beecher, or what?" Tot asks.

As I circle around to the passenger side, I notice a redheaded woman walking a little brown dachshund. The thing is, it looks like the exact same dog that man with the plaid scarf was walking outside of my house yesterday. Still...that can't be the same dog.

"C'mon, we're late enough as it is."

As I plop into the passenger seat, Tot punches the pedal and blows past them without a second glance.

I watch them in my rearview until they fade from view.

With a flick of the dial, Tot turns the radio to his favorite country music station. If Dallas is right, and Tot's in with the Plumbers—though I'm absolutely unconvinced he's in with the Plumbers—this is the moment he'll try to gain trust by offering me another bit of *helpful* advice.

"So guess what else I found last night while I was waiting for you?" Tot asks as we join the morning traffic on Rockville Pike.

From his pocket, he takes out his own photocopy of the message that was in the dictionary:

FEBRUARY 16

26 YEARS IS A LONG TIME TO KEEP A SECRET

WRITE BACK: NC 38.548.19 OR WU 773.427

"Get ready to thank me, Beecher. I think I know what happened on February 16th."

59

Y ou know who's the greeter this morning, right?" asked the President's young aide, a twenty-seven-year-old kid with a strict part in his brown hair.

In the backseat of the armored limousine, President Wallace didn't bother to answer.

Outside, there was a loud *crunk*, like a prison cell being unlocked. Through the Cadillac's green bulletproof glass, the President watched as one of the suit-and-tie Secret Service agents pressed a small security button underneath the door handle, allowing them to open the steel-reinforced door from the outside.

As Wallace knew, at any event, the first face he saw was always a super-VIP—someone with enough tug to wrangle the job of greeter. But in this case, as the door cracked open and revealed a heavyset woman in a navy blue dress, he knew this greeter was a familiar one.

"You're late," his sister Minnie barked.

"I'm always late. That's how I make an entrance," Wallace shot back, quickly remembering why he should've canceled this appearance.

Minnie flashed the largest half-smile that her stroke allowed, and then, like the nuns at their old school, rapped her flamingo-headed cane against her brother's polished shoes. "C'mon, I got people waiting."

With his big strides, it took no time for the President to make his way past the throngs of agents to the loading dock that led into the back entrance of the Capital Hilton. Barely a few steps down the sparse concrete hallway, Wallace heard the click-clack of Minnie's cane as she fought to speed-limp behind him. It'd been a while since they walked together. He slowed down—but he knew his sister too well. Even without the limp, she was forever trying to keep up.

"They tell you to thank Thomas Griffiths?" Minnie asked her brother.

"He knows about Thomas," the young aide called out, barely half a step behind them.

"What about Ross? You need to make a big deal. He's the one I answer to. Ross the Boss."

"He knows Ross too," the aide challenged as the smell of fresh croissants wafted through the air. Passing through a set of swinging doors, they followed the agents to their usual shortcut. Presidents don't arrive through front doors. They arrive through hotel kitchens.

"Just please…make him feel important," Minnie begged.

"Minnie, take my word on this one," the President said, nodding polite nods and waving polite waves to all the kitchen staff who stopped everything to turn and stare. "I know how to make people feel important."

"This way, sir," a short agent announced, pointing them to the left, through a final set of swinging doors. From the dark blue pipe-and-drape that created faux-curtains around the doorway, Wallace knew this was it. But instead of being in the main ballroom, he found himself in a smaller reception room filled with a rope line of at least two dozen people, all of them now clapping as he entered. Truth be told, he still loved the applause. What Wallace didn't love were the two private photographers at the front of the reception line.

"A photo line?" the aide hissed at Minnie.

"These are our top scientists—you have no idea how much they've done for brain injuries," Minnie pleaded.

"You said *one photo*...with just the executive director," the aide told her.

"I didn't agree to *any* photos," the President growled. Palmiotti was right. When it came to Minnie, he *was* a sucker.

"Sir, I apologize," the aide began.

With a cock of his head, the President flashed the aide a final look—the kind of angry, split-second daggers-in-the-eye that spouses share when they're entering a party but still want to say that this won't be forgotten later.

But as Wallace approached the crowd and waved the first guest into position, he couldn't help but notice how quickly Minnie stepped aside, leaving him alone in the spotlight. He'd seen it before—Minnie never liked cameras. All her life, she'd been self-conscious about her masculine looks that she got from the Turner syndrome. He knew that's why she didn't like the campaign trail, and why she never took a yearbook photo. But right now, as her colleagues gathered around her, there was a brand-new half-smile on her face. A real smile.

"Minnie, thank you so much for doing this," one of them said.

"—no idea what this means," another gushed.

A flashbulb popped in front of Wallace, but as the next person headed his way, he couldn't take his eyes off the...it was pride...real pride on his sister's face. And not just pride from being related to a President—or even from being an instant bigshot. This was pride in her work—for what she had done for this organization that had helped her so much all these years.

"Sir, you remember Ross Levin," the President's aide said as he introduced a bookish but handsome man with rectangular glasses.

"Of course, Ross," Wallace said, taking the cue and offering the full two-fisted handshake. "Can you give me one second, though, Ross? I want to get the real hero for these pictures. *Hey, Minnie!*" the President of the United States called out. "I'm feeling a little stage fright here without my sis near me."

There was a collective *awww* from Minnie's colleagues. But none of it meant as much as the bent half-smile that swelled across Minnie's face as her brother wrapped an arm around her shoulder and tugged her into the rest of the photos.

"On three, everyone say *Minnie!*" the President announced, hugging her even closer as the flashbulbs continued to explode.

Sure, Wallace knew he needed to get out of here. He knew he needed to deal with Beecher—just like they'd dealt with Eightball all those years ago. But after everything his sister had been through—from the teasing when she was younger, to the days right after the stroke, to the public hammering by Perez Hilton—would an extra ten minutes really matter?

No, they wouldn't.

Last night was a mess. But today...Beecher wasn't going anywhere.

60

Y'hear what I said?" Tot asks, his cloudy eye seeming to watch me in the passenger seat as he waves the photocopied sheet between us. "February 16th. Don't you wanna know?"

I nod, trying hard to stay focused on the traffic in front of us.

"Beecher, I'm talking to you."

"And I hear you. Yes. I'd love to know."

He turns his head even more. So he sees me with his good eye. I don't know why I bother. He's too good at this.

"You already know, don't you?" Tot asks. "You know what happened on February 16th."

I don't answer him.

"Good for you, Beecher. What'd you do—look it up when you got home?"

"How could I not?" I spend every day doing other people's historical research. All it took was a little extra footwork to do my own. "Khazei wants to pin the murder on me. This is my life on the line, Tot."

"So you saw the story? About Eightball?"

I nod. Even without his training, it wasn't hard to find. When it comes to figuring out what happened twenty-six years ago on February 16th, all you really need is a newspaper from the following day: February 17th.

Twenty-six years ago, President Orson Wallace was in his final year of college at the University of Michigan.

"You did the math, didn't you?" Tot asks.

"That what? That February 16th was a *Saturday*?"

This is when I'd usually see Tot's smile creeping through his beard. Right now, though, it's not there— even though I know Saturday was the breakthrough for him too. At this point, nearly every American has heard the story of how Wallace used to come home every weekend to check on his mom and his sick sister, who suffered from Turner syndrome. So if young Wallace was home in Ohio...

All I needed was the Cleveland News Index and their digital archives of the *Cleveland Plain Dealer*. I searched every keyword I could think of, including the names of family members. Not a single article on February 17th mentioned Wallace. But there was one—and only one— that did mention Wallace's hometown of Journey, Ohio:

Local Man Goes Missing

From my inside jacket pocket, I pull out the printed-out story, which was buried in the back of the newspaper. Just like Orlando. According to the piece, a twenty-year-old man named Griffin Anderson had gone missing the previous night and was last seen voluntarily getting into a black Dodge Diplomat with two other twenty-year-olds. All three men had tattoos of a black eight-ball on the inside of their forearms—a sign that police said made them a part of a Cleveland gang known as the Corona Kings.

"And that's all you found?" Tot challenges.

"Was there something else to find?"

"Tell me this first: Why were you testing me?"

"What're you talking about?"

"What you just did—you were testing me, Beecher. You came to pick me up, you knew you had done the same research, yet you stayed quiet to see what I offered up." If Tot were my age, this is the part where he'd say I didn't trust him and turn it into a fight. But he's got far more perspective than that. "So what's my grade?" he asks. "When I said the word *eight-ball*, does that mean I passed?"

"Tot, if you know something else..."

"Of course I know something else—and I also know I'm the one who told you not to trust anyone, including me. So I don't blame you. But if you're gonna insult me, try to be more subtle next time."

"Just tell me what you found!"

He ignores the outburst, making sure I get his real point: No matter how good I think I am, he's still the teacher. And still on my side.

"It's about the eight-ball tattoo, isn't it?" I ask. "I was going to look it up..."

"There's nothing else to look up—not unless you also

happen to have an old colleague who still works in the Cleveland Police Department."

"I don't understand."

"You will," Tot says. "Especially when you hear who, twenty-six years ago, also happened to be in the original police report."

61

The barber knew the hotel well. But as he followed the curving staircase from the Capital Hilton lobby up to the second floor, it didn't stop the sense of dread that was now twisting into the small of his back.

"Sir, can I help you?" a passing hotel employee with close-cropped red hair asked just as Laurent hit the final step.

Laurent was nervous, but he wasn't a fool. He knew that when the President was in the building, the Secret Service disguised their agents in hotel uniforms.

"I'm fine, thanks," the barber said.

"And you know where you're going?" the hotel employee asked.

No question. Secret Service.

"I do," the barber said, trying hard to keep it together as he headed left and calmly turned the corner toward his destination: the far too appropriately named Presidential Ballroom.

"Good morning!" an older blonde with a homedone

tint job sang out. "Welcome to the Caregivers' Conference. What can I do for you?"

"I should be on the list," Laurent said, abruptly pointing to the few unclaimed nametags—including the one he'd been using for so many months now. "Last name *Gyrich*."

"Mmm, let's find you," the woman said, scanning the names one by one, but also stealing a quick glance at his face.

Laurent felt the dread digging deeper into his back. It wasn't supposed to be this way. When Orson (he'd known the President since Wallace was little—he couldn't call him anything but Orson) first showed up all those years ago...in that rain...Laurent was just trying to do what was right. And when they first started in D.C....when he first agreed to help with the Plumbers, it wasn't much different: to do what's right...to serve his friend...to serve his country.

"Here we go! We have you right here, Mr. Gyrich," the woman said, handing the barber the nametag. "You're the one they called about...the guest of the White House. You should go in—he's just started. Oh, and if you like, we have a coat check."

"That's okay," he said, sliding the nametag into the pocket of his pea coat. "I'm not staying very long."

"This way, sir," a uniformed Secret Service agent said, motioning him through the metal detector that was set up just outside the main doors of the ballroom. From inside, he heard the familiar yet muffled baritone of President Orson Wallace booming through the ballroom's speakers. From what he could tell, Orson was keeping this one personal, telling the crowd about the night of Minnie's stroke and that moment in the ambulance when the paramedics asked her where she went to school, and the twelfth-grade Minnie could only name her elementary school.

In many ways, Laurent realized, it was the same problem at the Archives. The way they were rushing around—to even let it get this far—Orson was letting it get too personal.

"Enjoy the breakfast, sir," the Secret Service agent said as he pulled open the ballroom door. Underneath the brightly lit chandelier that was as long as a city bus, every neck was craned upward, all six hundred people watching the rosy-cheeked man who looked so comfortable up at the podium with the presidential seal on the front of it.

As always, the President glanced around the crowd, making eye contact with everyone. That is, until Laurent stepped into the room.

"...which is no different from the personal myths we tell ourselves every day," the President said, his pale gray eyes turning toward the barber in the back of the bright room. "The myths we create about ourselves are solely there so our brains can survive."

Across the red, gold, and blue carpet, the barber stood there a moment. He stood there waiting for the President. And when the two men finally locked eyes, when Laurent nodded just slightly and Orson nodded right back, the barber knew that the President had seen him.

That was it. Message sent.

Pivoting on his heel, the barber headed back out toward the welcome desk. The President cocked his head, flashing a smile and locking on yet another stranger in the crowd.

For the first time since this started, the Plumbers finally had something going their way.

62

So you've never heard of this guy Griffin?" Tot asks, stealing a glance at me as the Mustang zips through Rock Creek Park and we make our way to Constitution Avenue.

"Why would I've heard of him?"

"And there's no one you know who has an eight-ball tattoo?"

"Is this *you* testing *me* now?" I ask.

"Beecher, I'm seventy-one years old."

"You're actually seventy-two."

He thinks on this a moment. "I'm seventy-two years old. I have plenty of patience. I just don't like having my time wasted—and right now, since you're treating me like the enemy, you seem to be wasting it," he explains without any bitterness.

"I know you're not the enemy, Tot."

"Actually, you know nothing about me. For all you know, this is just another attempt to reel you in and grab you with the net. Do what you're doing, Beecher—keep asking the tough questions. And as for the toughest one so far: Every neighborhood in the country has a guy like Griffin."

"Meaning what?"

"Meaning according to the police report, Griffin's first arrest came when he was in high school—selling fake marijuana to a bunch of ninth graders. Then he got smart and started selling the real thing. His dad was a pharmacist, so he quickly graduated to selling pills. During one arrest—and remember, this is still in high school—Griffin spit in a cop's face, at which point he became the kid that even the tough high school kids knew you didn't mess with."

I see where he's going. "So when Griffin was kidnapped—"

"Not *kidnapped*," Tot corrects, approaching the end of Rock Creek Park. "They never use the word *kidnapped*. Or *abducted*. In the report, they don't even call it a *crime scene*. But you're painting the picture: When this guy Griffin finally disappeared, neighbors weren't exactly tripping over themselves to form a search party."

"It's still a missing kid."

"You sure? Griffin was twenty years old, no longer a minor. He got in a car—voluntarily—with two guys from his gang. And then he drives off into the sunset," Tot says as we make a left on Constitution Avenue and momentum presses me against the passenger door. "A crime? Where do you see a crime?"

"Okay," I say. "So where's the crime?"

"That's the point, Beecher. There isn't one. Griffin's dad goes to the newspaper. He begs the cops to find his son. But the cops see it as a young man exercising his independence. And they shut the case, I'm guessing secretly thrilled that Griffin and his eight-ball friends are someone else's problem."

"And now, all these years later, the case is back. So for the second time—where's the crime?"

Tot points his beard at the famous landmark all the way up on our left: the breathtaking home of President Orson Wallace. The White House.

"Don't tell me Wallace has an eight-ball tattoo," I say.

"Nope. Near as I can tell, Wallace was nowhere near this one."

"So what makes you think he's involved?"

As we pass the White House and weave down Pennsylvania Avenue and toward our building, Tot's smile finally pokes through his beard. "Now you're seeing the real value of an archive. History isn't written by the winners—it's written by everyone—it's a jigsaw of facts from contradictory sources. But every once in a while, you unearth that one original document that no one can argue with, like an old police report filed by two beat cops twenty-six years ago."

"Tot…"

"He was the one who gave them the info—the one eyewitness who told the cops everything he saw."

"The President was?"

"No. I told you, Wallace was nowhere near there." As we make a sharp right onto 7th Street and pull toward the garage, Tot picks up his photocopied sheet of paper and tosses it in my lap. It's the first time I notice the name he's handwritten across the bottom. "*Him!* He was there!"

I read the name and read it again. "*Stewart Palmiotti?*"

"Wallace's personal doctor," Tot says, hitting the brakes at the yellow antiram barrier outside the garage, just as the security guard looks up at us. "That's who we want: the President's oldest friend."

63

The cemetery reminded him of his mother.

Not of her death.

When she died, she was already in her eighties. Sure, she wanted a year or two more—but not much. She always said she never wanted to be one of those *old people*, so when it was her time to go, she went calmly, without much argument.

No, what the cemetery reminded Dr. Palmiotti of was his mother when she was younger...when *he* was younger...when his grandfather died and his mom was screaming—her face in a red rage, tears and snot running down her nose as two other family members fought to restrain her—about the fact that the funeral home had neglected to shave her father's face before putting him in his coffin.

Palmiotti had never seen such a brutal intensity in his mother. He'd never see it again. It was reserved solely for those who wronged her family.

It was a lesson Palmiotti never forgot.

Yet as he leaned into the morning cold and followed

the well-paved, hilly trail into the heart of Oak Hill Cemetery, he quickly realized that this was far more than just a cemetery.

All cities have old money. Washington, D.C., has old money. But it also has *old power*. And Oak Hill, which was tucked into one of the toniest areas of George-town and extended its sprawling twenty-two acres of rolling green hills and obelisk-dotted graves deep into Rock Creek Park, was well known, especially by those who cared to know, as the resting place for that power.

Founded in 1849, when W. W. Corcoran donated the land he had bought from a great-nephew of George Washington, Oak Hill held everyone from Abraham Lincoln's son Willie, to Secretary of War Edwin Stanton, to Dean Acheson, to *Washington Post* publisher Philip Graham. For years, the cemetery management refused to take "new members," but demand grew so great, they recently built double-depth crypts below the main walking paths so that D.C.'s new power families could rest side by side with the old.

Welcome to Oak Hill Cemetery, the wooden sign read just inside the wrought-iron gate that was designed by James Renwick, who also designed the Smithsonian Castle and St. Patrick's Cathedral in New York. But what Palmiotti couldn't shake was the message at the bottom of the sign:

All Who Enter Do So At Their Own Risk

So needlessly melodramatic, Palmiotti thought to himself. But then again, as he glanced over his shoulder for the fourth time, that didn't mean it was any less unnerving. Using the Archives, or a SCIF, or even the barbershop was one thing. But to pick a place like this— a place so public and unprotected...

This was where they were going wrong. He had told the President just that. But right now, like that night in the rain with Eightball back when they were kids, Palmiotti also knew that sometimes, in some situations, you don't have a choice. You have to take matters into your own hands.

With a quick look down at his iPhone, Palmiotti followed the directions that took him past a headstone carved in the shape of an infant wrapped and sleeping in a blanket. He fought against the ice, trudging up a concrete path and a short hill that eventually revealed...

"Hoo..." Palmiotti whispered as he saw it.

Straight ahead, a wide-open field was sprinkled in every direction with snow-covered headstones, stately family crypts, and in the far distance, a circular Gothic family memorial surrounded by thick marble columns. Unlike a normal cemetery, there was no geometric grid. It was like a park, the graves peppered—somehow tastefully—everywhere.

Leaving the concrete path behind, Palmiotti spotted the faint footprints in the snow and knew all he had to do was follow them to his destination: the eight-foot-tall obelisk that sat next to a bare apple blossom tree.

As he approached, he saw two names at the base of the obelisk: Lt. Walter Gibson Peter, aged twenty, and Col. William Orton Williams, aged twenty-three. According to the cemetery visitor guide, these two cousins were relatives of Martha Washington. But, as Palmiotti continued to read, he saw that the reason they were buried together—both in Lot 578—was because during the Civil War they were both hanged as spies.

Crumpling the brochure, Palmiotti stuffed it in his coat pocket, trying to think about something else.

Behind him, there was a crunch. Like someone stepping through the snow.

Palmiotti spun, nearly slipping on the ice. The field was empty.

He was tempted to leave...to abort and walk away. But as he turned back to the grave, he already saw what he was looking for. Kneeling down, he brushed away the snow that had gathered at the base of the obelisk. A few wet leaves came loose. And some clumps of dirt. Then he heard the hollow *kkkkk*—there it was, the pale beige rock that was about the size of his palm.

The rock was round and smooth. It was also plastic. And hollow.

Perfect for hiding something inside.

Just like a spy would use, he thought to himself as he reread the inscriptions for Lt. Walter Gibson Peter and Col. William Orton Williams.

As a blast of wind galloped across the hill, Palmiotti reached into his jacket pocket and pulled out the folded-up note that said: *I Miss You.*

Simple. Easy. And if someone found it, they wouldn't think twice about it. Not unless they knew to read between the lines.

And so far, even if Beecher had figured out the ink, he still hadn't figured out how to read the true message inside.

With a flick of his thumb, Palmiotti opened the base of the rock, slid the note inside, and buried the rock back in the snow.

It took less than a minute in all. Even if someone was watching, he looked like just another mourner at another grave.

But as Palmiotti strode back to the concrete path and the snow seeped into his socks, he could tell—by the mere fact he was out here, and the fact that someone else had found out what they had done all those years ago— the end was coming.

This would all be over soon. It had to be.

To get this far, to climb this high, you had to be capable of a great many things. And on that night all those years ago—to protect their future...to protect his and Wallace's dreams—Palmiotti found out exactly what he was capable of.

It wasn't easy for him. And it wasn't easy for him now. But as he learned from his own father, big lives required big sacrifice. The thing is, growing up in Ohio, Palmiotti never thought he'd have a *big* life. He thought he'd have a *good* life. Not a big one. Not until that first day of fifth grade, when he met Orson Wallace. But if Wallace was proof of anything, it was that, for Palmiotti, the big life was finally possible.

Still, to look at all that Palmiotti had sacrificed over the years—his time, his marriage, his defunct medical practice—to look at his life and realize that all those sacrifices were about to become worthless...

No. Palmiotti was capable of far more than anyone expected. And that's exactly why the President kept him so close.

No matter what, this would be the end.

And there was nothing Beecher could do to stop it.

64

As Tot and I wait at the guardhouse, blocked by the yellow metal antiram barrier that sticks out from the concrete, we both reach for our IDs.

"Beautiful morning," the guard with the bright white teeth calls out, waving us through without even approaching the car.

The metal barrier churns and lowers with its usual shriek, biting into the ground. We both wave back, confused.

There's no ID check, no bomb sweep. Yesterday, we were enemies of the state; today we're BFFs.

The guard even adds a wink as we pass his booth and ride down to the garage. A wink.

"Something's wrong," Tot insists.

Of course something's wrong. But as I mentally replay Dallas's words from last night, my mind wanders back to a few years ago when the Archives released all the personnel records of the OSS, the early version of the CIA. Historians had estimated that there were about six thousand people who had spied for the agency back during World War II. When the records were unsealed, there were actually twenty-four thousand previously unknown spies, including Julia Child, Supreme Court Justice Arthur Goldberg, and a catcher for the Chicago White Sox.

The OSS lasted a total of three years. According to Dallas, the Culper Ring has been around for two hundred.

As Tot pulls into his parking spot, I look over my shoulder and up the ramp of the garage, where White Teeth is still watching us. And smiling.

Dallas never said it...never even hinted it...but only a fool wouldn't think that maybe this Culper Ring has a deeper reach than I originally thought.

"Look who else is visiting," Tot whispers, working hard to climb out of the Mustang. As I elbow open the car door and join him outside, I finally see who he's looking at: Over by the metal door that leads inside are two men in black body armor, both of them holding rifles. Secret Service.

From the look on Tot's face, he has no idea why they're here.

"Think Wallace is coming back?" he whispers.

"He's definitely coming back."

He shoots me a look. "How do you know?"

I take a breath, repracticing what I've been practicing all morning. It's one thing to play it safe—for now, while I gather info—by not mentioning Dallas and the Culper Ring. But to hide that I'll be with the President...to hide what I know Tot'll find out...

"I'm the one staffing him," I say as I slam the car door and head for the Secret Service.

Limping behind me, Tot's too smart to make a scene. But as we flash our IDs and give quick head-nods to the Service, I can tell he's pissed.

He doesn't say a word until we're in the elevator.

"When'd you find out?" Tot hisses just as the doors snap shut and we ride up to our offices.

"Last night. They emailed me last night."

His good eye picks me apart. I know what he's thinking.

"I was trying to tell you all morning," I add as the elevator bobs and stops at our destination. "But when you brought up this Dr. Palmiotti— Who knows, maybe being alone with the President is a good thing. Maybe he'll make me an offer or something."

"Make you an offer? Who gave you a stupid idea like that?"

"I-I just thought of it," I say, still thinking about what Dallas said last night. Whatever's been happening in that SCIF, it's between the President and someone on staff— or at least someone with access to the room.

Tot shakes his head, stepping out on the fourth floor. I'm right behind him, but as Tot throws open the door to our office and I follow him inside, there's a flash of movement on my right.

Like a jack-in-the-box, a head pops up from the far end of the grid of cubicles, then cuts into the main aisle. From the Mona Lisa hair, I recognize Rina immediately, but what catches me off guard...she was in my cube.

"What're you doing!?" I call out before I even realize I'm shouting.

Rina whips around, still standing in the aisle. "What? *Me?*"

"You heard me...!" I say, already whipping around the corner.

Like whack-a-moles, three more heads—all of them other officemates—pop up throughout the grid. One of them is Dallas. Everyone wants to see the fuss.

Still looking shocked, Rina stands there frozen.

My cube is next to Rina's. Yet as I race up the main aisle, Rina is standing outside *her* cube—not mine.

"W-What'd I do?" Rina asks. "What's wrong?"

I step back, confused. I double-check to make sure I have it right. I know what I saw.

"Beecher, you okay?" she asks.

I glance over my shoulder. Tot must've seen it too. But as I turn around, Tot's all the way by his desk, refusing to look my way. I get the picture. He's still pissed I didn't tell him about the President. This is my punishment: leaving me on my own.

That's fine. I know what I saw.

From his cubicle, Dallas shoots me his own glance. He saw it too. When Rina ducked into the aisle...she moved...she must've moved.

Relax, Dallas says with a slow nod. *Not in public.*

My cell phone rings. I pick up quickly.

"Is Mom okay?" I ask my sister Sharon.

"She's fine. Going to Jumbo's for lunch," my sister

says. Hearing the strain in my voice, she adds, "What's wrong there?"

"Office politics. I'll call you later," I say, hanging up before she can pry.

"Beecher, you sure you're okay?" Rina asks.

"He's fine." Dallas tells her as he joins us in the main aisle. "He's just having one of those mornings."

"I can imagine," Rina says, cupping her palms and tapping her fingers together, more than happy to be rid of any confrontation. "I mean, it's not every day you get to staff the President, right, Beecher?"

I look back at Tot. His head's below the sightline of his cubicle, which means he's not even watching me anymore. The sad part is, I'm not sure if that's good or bad.

"Listen, if there's anything you need when you're in there," Rina offers, "I'm happy to help. I can even stand outside in case there're any new records the President might request."

"Thanks, but I'm okay, Rina," I say as I step into my cubicle and slide into my chair. On my desk, my eye immediately goes to my keyboard, which is slightly askew.

I hold my breath as I see it. My keyboard's never askew. I keep two neat piles on my desk. Both of them look messy. Like someone's thumbed through them.

Before I can react, my phone vibrates in my pocket. I assume it's my sister, but as I flip it open, caller ID says: *USSS*.

United States Secret Service.

"Beecher here," I say as I pick up.

"We've got Homerun ready to move," an agent with a stubborn Boston accent says. "You ready for us?"

"I'll be there in a minute," I tell him.

"You need to be there *now*," he challenges.

As he hangs up on my ear, I know the mess on my desk has to wait. I quickly dart for the stairs. I've got bigger problems to deal with.

65

During his early days at the White House, this was Orson Wallace's favorite part.

"Just an honor, Mr. President," an older man with a graying goatee offered.

"So nice to meet you, Mr. President," a woman wearing two diamond rings added.

"Thank you so much, Mr. President," a tall woman with wide black eyes said as she reached to shake his hand.

The speech was over, the applause was still going, and as President Wallace followed his aide to the swinging doors of the hotel's kitchen, he was riding such a swell of enjoyment, he tried to touch every outstretched hand of the insta-crowd that was now pressing so hard against the rope line.

It wasn't the adulation that got him going. What Wallace appreciated was just…the appreciation. The simple act of people saying *thank you*. These days, in this economy, that kind of crowd seemed to appear less and less often.

"Thank you so much, Mr. President."

"—just an inspiration, sir."

"—reinvigorated all of us, Mr. President."

"I hope you enjoyed the breakfast, Mr. President," the chef called out as Wallace weaved back through the kitchen.

"Just fantastic. We need to have you cook at the White House," Wallace called back, using the same compliment he saved for every chef in every hotel kitchen.

"—just want to thank you so much," Ross the Boss chimed in, leading the final row of handshakes—the VIP goodbyes—that waited for Wallace at the far end of the service entrance and would take him to the waiting door of his armored limo.

"Hey—!" a female voice called out.

Wallace's arm was already extended in a handshake as he finally looked up at the last person in line: a heavy-set woman in a royal blue dress.

"I love you," his sister Minnie said, leaning in and kissing him on the cheek.

"You're just saying that because I'm the President," Wallace teased.

With a whack, Minnie rapped her pink flamingo cane against his shin.

The President was still laughing as the Secret Service agent pushed the hidden button under the door handle, which unlocked the door so he could usher Wallace into the car. And for that moment, as he ducked inside and brother and sister shared their laughter, Wallace almost forgot about where he was headed next.

Almost.

"Homerun moving," one of the Secret Service agents whispered into his wrist, using the President's official Service code name. "Arrival at the Archives in approximately four minutes."

66

As I tear full speed around the corner, my shoes slide across the twelfth floor's green terrazzo squares. If my timing's right, I've still got a few minutes on the President. I need them. Especially if I want to be ready.

"I need some ID," a calm voice announces just as I make the turn. His voice draws out each syllable so it sounds like *Eye. Dee.*

I know that voice.

But as I nearly plow into the man in the black body armor, I'm not focused on him or his black rifle. I don't even see the SCIF that sits at the end of the hall. All I see are ghosts. Ghosts of myself. And Clementine. And Orlando. Forty-eight hours ago, we were standing in this same pale blue hallway, with the same marble wainscoting, studying this same room with the matching pale blue metal door. I wish it were just déjà vu. Déjà vu is easy to dismiss. But this…this is like stepping on Orlando's grave.

A cold dread grips me, squeezing my Adam's apple until I barely remember how to breathe. It reminds me that the only reason to search for these Plumbers—and for what they put in that dictionary—is to prove that they're the ones who killed my friend.

"I said, *ID*," the agent insists.

"Y-Yeah...sure...sorry," I say, holding up my badge.

"Arms up," he barks, pulling out a black-and-yellow wand that looks like a flattened flashlight. Metal detector.

Of course. He saw my name. He knows I'm staffing him. No way they're letting me get close without making sure I'm clean.

As he waves the wand under my armpits, I blink once and see Orlando's dimpled chin and big-toothed smile as he clutched his little coffee cup and ushered me and Clementine inside. I blink again, and there's nothing but the empty pale blue hallway.

"Don't be so nervous," the Secret Service agent calls out, pinning a temporary metal clearance button on my lapel and motioning me toward the SCIF. "The President doesn't bite. Unless he's pissed."

I can't even pretend to laugh as I speedwalk up the hallway and stop at the call box that hangs on the wall. As I press the silver intercom button, a red indicator light blinks on.

"This is Beecher," I say into the intercom. "I'm opening SCIF 12E1." They're the same words Orlando said to Khazei two days ago.

I wait to hear Khazei growl something back. The way

he's been watching, there's no way I'm seeing the President without him weighing in. But to my surprise...

"You're all set," a female voice replies. "Moses is four minutes away," she says, using our internal code name for him. "Enjoy."

The intercom goes silent, and I dart for the entrance to the SCIF. As I spin the combination lock, a sting of bile burns my throat.

I step inside the vault and catch a flash of shadow moving on my left. I'm not the only one in here.

"Oh, c'mon now," Khazei says as he slams the metal door shut and locks the two of us inside. "You really thought I'd miss this one?"

67

"You shouldn't be here," I warn Khazei.

"Let me just say that's one of a variety of things you're wrong about," he counters.

As always, he's trying to keep me cornered. But just seeing Khazei here—just seeing his polished fingernails and his cocky grin—even I'm surprised how fast my fear gets swallowed by anger. "You're interfering with my work. And the work of the President," I shoot back.

"Oh, so now you and the President are a *team*?"

"I never said that. What I said was you were interfering."

"Beecher, do me a favor and take a seat," he says, pointing to the single table at the center of the room and the rolling research cart stocked with documents that sits next to it.

I stay where I am. He doesn't seem to care.

"Beecher, I've thought long and hard about this. I know I can keep putting the pressure on you. I can keep huffing and puffing and trying to blow your house down. Or I can be honest with you," he says, his voice softening to nearly a whisper.

"Before I started working here, y'know what my old job was?" Khazei asks as he leans a hand on the research cart. "I used to be a cop out in Virginia. The pay was good. The hours were bad. And the pension couldn't even touch what I get here, which is why I made the switch. But there's one thing I learned as a cop: Sometimes good people don't know how to be good to themselves. Y'understand what that means?"

"It means you've been reading too many self-help books."

"No, it means you have no idea how many guns are aimed at your head. So let me do you one favor and tell you what I know: I know who your girlfriend Clementine is. I know who her dad is—which explains why you've been trying to hide her. Sure, I don't know why Orlando died—yet—but I do know that President Orson Wallace was scheduled to be in this room two days ago. I know that the Secret Service did everything in their power to clear out the CSI investigative folks from being here. And I know that despite the fact that there are over two dozen other SCIFs in this building that the President could've picked, he for some unexplainable reason asked for this room, *with you*, which puts him right back in the exact same place that, less than forty-eight hours ago, was the last known location that Orlando was seen before they found him lying downstairs on the carpet with his eyes permanently open. Now I know you're one of the smart ones, Beecher. Whatever deal you're working with the President—"

"I'm not working any deals!" I insist.

"Then you have even bigger problems than I thought. Look up and down at that totem pole you're stuck in. You're the lowest man. And when it comes to presidential scandals, when that totem pole finally tips and everyone starts yelling 'Timber,' you know what they call the lowest man? *The scapegoat*," he says, his dark eyes locked on mine.

"*We've got Moses outside the building*," Khazei's walkie-talkie squawks through the room.

"Beecher, I know you need a life preserver. This is me throwing you one. All you have to do is take hold."

"*Moses is in the elevator*," the walkie-talkie announces. "*One minute to arrival...*"

There's a hollow knock on the metal door. Secret Service wants the SCIF opened and ready. Even Khazei knows he can't stop a request like that.

"Please, Beecher," he says as he reaches out and twists the metal latch on the door. My ears pop from the change in pressure as the door swings inward and the vacuum seal is broken. "I'm begging you to take hold."

It's the last thing I hear from Khazei. Without looking back, he steps out into the hallway, where three suit-and-tie Secret Service agents motion him out of the way.

An agent with blond hair and a tiny nose joins me in the SCIF, taking a spot in the back left corner. "Thirty seconds," he whispers to me as a courtesy. "Oh, and he's in a good mood."

I nod, appreciating the news.

Within a few seconds, everything goes silent.

The calm before the storm.

From outside, there's a quiet *clip-clop* as a set of finely polished dress shoes makes its way up the long hallway.

As Orson Wallace turns the corner and steps inside, I instinctively step back. I've never seen him face-to-face. But I know that face. Everyone knows that face. And those rosy cheeks. And those calming gray eyes. It's like the front page of a newspaper walking right at me.

"Sir, this is Beecher White. He'll be staffing you today," the blond agent announces as I realize that Wallace has come here without any staff.

There's another audible *pop* as the two-ton metal door slams shut and metal bolts *kunk* into place, sealing me in this windowless, soundproof, vacuum-packed box with the President of the United States.

"Nice to meet you, Beecher," Wallace says, heading straight for the desk, the research cart—and the single wooden chair—at the center of the room. "I appreciate your helping us out today."

68

That's the single dumbest idea I've ever heard," the barber snapped. "Why would you send him in like that!?"

Through the phone, Dr. Palmiotti didn't answer.

"I asked you a question!" the barber added.

"And I heard you. Now hear me: Be careful of your tone," Palmiotti warned through the receiver.

"There's no reason to put him at risk!"

"Be careful of your tone," Palmiotti warned again.

Taking a breath, the barber stared up at the brick walls of the narrow alleyway that was used as a breakroom behind the barbershop. An unkind wind shoved the rotting stench from the nearby garbage cans into his face.

"I'm just saying, he didn't have to go there," the barber said, far more calmly. He knew he was already out of bounds by making the phone call. But he never forgot the rules—especially after what they think happened. Not once did he refer to the President by name.

"I appreciate your concern," Palmiotti shot back, doing a poor job at hiding his sarcasm. "But we know what we're doing."

"I don't think you do. By bringing him in like that—"

"We know what we're doing, okay? He's not at risk. He's not in danger. And right now, he's in the best possible position to find out exactly who's holding the tin can on the other end of the string. So thank you for the concern, but this time, why don't you go back to doing what *you* do best, and we'll go back to doing what *we* do best?"

Before the barber could say a word, there was a click. Dr. Palmiotti was gone.

Even when he was little, he was a prick, Laurent thought as he shoved his way through the back door of the barbershop, anxious to refocus his attention on his next haircut.

69

I'm waiting for it.

And watching.

And standing there, swaying in place as my hands fiddle in the pockets of my blue lab coat, pretending to fish for nothing at all.

The President's been here barely two minutes. He's sitting at the long research table, eyeing the various boxes and documents that are stacked in neat piles on the rolling cart.

"Do you need help, sir?" I ask.

He barely shakes his head, reaching for a file on the second shelf of the cart: a single-page document encased in a clear Mylar sleeve. I saw the request list. It's a hand-written letter by Abraham Lincoln—back when he was a regular citizen—requesting that better roads be built by the government. There's another on the cart from Andrew Jackson, petitioning for money well before he was elected. From what I'd heard, Wallace loves these records: all of them written by our greatest leaders long before they were our greatest leaders—and proof positive that life exists *before* and *after* the White House.

But today, as Wallace squints down at Lincoln's scratchy, wide script, I can't help but think that he's after something far bigger than life advice from his predecessors.

If Dallas and his contacts in the Culper Ring are to be believed—and that's a big *if*—they think Wallace is here to talk. With me.

I eye the blond Secret Service agent who's still standing in the opposite corner. He stares right back, unafraid of the eye contact. At the table, the President leans forward in his chair, both elbows on the desk as he hovers over the document. I watch him, picking apart his every movement like a mall cop studying a group of loud kids with skateboards.

The SCIF isn't very big. With three of us in here, the room temperature inches up just enough that I'm feeling it.

But that's not what's causing the heat that's swallowed my palms and is now plotting to take over the rest of my body.

At the table, Orson Wallace is calm as ever—ridiculously calm—like he's reading the Sunday paper.

For ten minutes, I stand there, my lab coat making me feel like a baked potato in tinfoil. The only movement I allow myself is licking the salty sweat mustache that's staked a claim on my upper lip.

Ten feet away, the President gives me nothing.

At twenty minutes, my back starts to ache from the lack of movement, and the sweat mustache doesn't even taste that salty anymore.

Still nothing from the President.

At the half-hour mark, he pulls a pencil—usually only archivists and researchers use pencils—from his jacket pocket and then flips to another set of presidential letters.

But otherwise, more nothing. And more nothing. Until…

Diagonally across the room, the blond agent puts a pointer-finger to his ear. Something's being said in his earpiece.

Without a word, the agent heads for the door and twists the metal latch. The President's used to people moving around him. He doesn't look up, even as our ears pop.

Sticking his head out the door, the blond agent listens to something being whispered by the agent outside. Something's definitely up. And the way the agent keeps looking back at me, then back to his boss, I can tell—clearance or no clearance, secure room or unsecure room—there's no way they're leaving me alone with the President.

"I need two minutes," the agent calls to me. He steps outside.

Before I can react, there's a sharp sucking sound as the door shuts and the vacuum again takes hold.

I look over at the rosy-cheeked President, who's still lost in his reading. But like before, all I see are the ghosts that float behind him: Orlando and Clementine…the spilled coffee…then the chair crashing to the floor. If it weren't for this room…and what we found…and what Orlando was fast enough to…

I almost forgot. What Orlando grabbed.

I glance up at the corner of the ceiling. The videocamera is right where it's always been. Watching us.

The sweat mustache puddles in the dimple of my lip.

That's why the President hasn't said a word. That's why he hasn't moved as he leans over the old documents. And that's why Dallas said Wallace created his so-called Plumbers in the first place.

He knows he's being watched. He's always being watched.

If he's sending a message, it has to be a subtle one.

That's fine.

I'm an archivist. I know how to wait.

Sticking to my corner and tightening the microscope, I study him sitting there—the way he favors his right arm, putting more weight on it as he leans on the desk.

I notice that he never touches the documents, always being respectful of their value.

I even observe the way he keeps both his feet flat on the floor. But beyond that...

Still nothing.

I wait some more.

More nothing.

He doesn't look up. Doesn't make eye contact. Doesn't ask any questions—just another five minutes of...

Nothing.

The door to the room unpuckers on my right as the blond Secret Service agent rejoins us. But he doesn't take his spot in the back corner.

"Sir, we really should get going," he says, staying by the door, which he holds open with his hand.

The President nods, tapping the eraser of the pencil against his chin. Still trying to get the last few seconds of reading done, he's quickly out of his seat, twisting himself so that it looks like his body is leaving the room even as his head is still reading.

"You have a good one now," the blond agent says to me.

As the President heads for the door—and toward me—it's the only other time the President's heavy gray eyes make contact with me.

"Thanks for helping us out," the leader of the free world offers as I crane my neck up to take in his six-foot-one frame. "Just amazing what you have here."

Then he's gone.

Poof.

He doesn't offer a handshake or a pat on my shoulder. No physical contact at all. All I get, as he cuts past me, is that he smells like talcum powder and Listerine.

As the silence sets in, I look over my shoulder, searching the room. The chair...the cart...everything's in place. Even the Mylar-encased document he was reading is still sitting there, untouched, on the desk. I rush over to it to make sure I didn't miss anything.

There's nothing.

Nothing.

Nothing.

And then I see it.

Something.

70

That's your great find? A *pencil*?" Dallas asks.

"Not just *a* pencil. *His* pencil," I say, pushing open the doors to all the bathroom stalls to make sure we're alone. "The President's pencil. That's what he left behind."

"Okay, so Wallace left a pencil. It's hardly the nuclear codes."

"You're really not seeing this? We were in the room…"

"I heard the story—you were in the SCIF, Wallace came in, and then, instead of reaching out to you, he spent the next forty minutes reading through old records. So fine, he held back. Maybe he got scared."

"He wasn't scared! Look at what he did: In the middle of everything, he reaches into his jacket and takes out a pencil—not a pen, like every other person outside the Archives uses. A pencil."

"Oh, of course—now I see it," he says sarcastically as he starts washing his hands in the bathroom sink. I'm not thrilled to be dealing with Dallas, but at this point—based on the info he gave me yesterday...based on his explanation of the inner and outer rings...and everything he anticipated about the President...and the safehouse and the videotape and the wireless ear thingie...plus with Tot now giving me the silent treatment—I can fight alone, or I can fight with his Culper Ring behind me. The answer's easy. Dallas may not have my complete trust, but for now, he's got some of it.

"I think Khrushchev and Mussolini were also pencil men," he adds with a laugh.

"I'm serious, Dallas. Think about it: Why does someone pull out a pencil? To follow our procedures for the research rooms—and to take notes, right? That's fine—that makes sense. But here's what doesn't make sense. Wallace *wasn't* taking notes. The entire time, he didn't have paper...didn't have a notebook...didn't have or ask for a single thing to write on."

"Maybe he would've—but instead, he didn't find anything worth writing about. And even if that weren't the case, what's the big deal about having a pencil?"

"The big deal isn't *having* it. The big deal is that he *left it behind*! And truthfully, I wouldn't think it was such a big deal, except for the fact that—oh yeah—two days ago, we found a book in the same room that also wasn't a big deal...until we found it had a hidden message written in invisible ink."

At the sink, Dallas opens and closes his fists, shaking the excess water from his hands. He's listening. "So where's the hidden message in the pencil?"

"There are marks. Look at the pencil. Those indentations."

He picks up the pencil from the sink counter, holding it just a few inches from his nose.

He wants to tell me they're bite marks. But he knows they're not. In fact, as he looks close, he sees that the length of the pencil is dotted with perfect tiny pockmarks—like someone took the sharp point of a pin and made a few dozen indentations.

"Who does that to a pencil?" I ask.

"Beecher, I know you're all excited about the Culper Ring, but I think you're reading too many mystery novels. Not everything has to be a clue," he says, tossing me the pencil and rewashing his hands.

"You really don't see it?" I ask.

"I really don't—and even if I did, invisible ink is invisible ink. Since when are a few random dots a secret code?"

"Maybe now."

I toss him back the pencil. He tugs hard on the eraser.

"The eraser's attached. There's nothing hidden inside."

"You don't know that for sure," Dallas says.

"I do. I brought it downstairs and ran it through the X-ray. It's not hollowed out."

Dallas again brings the pencil close to his face—so close it almost touches his patchy beard.

"It still could be nothing," he says.

"It's *supposed* to look like nothing. And that dictionary was *supposed* to look like a dictionary. Until you find the exact right someone who knows how to read what's hidden underneath."

Standing at the sink, Dallas glances back at me. "You got someone in mind?"

For the first time today, I smile. "I very much do."

71

The archivist knew there was trouble when the cell phone started ringing.

The sound came from across the office, back by Beecher's desk.

Of course, he knew the ringtone—the theme song from the History Channel's *Last Days of the Civil War*. Everyone knew Dallas's phone.

But it wasn't until Dallas went darting out of the office that the archivist got concerned.

Being smart, the archivist didn't stand up...didn't panic...didn't even look up above the sightline of the cubicle.

Instead, all it took was the best tool in his arsenal— the one tool every historian must have.

Patience.

For sixteen minutes, the archivist sat there.

For sixteen minutes, the archivist waited.

He heard the door to the office again slam open. Dallas rushed in, bursting back into the office to grab something—sounded like winter coats sliding together—then darted back out again.

And then, giving Dallas time to make his way downstairs, the archivist turned to the one tool that served him, at this moment, even better than patience: the large plate glass window that doubled as an entire wall of his cubicle—and that gave him a perfect bird's-eye view of Pennsylvania Avenue.

Staring outside, the archivist watched as the two familiar figures bolted out of the building, racing across the street.

There they were.

Dallas. And Beecher.

Dallas and Beecher.

Definitely together.

The archivist's phone vibrated in his pocket. Just like he knew it would. No way would they let something like this slip by.

"Yeah, I see it," the archivist answered.

As they talked it through, an old silver Toyota—Dallas's Toyota—eventually stopped in front of the Archives. That's where Dallas and Beecher ran: to get Dallas's car. And from what it looked like, Beecher was the one driving. The car stopped and Dallas got out. From this height, four stories up, the archivist couldn't hear the screech. But he saw how fast Beecher drove off.

Like he was on a mission.

The archivist wasn't thrilled.

Now there was definitely no choice.

"I know . . . I see it too," Tot said into the phone, pressing his forehead against the cold plate glass window and watching as Beecher turned the corner and disappeared down 9th Street. "No, I don't know for sure, but I can guess. Yeah. No, of course we tagged the car. But it's time to tell the others," Tot added. "We've officially got ourselves a problem."

72

W ho you here to see?" the female guard with the bad Dutch-boy hair asks through the bullet-proof glass window.

"We're on the list," I say, handing over my ID and stepping aside so she sees who I'm with.

From behind me, Clementine steps forward and slides her driver's license, along with her own temporary ID badge (the one that says she's a graduate student), into the open metal drawer just below the glass. With a tug, the St. Elizabeths guard snaps the drawer shut, dragging the contents to her side of the glass, but never taking her eyes off me. No question, she remembers me from yesterday.

"He's my assistant," Clementine explains.

"I don't care who he is. He still needs to be checked in," the guard pushes.

"I did. I called," Clementine pushes right back, tapping her thumb ring against the counter. Unlike last night with her grandmother, her voice is back to pure strength. "Check your computer."

The guard hits a few keys, and as her face falls, it's clear I was right to bring in Clementine. But as I take back my ID and the new sticker, and the guard motions us through the X-ray, it's also clear that Clementine's not exactly ready for the victory dance. "End of the hall," the guard says. "Escort'll meet you upstairs."

With a baritone *tunk*, the thick steel door on our left pops open, and we head inside to the heart of the building. Barely two steps in, we come to another steel door. This one's closed. It's the same system they have in prisons—a sally port—the next door won't open until the previous one is shut. That way, the patients can't escape.

Behind us, the first door clamps shut. I'm barely half a step behind Clementine. All I see is the back of her head, and a black beauty mark on the curve of her neck. But you don't have to be fluent in body language to see the way she's not moving. This is harder than yesterday. She knows what she's about to face.

"You don't have to do this," I whisper.

She doesn't look back.

"Clemmi, I'm serious," I add. "If you want, just wait here."

"How come you haven't asked me about last night?" she blurts.

"Wait. Are we fighting now? Is this about the kiss?"

"Forget the kiss. Last night. What you saw with Nan...why haven't you asked me about it?"

"I *did* ask you. You said you didn't want to talk about it."

"Well, now I do. Especially as I'm starting to hyperventilate in this tiny metal box."

Another metal *tunk* makes us both jump—the next door unlocks—and there's another long lime green hallway with an elevator at the far end. Clementine doesn't move, though it looks like she's trying to. In the past few days, I've seen her be both strong and weak, fearless and terrified, and also kind and protective. There are so many Clementines in that body. But when it comes to her family—especially her father—the girl who used to be prepared for anything reminds me that the number one thing she's not prepared for are her own insecurities.

"Y'know I don't judge you based on how you're treated by your grandmother," I tell her.

"I know you don't. But it's not just about how she treats me. It's about how I *let her* treat me. You saw it yesterday—I'm not...when she..." She presses her lips together. "I'm not my best with her."

I stand there, pretending I didn't see exactly that last night. "Sometimes you're so strong, I forget you can be hurt."

She shakes her head. "We can all be hurt."

I nod, thinking about the fact that Iris's bicycle is still sitting in my garage from where she accidentally left it. Iris loves that bicycle. But she still won't come pick it up.

As I study the single beauty mark on the back of Clementine's neck, it reminds me that there's nothing more intimate in life than simply being understood. And understanding someone else.

"How long've you been taking care of your grandma?" I finally ask.

"Four years. Ever since my mom died. And yes, I

know it's good to take care of the elderly, but…living
with a nasty old woman…having no job…which, also
yes, I should've told you…and then finding out that Nico
is my…*y'know*…I'm not saying I needed my life to be
a symphony—I just never thought it'd turn out to be a
country song."

"Yeah, well…it's better than realizing that your life
is elevator music."

"Some people like elevator music," she counters.

I look over at her. She stands her ground, fearlessly
locking eyes and reminding me exactly why her reap-
pearance has slapped me out of the safe hibernation that's
become my life. Even when she's afraid, this girl isn't
afraid of anything. Or at least she's not afraid of me.

As she studies me, I want to kiss her again. I want to
kiss her like last night—and I know this is my chance,
a true second chance in every sense. A golden moment
where the earth stops spinning, and the clouds roll away,
and I get the opportunity to say the perfect words and
prove that I can actually change my life.

"So…buh…your grandmother…" I stutter. "Her
cancer's really bad, huh?"

"Yeah. It's bad," Clementine says, heading up the
hallway. "Though mark my words, Nan's got eighteen
lives. She'll bury us all and tap-dance on our graves."

I curse myself and contemplate cutting out my tongue.
How's the cancer? That's the best I could come up with?
Why didn't I just blurt out that I know she's pregnant and
then make it a perfectly horrible social moment?

"Beecher, can I ask you a question?" Clementine adds

as she jabs at the elevator call button. "Why'd you really come here?"

"What?"

"Here. Why here?" she says, pointing up. Three flights up to be precise. To her father. "You saw how crazy he is. Why come and see him?"

"I told you before—of all the people we've spoken to, he's still the one who first cracked the invisible ink. Without him, we'd still be thumbing through the dictionary."

"That's not true. He didn't crack anything. Your guy at the Archives…in Preservation…"

"The Diamond."

"Exactly. The Diamond," she says. "The Diamond's the one who cracked it."

"Only after Nico pointed out it was there. And yes, Nico's loopy, but he's also the only one who's handed us something that's panned out right."

"So now Tot's not right? C'mon, Beecher. You've got a dozen other people in the Archives who specialize in Revolutionary War stuff. You've got the Diamond and all his expertise about how the Founding Fathers used to secretly hide stuff. But instead of going to the trained professionals, you go to the paranoid schizo and the girl you first kissed in high school? Tell me what you're really after. Your office could've gotten you in here. Why'd you bring me with you?"

As I follow her into the elevator and press the button for the third floor, I look at her, feeling absolutely confused. "Why *wouldn't* I bring you? You were in that room when we found that dictionary. Your face is on that videotape just as much as mine is. And I'm telling you right now, Khazei knows who you are, Clementine. Do you really think all I care about is trying to protect myself? This is *our* problem. And if you think I haven't thought that from moment one, you really don't know me at all. Plus...can't you tell I like you?"

As the elevator doors roll shut, Clementine takes a half-step back, still silent. Between her missing dad, her dead mom, and the evil grandmother, she's spent a lifetime alone. She doesn't know what to do with *together*.

But I think she likes it.

"By the way," I add, standing next to her so we're nearly shoulder to shoulder. "Some of us like country music."

Clementine surprises me by blushing. As the elevator rises, she grips the railing behind her. "You were supposed to say that two minutes ago, genius—back when I said I liked elevator music."

"I know. I was panicking. Just give me credit for eventually getting there, okay?" Within seconds, as the elevator slows to a stop, I reach down and gently pry her fingers from the railing, taking her hand in my own.

It's a soaking, clammy mess. It's caked in cold sweat.

And it fits perfectly in mine.

For an instant, we stand there, both leaning on the back railing, both entombed in that frozen moment after the elevator bobs to a stop, but before the doors...

With a shudder, the doors part company. A short black woman dressed in a yellow blouse is bouncing a thick ring of keys in her open palm and clearly waiting to take us the rest of the way. Clementine prepared me for this: To help the patients feel more at ease, the staff doesn't wear uniforms. The silver nametag on her shirt says FPT, which is the mental hospital equivalent of an orderly. Behind the woman is another metal door, just like the ones downstairs.

"You're the ones seeing Nico Hadrian?" she asks, giving a quick glance to our IDs.

"That's us," I say as the woman twists a key in the lock and pushes the door open, revealing dull fluorescent lights, a scuffed, unpolished hall, and the man who's waiting for us, bouncing excitedly on his heels and standing just past the threshold with an awkward grin and a light in his chocolate brown eyes.

"I told everyone you'd be back," Nico says in the kind of monotone voice that comes from solid medication. "They never believe me."

73

That your pop or your granpop?" the muscular
white kid with the laced-up army boots asked as
the barber mowed the clippers up the back of the
guy's head.

"My dad," Laurent replied, not even looking up at the
crisp black-and-white photo of the soldier in full army
uniform that was tucked next to the shiny blue bottle of
Barbasol. In the photo—posed to look like an official
army portrait in front of an American flag—his father
was turned to the camera, a mischievous grin lighting his
face.

"Those bars on his chest?" the client asked, trying to
look up even though his chin was pressed down to his
neck.

Laurent had heard the question plenty of times
before—from people who wanted to know what medal his
dad was wearing on his uniform.

The amazing part was, despite the photo, the barber
rarely thought of his father as a soldier. As a strict
Seventh-day Adventist, his dad was a pacifist, so committed to his faith that he refused to have anything to

do with military service. But three days after Pearl Harbor, when the country was reeling and his prayers weren't bringing the answers he needed, his father walked into the recruitment office and enlisted.

He told his sergeants he wouldn't carry a weapon or dig ditches on Sabbath. They made him a cook, and of course let him cut hair too. Years later, after he returned home, Laurent's father remained just as committed to his faith. But the lesson was there—the one lesson he forever tried to drill into his children: Sometimes there's a greater good.

"He was actually a kitchen man," the barber said to his client, pointing the clippers back at the photo. "The medal's a joke from his first sergeant for being the first one to catch a lobster when they were stationed in San Juan."

The client laughed...and quickly rolled up his sleeve to reveal a crisp tattoo of a cartoony Marine Corps bulldog that was flexing his biceps like a bodybuilder and showing off his own tattoo, which read *Always Faithful* across his bulging dog arm.

The barber felt a lump in his throat, surprised by the swell of emotion that overtook him as he read the tattoo. No question about it, there was a real power that came with being faithful.

But.

He looked up and stole a quick glance at the photo of his father. At the miniature lobster that was pinned to his chest. And at the mischievous grin on his dad's young face.

There was also something to be said about the greater good.

74

Leading us past the nurses' station, past the TV alcove, past the section of small square tables covered by checkers sets, Nico keeps his chin up as he purposefully strides to what is clearly our destination: the only round table in the entire day room—and the only one with a green laminated card with the words *Don't Sit* on it.

"I made the card. So people don't sit here," Nico says.

"We appreciate that," I say, noticing that Clementine still hasn't said a word. It hasn't gotten any easier for her to be here. But the way Nico is staring more at me instead of her, I realize he still doesn't know she's his daughter. No question, that's better for all of us.

We all sit down. There are three of us at the table—and four seats. But as Nico's attention turns to the empty one, I have no doubt that, in his head, that empty seat is filled.

"It'll be quiet back here. That's why I like the round table," Nico says. Like every other table in the room, it's got a Plexiglas top. Makes it easier for the nurses to see what we're doing. Back by the nurses' station, the escort who walked us in is sitting at a computer, pretending not to stare at us. Pointing across the room to a set of swinging doors, Nico adds, "My room's back there."

There's a loud *kuh-kunk*. I follow the sound over my shoulder, where a soda machine—*kuh-kunk*—spits out a Diet Dr Pepper that's retrieved by a male patient with curly black hair.

"I can get us apple and orange juice for free. They make us pay for soda," Nico explains.

"I think we're okay," I say, hoping to move us along.

"You talk to me like the doctors," Nico says, placing both his hands flat on the see-through table. His feet are pressed perfectly together on the floor. "Like the newer doctors who are worried I might hurt them."

"Nico, I wasn't—"

"I know you're not her assistant. I know you said that just to get in here." There's a *kuh-kunk* behind us— another Diet Dr Pepper to another patient. "The Secret Service can arrest you for that, Benedict."

He's trying to take control, especially with the hokey move of calling me Benedict Arnold. But unlike last time, I've done my homework. Especially about him.

When Nico was first arrested for shooting the President, he was charged with a *federal* crime, which means he had *federal* records—including a psych profile— which means those records eventually came to the Archives, which also means it took nothing but a phone call to get them from our record center out in Suitland, Maryland.

To be honest, most of what I read was typical Psych 101 nonsense, but one thing did stand out: Yes, Nico's hyper-paranoid, and used to claim God talks to him…and yes, he's clearly well versed in all sorts of historical conspiracy theories, including delusional concerns about Thomas Jefferson and George Washington and a hidden pentagram in the street layout of Washington, D.C. But as a former decorated soldier in the army, the one thing Nico has always responded to best is a sure voice of authority.

"Nico, I'm here to talk about the Culper Ring," I announce. "Would you like an update or not?"

His hands stay flat on the table. His eyes flick back and forth, picking me apart. Then Clementine. Then the empty chair next to him. The profile said how methodical he was. But the way he starts biting the inside of his lip, he's also excited.

"I was right, wasn't I?" he blurts. "About the invisible ink…"

"You were. Messages were being sent."

"I knew! I—" He lowers his voice, glancing over at the nurses' station. The escort who brought us in is on the phone. Nico definitely hears what she's saying. And he's been here long enough to know what happens if he gets too excited. "I told you you were being tested," he insists, fighting to keep his composure. "I told you, didn't I?"

"We're all being tested," Clementine says, just like we practiced. "That's what life is."

"And here's your newest test," I jump in, already feeling guilty, but knowing that this is our only chance. "*This* is the message that came back."

From my front pants pocket, I pull out the pencil that was left behind by President Wallace and gently place it on the open table.

75

Nico's hand snaps out like a snake, snatching the President's pencil and cradling it in his open palm. His eyes again flick back and forth, soaking in every detail.

Eventually, he looks up. "I don't understand."

"The pencil...the indentations..." I say. "We think a message was hidden on that."

"On the pencil?" he asks.

"In the indentations," I say, pointing him back.

There's another *kuh-kunk* behind us. Diet Dr Pepper for another patient.

Clementine jumps and Nico blinks hard as the soda can hits. But Nico never loses sight of the pencil. Holding both ends, he twirls it slowly like the tips of a cartoon mustache. He devours every mark, every groove, every detail.

Eventually he looks up, his brown eyes peeking just above the pencil. "Tell me what it said in the invisible ink."

"Pardon?" I ask.

"The message. In the dictionary. I want to know what it said first. I want you to tell me."

"No. Absolutely no," I say, eyeing Clementine, who's staring through the see-through table at her own feet. She's not gonna last long. "That's not the game, Nico— I've got no time."

"Then I have no time for you," Nico challenges.

"That's fine. Then we'll leave. And you can sit here waiting another two years for your next visitor," I say, standing up from my seat.

"Sit."

"No. You're not driving this," I shoot back.

"Sit," Nico repeats, lowering his chin and trying hard to keep his voice down.

"Are you listening? You're not driving. So tell me what it says on the pencil, or have fun spending the rest of your afternoon with your free orange juice."

Next to me, Clementine rises from her seat, joining me to leave.

Nico looks over at the table's empty chair. He nods a few times. Whatever he's hearing, I pray it's good advice.

"It doesn't say anything," Nico blurts.

"Excuse me?"

"The pencil," Nico says. "There's no message."

"How do you know?"

"I can see. I can— I'm good with patterns. The doctors...they've told me...I can see what others can't. God gave me that gift," he says, again glancing at the empty chair. "The marks on the pencil...the indentations...there's nothing recurring. No repetition."

"So the Culper Ring…back in the day…they never used old carvings as codes?" I ask.

"These aren't carvings. These are…they're nothing. Nothing I can see. Now tell me what you haven't been saying. Tell me what was written in the invisible ink."

He says the words matter-of-factly, as if there should be no argument.

Clementine and I both stand there, silent.

"I know you came here for my help," Nico says. "You wouldn't be here if you weren't stuck. I can help with—"

He stops.

I know it's a trick. Nico isn't sly. He's not subtle. He's a whack job who acts like a giant child and thinks he's the reincarnation of George Washington. So I know he's just trying to get me to say…

"You can help me with *what*?" I ask, plenty annoyed, but curious enough to play along. I return to my seat.

He looks over toward the nurses' station, once again scanning the brightly lit room. Taped to a nearby square concrete column is a laser-printed sign that says:

Please keep voices low
And spirits up

"Nico, what can you help us with?" I repeat.

"I know about the Purple Hearts," Nico says.

"Okay, we're done—I've seen this scam already," I say as I again stand up.

"Where are you going?" Nico asks.

"This is the exact same thing you did last time—first

you offer to help, then you start shoveling your whacky ghost stories."

To my surprise, Clementine grips my wrist, keeping me in place. "What about the Purple Hearts?" she asks.

"The medals. The military medals. Do you know who created the Purple Heart?"

"George Washington," I shoot back.

"I appreciate that. I appreciate you knowing your history," Nico says. "Yes, George Washington created it. It was one of the first medals introduced in the United States. But he didn't call it the Purple Heart—"

"He called it the Badge of Military Merit," I interrupt. "It got its name from the fact that the medal itself was a purple cloth in the shape of a heart. What else do you want to know?"

"Do you know how many Purple Hearts George Washington gave out?" Nico challenges.

This time, I'm silent. I'm good, but I'm not Tot.

"Three," Nico says. "That's it. Three. Three men—all of them from Connecticut. As part of the honor, Washington wrote their names into a special book he called the Book of Merit. And do you know where this Book of Merit is today?"

"In that warehouse with the Ark of the Covenant?" I ask.

"No one knows where it is," Nico says, oblivious to my joke as he flashes us a grin of excitement. Clementine looks even worse than she did yesterday. She's not lasting much longer. "Washington's book disappeared. Forever. In 1932, they revived the honor of the Purple

Heart—it's been given in our military ever since. But to this day, no one—not anyone—has any idea where Washington's original Book of Merit—with the original names—actually is."

"And this matters to us because...?"

"It matters because today, the Purple Heart goes to those who are wounded in battle. But originally, back then, Washington's badge had nothing to do with injuries. In his own words, Washington said it was for *extraordinary fidelity*. Do you know what *extraordinary fidelity* means?"

"It means someone who's loyal," I say.

"It means someone who can keep a secret," Nico counters. "I didn't know this. I looked it up. I found it after your visit. I have a lot of time here."

"Just get to the point."

"I have been. You're not listening to it. Like your predecessor—"

"Don't compare me to a predecessor. Don't call me Benedict Arnold. Don't start with all that reincarnation hoo-hoo," I warn him, still standing across from him. "If you want us to listen, stay in reality."

His eyes flicker back and forth. His chest rises and falls just as fast. But to his credit, Nico bites the inside of his lip and stays on track. "The very first recipient of the Purple Heart was a twenty-six-year-old named Elijah Churchill," Nico explains. "Elijah served under someone I think you've heard of— Benjamin Tallmadge."

Clementine looks my way.

"Tallmadge was the organizer of the original Culper Ring," I say.

"Then when you look at the third name on that list—Daniel Bissell from Windsor, Connecticut—guess why his name was put in the Book of Merit? He was one of our best spies, who helped infiltrate Benedict Arnold's own corps," Nico says, his eyes flicking faster than ever. "And according to some, that's the *real* reason the Book of Merit disappeared. It wasn't stolen. It was hidden—by Washington himself, who collected our best men and used them to build the greatest secret corps that history never knew…"

"The Culper Ring," Clementine says.

"I'm not asking you to believe it," Nico says. "But even America's secret history has its experts. Let me help you with this. You know I can help you. This is the world I know best."

I'm tempted to argue, but we both know he's right. When it comes to conspiracies, Nico's got a PhD.

"Tell me what you found in the invisible ink," Nico says. "Tell me and I'll share what I know. If I fail, you can leave and we're done."

I look over at Clementine, who replies with an awkward shrug. I can't help but agree. At this point—especially with the President's pencil apparently being a bust, and still not knowing why Wallace brought me to that room—what do we have to lose?

From my back pocket, I unfold the photocopy of the dictionary page and slide it across the round table.

Unlike before, Nico doesn't snatch it. He stays calm,

hands again flat on the table. But as he leans forward and reads the words, I see the thick vein starting to swell on his neck.

FEBRUARY 16

26 YEARS IS A LONG TIME TO KEEP A SECRET

WRITE BACK: NC 38.548.19 OR WU 773.427

There's a loud *kuh-kunk* behind us. Another Diet Dr Pepper for another patient, this one a young Asian man with a dyed blond stripe running down the middle of his head like a skunk streak.

"Get away from us, Simon—this isn't your business!" Nico growls without turning around as he covers the photocopy by pressing it against his own chest. The Asian man flips Nico the finger, then heads for the swinging doors that lead back to patients' rooms.

Barely noticing, Nico focuses back on the photocopy. His lips move as he reads.

His lips move as he reads it again.

Over and over, he rereads the document. The vein on his neck swells larger than ever.

He finally looks up—not excited, not energized…not anything.

"I know where you need to go," he says.

76

The barber had gloves in his pocket. But he didn't put them on.

It wasn't that he wasn't cold. Out here—especially out here in the snow-covered graveyard—the weather was freezing. He was most definitely cold.

But for now, he wanted to feel it.

In fact, as he walked up the twisting concrete path of Oak Hill Cemetery, he knew that was his real problem. For too long now, especially the past few years, he hadn't felt the cold, or fear—or most anything at all. Instead, he'd been lulled. And worst of all, he hadn't been lulled by anyone. He'd been lulled by himself.

It was the same reason he came here today.

He knew he shouldn't. Palmiotti would tear him apart if he found out he'd trekked all the way out here in the snow. But as he spotted the headstone that was carved in the shape of a baby swaddled in a blanket, the barber couldn't help but think what else he'd lulled himself into.

He'd only lived in Washington a few years now. But he'd been here long enough to know where the real strings were pulled. Right now, Palmiotti was the one with the office in the White House. And the private parking spot in the White House. And the best friend who sat in the Oval Office. All the barber had was high rent on his barber chair and a set of presidential cuff links. So if this really was the moment where the tornado was about to uproot the house, Laurent knew who'd be the first one that house was landing on.

Damn right he needed to come out here and start feeling this stuff for himself.

But as he took his first step off the concrete path and into the snow, he heard the faint rumbling of voices behind him.

Hobbling and hiding behind a section of trees that surrounded the edges of the wide-open graveyard, Laurent didn't have any trouble staying out of sight. Out here, no one was looking for anything except the dead—which is why it made such a perfect drop point.

In the distance, two voices were fighting, arguing, and far too busy to see what was really going on in the cemetery.

Still, it wasn't until they reached the top of the path that Laurent peered out from behind the apple blossom tree and spied who was making all the noise.

That's him, the barber thought as the bitter cold settled between the thin bones of his fingers.

"Stop!" the girl called to the guy with the sandy blond hair.

The guy wasn't listening. But there he was. The one who could take away everything they had worked for.

Beecher.

77

Beecher, *stop*...!" Clementine calls out, chasing behind me.

I keep running, my lungs starting to burn from the cold, my shoes soaked from the snow as I climb the concrete path and pass a double-wide headstone with an intricate carved stone owl taking flight from the top.

No doubt, Oak Hill Cemetery is for people with money. But if Nico's right, it's also for people with something far more than that.

"Beecher, you need to be smart!" Clementine adds. "Don't jump in without knowing where you're going!"

I know she's right. But thanks to the GPS in my cell phone, I know exactly where I'm going.

"*542 feet northwest*," it says in glowing green letters. There's even a red digital arrow that points me in the right direction. Yet as I look down to check it, my phone vibrates in my hand.

Caller ID says it's the one archivist who I know is a member of the actual Culper Ring. Dallas.

"Beecher, that's it! You cracked it!" Dallas blurts before I even say hello.

I know what he's talking about. The note. The invisible ink. *Twenty-six years is a long time to keep a secret. Write back: NC 38.548.19 or WU 773.427.* Since the moment we found it, we knew those numbers weren't call numbers on books. So then we kept thinking, *What's NC? What's WU?*

Until Nico said it was another old George Washington trick.

"Nico's the one who cracked it," I remind him.

"The point is, he was right. One of our guys—he works at the Supreme Court of all things—he said Nico's story checked out: Washington apparently used to write these long rambling letters that seemed to go nowhere...until you read just the first letter, or third letter, or whatever letter of every word. When we tried that here, it's like he said: NC and WU became..."

"N and W. North and West," I say, repeating what Nico told me, and I told Dallas a half hour ago when I said to meet us here.

As I head up the main path, I understand why no one wants to take Nico at his word, but even I have to admit, it was amazing to watch. Once Nico had the N and W, he played with the decimals and the message became a bit more familiar: *Write back: N 38° 54.819 W 77° 3.427*—a GPS address that converts to the same latitude and longitude system that's been in place since Ptolemy put them in the first world atlas nearly two thousand years ago. That's why we were stuck for so long. We were looking for *book* coordinates. These were *map* coordinates. "Where are you anyway?" I ask.

"Just getting to Oak Hill now," Dallas explains. "I just passed the front gate. Where're you?"

"I don't know—where all the headstones and dead people are. Up the hill on the left. There's..." I glance around, searching for landmarks. "There's a wide-open field and a huge stone statue of a...she looks like a farm girl, but her face is all flat because the weather's worn away her nose."

"Hold on—I think I...I see you," Dallas says. "I see you and—" He cuts himself off. "Please tell me that's not Clementine with you."

"Don't even start. Y'know I needed her to get into St. Elizabeths."

"And what about here? Why bring her here? We talked about this, Beecher. No matter what you think, we don't know this girl."

I hang up the phone, tired of the argument. It's no different than what Tot said. But what neither of them understands is, without Clementine, I never would've made it all the way here. And like I told her earlier, she was in that SCIF too. I can't leave her behind.

"*Beecher, hold up!*" a faint voice calls out behind us.

I turn, spotting Dallas just as he comes around the corner, halfway down the crooked path. He's less than fifty yards away. He's running fast to catch up.

But not as fast as me.

"Who's that?" Clementine calls out, clearly freaked out.

"Don't worry. Just Dallas," I say.

"Why'd you tell him we were coming here?" Clementine asks, remembering Tot's advice to not trust anyone.

I don't answer.

On my cell phone, GPS says we've got another 319 feet to go. But I don't need a snazzy cell phone to see my true destination.

An expansive pie crust of snow covers the ground, and a narrow minefield of footprints burrows straight at a single grave: an eight-foot-tall obelisk that looks like a miniature Washington Monument.

"That's it, isn't it?" Clementine whispers behind me.

As I sprint from the paved path, my feet are swallowed by the ice. I stick to my left, careful to steer clear of the evidence. The footprints look new—like they were made this morning. There's also another set of prints that leads back, back, back to the ring of trees that surround the field.

"You think someone's out there?" Clementine asks, spotting the same prints I do.

I don't answer. But what catches my eye is what's sitting at the base of the obelisk: wet leaves…clumps of soil…and a neat little hole in dirty brown snow…

Like something's buried underneath.

Scrambling forward, I dive for the little rabbit hole, stuff my hand down it, and pat around until…

There.

The beige rock is smooth and flat, perfect for skimming in a lake. Dallas and Clementine both rush to my side. But as I pull the rock out, I know something's wrong. The weight's not right.

"It's plastic," I say. "I think...I think it's hollow."

"Of course it's hollow. That's how they hide stuff in it," Dallas says as if he sees this all the time. "Open it up. See what it is."

I flip the rock over. Sure enough, the bottom swivels open.

All three of us hunch over it like mother birds over an egg.

And we finally get to see what's inside.

78

Tot purposely chose one of the SCIFs on the opposite side of the building.

He picked one that was assigned to the Legislative folks. The head of the Legislative SCIFs was a middle-aged guy who spent his nights playing Adams Morgan clubs with a happy but untalented rocksteady and reggae band. He'd never know the room was being used.

Still, Tot was careful as he came over. He did his usual weaving through the stacks, kept his face off the cameras, and even knew to avoid the elderly volunteers who they'd packed into one of the suites on the eighteenth floor to sort through the recently unearthed Revolutionary War widow pension files.

In fact, to actually get in the room, he was smart enough to avoid using the regular door code.

And smart enough to instead use the security staff's override code.

And smart enough to pick one of the few SCIFs in the building that didn't have a single surveillance camera (which is how most Senators and Members preferred it).

But the one thing Tot did that was smartest of all?

He made sure he wasn't working this alone.

On his right, the quarter-inch vault door clicked and thunked, then opened with a pneumatic pop.

"You're late," Tot said.

"You're wrong," Khazei said as the door slammed behind him. "I'm right on time."

79

N othing."

"No. Can't be," Dallas says.

"It can. And it *is*," I say, tipping the hollow rock so he and Clementine can get a good view.

Dallas squints and leans in, examining the small rectangular compartment inside the rock. No question, there's nothing there, which means...

"Someone already picked up the message," Clementine says, looking back at the footprints that lead out to the treeline, which curves like a horseshoe around us.

"Or no one's put one in yet," I say, trying to stay positive, but unable to shake the feeling that Clementine may be right. I follow her gaze to the treeline in the distance. Nothing moves. Nothing makes a sound. But we all recognize that out-of-body gnawing that comes when you think you're being watched. "I think we need a place to hide. Someone could still be coming."

Dallas shakes his head, pointing down at the grave. "If that were the case, where'd these footprints come from?"

"Actually, I was thinking they came from you,"

Clementine challenges, motioning at Dallas even as she eyes the ones back to the treeline. "I mean, even with Beecher calling you, that's a pretty amazing coincidence that you show up at the exact moment we do."

"Funny, I was thinking the same about *you*," Dallas shoots back. "But I was going to be cordial enough to wait until you left and tell Beecher behind your back."

"Can you both please stop?" I plead. I'm tempted to tell Clementine what Dallas did last night—how he spotted that person in the taxi...and gave me the video of us in the SCIF, keeping it away from Khazei...and told me the true story about the Culper Ring and the President's private group of Plumbers. But it doesn't change the fact that with this rock being empty..."We're more lost than ever."

"Not true," Dallas says, licking flicks of snow from his beard.

"What're you talking about? This was the one moment where we had the upper hand—we knew the location where the President and his Plumbers were dropping their message, but instead of catching them in the act, we're standing here freezing our rear ends off."

"You sure this message is between the President and his Plumbers?" Dallas asks, his voice taking on that timbre of cockiness that it gets when he thinks he's in control.

"What's a Plumber?" Clementine asks.

"His friends. Like Nixon's Plumbers," I explain. "The people Wallace is working with."

"But you see my point, right?" Dallas adds. "If this

note really was between the President and his Plumbers—and they knew you found out about it—"

"Why didn't they simply change the meeting spot?" I ask, completing the thought and looking again at the mess of footprints.

"And on top of that, if the big fear was the fact that you'd rat him out, why didn't the President make you an offer when he had you in the SCIF? He's supposedly who the message in the dictionary was for, right?"

It's a fair question. And the one assumption we've been relying on since the moment this started: that when we found the dictionary in the SCIF, it held a message between the President and someone from his inner circle. But if that's not the case . . .

"You think the President may've been trying to communicate with someone *outside* his circle?" I ask.

"Either that or someone outside his circle may've been trying to communicate with the President," Dallas replies.

As I turn away from the treeline, my brain flips back to the original message: *February 16. Twenty-six years is a long time to keep a secret.*

"Maybe that's why the President asked for you to staff him this morning, Beecher. Maybe he wasn't trying to *give* you a message—maybe he was waiting to *get* one. From *you.*"

I see where he's going. It's the only thing that makes sense. All this time, we thought the dictionary held a letter that was written to Wallace by one of his friends. But if this is really from someone who's *not* on his side . . . and they somehow found out about his Plumbers, and were hoping to reveal something from twenty-six years ago...

"You think someone's threatening Wallace?" Clementine asks.

"I think they're way beyond threats," I say as a cloud of frosty air puffs out with each syllable. "If this is what I think it is, I think someone's blackmailing the President of the United States."

80

Entering the SCIF, Khazei did his own quick scan of the windowless room.

"You think I'm stupid?" Tot asked as he fiddled with the TV that sat atop the rolling cart. "There're no cameras."

Khazei checked anyway. For himself. Sure enough, no cameras.

But that didn't mean there was no VCR.

"Where'd you even find it?" Khazei asked, motioning to the videotape as Tot slid it in and turned on the TV.

"In his house. He had it hid in a box of tampons."

"Why'd he have tampons? I thought he lived alone."

"He's got a sister. And had a fiancée. He's not throwing their stuff away," Tot scolded.

Khazei didn't respond. Instead, he looked down at his recently polished nails, tempted to start biting the cuticle of his thumb.

On TV, the video began to play, showing Orlando, Clementine...and of course Beecher—and what they found in the SCIF that day.

"Eff me," Khazei muttered.

Tot nodded. "I think they already did."

81

Eightball?" Dallas asks.

"Has to be Eightball," I agree with a nod.

"What's Eightball?" Clementine asks.

I look over at Dallas, who shakes his head. He doesn't want me telling her. He also didn't want me bringing her to see Nico. But that's the only reason we got in. And got here.

"Beecher, if you don't want to tell me, you don't have to," Clementine says. "It's okay. I understand."

"Listen to the girl," Dallas whispers.

But what Dallas will never understand is what Khazei said this morning—once everything finally gets out and they verify that Orlando's been murdered, Clementine's just as high on the suspect list as I am, and therefore has just as much of a right to know what the hell is really going on.

"Eightball's a person," I say as Clementine stands frozen in the cold. "He's a kid, really—or *was* a kid—named Griffin Anderson. He was twenty years old when he disappeared."

"*Disappeared?* As in abducted?"

"No one knows. This guy Eightball was the town bully, complete with an eight-ball tattoo on his forearm. The point is, *he's* what happened twenty-six years ago. February 16th. That's the night he disappeared from the President's hometown in Ohio."

"Which means what?" Clementine asks as a twig snaps back by the treeline. We all turn to look. It's too hard to see anything. "You think that when the President was younger, he had some hand in this?"

"I have no idea, but...well...yeah," I say, still scanning tree by tree. "Think about it. Something happens that night, Wallace loses his cool, and—I don't know— the future President goes all *Mystic River* and he and his boys somehow make Eightball disappear..."

"Until somehow, someone from the past suddenly shows up out of nowhere and starts resurrecting the story," Dallas says, his eyes tightening on Clementine.

"Dallas, leave her alone," I say.

"No, Dallas, say what you're thinking," Clementine says.

"I just did," he shoots back.

"And that's your grand scenario? You think I got my hands on some old info, and then what? I've been using Beecher in hopes of terrorizing the President?"

"There are more ridiculous ideas out there."

"And just to complete your delusion, tell me what my motive is again?"

"I've seen where you live, Clementine. I was out there last night," Dallas says. "No offense, but that house...that neighborhood...you could clearly use an upgrade."

"Dallas, that's enough!" I say.

"You do *not* know me," Clementine growls, making sure he hears each syllable, "so be very careful what you say next."

"Ooh, nice threatening ending. I didn't even have to bring up how far the apple tumbles from the tree. Like father, like dau—"

Springing forward, Clementine leaps for Dallas's throat. *"You smug piece of—!"*

I dart in front of Dallas, catching Clementine in midair, inches before she clobbers him. She's a whirl-wind of wild punches, her weight hitting my chest at full speed and knocking me backward.

"Clemmi, relax!" I insist as I dig my feet into the snow. She still fights to get past me, our chests pressing against each other.

"Don't you dare compare him to me! You take those words back!" she continues, still raging at Dallas.

"He didn't mean it," I plead as I try to hold her in place.

"You take it back!" she howls, her hot breath pounding against my face. It's even worse than when she lost it with Khazei.

"Clementine! Stop!" I order, gripping her shoulders hard enough that I know she feels it.

Her eyes turn my way, her anger still at full boil. The scariest part is, for that half a second, she looks *exactly* like her father. She again grits her teeth, and the big vein swells. I wait for her to attack.

"You can let go now," she says in a low voice. Her arms are still tensed.

"You sure?" I ask.

"Let go, Beecher. I want you to let me go. Now."

As she tugs free of my grip, I shoot Dallas a look, hoping he'll apologize. He doesn't.

"Dallas didn't mean it," I tell her.

"I know who I am!" she shoots back, struggling to find control. "I know I'm impulsive. And passionate. I know I have a temper—but I'm *not him*, Beecher! I'm not *that*," she insists, refusing to say her father's name.

I reach out to calm her.

She again pulls away. By now, I know she's good at hiding her wounded side. And her scared side. But this anger...this venom that erupts and stings so brutally...Some things can't be hidden—especially when it's who we really are.

"The least you can do is pretend to stick up for me," she adds, catching her breath.

"C'mon, you know I don't think you're like Nico."

"I know you can *say* it, Beecher. The point is to *mean* it."

The words bite as she lets them freeze in the air.

Before I can say a word, she turns around, walking back to the path alone.

"Apologize later," Dallas says, gripping my arm as I go to chase her. "Right now, let's get back to the group so we can figure out what's going on."

"The group? Your super-bad-ass Culper Ring?" I ask, my eyes still on Clementine, who needs some time to calm down. "In case you haven't noticed, Dallas, for all the bragging you've done, they didn't get anywhere until I gave them Nico's answer. And in case you hadn't noticed that, everything else has failed: The rock was empty, all the messages are gone, and we've got no leads to follow."

"That's not true. You said Tot found that police report—the one that had the President's doctor..."

"Stewart Palmiotti."

"...that when Palmiotti was home from college, he was the last one who saw Eightball alive...that he told the police he saw Eightball voluntarily get into that car. While you were running around with Clementine, I had our guys confirm it. They found the report. Palmiotti knows what really happened that night, which means we can—"

"We can *what*? We can send some Culper Ring guys to go confront Palmiotti? Is that the new master plan—that they march into the White House, stick a finger in his face, and accuse the President's oldest and most trusted friend of harboring an old secret?"

"You'd be surprised what people will say when they think you have the upper hand."

"But we don't have the upper hand! All we have is a sheet of paper with someone saying, *I know what you did last summer*, which is proof of *nothing*! And I'm telling you right now—I don't care how many brainiacs you've got in that Ring—if you go in there with nothing and start yanking on the tail of the lion, that lion is going to take out his claws and show us firsthand why they crowned him king of the jungle. And the first claw's coming at me."

As Clementine heads back down the curving concrete path, Dallas for once doesn't argue. He knows I'm right. He knows that the moment those tox reports come back and Khazei can prove that Orlando was murdered, every single eye is going to be aimed at the last person Orlando was seen with: me. And when that black hole opens, there's no slowing it down. Not until it swallows every one of us in its path.

"That still doesn't mean we shouldn't focus on Palmiotti," he says, again motioning to the footprints. "Our people are looking. They can find anything. So whatever happened all those years ago, we'll find out what they saw, or who was there…or even where they were—"

"Wait," I blurt. "Say that part again."

"We'll find what they saw?"

"No. *Where they were.* If we find where they were…" I pull out my phone, quickly dialing a number.

"What're you doing?" Dallas asks.

"If we want to take down the lion," I tell him, "we need to get a bigger gun."

82

What're you doing?" Dallas asked.

"*If we want to take down the lion*," Beecher replied, "*we need to get a bigger gun.*"

Still watching from the treeline, the barber had to hold his breath to hear what they were saying. He tried to tell himself it was still okay. But as Beecher dialed whatever number he was dialing in the distance, Laurent knew the truth—and he knew just how far he was from *okay*.

From what he could hear, Beecher and his group weren't just guessing anymore. They had details. They had names—and not just the President's. They had Palmiotti...plus, he heard them say *Eightball*...

If they—for them to know about that...for them to know what happened that night...

On the side of the apple blossom tree that hid Laurent from sight, a small patch of snow, clinging like a white island to the bark, was slowly whittled down by the intensity of the blowing wind. As he watched the island shrink, flake by flake, Laurent knew it was no different here.

Erosion over time.

For a while now, Palmiotti said he could stop it. That somehow, he could make it all go away. But confidence is no different than friendships or secrets. They're all susceptible to the same fate...

Erosion over time.

It was so clear to Laurent now. This wasn't the beginning of the tornado.

This was the beginning of the end of it.

A few inches in front of the barber, the island of snow was the size of a quarter, worn down by another slash of wind. Across the snowy field, Beecher was having much the same effect. Indeed, as the last bits of snow were tugged from the bark, Laurent once again felt a thick lump in his throat and the matching swell of emotion that overcame him earlier when he read his client's tattoo.

If Laurent wanted to stop the tornado, there was only one way to make it go away. Until this exact moment, though, he didn't think he had the courage to do it.

But he did.

Reaching into his jacket pocket, Laurent gripped tight to the item he'd instinctively grabbed from the shop, one of only a few mementos his father brought back from the war: the Master Barbers straight-edge razor with the abalone handle.

As he slid it out and flipped the blade open, the last bits of snow were blown from the tree bark.

Across the field, both Beecher and Dallas had their backs to him.

The tornado was about to start swirling a whole lot faster.

83

ational Archives," a familiar voice says through my phone. "How may I direct your call?"

"Katya, it's Beecher. Can you transfer me over to Mr. Harmon in Presidential Records?" Standing in the snow and reading the confusion on Dallas's face, I explain, "The goal is to find what really happened on February 16th, right? The problem is, the only record from the sixteenth is that police report, which is a record that Palmiotti created himself. But what if we could find out where Palmiotti and Wallace were on the seventeenth...or even the eighteenth?"

Dallas's eyes tighten as he tries to put it together. He knows the problem. Twenty-six years ago, Wallace wasn't President. But that doesn't mean there aren't any presidential records.

"Okay, so when this happened...Twenty-six years ago, the President was...back in college," Dallas adds, quickly doing the math.

Dallas knows how the Archives work. He knows what we keep. And knows that when Wallace or any other

President gets elected, the very first thing we do is start a file for them. But most of all, we start *filling that file*—by preserving that person's history. We start collecting photos and family pictures, mementos and birth records and elementary school reports.

It's how we have those baby photos of Clinton—and how we know what was written in Bush's and Obama's fifth-grade report cards. We know those documents are eventually headed for a presidential library, so the moment a new President is elected, the government starts grabbing everything it can. And best of all, guess who's in charge of storing it?

"You think there're records from where Palmiotti was on February 16th?" Dallas asks.

"We know he was in Ohio. The police report says so. He and Wallace were both home from college, which means—"

"This is Mr. Harmon," a curt voice snaps through the phone. As one of our top people in Presidential Records, Steve Harmon doesn't apologize for being impatient, or for referring to himself as Mr. Harmon. A former navy man, all he cares about are facts.

"Mr. Harmon, this is Beecher calling—from Old Military."

"Katya told me."

"Yes, well, er—I have a request here for some records from when President Wallace was in college, and—"

"Most of those records haven't been processed yet."

"I know, sir, but we're trying to track down a particular date—the week of February 16th—back during the

President's final year of college." As I say the words, even though she's way down the path and nearly a football field away, Clementine glances over her shoulder. I don't care whose daughter she is. No way can she hear me. She turns away and continues walking. "It's for a friend of the foundation," I tell Harmon.

In Archives terms, *friend of the foundation* means one of the bigshot donors who help sponsor so many of our exhibits.

From the silence on the phone, I know Mr. Harmon's annoyed. But he's also well aware that the only reason we're still allowed to display one of the original Magna Cartas is because a friend of the foundation—the head of the Carlyle Group—loans it to us.

"Put the request in writing. I'll take a look," Mr. Harmon says.

The click in my ear tells me he's gone.

"Wallace's college records?" Dallas asks as I put away my phone and we both stand there, our feet eaten by the snow. "You really think the smoking gun's in some old English paper? 'What I Did During Spring Break— And How We Hid Eightball's Body,' by Orson Wallace?"

"There's no smoking gun, Dallas. What I'm looking for is a timeline. And if we're lucky, this'll tell us whether, during that week, Wallace came back to class or was so traumatized by what happened, he spent some time away."

"So you're looking for attendance records? Hate to remind you, but they don't take attendance in college."

"And I hate to remind you, but you have no idea what they take. Maybe when Wallace got back to school he spoke to a guidance counselor, and there's an incident report still floating in his old student file," I say as I look over Dallas's shoulder, where Clementine is just a tiny speck of coal in the white distance.

Another twig snaps back by the treeline. "We should get out of here," I say.

Watching me watching Clementine, Dallas follows me to the graveyard's concrete path, which still holds the trail of her impacted-snow footprints. "Beecher, do you have any idea how the Culper Ring has managed to successfully stay secret for over two hundred years?"

"Trust."

"Exactly. Trust," Dallas says. "Two hundred years of trusting the right people. Now let me ask you a question: Did you tell Clementine everything I said about the Culper Ring?"

"You told me not to."

"I did. But the point is, you listened. And y'know why you listened? Because even though, when it comes to Clementine, there's a little voice in your pants that's been telling you what to do—when you thought about telling her about the Culper Ring, there was a second voice—the voice in your head—that told you *not* to. For whatever reason, something in your brain told you that Clementine shouldn't know this one. And that's the voice you need to listen to, Beecher. It'll lead you far better than the voice in your pants," he says as he steps out onto the concrete path and plants his own snow footprint right over Clementine's.

"I appreciate the talking-penis analogy, but let's be honest, Dallas—if I didn't have Clementine with me this morning, I never would've even gotten in to see Nico."

"And that's so bad?"

"If Nico didn't see that sheet, we wouldn't've gotten here," I point out, catching up to him and holding out the empty rock.

"What're you talking about?"

"The coordinates. North 38 degrees, west 77 degrees—"

"Go back," Dallas says, stopping on the path. "You showed him the actual invisible ink sheet?"

"No, I—" I pat my jacket pockets, then my jeans. Don't tell me I—

"*What*, Beecher? You *gave* Nico the sheet?"

"Of course not. In the rush...we were so excited...I think I left it."

"You didn't *leave* it, Beecher. He *took* it. Didn't you see *Silence of the Lambs*? He absolutely *took* it—which means in your quest to figure out who's messing with the President, you gave the full story to the mental patient who once tried to assassinate one!"

I try to tell myself that Nico doesn't know that the note was for Wallace, but it's drowned out by the fact that there are only two types of people who ever come to see Nico: fellow crazies and desperate reporters.

"You better pray he doesn't have access to copiers or scanners," Dallas says, reminding me exactly what'll happen if Nico puts that sheet of paper in the hands of either of those two groups.

I look downhill, checking for Clementine. She's gone. In her place, all I see is Nico and the calm, measured way he said *thank you* when I left. He definitely took it.

"Don't tell me you're going back to St. Elizabeths," Dallas calls out, though he already knows the answer.

"I have to," I tell him as I pick up speed. "I need to get back what Nico took from us."

84

It was something that the one with the ungroomed beard—Dallas—it was something Dallas had said.

Squinting through the front windshield as the morning sun pinged off the piles of soot-capped snow, the barber couldn't help but notice the sudden increase in the number of the neighborhood's liquor stores and laundromats. Of course, there was a barbershop. There was always a barbershop, he knew, spying the hand-painted sign with the words *Fades To Braids* in big red letters.

Kicking the brakes as he approached a red light, he didn't regret holding back at the cemetery. He was ready. He'd made his peace. But when he heard those words leave Dallas's lips, he knew there was still one box that needed to be checked.

Twenty-six years ago, he'd acted in haste. Looking back at it, though, he didn't regret that either. He did the best he could in the moment.

Just as he was doing now.

As the light winked green, he twisted the wheel into a sharp left turn, fishtailing for a split second in a mass of gray slush. As the car found traction, Laurent knew he was close.

This was it.

He knew it from the moment he saw the building in the distance.

He knew it as he felt the straight-edge razor that still called to him from his pocket.

He knew it as he saw—parked at the top of the hill—the silver car that Beecher had been driving.

And he knew it when he spotted, just next to the main gate, the thin black letters that spelled out those same two words that had left Dallas's lips back in the cemetery.

St. Elizabeths.

The greater good would finally be served.

85

It takes me nineteen minutes to drop Dallas at the Archives, eleven minutes to drive his silver Toyota back to St. Elizabeths, and a full forty seconds for me to stand outside, working on my story, before I push open the front door of Nico's building.

"I...hi...sorry...I think I left my notebook upstairs," I say to the guard, feigning idiocy and holding up the temporary ID sticker that she gave me a little over an hour ago.

The guard with the bad Dutch-boy hair rolls her eyes.

"Just make it quick," she says as a loud *tunk* opens the steel door, and I take my second trip of the day through the metal detector.

"Don't worry," I tell her. "I'll be lightning."

Trying hard to stand still, I fight my body as it follows the rhythmic sway of the rising elevator.

An hour ago, when I was standing here, I was holding Clementine's hand. Right now, I lean hard on that thought, though it does nothing to calm me.

As the doors rumble open and I step out, the same black woman with the same big key ring is waiting for me.

"Forgot your notebook, huh?" she asks with a laugh. "Hope there's no phone numbers in there. You don't want Nico calling your relatives."

I pretend to laugh along as she again opens the metal door and leads me down the hallway, back to the day room.

"Christopher, can you help him out?" the woman asks, passing me to a heavy male nurse in a freshly starched white shirt. "We got some more visitors coming up right now."

As she leaves me behind, I take a quick scan of the fluorescent-lit day room: patients watching various TVs, nurses flipping through various clipboards, there's even someone feeding coins into the soda machine. But as I check the Plexiglas round table in the corner...

No Nico.

"Who you here for again?" the heavy male nurse asks as he fluffs pillows and straightens one of the many saggy sofas.

"Nico," I say, holding up my ID sticker like it's a badge. "I was here seeing Nico, but I think I left my notebook."

He does his own scan of the area, starting with the round table. He knows Nico's routine.

"I bet he's in his room—711," he says, pointing me to the swinging doors on the far left. "Don't worry, you can go yourself. Nico's got room visitor privileges."

"Yeah…no…I'll be quick," I say, taking off for the swinging doors and reminding myself what they first told me: This is a hospital, not a prison. But as I push the doors open and the bright day room narrows into the far smaller, far darker, far quieter hospital hallway, the sudden silence makes me all too aware of how alone I am back here.

At the end of the hall is an internal metal staircase that's blocked off by a thick glass door so no one on this floor can access it. I still hear the soft thud of footsteps as someone descends a few floors above.

Counting room numbers, I walk past at least three patient rooms that have padlocks on the outside. One of them is locked, bolted tight. I don't even want to know who's in there.

By the time I reach Room 711, I'm twisting out of my winter coat to stop the sweat. Nico's door also has a padlock and is slightly ajar. The lights are on. But from what I can tell, no one's inside.

I look back over my shoulder. Through the cutaway in the swinging doors, the male nurse is still watching me.

"Nico…?" I call out, tapping a knuckle softly on the door.

No one answers.

"Nico, you there?" I ask, knocking again.

Still nothing.

I know this moment. It's just like the moment in the original SCIF: a scary door, an off-limits room, and a spectacularly clear opportunity. Back then, I told Orlando we shouldn't be that guy in the horror movie who checks out the noise coming from the woods. The thing is, right now, I need what's in those woods.

Clenching my jaw, I give the door a slight push, and the whiff of rosewater perfume takes me back a dozen years. It's the same smell as Clementine's old house. As I lean forward, the nylon on my winter coat rubs the door like sandpaper. I crane my neck just enough to see—

"*What the hell you doing?*" an angry voice snaps behind me.

I spin around to find a tall brown-haired man— nurse...another nurse—standing there wearing plastic gloves and carrying a stack of Dixie cups in a long plastic sheath.

"*You got no business being back here!*" the nurse scolds, plenty pissed.

"The other nurse...the guy up front...in the white," I stutter, pointing back the way I came. "He said Nico had visitor privileges."

"*Christopher?* Christopher ain't no nurse! He runs the juice cart! And don't think I don't know what you're doing..."

"*Doing?* I-I'm not doing anything."

"You say that. But then every year or so, we still get one of you showing up, hoping to get an autograph or grab some personal item—last year, some guy put a Bible that he said belonged to Nico up on eBay. I know you think it's cool, but you've got no idea how hard Nico's working. It's not easy for him, okay? Let the man live his damn life."

"I am. I want to. I'm...I'm just trying to get my notebook," I tell him.

"The what?"

"My notebook. I was visiting with him earlier. Doing research. I think I left my notebook."

The nurse cocks his head, studying me for a full two seconds. He believes me. Pointing me back to the swinging doors of the day room, he explains, "Nico's doing his janitor work in the RMB Building. You wanna ask him something, go find him there. You're not going in his room without his okay. Now you know where RMB is?"

"The redbrick building, right?" I say, rushing for the door, remembering where Nico feeds the cats. "I know exactly where it is."

86

"N ippy out today, huh?" a young guard with a big gold class ring asks as I shove my way out of the wind and into the toasty lobby of the redbrick RMB Building.

"I'm from Wisconsin. This is summer for us," I say, working extra hard to keep it light as I approach the desk and yet again scribble my name in a sign-in book. "So who'd you play for?" I add, motioning to the gold football that's engraved into his ring.

"Floyd County High School. Out in Virginia," he says. "It's class A, not AAA, but still... state champs."

"State champs," I say with a nod, well aware that there's only one thing I really care about from high school.

"So you're the Nico guy?" the guard asks.

"Pardon?"

"They called me from the other side—said you'd be coming. You're the one looking for Nico, right?" Before I can answer, a lanky black woman with bright red statement glasses shoves open the locked metal door that leads to the rest of the building. After finding me outside Nico's room, they're not letting me get in this building unattended.

"Vivian can take you back," the guard says, motioning me through what looks like a brand-new metal detector. But as the red-glasses nurse swipes her ID against a snazzy new scanner to open the metal door, I'm all too aware that this building has a far more high-tech security system than the ancient giant key ring that the nurses rely on in the other one.

"So you a reporter?" Red Glasses asks as she tugs the door open and invites me inside.

"No...no...just...I'm doing some research," I say, following behind her.

"Like I said—a reporter," she teases as I notice a sign on the wall that says:

Gero-Psych Unit

In the hallway, there's an empty gurney, an empty wheelchair, and a state-of-the-art rolling cart. Everything's scrubbed neat as can be. Outrageously neat. Even without the industrial hand sanitizer dispensers along the walls, I know a hospital when I see one.

"I didn't realize you had a full medical unit back here," I say as we pass an open room and I spot an elderly man in a hospital bed, hooked to various monitors and staring blankly at a TV.

"Our population's aging. We need someplace to take care of them. You should put that in one of your articles, rather than all the usual stuff you write about us." She's about to say something else, but as we reach our destination—the nurses' desk that sits like an island at the center of the long suite—she stops and arches an eyebrow, looking confused.

"Everything okay?" I ask.

"Yeah, I just...Nico was just mopping back here."

I follow her gaze down to the floor. Sure enough, the tiles are still shiny and wet.

"Gimme half a sec," the nurse says, picking up the desk phone and quickly dialing a number. As she waits for it to ring, I trace the wet streaks on the floor to...

There.

Just a few feet ahead, along the tile, there're two parallel streaks—from the wheels of a mop bucket rolling along the wet floor—that run like train tracks, then make a sharp right into one of the patient rooms.

"Pam, you see Nico up there?" the nurse says into the phone.

As she waits for an answer, I follow the streaks a few steps toward the open room. Inside, the lights are off, but there's sunlight coming in from the window. Stretching my neck, I peek around the corner, into the room, and...

Nothing. No mop bucket...no Nico...nothing but another patient hooked up to another set of machines.

"Great—he's up there?" the nurse says behind me, still talking on the phone. "Perfect. Great. Sure, please send him down."

As she hangs up the phone, I take one last glance at the patient in the bed. He's maybe sixty or so, and propped on his side, facing me. It's not by his choice. There are pillows stuffed behind his back. His body's frozen, and his hands rest like a corpse's at the center of his chest. They did the same thing when my mom had her heart surgery: turning him to prevent bedsores.

The oddest part are the man's eyes, which are small and red like a bat's. As I step in the room, he's staring right at me. I raise my hand to apologize for interrupting, but I quickly realize...he's barely blinking.

I tighten my own gaze. There's nothing behind his eyes. He's not seeing anything at all. He just lies there, his whole body as stiff as his arms on his—

Wait.

His arm. There's something on his arm.

My face goes hot, flushing with blood. Every bone in my body feels paper-thin and brittle, like a fishbone that's easily snapped.

I didn't see it when I first walked in—I was too busy looking at his empty eyes—but there it is, faded and withered on the lower part of his forearm:

A tattoo.

A sagging, faded black tattoo.

Of an eight-ball.

87

Twenty-six years ago
Journey, Ohio

That'll be seventeen dollars and fifty-four—"

"No...hold on...I got coupons," the heavy customer with the thick neck interrupted, fishing out wads of crumpled coupons and handing them to the supermarket cashier.

The cashier shook her head. "Son, you should've—" But as the cashier finally looked up and made eye contact, she realized the customer with the ripped black concert tee and the matching punk black Converse wasn't a *he*. It was a *she*. "I...hurrr...lemme just...ring these up," the cashier stuttered, quickly looking away.

By now, after sixteen years of living with Turner syndrome, Minnie Wallace knew how people saw her. She was used to awkward stares. Just like she was used to the fact that as she stepped past the cashier and into the bagging area, every single bagboy in the store had somehow subtly made his way to one of the other cashier lanes.

No way around it—people always disappoint, Minnie thought as she sorted cans of cheap tuna fish away from the cheap generic aspirin, and bagged the rest of her groceries herself.

"New grand total...fifteen dollars and four cents," the cashier announced, stealing another quick glance at Minnie's broad chest and low, mannish hairline. Minnie caught that too, even as she brushed her black bowl-cut hair down against her forehead in the hopes of covering her face.

With a final hug around the two brown bags of groceries, Minnie gripped them tightly to her chest, added a sharp lift, and headed for the automatic doors.

Outside, the drab Ohio sky was still laced with a few slivers of pink as the sun gave way to dark.

"Y'need some help?" a voice called out.

"Huh?" Minnie asked, turning off balance and nearly dropping both bags.

"Here, lemme...*Here*," a boy with far too much gel in his spiky brown hair said, taking control of both bags before they tumbled.

"Man, these *are* heavy," he teased with a warm smile as he walked next to her. "You're strong."

Minnie stared, finally getting her first good look at his face. She knew him from school. He was a few years older from being left back. Twelfth grade. His name was Griffin.

"Whattya want?" she asked, already suspicious.

"Nothing. I was— You just looked like you needed—"

"If you want my brother to buy you beer, go ask him

yourself," she said, knowing full well what Orson had been doing since he'd been back on spring break.

"No...that's not—Can you just listen?" he pleaded, readjusting the bags and revealing the tattoo on his forearm. A black eight-ball. "I just was hoping—I don't know...maybe..." Griffin stopped at the corner, working hard on the words. "Maybe we could...maybe go out sometime?"

"You're serious?"

"Sure...yeah. It's just...I've seen you around school—always wearing that concert shirt—the Smiths," he said as Minnie's big cheeks burned red. "The Smiths are cool."

"Yeah, they're...they're kinda cool," she replied, unable to do anything but look straight down, study her black Converse, and try extra hard to slide open her leather jacket so he could see her current English Beat concert tee, which was stretched tight by her round belly.

"Yeah, English Beat's cool too," Griffin added, nodding his approval as he readjusted the brown paper bags and stole another glance at her.

As they crossed the street, Griffin pointed to a parked black Dodge Aspen that had been repainted with a cheap paint job. "If you want, I can drive you home," he offered.

"You don't have to do that."

"I know," he said, again peering over at her, this time for longer. "I'd like to. I'd really like to."

It wasn't the offer that caught Minnie off guard. Or even his smile. It was the way he looked at her. Right at her. For sixteen years, unless someone was staring, no one looked at her.

But Griffin did. He looked. And smiled.

He was still smiling, even as Minnie shyly looked away.

Feeling like a cork about to leave a bottle, Minnie couldn't look away for long. Standing up straight—completely unafraid—she looked back at him. "Okay," she said, standing by the passenger side of the car and waiting for him to open the door.

Still holding both bags, he leaned in and reached past her, his forearm about to brush against her own. He was so close, she could smell the Wonder Bread in the grocery bag—and the black cherry soda on his breath.

She looked right at him, waiting for him to say something.

The only sound was a muffled *rat-a-tat-tat*...

...of laughter.

It was coming from her left. She followed the sound over her shoulder, just around the corner, where two guys—one black with a high-top fade, one white wearing an Oakland Raiders jersey—were snickering to themselves.

"No, ya Guido—the deal was you gotta do the kiss!" the white one shouted.

"You lose, brother! Game over!" the black one added.

"That's not what we said!" Griffin laughed back.

Minnie stood there, still struggling to process.

"C'mon, you should be thanking me," Griffin said, turning back to Minnie. "I gave you a full two minutes of what it's like to be normal."

Minnie wanted to scream. She wanted to hit him. But her body locked up and her legs began to tremble. Still, there was no way she'd cry for him. No way. She tried steeling herself, but all she saw was how hard all three of them were laughing. From her nose, twin waterfalls of snot slowly ran down.

"Bye, freak," Griffin said, dropping both bags of groceries. The eggs shattered in one bag. From the other, a single can of tuna fish cartwheeled down the sidewalk.

"You even realize how much you look like a boy? Whatchu got down there, boy parts or girl parts?" Griffin asked, flicking his fingers against her crotch. The trembling in her legs only got worse. "It's boy parts, innit?"

Minnie shook her head, fighting the tears. "I'm a girl," she whispered.

"And you're telling me all those girl parts work? No chance," Griffin challenged, getting right in her face. "No chance those parts work."

Minnie watched the can of tuna fish roll into the street and tip on its side, making a small repeating circle like a spun nickel approaching its stop.

"I'm right, ain't I?" Griffin added as the can of tuna continued to spin in front of the car. Minnie shut her eyes, her legs trembling worse than ever. "You got nothing working down there, do ya?" he shouted. "Take the hint, animal. God did it for a reason—He don't want no more mongrels like you!"

Minnie's legs finally stopped trembling. She could feel the result running down her legs.

"Did you just wet your—!?" Griffin took a step back, making a face. That smell… "Is that—? Ohh, *nasty*!"

"She just took a dump in her pants?" the white kid asked.

"She crapped her pants!" Griffin laughed.

Scrambling backward, Minnie tripped over the rest of her groceries, landing on her rear with an awful squish that set Griffin and his friends howling.

In the street, the can of tuna sat there.

Climbing to her feet, Minnie looked up at Griffin and his eight-ball tattoo as the world melted in a flush of tears.

"Check it out—a face made for an abortion—and the stench of one too!" one of them said, laughing.

"Where you going, Elephant Man!? You forgot your groceries!" Griffin called out as she fought to her feet and started running up the block. "Whatcha gonna do— go tell your mom!?"

She didn't respond, but as she ran as hard as she could and tried to avoid thinking of what was running down her legs, Minnie Wallace knew the answer. She knew exactly what she was going to do.

She was going to get her brother.

88

I stumble backward, bumping into the spine of the open hospital room door.

"Good news!" the red-glasses nurse calls out behind me. "Nico's upstairs. He's on his way down."

I barely hear the words. I'm too focused on the patient with... eight-ball. He's got an eight-ball...

"I-Is he...? Is that...?"

"Relax. He's fine," the nurse says. "He's PVS. Persistent vegetative state. Been like that since he got here—though actually, you should talk to Nico. We ask our patients to go in and do therapy for him: play music, rub his face. But Nico swears that he's heard him speak—just mumblings, of course."

I spin back to face her. It's the first time she sees the panic on my face. "You okay?" she asks.

"Is that his name? *R. Rubin?*" I blurt, reading the name from the medical chart clipped to the foot of his bed. "How long has he been here?"

"Actually, that information is—"

"*How long's he been here!*" I explode.

The nurse steps back at the outburst. Eightball doesn't move, his bat eyes barely blinking.

"Ten years," the nurse says coldly. "Now I need to ask you to leave. If you want to speak to Nico—"

Nico. I almost forgot. Nico's headed here right now.

"I changed my mind. I don't need to see him," I say, cutting past the nurse and rushing back to the lobby. "And don't tell him I came. You'll only upset him," I warn, meaning every word.

As I shove the metal door open and dart back into the cool air of the lobby, my brain is still swirling, trying to do the math. If Eightball's here, then—No. Don't even think it. Not until I know for sure.

"Well that was fast," the guard with the big football ring calls out from behind the security desk.

"Can I—? Your sign-in book," I blurt, pointing to the black binder on the edge of his desk. "You need me to sign out?"

"Nah. I can do it for you."

"It's fine, I'm right here," I say, flipping open the book and grabbing the pen. My name's on the last page. I purposely flip to the first, scanning names as quickly as I can.

For Eightball to be here...If Nico knew—or even if he didn't know—there's no way this was pulled off without help.

The first page in the overstuffed book dates back to June, over six months ago. There're only two or three visitors per day, which, as I continue to flip through the pages, makes it easy to see who's been in this building five months ago…four months ago…three months ago…

Oh. Shit.

No…it can't be.

But it is.

My ribs contract, gripping my lungs like thin skeleton fingers. But before I can react, my phone vibrates in my pocket.

Caller ID tells me it's Dallas.

"You ready to pass out?" I ask as I pick up.

"Don't talk. Just listen," he insists. "We've got an emergency."

"Trust me, the emergency's here."

"No, Beecher. The emergency's *here*. Are you listening? I had some folks—some of our folks here—I had them run Clementine's info to see if they could find something new. But when they looked up her address—"

"The address isn't in her name. I know. It's her grandmother's place. Her grandmother owns the house."

"You said that last night. But that's the problem, Beecher. When they ran her name—according to everything we found…" He takes a breath, making sure I'm listening. "Clementine's grandmother died eight years ago."

Inside my ribcage, the skeleton fingers tighten their grip. I'm still flipping through the sign-in book. But I can't say I'm surprised.

"I know," I tell him.

"What're you talking about?"

I look down at the sign-in book and reread the one

name that is in here over and over and over again. Three months ago, two months ago, even last month—the signature is unmistakable. An effortless swirl from the one person who I now realize has been coming to see Nico not just since yesterday, but for over three months now.

Clementine.

89

Twenty-six years ago
Journey, Ohio

It was Thursday, and the barbershop was open late.

The young barber wasn't thrilled—in fact, if it were any other client, he would've already locked up and left. Especially tonight. Tonight was card night, and with Vincent hosting, that meant they'd be playing bid whist and eating those good pierogies Vincent always ordered from around the corner. They were probably already eating them now, Laurent thought as he glanced down at his digital watch and then out the plate glass window where the rain had just started to springboard from the black sky.

Ten more minutes. I'm not waiting a minute more than that, he promised himself, even though he made the same promise ten minutes ago.

And ten minutes before that.

Again, if it were anyone else, Laurent would've already left. But he wasn't waiting on just any client. This was one of Laurent's *first* clients—back from when Laurent was still in high school and his dad first gave him the scissors and a chair of his own.

In a town like Journey, where the same man has been cutting the same hair for nearly four decades, it takes more than just bravery to try out the untested new barber.

It takes trust.

And like his father with his own first clients, Laurent would never—not ever—forget that fact, not even years later when he was asked to stay late on a cold, rainy card night, when every store on the block was closed and every second waiting here decreased the chances of him seeing a pierogi or—

Diiiing, the bell rang at the front of the barbershop.

Laurent turned as the door slammed hard into the wall, nearly shattering the plate glass. It wasn't his client. It was a crush of young men in their twenties rushing in from the rain, stumbling at the threshold. They were soaked...slipping...dripping puddles across the black-and-white tile floor.

For those first seconds, Laurent was pissed. He hated dealing with drunks, especially drunk college kids who suddenly see a barbershop and think they want a Mr. T mohawk. But it wasn't until they tumbled inside that Laurent finally saw the true cause of their lack of balance: The young man in the middle sagged facedown to the ground. His friends weren't walking with him. They were carrying him.

As he lay there, not moving, his right arm was bent awkwardly in a way that arms don't bend. Sliding down from his soaked hair, drips of blood tumbled into the new puddle of rainwater, seeping outward as they turned the floor a strangely beautiful light pink. But even in the midst of the chaos, even with the blood still coming, the young barber, who would forever regret staying late that night, immediately recognized the tattoo on the bleeding man's forearm.

An eight-ball.

He'd cut the hair of one other person with the same mark. He knew what it meant—and what gang it came from.

"Get inside! Shut the door!" one of the boys said, screaming at the overweight boy—no, that was a girl—who was still standing out in the rain, looking like a chubby phantom and not saying a word.

"They're gonna kill us!" the other boy called out, his haunting gray eyes locking on the barber with an almost spiritual clarity. Laurent knew him too—he'd known him for years—back from when the boy was little and his father would bring all sorts of trouble to the shop. Even back then, even when it got bad, Laurent never saw the boy get riled. Until now.

"I mean it, Laurent. *Please*..." the young twenty-year-old who would one day be the President of the United States pleaded as his gray eyes went wet with tears. "Please can you help us?"

90

Beecher…" Dallas warns through the phone.

"I'm already gone," I say, shoving open the lobby's glass door and darting out into the cold. My body bakes in the weird sensation from the heat in my winter coat mixing with the brutal wind from outside. But as I weave past the concrete benches in front of the brick building…

"Make sure Nico's not following," Dallas says, reading my mind.

I check. And check. And recheck again.

The glass door is shut. From what I can tell, there's no movement inside.

"Get out of there!" Dallas adds as I run for the narrow black path that snakes through the snow and leads back up to the parking lot. I recheck one more time, but as I turn around, my legs feel like toothpicks, ready to snap and unable to hold my weight. But this time—all the times—I'm not looking for Nico. I'm looking for *her*.

For Clementine.

My mind swirls into rewind, replaying every moment,

every interaction, every conversation we've had since she "magically" returned to my life. I thought I was lucky. I thought I was blessed. How many guys get to reconnect with the girl they used to dream of? The answer's easy. None.

I replay our night on the bridge...and the homemade photo she made of us...and how she understood me in a way that Iris never did. I try to tell myself how stupid and cliché and dumb every precious moment was—but the toughest truth, as the bitter pain in my belly tells me, is how bad I still want every damn second of it to be real.

Still running on toothpicks, I tear as hard as I can, putting as much space between myself and the building as possible. My stomach nearly bursts, feeling like a rolled-over carcass. *How could she do this to me?*

"Beecher, are you—?"

"I-I saw him," I tell Dallas.

"Nico?"

"No. I saw him. He's here. I saw *Eightball*!"

"What're you talking about?"

"He's alive. We assumed he was dead—that Wallace killed him all those years ago—but he's—" At the top of the hill, the path dumps me back in the parking lot that sits right across from Nico's home building. Within seconds, I beeline for Dallas's old Toyota and fish the keys from my pocket. "Don't you see, Dallas? We were right—about Eightball...and the blackmail...That's what they were doing. That's how they found out what happened all those years ago," I add as I whip open the car door and slide into the front seat. "Maybe they found

Eightball…or Eightball whispered it—either way, they used that to blackmail—"

"I think it'd be best if you put down the phone now," a soft gentlemanly voice suggests from the backseat.

"Whatthef—!" I jump so high, my head slams into the roof.

"I also highly recommend not turning around," the man warns. "I see what you're doing," he adds as we lock eyes in the mirror. He's an older black man with silver hair and a matching silver mustache. "I'm begging you, Beecher—this is the time when you want to use that big brain of yours. Now please…put the phone down, and put your hands on the steering wheel."

His voice is kind, almost soothing. But there's no mistaking the threat, especially as I spot his shiny silver weapon just above the back of my headrest.

At first, I assume it's a gun. It's not.

It's a straight-edge razor.

91

Twenty-six years ago
Journey, Ohio

U p here...left up here!" the kid with the tight
curly hair—the one called Palmiotti—insisted,
sitting in the passenger seat and pointing out the
front windshield of the young barber's white van.

"The hospital's to the right!" Laurent shouted, refusing to turn the wheel.

"No...go to the other hospital—Memorial. Stay left!"
Palmiotti yelled.

"Memorial's twenty minutes from here!" Laurent shot
back. "You see how he's bleeding?"

Behind them, in the back of the van, Orson Wallace
was down on his knees, cradling the head of the unconscious kid with the eight-ball tattoo, trying to stop the
bleeding by tightly holding towels from the barbershop
against his head.

An hour ago, Wallace threw the first punch. And the
second. He would've thrown the third too, but Eightball

got lucky, knocking the wind out of Wallace's stomach. That's when Palmiotti jumped in, gripping Eightball in a tight headlock and holding him still as Wallace showed him the real damage you can do when, in a moment of vengeful anger, you stuff your car keys between your knuckles and stab someone in the face.

Years later, Wallace would tell himself he used the keys because of what Eightball did to Minnie.

It wasn't true.

Wallace was just pissed that Eightball hit him back.

"He's not moving anymore," Wallace's sister whispered from the back corner of the van. She was down on her knees too, but just like in the barbershop, she wouldn't get close to the body. "He was moving before and now he's not."

"He's breathing! I see him breathing!" Wallace shouted. "Stewie, get us to Memorial!"

Palmiotti turned to the barber. His voice was slow and measured, giving each syllable its own punch. "My father. Works. At Memorial," he growled. "Go. Left. Now."

With a screech, the van hooked left, all five of them swayed to the right, and they followed Spinnaker Road, the longest and most poorly lit stretch of asphalt that ran out of town.

Passing field after field of pitch-black farmland, the barber used the silence to take a good look at Palmiotti in the passenger seat. New jeans. Nice Michigan Lacrosse sweatshirt. Frat boy hair.

"Can I ask one thing?" the barber said, finally breaking the silence. "What was wrong with your car?"

"What's that?" Palmiotti asked.

"You got those nice clothes—the new Reeboks. Don't tell me you don't have a car. So what's wrong with yours that we gotta be driving in mine?"

"What'd you want me to do? Run home and get it? My brother dropped us off downtown—then everything else exploded with the fight."

It was a fast answer. And a good one, Laurent thought to himself. But as he looked over his shoulder and saw the pool of blood that was now in his van—in his carpet—and could be linked just to *him*, he couldn't help but notice the look that Palmiotti shot to Wallace in the passenger-side mirror.

Or the look that Wallace shot back.

As a barber who spent every day watching clients in a mirror, Laurent was fluent in talking with just your eyes. He knew a *thank-you* when he saw one. And right there, in that moment, he also knew the hierarchy of loyalties that would drive their relationship for the next twenty-six years.

"There…*pull in there*!" Palmiotti said, eventually motioning to the putty-colored building in the distance with the backlit sign that read *Emergency Room*. "There's parking spots in front."

Even before the van bucked to a stop, Palmiotti was outside in the rain. With a tug, he whipped open the side door of the van, and in one quick motion, he and Wallace scooped up Eightball and—shouting the words "Wait here!"—carried him off like tandem lifeguards toward the sliding doors of the emergency room.

There was a hushed *whoosh* as they disappeared, leaving the barber breathing heavy in the driver's seat, still buzzing with adrenaline. But as fast as reality settled in, all the mental avoidance of the past half hour faded with equal speed. To drive out here…to even take them at all…Laurent had said they should call an ambulance—but in the rush of chaos…the way Eightball was bleeding…and all that screaming…Wallace seemed so sure. And when Wallace was sure, it was hard to argue. They had to take him themselves. Otherwise, he would've died.

"You okay?" a soft female voice coughed from the back of the van.

Laurent nodded.

"I-I'm sorry for this—I really am," she added.

"You have nothing to apologize for," Laurent insisted, staring out at the raindrops that slalomed down the front windshield. "This has nothing to do with you."

"You're wrong."

"I'm not. They told me what happened when you came back—Eightball grabbing a baseball bat…It shouldn't've escalated like that, but lemme tell you—"

"You weren't there."

"—if someone did that to my sister…and *I* was your brother—"

"You weren't there," Minnie insisted, her voice cracking. "You didn't see what happened. Orson wasn't the only one who made him bleed."

The words hung in the van, which was battered by the metal pinging of raindrops from above. Laurent slowly twisted in his seat, turning to the chubby girl with the wet hair and the now dried train tracks of black mascara that ran down her face. She sat Indian-style, looking every bit her young age as she picked at nothing in the blood-stained carpet.

The barber hadn't noticed it before. Hadn't even registered it. But as he thought about it now, Orson's clothes—just like Palmiotti's—were mostly clean. But here, in the back of the van...

The front of Minnie's leather jacket...her neck...even her English Beat T-shirt...were covered in a fine spray of blood.

Just like you'd get if you hit something soft. With a baseball bat.

Still picking at nothing in the blood-soaked carpet, Minnie didn't say a word.

In fact, it took another ten minutes before her tears finally came—pained, soft whimpers that sounded like a wounded dog—set off when her brother exited from the sliding doors of the emergency room, stepped back into the rain, and told them the news: Eightball was dead.

92

Y ou have no idea how hard this is," the man with the razor says as he sits directly behind me in the backseat of the car.

"Listen," I plead. "There's no reason to—"

"Beecher, I've asked you two times now. Please put your phone down."

"It's down...I put it down," I say, though I don't tell him that I haven't hung up. If I'm lucky, Dallas can hear every word we're saying. "Just please...can you lower the razor?"

In the rearview, the man barely reacts, though the razor does disappear behind my headrest. Still, the way he manically keeps shifting in his seat—sitting up so close I hear him breathing through his nose—he's panicking, still making his decision.

"I'm sorry you found him," the man says, sounding genuine as he stares down at his lap. "That's why you were running just now—all out of breath. You saw him, didn't you?"

"I don't know what you're talking about. I was here picking up a notebook—"

"Please don't do that to me. I was being honest with you," he says, sounding wounded, his head still down. I feel a slight nudge in my lower back. From his knees. His feet tap furiously against the floor, making the whole car shake. Whatever he's about to do, it's weighing on him. "I know it's over, Beecher. I know you saw Griffin."

"If you think I'm the one doing this…with the blackmail…It's not me," I tell him. "I swear to you—Clementine's—"

"They know the roles. They know who's done this. And when it comes to the fight you've picked…the poor girl's as dead as you are."

It's the second time in two days someone's mentioned my death as if it's inevitable. It's starting to piss me off.

Behind me, the man with the razor continues to lean forward, elbows resting on his still bouncing knees. He again takes a heavy breath through his nose. It's not getting any easier for him. "You're a history guy, right, Beecher?" Before I can answer, he asks, "Y'ever hear of a guy named Tsutomu Yamaguchi?"

I shake my head, searching the parking lot and scanning the grounds for a guard…for an orderly…for anyone to help. There's no one in sight.

"You never heard of him? Tsutomu Yamaguchi?" he repeats as I finally place his accent. Flat and midwestern. Just like the President's. "In 1945, this man Yamaguchi was in the shipbuilding business. In Japan. Y'know what happened in 1945 in Japan?"

"Please...this—whatever this is about. You can let me go. No one'll ever know. You can say I—"

"Hiroshima. Can you imagine? Of all the towns that this guy's shipbuilding business sends him to, on August 6, 1945, Yamaguchi was visiting Hiroshima at the exact moment one of our B-29s dropped the atomic bomb," he continues as if I'm not even there. "But ready for the twist? Yamaguchi actually *survives*. He suffers bad burns, spends the night in the city, and then quickly races to his hometown, which is guess where?"

I don't answer.

"Nagasaki—which gets hit with the second bomb three days later. And God bless him, Yamaguchi *survives that too*! Blessed by God, right? A hundred and forty thousand are killed in Hiroshima. Seventy thousand die in Nagasaki. But to this day, this one man is the only person certified by the Japanese government to have survived *both* blasts. Two atomic bombs," he says, shaking his head as he continues to stare down at the blade in his lap. "It may be on a smaller scale, but I can tell you, Beecher. In this life, there are days like that. For all of us."

I nod politely, hoping it'll keep him talking. On my phone, it says my call has been connected for four minutes and twenty-seven seconds. If Dallas and his Culper Ring are as good as I think they are, it won't be long until the cavalry comes running.

In the small of my back, the man's knees stop shaking.

"Mine was that night in the rain," he adds as his voice

picks up speed. "I knew it the instant they brought him in. Forget the blood and the bits of bone that they said she drove into his brain..."

She? Did he just say she*?*

"...I knew it from the split second I saw the looks on those boys' faces. It was more than terror, more than remorse. The pain in their eyes was like...it was like they knew they'd never be able to face God Himself again." He looks up from the blade. His eyes are red and bloodshot. "Y'ever been around a victim of crime—someone who's been raped or beaten or even mugged? The depth of their horror—you feel that pain through the pores of your skin. I didn't want to admit it, but that night...that was my own Hiroshima sitting right there in front of me."

As he says the words, my own pores—my whole body—I feel the despair rising off him. He doesn't have a choice. From here on in, there's only one way to keep me from talking. Outside, I eye the service road that leads up from the front gate. Still no cavalry. If I run, the knife's close enough that he can still do damage. My hands stay gripped to the steering wheel. I search between the seats...across the floor...looking anywhere for a weapon.

"The worst part was how easy it was to pretend otherwise and keep it all silent. Not just with Griffin. With her too. With the stroke..."

The stroke? I think for a second. He said *her. Does he mean...?*

"They blamed it on the Turner syndrome, but when someone takes the long accordion hose from her vacuum cleaner, hooks one end to the tailpipe of her family's Honda Civic, and then loops the other end into the window of the driver's seat? That's not Turner syndrome. That's *penance*," he says. "Palmiotti didn't find her for four hours. To this day, him pulling her out...it's a miracle she even survived."

My chest cavity feels hollow—all my organs gone—as I try to take a breath. All this time, we thought Wallace was protecting himself. But he was actually trying to protect...*her*. His sister. "You're saying Minnie...that Minnie Wallace was the one who...and she tried to commit—?"

"You're not listening! *I need you to listen to me!*" he explodes, his face contorting with pain. "I was just the driver! I didn't do anything—I was just trying to help some...they were *kids*!"

"Then you need to listen to me now," I interrupt, trying to make eye contact in the rearview. "If that's the case, you need to tell your story. You have nothing to worry about. You didn't do anything wrong."

"I didn't," he agrees as the pain on his face only gets worse. "I just took them to the hospital. They told me Griffin was dead."

"Then there you go. That's what matters," I say, knowing the benefits of agreeing. The sooner I win him over, the more I can buy myself more time. "All these years...you had no idea."

"It's true...I-I was just the driver. How am I supposed to know they gave him a fake name—or—or—or transferred him here once Wallace got his Senate seat? They told me he was dead."

"Exactly—they told you he was dead. That's all you knew, right?"

I wait for his answer, but this time there's only silence from the backseat.

I glance again in the rearview. Our eyes lock.

"That's all you knew, right?" I ask for the second time.

But as a watery glaze fills his bloodshot eyes, I quickly understand. The worst lies in life are the ones we tell ourselves.

"You knew..." I say. "You *knew* Eightball was here."

"Only recently."

"How recently? A week? A month?"

His face goes pale like an onionskin. "I lied to my own soul."

"How long?" I ask.

"Two years. Two and a half years," he whispers, his head sloping down as if his neck no longer works. The car still sits in the parking lot. I search the service road. Still no one there. "You have to understand, when I found out...when I confronted Palmiotti...They said they moved him here to keep an eye on him—to take care of him—but I was the only one who came to visit him. He needed to know...I needed to tell him what Wallace had done. For me. I didn't do it for the greater good. It was only good for me. But I had no idea Nico heard me," he adds, his voice at full sprint. "That's why, at the cemetery...when you said you were coming here...I knew. I knew it! This was my chance to end it. I'm sorry for being so weak, Beecher—but this is what I should've done the moment this started..."

Over my shoulder, he raises his blade to cut me.

But in the mirror, I see it.

It's already covered in blood.

I look down, patting my neck. I didn't feel any-thing...

Without warning, the blade drops from his hand, bouncing and falling into the front seat.

His onionskin face goes practically transparent. He sags backward, sinking in his seat.

Oh God. Has he been shot?

I check the front window...the sides. All the glass is intact. But as I spin back to face him...in the seat...There's blood. So much blood. It's not splattered. It's contained. A small pool. On the seat...on his arms...No. Not his arms...

It's coming from his wrists.

"What'd *you do*?" I yell.

"She paid her penance," he whispers through a hard cough. "I need to pay mine."

"*What the hell'd you do!?*" I repeat as a slow red puddle blooms in the backseat, raining down to—On the floor. I couldn't see it before.

At his feet, a larger pool of blood seeps into the carpet. From the size of the puddle...all that red...He did this. When we were talking. He wasn't just staring down at the razor. He'd used it.

"You tell them—you tell them there's a cost," he sput-ters, about to pass out. "Every decision we make in life, there's always a cost."

"Gimme your wrists! I can stop it!" I tell him.

"You're missing the point," he stutters, no longer cringing. Whatever pain he was feeling is finally gone. "For thirty years, I wondered why they stumbled into my store that night. They could've picked any store. Or no store. But it's no different than that guy...from Hiroshima. It's no different than Yamaguchi. We spend our lives thinking history's some arbitrary collection of good and bad moments stirred together in complete randomness. But look at Yamaguchi. When history has your number, there's...there's nowhere on this planet you can run."

He sags sideways, his breathing sputtering as he collapses against the back door.

I kick open my own door, rushing outside. Whatever I think of him, he still needs my help. But as my feet hit the concrete and I reach for his door, my face nearly collides with the chest of the man who's just arrived outside the car and is now blocking my way.

I know he's got ground privileges. He followed the path right back the way he came. To the parking lot across from his building.

"Don't look so scared, Benjamin," Nico says, barely noticing that he's standing in my personal space. "I'm here now. Everything's going to be all right."

93

Y ou need to move," I say to Nico as I try to cut around him to get to the back door of the car.

Nico doesn't budge. Doesn't move. But he does see what I'm looking at. In the backseat. The black man covered in blood.

"I know him," Nico blurts. "He's the barber."

"What?"

"He comes to give haircuts. To Griffin. But sometimes when he leaves—I check. Griffin's hair isn't cut at all. I told them, but they never—"

"Nico, get out of the way!"

"The barber...for you to do this to him...he was watching me, wasn't he? I know their eyes are everywhere."

"Nico..."

"That's why you came back, isn't it? To do this. To protect me..."

"Protect you?"

"I see your razor. In the driver's seat," he says, his eyes flicking back and forth as he dissects the contents of the car. "I see how you killed him."

"That's not—"

"It makes perfect sense," he adds, nodding feverishly. "It's what I said. This was your mission . . . your trial. The test of Benedict Arnold. And you—you—don't you see?—you finally passed, Benjamin! Instead of betraying George Washington, you were given a chance . . . a chance to protect him. *And you did!* You risked your life to protect me!"

Annoyed by the nuttiness, I shove him aside, tear open the back door of the car, and feel for a pulse. Nothing. No heartbeat.

Across the long field that leads back to the medical building, a security guard turns the corner, heading our way.

"You need to go," Nico says to me, eyeing the guard. "They can't know you did this."

"I didn't do anything!" I say, still staring at the barber.

"There's no need to mourn him. He's moved on to his next mission."

"Will you stop? *There is no mission!*" I explode, slapping his hand from my shoulder. "There's no test! There's no trials! There's no George Washington—and stop calling me Benedict Arnold! All that matters is *this*! This, *right here*," I hiss, pointing back at the body of the barber. "I know you and she . . . you *caused* this! I saw the sign-in sheet! I saw Clementine's name! And if it'd help you get out of here, I know you'd do anything, including making your daughter blackmail the Pr—!"

"What'd you call her?"

"Don't tell me you don't know she's your daughter," I challenge.

He takes a half-step back and stands perfectly still. "She told me she was a graduate student. But students...students don't come to see me. That's how I knew," Nico admits, blinking over and over and suddenly looking...he actually looks *concerned*. He opens his mouth to say something, then closes it just as fast. He's fitting his own pieces together. But as his eyes stop blinking and the concern on his face slowly turns to pain, I can't help but think that I have it wrong. Maybe this isn't the father-daughter operation I just thought it was.

"When I fed the cats, Clementine used to— I saw her one Wednesday. When the barber was cutting hair," Nico blurts. "She helped him. She told the barber Griffin's hair looks better when it's long in front. He listened. It made her smile more."

On my right, across the field, the security guard is less than fifty yards away. On my left, down by the front gate, the guardhouse's white-and-orange-striped gate arm rises in the air. A black car pulls up the service road. Someone's just arrived.

"It made me smile more too," Nico adds, barely noticing. "But she heard the barber, didn't she? She heard his confession."

"Nico, you need to get away from here," I tell him as the guard picks up his pace, coming right at us.

"She did this...she caused this, didn't she?" Nico says, motioning to the barber.

On the service road, the black car picks up speed.

"The doctors here...they say I have a sickness," Nico says. "That's what put the evil in my body—the sickness did. And so I prayed—I begged God—I begged God since the first day she came to visit . . . I worried she had it too."

"Nico, get out of here," I insist, tempted to jump in the car and take off. But I don't. The barber's dead—I can't take him with me. But if I stay and try to explain, there's only one place I'm going if they find me with Nico and a bloodied corpse.

"All these years, I knew my fate. I always knew what God chose me for," Nico adds. "But when Clementine came . . . when she reached out to me like that . . . I thought I finally got— I was lucky. Do you know what that means, Benjamin? To be a lucky man?" he asks, his voice cracking.

"Nico, please get out of here," I beg, grabbing my phone from the front seat.

The black car knifes to the left, heading straight for our parking lot.

The security guard is now running.

"But there is no luck, is there, God?" he asks, talking to the sky. "I knew that! I knew it all along! But when I met her . . . when I saw her . . . how could I not hope? How could I not think that I'd finally been blessed—the truest blessing—that despite the sickness inside myself, that You made her different than me." He stares up at the sky, his eyes swollen with tears. "I begged You, God! I begged You to make her different than me!"

"Nico, back to your building! *Now!*" the security guard shouts in the distance.

Behind me, the black car speeds up the service road, its engine roaring.

"*You!* Away from Nico!" the guard yells at me.

There's a loud screech. The black car skids into the parking lot, punting bits of frozen gravel at us. But it's not until the passenger door bursts open that I finally see who's driving.

"Get in! Hurry!" Dallas shouts from behind the steering wheel.

"*Nico, don't you move!*" the guard yells as he reaches the parking lot. That's still his priority.

"Nico, I'll see you next week!" I call out, trying to make it all sound normal as I dart to the black car, which is already pulling away.

As I hop inside and tug the door shut, Dallas kicks the gas and we're off. Behind us, the guard grabs Nico by the arm. The guard looks relieved. Problem solved. That's still the top St. Elizabeths priority. No escapes.

The road isn't long. Within ten seconds, we're rolling past the main gate. Dallas offers a casual wave to the man in the guardhouse. The fact that he waves back tells us the guard in the parking lot still hasn't found the barber's body. Word's not out yet.

"That guy with the knife...the barber—" I say.

"I know. I could hear," Dallas says, holding up his phone as we pull out of the gate and reach the main street. "I think I was able to get most of it on tape."

"Then we should—"

"No," Dallas says, twisting the wheel as we speed toward the highway. "Right now, there's only one place we need to go."

94

From the front seat of the white van that was parked down the block, it wasn't hard to spot Beecher.

Or Dallas.

There are two of them now, the driver of the van thought, watching their black car bounce and rumble as it left St. Elizabeths. Two of them to deal with.

From the look on Beecher's face, he was terrified, still processing. Dallas wasn't doing much better.

It was no different for the driver of the white van.

It had all gone so bad, so quickly.

But there was no choice. That's what Beecher would never understand.

For a moment, the driver reached for the ignition, but then waited, watching as Dallas's car coughed up a small choke of smoke and disappeared up the block.

This wasn't the time to get spotted. More important, the driver wanted to see if anyone else was following.

For a full minute, the driver sat there, watching the street and every other parked car on it. No one moved.

Beyond the front gate, up the main service road that

ran inside St. Elizabeths, there was a swirl of orange sirens. On-campus security. No doubt, Nico was already being medicated for whatever mess the barber's panicking had caused.

The driver was tempted to go up there, but again, there was no choice.

There was never any choice.

Not until the one problem that had caused so many others was dealt with. The problem that she could only blame on herself.

Beecher.

By now, the black car was long gone, zipping toward its destination.

With a deep breath, Clementine pulled out onto the road and did her best to stay calm.

Beecher's head start didn't matter.

Not when she knew exactly where they were going.

95

Four months ago
St. Elizabeths Hospital

The man with the black leather zipper case was never late.

He always came on Thursdays. At 4 p.m. Always right on time.

But as Clementine glanced down at her watch and saw that it was already a few minutes past four...

"Heya, Pam," the older black man with the silver hair and silver mustache called out as he shoved his way through the swinging doors, approached the nurses' station, and eyed one of the many open rooms. Like an ICU, the rooms of the Gero-Psych Unit didn't have any doors. "How's your Thursday?"

"Same as my Wednesday," the nurse replied, adding a flirty laugh and crumpling up the foil wrapper of her California Tortilla burrito.

Over by the sinks, Clementine pretended to fill one of the cats' water dishes as she watched the same exchange she'd witnessed the week before—and so many weeks before that. By now, she knew his patterns. That's how she knew when to send her dad upstairs for more cat food. She knew the old black man wouldn't be late. Like all barbers, he knew the value of keeping an appointment.

"They ready for me?" the barber asked.

"Not like they got much choice," the nurse added along with another flirty laugh.

Dumping and refilling the same water bowl and strategically using the room's pillars to stay out of sight, Clementine watched as the barber unzipped the leather case that held his sharpened scissors. It had been nearly two months since she first saw him enter the unit, saying he was there to give haircuts to patients. No reason to look twice at that—until Clementine noticed that although he rotated through a few of the rooms, he always finished with the exact same patient:

The guy with the tattoo of the eight-ball.

Clementine tried not to think about it. She didn't want to be a suspicious person, or assume the worst about people. But as she learned when her mom was lying there in hospice and finally told Clemmi her father's real name, there are certain traits that God puts in each of us. There's no escaping them.

It's who we are.

Indeed, when Clementine first peered across the unit and into the room, she couldn't help but notice how the barber, with his back to her, was standing next to Eightball's bed, clutching the bed's guardrail as if he needed it to stand. He wasn't cutting Eightball's hair.

His hands didn't move...his shoulders were slumped. He was crying. And more than anything else, that's what drew Clementine to take that first step toward them.

She told herself she wasn't trying to pry—she was just hoping to console him—but as she neared the room, she heard those two words that made her stop midstep. The two words that forced her to cock her head and look twice at the barber, and that had her coming back week after week to fill in the rest of the story. Two simple words: *Orson Wallace*.

From that moment, Clementine knew she'd never mention it to Nico. She still hadn't told him she was his daughter—and there were plenty of reasons for hiding that. So she certainly wasn't going to tell him this. Indeed, over the next few months, as she eventually put together the full picture, Clementine knew that what she'd been witnessing was far more than just a simple visit from a barber. What she'd been given was a chance. A real chance to answer the original questions she'd come searching for—to find out the things even her father didn't know.

With the changes in her body and everything she was going through—was it really such a sin to want to know the truth?

"Laurent here," the barber said today, flipping open his cell phone and pacing back and forth in Eightball's small room. "Yeah. I can do it tonight or first thing tomorrow. Just tell me when."

Dumping and refilling the cat's water bowl for the fifth or sixth time, Clementine listened carefully to every detail she could hear. She knew she was getting close. She knew about Wallace and his group of Plumbers, who were running errands for him. Of course, there was only so much one could get from eavesdropping. She had no idea what Minnie did with the baseball bat—or about how Palmiotti held Eightball down while Wallace worked on his face with his car keys. But she did know the Plumbers were helping him hide Eightball. No way could Wallace afford to let that get out. And best of all, after all this time, she knew where the barber was talking about.

"Same place?" the barber asked. "At the Archives?"

Ducking back toward the sink, Clementine had heard him mention the Archives before.

"I found a salmon flavor," Nico interrupted, reentering the room with a big bag of Meow Mix cat food under his arm. "They like salmon flavor."

Across the unit, the barber shut his phone, knowing better than to make eye contact with Nico. Clementine stayed by the sink, so as to not look out of place.

"Anything we're forgetting?" Nico called out to Clementine.

"I don't think so," she replied, shutting off the water and stealing one last glance at Eightball's room. She was definitely getting close. And as she thought about it, if she needed to, she even had a way to get into the Archives. That guy whose name she saw on the high school page. On Facebook.

Beecher.

For a moment, she felt that familiar pang of guilt. It

didn't last long. If she'd learned anything during this time with her father…There was no avoiding it. Or escaping it.

This was who she was—or at least who she had to be…if she wanted to find the truth.

"I think we're set," Clementine said, balancing the full bowl of water as she followed her dad back outside. "I've got everything we need."

96

D on't say those words to me," Tot warned, gripping the receiver at his desk.

"Will you just listen?" Khazei asked through the phone.

"Do you know where Beecher is or not?"

"Don't blame this on me. You said Dallas's car was tagged last night—that all I had to do was track them on GPS."

"That *is* all you had to do. In fact, isn't that why you went racing to St. Elizabeths? To find them?" Tot asked. "So are they there or not?"

"The car's here, sure. But you should see what else is here—sirens swirling…there's no going in or out—total lockdown. As I pulled up, they had half their security force gathered around Dallas's car that Beecher drove here. So yes, that gray car is still in the same GPS spot as it was a half hour ago. But I'm telling you, Tot—there's no Beecher…no Clementine…no one's here."

Glancing out the plate glass window of his office, Tot stared down at Pennsylvania Avenue, then tightened his focus so that all he saw was his own gray beard in his reflection. "Something's wrong."

"Do not panic on this."

"You're not listening. Something's wrong, and Beecher's gone," Tot insisted. "And the only way we're salvaging this is if we somehow find him."

"That's fine. You're the one who knows him so well. Tell me what's next?"

Tot thought about it for a moment. He thought about it again. And for the first time in a long time, he had no idea.

97

S he hasn't said *yes* yet?" the President challenged.

"It's not that simple," the young aide replied as they rode up in the White House elevator.

"It *is* that simple, son—you ask a girl out, she says yes or she says no," Wallace teased, tossing a wink at the usher who ran the elevator. "You want me to issue an executive order for you? I'll handwrite it on the good stationery: *Go out with my aide Patrick, or face formal charges. Signed—Me.*"

The young aide forced a laugh, pretending he hadn't heard the joke fifty times before. He didn't mind, though. Like any job, everyone's happy when the boss is in a good mood.

The elevator door unclenched on the second floor of the White House Residence, and as the President made a sharp right up the hallway, the aide knew that mood was about to get even better.

"You tell him who he's eating with?" the usher in the elevator whispered to the aide.

"Why you think he's walking so fast?"

At the far end of the hallway, the President spotted the small antique Georgian serving table that every day would hold a silver tray filled with small place-cards, each one in the shape of a thin, pointed collar-stay that was made of fine thick paper. On each one would be a calligraphed name, and the way the place-cards were organized in two neat columns—that same order would be the seating assignment for the day's presidential lunch.

Today, however, there were no place-cards.

No seating chart.

No calligraphed names.

"Okay, who's ready for mac and cheese?" Wallace called out playfully, clapping his hands together as he made a final sharp right and entered the narrow Family Dining Room, with its pale yellow walls and long mahogany table.

On most days, there'd be two dozen people gathered here.

Today, the table was set for two. Him and Andrew.

"No mac and cheese," announced a disappointed eight-year-old boy with a mess of brown hair and glowing gray eyes. Just like his father's. "They said we can't."

"*Who* says we can't?" the President challenged.

Just outside the dining room—and knowing better than to come inside—the nanny who was in charge of Wallace's son shook her head. Wallace knew that look. Andrew had mac and cheese last night. And probably the night before that.

"He'll live," Wallace said. "Two mac and cheeses."

As young Andrew's gray eyes lit up, Wallace couldn't even pretend to contain his own smile.

"Chocolate milk too?" the boy asked.

"Don't push it," Wallace teased.

It was tough being President. But it was even tougher being a father in the White House. So at least once a week—or at the very least every other week—there was an uninterrupted meal with no staff, no scheduling, no briefings, no press, no VIPs, and no Members of Congress who will vote your way if you invite them to have lunch with you at the White House.

Some days, the Family Dining Room had to be for just that. Family.

With a playful shoo of his hand, the President got rid of the nanny and the other staffers, closed the door to the dining room, and flicked off the lights.

"Dad, I got two new ones—and found the one where they're plumbers." Andrew beamed, flipping open his laptop and angling it so they could both see. With the push of a button, a black-and-white episode of *The Three Stooges* started playing onscreen.

As President, Wallace knew he could use the White House movie theater downstairs. But as a father, just as he'd done long before he won the election, there was nothing better than being hunched over some mac and cheese, watching the classics with his son.

Kuuk-kuuk-kuuk.

Someone knocked on the door.

Wallace turned, all set to unleash on his staff—until the door opened and he saw who was knocking.

"It'll take only a second," Dr. Palmiotti said.

The President shot him a look that would need ice later. Sliding inside, Palmiotti didn't care.

"Sorry, Andrew—I'll be fast," the doctor added, trying to sound upbeat. "It's about your haircut," he told the President.

As Palmiotti leaned to whisper in his ear, Wallace knew lunch was over.

"I'm on this. I'm taking care of it. And I'm sorry," Palmiotti whispered. "He's gone. They found him dead. Slit wrists."

Nodding as if he were hearing a baseball score, the President stared across the table at his eight-year-old son.

"Y'have to go now, don't you?" the boy asked his father as Palmiotti left the room.

"You kidding?" the President asked, reaching for the laptop and hitting the play button himself. "What kinda dad misses mac and cheese with his boy?"

As the theme music began and Moe, Larry, and Curly jumped around onscreen, Wallace sat there in the semi-dark room, listening to his son laugh hysterically, while trying hard not to think about the dead friend he'd known since he was nearly the same age as his boy.

98

Y ou don't have to come if you don't want to," Dallas says.

"I'm coming," I tell him. "It's just— The caves?" I ask from the passenger seat. "They're far."

"They're in Pennsylvania," Dallas says, gripping the steering wheel with both hands. "We just cut through Maryland and the facility's right there."

I know where he's talking about. In our downtown building, we house nearly one billion documents. There're another 3.2 billion out in College Park, Maryland. And there's overflow storage in places like Suitland, Maryland, whose building is the size of more than twenty football fields and houses over 6.4 billion documents. But since the most important issue—and biggest cost—surrounding document storage is room temperature, the Archives saves millions of dollars each year by using the natural cold of underground caves all across the country, from Lee's Summit, Missouri, to Lenexa, Kansas, to, in the case of documents coming in from Ohio, the caves in Boyers, Pennsylvania.

"Can I ask you one last question?" I say, my eyes catching my own reflection in the windshield. "When you were back at the office...why'd you pick up my phone?"

"What?"

"Before. After we left the cemetery. You went back to the office; I was going back to see Nico. You said they called. You said you spoke to Mr. Harmon yourself," I add, referring to the guy from Presidential Records who I called from the cemetery. "You said that while they didn't find anything in Wallace's old college records—"

"Which I said they wouldn't."

"—I was still right about one thing: Our Archives staff collects every document from every place Wallace ever visited, including elementary school, junior high, and...even the records from the hospital he was born at."

"But do you understand what happened, Beecher? That hospital—sure, it's great that they have the President's birth records. But when Mr. Harmon started digging, he also found another file with Wallace's name on it: for a broken finger that Wallace had treated in the emergency room *twenty-six years ago*. That means that emergency room—"

"—is the same emergency room they took Eightball to that night. I know. The barber told me they were there. I know what happened."

"I'm sure you do. But every word that barber said to you—from Minnie being the one to swing that bat, to Wallace covering it up to protect his sister, to transferring Eightball and keeping him hidden all these years, to however Clementine found out about it and started black-mailing them—y'know what that amounts to? *Nothing*. Not a single thing, Beecher. Every word that barber said is hearsay from a dead man. If you go and shout it in public, you'll get about as far as any other Kennedy con-spiracy nut who swears that Jack Ruby whispered all his secrets from his jail cell. But. If we get these hospital records, you have the one thing—*the only thing*—that works when you're going up against a sitting President. Proof. That file is *proof*, Beecher. Proof that Wallace was there that night. That file in Pennsylvania will save your life."

I know Dallas is right. And I know when it comes to the massive piles of incoming records, our office won't fax them or scan them until they're officially processed, which starts with the vital documents and takes years to work its way down to something as small as a child-hood broken finger. Yet…"You're not answering my question," I say, still locked on our reflection in the wind-shield. "You said Mr. Harmon *called*. That you spoke to him yourself. But when we were at the cemetery, I didn't give Mr. Harmon *your* number. I gave him mine."

Dallas turns, cocky as ever.

"And that's what you're all sulky about? That I picked up your phone? You were already at St. Elizabeths—I was back in the office and heard it ringing—so yeah, of course I picked it up. Considering what happened, you're lucky I did."

I nod. It's a perfect explanation. But it doesn't lift my mood.

"How're you not thrilled?" Dallas asks. "This is gonna be the nail for the coffin."

"I've already seen the coffins! Two men are dead! Orlando...and now this barber— He came to me! The barber came to me and died in front of me! All because of— Because she—" I stay with the reflection, trying hard not to see myself.

Outside, the sun argues with the snow that lines both sides of I-270. A brown-and-white highway sign tells me we're nearing Hagerstown and the Pennsylvania border. But I'm still staring at my own reflection.

"You didn't cause those deaths, Beecher. And just so you actually hear it: She wasn't exploiting your weakness. She was counting on your strength."

"What're you talking about?"

"What Clementine did—the only reason she was able to pull it off—was because you're someone who helps people. And that's a good thing."

"It doesn't feel so good right now," I say as I again replay every single moment over the past two days. The only thing that's worse is how easily she pulled it off. For Clementine to have everything that the barber confessed to Eightball...for her to somehow figure out all the Plumber details...and when we first were in the SCIF...I don't think she *found* that old dictionary. I think she was actually sneaking it in, but then when the coffee got spilled, she had to improvise...

"Listen, I know she and Nico stabbed you plenty deep—"

"No. Don't blame Nico for this. You didn't see him—

the way he reacted... Nico's not in this. And I know it's hard to believe because he's such a nutface, but when you listen to him—there was one thing Nico was always right about." Up above, the sun blinds me. But not for long. "Nico said we're all here for a reason. He's not wrong. So when this is done—when Clementine's captured, and Orlando's family has their answers, and we tell the world the real story about the President—"

"You don't have to say it, Beecher. They're watching," Dallas says, leaning hard on the word *they*, which is how he always refers to the Culper Ring. "They'll make sure you're taken care of."

I nod, pretending that's what I'm really after.

"So I assume they're the ones who gave you this car?" I ask.

"And the gray one too," Dallas says.

"Yeah, I was thinking about that. So I shouldn't be worried that the barber's body is still sitting in it?"

"If Jesus himself came down and searched that car, he'd still never be able to trace it."

"I drove it on the grounds. They're not going to link it to me?"

"They said not to worry about that either."

"So that's it? The Culper Ring just waves their hands and magically takes care of it all?"

"It's not magic, Beecher. It's loyalty. Loyalty and efficiency. They'll get there well before the cops, and then... well... think of what you're seeing with Wallace and Palmiotti. Especially in this town, never underestimate the power of loyalty."

"I'm not. That's why, when everything settles…" I take a breath and think again about that guy from Hiroshima. "I want to be introduced."

"What're you talking about?"

"To them. To the Culper Ring. When this is all done, I want in."

"Beecher, I know you've got a lot of adrenaline flowing…"

"This isn't adrenaline. And don't think it's some silly revenge fantasy either. I know what Clementine did to me. I know I let her do it. But when I was in that car at St. Elizabeths—when I thought the barber was about to take that knife and slit my throat—I kept waiting for my life to flash in front of my eyes…or for some hypersensitivity, or slow motion, or whatever the other clichés are, to kick in. But instead, all I could think was that it felt…*right*. Does that make sense?"

"It doesn't make any sense at all."

"I don't mean *right* that I was about to be murdered. I mean *right* that, when I was in that spot…when I was in that danger…I felt like I was shaken awake. After Iris…after everything she made me feel…I made a decision and went to sleep. Do you know what that's like— trying to go to sleep, and lose yourself in the hopes of burying the worst fears in your life? It was the one thing Clementine didn't lie about: I wasn't in love with the past. I was terrified of my own future—and then when Clementine came along, I thought she was my second chance. But she's not. *This* is. I want my second chance. It's like my life finally makes sense."

"That's still the adrenaline speaking."

"It's not adrenaline. It's what we're here for, Dallas. It's what I thought I was here for, but instead...Do you know how many years I've spent staring into old books and thinking I was touching history? But that's not where history is." I look at the rearview and lean to the side until I again see myself. All this time, I thought Clementine was the one reviving me. But when your world feels dead, there's only one person who can bring you back to life.

"I can do this, Dallas."

"I'm sure you can. You can do lots of things. But this isn't what you're meant for."

"You're not listening to me," I say, giving him a good long stare. "Look at my life. I'm tired of doing what I'm meant for."

From the driver's seat, Dallas peers my way, using his top teeth to chew the few beard hairs below his bottom lip.

"I can do it," I insist. "I'm ready."

He doesn't say a word.

And then, as we race for the caves...and for the proof...and for the records that will end this mess, he finally does.

"Y'know what, Beecher? I think you're right."

99

Carla Lee knew it was going to be a bad day. She knew it when her two-year-old son woke up at 5:40 in the morning all excited to play. She knew it when the little yellow tub of margarine for her morning English muffin was completely empty, even though her husband had put it back in the fridge. And she knew it when she was racing back from her 3 p.m. meetings and saw the dead animal on Franklin Road.

She'd seen dead animals before on the highway. In these parts of western Pennsylvania, there were always deer and foxes and loads of unlucky possums. Carla had even stopped for a few (she was a dog owner—she couldn't just ride past if it was a dog). But here, on Franklin Road, which was hilly and rarely traveled, if you did see a dead animal, it never looked like this.

Carla couldn't see the fur anymore—couldn't even tell what kind of creature it was. The animal was— Carla squinted as she veered around the tight curve in her banged-up maroon Camry. There was no other way to say it. The animal was run-through. Run-through over and over again. People probably couldn't even see it if they were coming fast around the turn. But Carla was a mother. With three kids. And a sweet Maltese that peed on the floor every time someone came in the door. It'd been years since she went fast around the turns.

For that reason, she had a perfect view of the poor creature that was a mess of twisted red and black organs covered in flies.

For Carla, the mother and Maltese owner, that was the worst part of her bad day—being stuck with that image in her head.

She couldn't shake the image as she turned onto Brachton Road.

She couldn't shake it as she pulled into the enormous employee parking lot that sat across the road from the underground storage facility known as Copper Mountain.

And as she left her car, stepped into the cold wind that was whipping off the nearby Pennsylvania hills, and rushed for the arriving white school bus that served as the employee shuttle, she still saw that mess of red and black.

It was that image, still floating in her mind, that took all of her attention as she and her fellow employees packed together to get on board the arriving bus.

It was because she was thinking of that image that Carla didn't even notice, in the usual crush to get on the bus, the young black-haired woman standing so close behind her.

"Please—go ahead—you were first," Clementine said, flashing a warm smile and motioning politely.

"Thanks," Carla replied, climbing aboard without

even noticing how much Clementine's hair and overall coloring matched her own.

Within minutes, the white school bus rolled through security and pulled up to the main entrance at the mouth of the cave. After all these years, Carla was used to working underground. But as they entered the cave, and a long slow shadow crept across the roof of the bus and swallowed the remaining daylight, Carla felt that familiar wiggle in her belly. Spotting the armed guards that always greeted them as they stepped off the shuttle, she then reached into her purse, fished for her ID, and—

"Craparoo," she whispered to herself. "I need to go back," Carla called out to the bus driver.

"Everything okay?" Clementine asked.

"Yeah. I think I just left my ID in my car."

"I do that all the time," Clementine said, heading for the front of the bus, where she took out the ID she'd lifted from Carla's purse, flashed it at the guard, and followed the other employees along the concrete path into Copper Mountain.

Carla Lee was definitely having a bad day.

But Clementine, so far, was having a great one.

Especially if they'd found the file she was looking for.

100

It's under us," Dallas says.

"Whattya mean?" I ask.

"The place. The caves," Dallas explains as the narrow two-lane road sends us rising and falling and rising again over yet another set of low twisting hills, which are getting harder to see as the 4 p.m. sky grows dark. "That's why the road's like this. I think the caves are right under us."

I nod, staring down at my phone, which casts a pale blue glow in the car and is still getting enough signal for me to search the websites of all the D.C. TV stations to see if anyone's covering the story.

I search for Nico's name...for my name...even for the word *homicide* or *murder*. Nothing. No mention of St. Elizabeths, no mention of a dead barber, and most important, no mention of me being wanted as a fugitive.

"Now do you understand why no one's heard of us in two hundred years?" Dallas asks, once again trying to put me at ease. It almost works—until I gaze out at the snow-covered trees and we blow past the red, white, and blue road sign with the picture of George Washington.

Welcome to the Washington Trail—1753

It's silly and a meaningless coincidence, but I can't help but imagine Nico's joy if he knew that we were driving the same path that George Washington marched on back in 1753.

"Beecher, stop thinking what you're thinking," Dallas warns.

"You have no idea what I'm thinking."

"I saw the sign. It's not an omen."

"I never said it was an omen."

Dallas hears my tone. He believes me. "Though it is kinda haunted house," he admits.

"It's definitely haunted house," I say with a nod.

With a few quick turns, Dallas weaves us deeper into the hills, where at every curve in the road the nearest tree has a red reflector sunk into its trunk. Out here, the roads don't have lights, which we need even more as the winter sky grows black.

"You sure this is right?" I ask.

Before he can answer, my phone vibrates in my hand. Caller ID tells me who it is.

"Tot?" Dallas asks.

I nod. It's the fourth time he's called in the last few hours. I haven't picked up once. The last thing I need is for him to fish and potentially figure out where we are.

As we round the final curve, the hills level out and

a brand-new glow blinds us in the distance, forcing us to squint. Straight ahead, giant metal floodlights dot the long field that stretches out in front of us. A familiar churn in my stomach tells me what my eyes can't see.

"This is it, isn't it?"

Dallas doesn't answer. He's staring at a white bus that slowly rumbles through the brightly lit parking lot on our left.

The only other sign of life is a fluorescent red triangle that looks like a corporate logo and is set into a haystack-sized man-made hill and serves as the sole welcome mat. You don't come this way unless you know what you're looking for.

Just past the red triangle, at the only intersection for miles, a narrow paved road slopes down to the left, toward a high-tech check-in building, then keeps going until it dead-ends at the base of the nearby stone cliffside that surrounds the little canyon that we're now driving in.

But as we make the left toward the check-in building, it's clear that the road doesn't dead-end. It keeps going, into a black archway that looks like a train tunnel, inside the cliff and down underground.

"Stay in your car! I'm coming to you," a guard calls out in a flat western Pennsylvania accent, appearing from nowhere and pointing us away from the check-in building and toward a small freestanding guardhouse that looks more like a construction shed.

I look again to my right. There are two more sheds and a bunch of workers wearing hard hats. The check-in building is still under construction.

"Here...right here," the guard says, motioning us into place outside the security shed—and into view of its two different security cameras. "Welcome to Copper Mountain," he adds as Dallas rolls down his window. "I assume you got an appointment?"

101

Racing in the golf cart, our hair blows in a swirl as Dallas and I whip down one of the cave's long cavities.

"…just so glad to have you both here," gushes Gina Paul, our driver, a short, overfriendly woman with a pointy-beak nose, smoker's breath, and straight blonde hair that's pulled back so tight, it acts as a facelift.

"I'm sorry it's such short notice," I tell her.

"Short notice…it's fine. Short notice is fine," she says as I realize she's just like my aunt who repeats everything you say. Her nametag says she's an account manager, but I don't need that to know she's in sales. "So, so great to finally meet you, Beecher," she adds even though she doesn't mean it.

She doesn't care who I am.

But she does care where I work.

Fifty years ago, this cave was one of Pennsylvania's largest limestone mines. But when the limestone ran dry, Copper Mountain, Inc., bought its 1,100 acres of tunnels and turned it into one of the most secure off-site storage areas on the eastern seaboard.

And one of the most profitable.

That's a fact not lost on Gina, who, by how fast this golf cart is now moving, realizes just how much money the National Archives spends here every year.

We're not the only ones.

The narrow thin cavern is about as wide as a truck, and on our right a painted red steel door is set deep into the rock, like a hanging red tooth on a jack-o'-lantern. Above the door, a military flag hangs down from the ceiling. I know the logo. *U.S. Army*. As the golf cart picks up speed, there's another door fifty yards down from that— and another flag hanging from the ceiling. *Marines*.

It's the same the entire stretch of the cavern: red steel door after red steel door after red steel door. *Air Force. Navy. Department of Defense.*

"I'm surprised they put their names on them," Dallas says as we pass one for the FBI.

"Those are the rooms they want you to see," Gina says with a laugh. "We've got over twenty-two miles of tunnels back here. You don't want to know how much more space they've got."

I pretend to laugh along, but as we go deeper into the cave I can't take my eyes off the ceiling, which seems to be getting lower.

"You're not imagining things," Gina says. "It *is* getting lower."

Dallas shoots me a look to see if I'm okay.

Throughout the cavern, the jagged rock walls are

painted white, and there are fluorescent lights hung everywhere, presumably to make it feel more like a workplace instead of an anthill.

To my surprise, it works.

On our right, two employees wait at an ATM that's built into the rock. Next to that, there's a red awning over a fully functioning store called the "Roadway Café."

I thought being this far underground would feel like I was being buried. Instead...

"You've got a full-blown city down here," Dallas says as we pass a new group of construction workers—this one putting the finishing touches on an area that holds vending machines.

"Almost three thousand employees. Think of us as the Empire State Building lying on its side and buried three hundred feet underground. We got a full-service post office...our own water treatment plant to make the toilets work...even good food in the cafeteria—though of course, it's all brought in. There's no cooking permitted on site. We get a fire and—forget burning the files that're stored down here—y'know what kinda death trap we'd be standing in?" she asks with a laugh.

Neither Dallas nor I laugh back—especially as we both look up and notice the cargo netting that's now running along the length of the ceiling and keeping stray rocks, cracked stalactites, and what feels like the entire cavern from collapsing on our heads. Back by the café and the ATM, we were in the cave's version of Times Square. But as the employees thin out and we head deeper into the catacombs, this is clearly one of its darker alleys.

"Home sweet home," Gina says, flicking on the golf cart's lights.

Straight ahead, it looks like the cave dead-ends. But as the golf cart's lights blink awake, there's no missing the yellow police tape that keeps people from turning the corner, or the enormous red, white, and blue eagle—part of the National Archives logo—that's painted directly on the cave wall. Above the eagle's head is a partially unrolled scroll with the words: *Littera Scripta Manet*, the Archives motto that translates as "The Written Word Endures."

Damn right it does, I think to myself, hopping out of the golf cart and darting for the bright red door that serves as the entrance to the Archives' underground storage facility.

102

Anything else I can help with?" Gina calls out, standing in the cave, outside the threshold of the open red door.

"I think we're fine," I tell her.

Dallas is already inside the storage unit.

I'm anxious to follow.

Gina never leaves her spot. As a sales rep, she's in charge of clearing our visit with Mr. Harmon and the Presidential Records Office, checking our IDs, and even putting in the six-digit code that opens the steel door (and the secondary door that sits just behind that). But without the necessary security clearance, she can't join us in here.

"Both doors open from the inside," she assures us as the cold air pours out from the room. Just inside the door, I take a quick glance at the hygrothermograph on the wall. The temperature is at a brisk fifty-eight degrees, which is colder than we usually keep it.

"If you think of anything else, just gimme a call," she adds, tapping the leather phone holster on her hip. Reading my expression, she says, "Reception's great. We've got cell towers throughout."

Her point hits home as my own phone starts to vibrate.

As I glance down, caller ID tells me it's Tot. Again.

"I should grab this," I say to Gina, who nods a quick goodbye, keenly aware of when a client needs privacy.

As the red steel door slams shut and my phone continues to vibrate, I spin toward our destination and step through the second door, where the damp darkness of the cave has been replaced by an enormous bright white room that's as big as an airplane hangar and as sterile as our preservation staff can possibly manage. In truth, it's just a taller, brighter version of our stacks in D.C., filled with row after row of metal shelves. But instead of just books and archive boxes, the specially designed shelves are also packed with plastic boxes and metal canisters that hold old computer tape, vintage film, and thousands upon thousands of negatives of old photographs.

There's a reason this stuff is here instead of in Washington. Part of it's the cold temperature (which is better for film). Part of it's cost (which is better for our budget). But part of it—especially the archive boxes that are locked in the security cage on my left—is what we call "geographical separation." It's one of the National Archives' most vital—and least known—tasks. If there's ever a terrorist attack that turns Washington into a fireball, we're fully ready with the documents and paperwork to make sure our most vital institutions survive.

But as I step into the room, the only survival I'm really worried about is my own.

"You find it yet?" I call to Dallas, who's racing up the center aisle, checking record group numbers on each row of shelves that he passes.

His only answer is a sharp right turn as he disappears down one of the far rows in back. We're definitely close.

My phone vibrates for the fourth time, about to kick to voicemail. I have no idea if Tot knows where we are. But now that he can't get in the way, it'd probably be smart to find out.

"Beecher here," I answer, waiting to see how long it takes him to fish.

"Where the hell are you?" Tot asks. "I left you half a dozen messages!"

"I didn't get them. I'm just…it's been a crazy day."

"Don't. I know when you're lying, Beecher. Where are you? Who're you with?"

I take a moment to think about a response. Even through the phone, I swear I feel Tot's good eye picking me apart. "Tot, you need to—-"

"Are you still with Clementine? I thought she left after the cemetery."

I pause. "How'd you know I was at a cemetery?"

"Because I'm not an idiot like the rest of the idiots you seem to be in love with!"

"Wait…time out. Did you have someone following me!?"

Before he can answer, my phone beeps. I look down and recognize the number. It's the only person who could possibly take me away from this one.

"Tot, hold on a sec."

"Don't you hang up on me!"

With a click, I put him on hold.

"*Mr. Harmon?*" I ask the man in Presidential Records who not only helped us get into the cave but also knows exactly what document we're looking for. "I-Is everything okay?"

"That's my question for *you*," he says, though his tone surprisingly seems softer and more helpful than usual. That's all I need to be suspicious. "Everything going okay down there?"

"It's ... we're fine." I pause a moment, confused. "Is there a reason we *shouldn't* be fine?"

"Not at all," he says, back to his military matter-of-factness. "Just making sure you got there. I'd asked the Copper Mountain folks to stay a little later when I heard you lost the directions."

"When I lost the *what*?"

"The directions I sent. Your secretary said—"

"My secretary?"

"The woman who called. She said you lost the directions."

Up on my left, back in the stacks, there's a metal *thunk*. The problem is, Dallas is all the way down on my right.

According to the hygrothermograph, it's still a cool fifty-eight degrees. But suddenly the long white room feels like an oven. Clearly we're not alone in here.

"Mr. Harmon, let me call you right back," I say, hanging up the phone.

"*Dallas, we got problems!*" I shout, racing up the aisle and clicking back to Tot.

"Wait—you're with *Dallas*!?" Tot asks, hearing the last bits through the phone.

"Tot, this isn't—!"

"Beecher, you don't know what you're doing!"

"You're wrong! For once, I know exactly what I'm doing!"

"*Pay attention!*" Tot explodes. "I know what Clementine did…I know her grandmother's long dead…I even know how she did it! We got the tox report—they found a dose of oral chemo in Orlando's blood, even though he never had cancer. That's how she poisoned him—she put it in his coffee! Now where in God's name are you so I can get you someplace safe?"

My brain kicks hard, fighting to find the right places for each new puzzle piece. What's amazing is how quickly each one fits.

"Where are you, Beecher?" Tot asks again.

There's a part of me that knows to stay quiet. It's the same part that has kept Tot at arm's length since the night I went out to Clementine's house. But no matter how easy it is to paint him as the enemy, the one picture I can't shake is the one from three years ago, at lunch in our dungeony cafeteria, when Tot finally trusted me enough to tell me about the first night, after fifty years, that he slept alone in his house after his wife died. He said he couldn't bring himself to sleep under those covers as long as she wasn't there.

I don't care what anyone says. There are some things that can't be lied about.

"Tot, listen to me: I think Clementine is here. With us."

"What're you talking about? Where's *here*? Who're you with besides Dallas?"

"Them. The Culper Ring."

I hear him take a deep breath.

"You need to get out of there, Beecher."

"We are...we're about to," I say as I reach the back of the room and spot Dallas down one of the rows. He's on his knees, rummaging through a cardboard file box—a new box—that's marked *Wallace/Hometown* in thick Magic Marker. "We're just getting—"

"Forget the Culper Ring. *Get out of there!*"

"But don't you see? You were right about them. Dallas brought me in and—"

"Dallas *isn't in* the Culper Ring!"

Turning the corner, I hit the brakes, knocking a square file box from the shelf. As it tumbles and hits the concrete floor, it vomits sheets of paper in a wide fan.

"What'd you say?" I ask.

"Dallas isn't in the Culper Ring. He never *was*."

"How do you know?"

Tot takes another breath, his voice more of a grumble than a whisper. "Because *I'm* in the Culper Ring, Beecher. And I swear to you—the moment he finds what he's looking for, Dallas is going to end your life."

At the end of the row, down on his knees and flipping through one particular file, Dallas looks my way and peers over his scratched black reading glasses. "Y'okay, Beecher?" he calls out. "You don't look so good."

103

I-I'm great," I tell Dallas, who quickly turns back to the file he's flipping through.

"Turn around and walk away from him!" Tot barks through the phone. "Dallas has been in the Plumbers from the start—his uncle is Ronald Cobb, the President's law school pal, who used to work at the Archives and got Dallas the job here! That's why they picked him!"

It makes no sense. If that's the case, why'd Dallas bring me here? But before I can ask it—

"If you think I'm lying, at least get out of there," Tot adds. "At the very worst, I keep you alive!"

I take a few steps back, my body still in shock. It's like staring at your reflection in the back of a spoon. In front of me, the spoon flattens—the distortion fades—and life slowly becomes crystal clear. Since the start of this, I've learned how good the Culper Ring was at keeping secrets...how they protect us like a big *outer ring* without ever revealing their existence...and how hard they've worked to shut down corrupt Presidents like Nixon or Wallace when they start their own private, self-serving *inner rings* like the Plumbers. But last night, within the first three minutes of being in that safehouse, Dallas spilled every secret, revealed his own membership, and took control of my entire search for the Plumbers, including making sure that I stopped sharing with Tot.

I thought it was for my own good.

But if what Tot says is true...if Tot's the one in the Culper Ring and Dallas has been lying...the only ones who really benefited were Wallace...Palmiotti...and...

"This is it...!" Dallas shouts, excitedly pulling out a few sheets of paper and slapping the file folder shut. "We got it, Beech. *Here it is!*" Closing the file box, he shoves it back on the shelf and rushes right at me.

"*Get away from him, Beecher!*" Tot yells in my ear.

Dallas stops right in front of me, the hospital file clutched at his side.

"Who're you talking to?" Dallas asks, pointing to my phone and sliding his reading glasses back into his jacket pocket.

"*He found the file? Do not let him have that!*" Tot adds as another noise—this one louder, a metal thud—erupts from this side of the stacks. Whoever's in here, they're getting closer.

"That noise...you think that's Clementine?" Dallas asks, sidestepping past me and racing into the main aisle, back toward the door. What Tot said first is still my best move. I can deal with Dallas later. Right now, though, I need to get out of here.

"*Watch him, Beecher!*" Tot says in my ear as we pick up speed.

With each row we pass, I glance down each one. Empty. Empty. Empty again.

The air feels frozen as we run. It doesn't stop the even colder sweat that's crawling up my back.

The red doors are just a few feet away.

We pass another empty row. And another.

"Do we need a code to get out!?" Dallas asks.

"She said it opens from—"

Kuh-kunk.

The metal door flies wide as Dallas rams it with his hip. It's the same for the next door, the outer red door, which whips open, dumping us both back into the dusty air and poor lighting of the cave. We're still moving, skidding, slowing down. It takes a moment for my eyes to adjust to the dark.

That's the reason we don't see who's standing there, waiting for us.

There's a soft click. Like the hammer on a gun.

"Put the phone down, Beecher," she says, and I drop it to the ground. To make sure Tot's gone, she picks it up and hangs up the phone herself.

I was wrong. She wasn't inside. She was out here the whole time.

"I'm sorry. I really am," Clementine adds as she points her gun at Dallas's face, then over to mine. "But I need to know what they did to my dad."

104

Y ou really think I believe a word you're saying?" I ask, my eyes narrowing on Clementine's gun.

"She's a liar," Dallas agrees. "Whatever she's about to tell you, she's a liar."

"Don't let Dallas confuse you," Clementine says. "You know what's true…you met Nico yourself. They ruined him, Beecher. They ruined my dad's life."

"You think that excuses everything you did? You killed Orlando! And then that lying…exploiting our friendship…!" I shout, hoping it's loud enough for someone to hear.

There's a small group of employees all the way down by the cave's cafeteria. They don't even turn. They're too far.

She points with her gun, motioning us around the corner as we duck under the yellow police tape with the word *Caution* written across it. Back here, the lights are dimmer than those in the main cavity. From the piles of metal shelving on our right, and the rolls of cable wire piled up on our left, it looks like this section of the cave is mostly used for maintenance and storage. No one's hearing us back here.

My brain whips back to our old schoolyard and when she tied that jump rope around Vincent Paglinni's neck. Two days ago, when Clementine saw her father, I thought the girl who was always prepared was finally undone. But I was wrong. As always, she was prepared for everything.

"Beecher, before you judge," she says. "I swear to you... I tried telling you the truth."

"When was that? Before or after you hired someone to play your dead grandmother?"

"I didn't hire anyone! Nan's the woman I live with— the landlord's mother-in-law. Instead of paying rent, I take care of her!"

"Then why'd you say she's your grandmother?"

"I didn't, Beecher! That's what *you* said! And then— You cared so much about it, and I just wanted— You have no idea what's at stake."

"That's your response!? You're not even pregnant, are you? That was just to suck my sympathy and lead me along!"

"I didn't tell her to blurt that! She saw me throwing up and that's what she thought! The woman hates me!"

"You still let me believe some old woman was your dead grandmother! You understand how sick that is?"

"Don't say that."

"You're sick just like Nico!"

"*Don't say that!*" she erupts.

"*You killed my friend!*" I erupt right back. "You murdered Orlando! You're a murderer just like your crazy-ass father!"

She shakes her head over and over, but it's not in anger. The way her chin is tucked down to her chest, she can't look up at me. "I-I didn't mean to," she pleads. "I didn't think he would die."

"Then why'd you bring that chemo with you!? I know how you did it—don't say it's an accident, Clementine! You came in the building with that chemo in your pocket—or was the real plan to use that on me?"

"It wasn't meant for anyone," she says, her voice lower than ever.

"Then why'd you bring it!?"

Her nostrils flare.

"Clementine..."

"Why do you think I brought it? Why does anyone carry around oral chemo? It's mine, Beecher. The medicine is for me!"

My eyebrows knot. Dallas shakes his head.

"What're you talking about?" I ask.

"Orlando...He wasn't supposed to be there," Clementine stutters. "When Orlando opened that SCIF and handed me his coffee...I thought the chemo would just...I thought he was in the Plumbers—that he was watching me for the President...that they'd found out about me. I thought it would knock him out...but I never thought it'd..."

"What do you mean, *the medicine's for you*?" I ask.

"Ask yourself the real question, Beecher: After all these years, why now? Why'd I pick *now* to track down my father?" Her chin is still down, but she finally looks up at me. "They diagnosed me eight months ago," she says, her hands—and the gun—now shaking. "I'm dying, Beecher. I'm dying from...back when Nico was in the army...I'm dying from whatever they did to my father."

105

S he's a liar," Dallas insists.

"They changed him!" Clementine shouts. "Whatever the army put in Nico...that's what made him insane!"

"You see that, Beecher? It's pure delusion," Dallas says.

"It's not delusion," Clementine says. "Ask him, Beecher. He's in the Plumbers, isn't he?"

"I'm not in the Plumbers," Dallas insists.

"Don't let him confuse you," Clementine says. "I knew it when I saw him at the cemetery. But when I first found out about Eightball...ask him what I was black-mailing Wallace for. It wasn't money. Even when they nibbled and replied to my message in that rock at the graveyard—I never once asked for money."

"Is that true?" I say to Dallas.

He doesn't answer.

"*Tell him!*" Clementine growls, her hand suddenly steady as her finger tightens around the trigger. "He knows you're working with the President and the barber and all the rest of his ass-kissers who've been hiding the truth for years!"

Dallas turns my way, but never takes his eyes off Clementine's gun.

"She asked for a file," Dallas finally says. "She wanted Nico's army file."

"His *real* file," Clementine clarifies. "Not the fake one they dismissed him with." Reading my confusion, Clementine explains, "My mother told me the stories. She told me how Nico...she told me how he was *before* he entered the army. How when they were younger... how she used to keep the phone on her pillow and he'd sing her to sleep. But when he finally came home...when he left the army—"

"He didn't *leave* the army. They *kicked him out*—for trying to use a staple remover to take out one of his superiors' eyes," Dallas says.

"No—they kicked him out because of what they put inside him...what they turned him into," Clementine shoots back. "Have you even bothered to read his fake file? It says he got transferred from army sniper school in Fort Benning, Georgia, to the one in Tennessee. But I checked. The address in Tennessee was for an old army medical center. Nico wasn't just a sniper! He was a patient—and he wasn't the only one!" she adds, looking right at me. "You know another one! You know him personally!"

"What're you talking about?" I stutter.

"My mother—before she died—she told me, okay. You think they came to our tiny town and just took one person? They took a group of them—a bunch of them. So you can think I'm as crazy as you want, but I'm not the only one with the results of their experiments in me, Beecher. You have it in you too! You have it from what they did to *your* father!"

I shake my head, knowing she's nuts. "My dad died. He died on the way to the recruitment office. He never even got a chance to sign up."

"And you believed that. You believed that because that's what they told you, okay. But he was there. He and Nico and the others...they were enlisted long before anybody knew it. Your father was alive, Beecher. And if I'm right, he still may be!"

My lips go dry. My stomach crumples, folding in on itself. She's a liar. I know she's a liar...

"You can look for yourself," she adds. "Ask them for the records, okay!" It's the third time she's ended a sentence with the word *okay*, and every time she uses it, every time her voice cracks, it's like a fracture, a faultline that's splintering through her, threatening to undo everything she always keeps so neatly packed in place. "My mom told me—the experiments were all going right—until everything went wrong—!"

"Do *not* listen to her!" Dallas says. "She spent months planning this—months to manipulate you and blackmail us. She's an even bigger psychopath than Nico!"

"Beecher, do you know what kind of cancer they found in me?" Clementine asks as I replay the last words Nico said to me back at the hospital: Nico begged God to make Clementine different from him. He wanted her to be different. "The kind of cancer no one's ever heard of. *Ever*," she adds. "Every doctor…every specialist…they said there're over one hundred and fifty types of cancer in the world, but when they look at mine, they can't even classify it. The mutation's so big, one doctor described it as a DNA spelling mistake. That's what my body is. That's what yours may be! A spelling mistake!"

"Beecher, I know you want to believe her," Dallas interrupts. "But listen to me—no matter what she's saying—we can still help you walk away from this."

"You think he's stupid!? Your Plumbers caused this!" Clementine yells.

"Will you stop?" Dallas insists. "I'm not in the Plumbers—I'm in the Culper Ring! I'm one of the good guys!"

"No," a brand-new voice—a man's deep voice—announces behind us. "You're *not*."

There's a hushed click.

And a muffled boom.

A small burst of blood pops from Dallas's chest. Lurching backward, Dallas looks down, though he still doesn't register the fresh gunshot wound and the blood puddle that's flowering at his chest.

Even before we spin to face his attacker, I know who pulled the trigger: the one man who benefits most from having all of us out here, in one place—the man who will do anything to get this file—and who's spent nearly three decades proving his loyalty while protecting his dearest friend.

"Don't look so surprised," Dr. Palmiotti says, his eyes burning as he turns the corner and points his gun at us. "You had to know this was coming."

106

That's not…No…" Dallas stutters, barely able to stand and still not registering his wound. "You told me…you said I was in the Culper Ring—"

Ignoring him, Palmiotti steps in close and snatches the file from Dallas's hands. "You need to know you were serving your country, son."

Dallas shakes his head, his body still in shock.

I try to take a breath as the stale air fills my lungs. Tot had it only part right. Yes, Dallas was in the Plumbers. But he didn't *know* he was in the Plumbers.

"Beecher, you see what these people are capable of?" Clementine snaps as all the doubt, all the sadness, all the weepiness she just showed us is suddenly gone. For the past few days, every time Clementine had a mood shift or revealed a new side of herself, I kept saying it was another door opening inside her. She had dozens of rooms. But as I look at her now, I finally understand that it doesn't matter how many rooms she has. It doesn't matter how striking the rooms are. Or how well they're decorated. Or how mesmerizing they are to walk through. What matters is that every one of her rooms—even the very best one—has a hell of a light switch. And it flips. Instantly. Without any damn warning. Just like her father.

On my left, Dallas looks down at his chest, where the blood puddle has blossomed, soaking his shirt. His legs sway, beginning to buckle.

Wasting no time, Palmiotti turns his gun toward me. I see the blackness of the barrel. I wait for him to make some final threat, but it doesn't come. "My apologies, Beecher," he says as he pulls the trigger and—

Ftttt.

The air twists with a brutal hiss.

Palmiotti doesn't notice. Not until he looks down and spots the singed black hole, like a cigarette burn, that smolders in his forearm. A thin drip of blood begins to run down.

It's not like the movies. There's no wisp of smoke twirling from the barrel. There's just Clementine. And her gun.

She saved me.

Palmiotti stands there, stunned. His gun drops from his hand, bounces along the floor, and makes a dull thud near Dallas's feet.

Dallas can barely stand, but he knows this is his chance. His last chance. He spots Palmiotti's gun.

But before Dallas can even bend for it, he grabs his own chest. He's bleeding bad. His legs buckle and he crumples, empty-handed, to the dusty floor.

"I'm leaving now," Clementine says, keeping her gun on Palmiotti and once again tightening her finger around the trigger. "You can hand me that file now, please."

107

*D*allas...!" I yell, sliding on my knees and trying to catch him as he falls forward.

I'm not nearly fast enough. I grab his waist, but his face knocks with a scary thud against the concrete.

Out of the corner of my eye, I see Clementine holding her gun inches from Palmiotti's face. Without a word, she plucks the file from his grip.

"Dallas, can you hear me!?" I call out, rolling him on his back.

"I-I didn't know, Beecher..." Dallas stutters, holding his chest, his eyes hopping back and forth, unable to focus. "I swear I didn't know..."

"Dallas, listen—"

"You shoot him back!" Dallas interrupts, reaching out and pointing to Palmiotti's gun. He wriggles—and reaches all the way out, finally grabbing it.

Next to us, Palmiotti's bent over, dealing with his own pain and putting maximum pressure on the bullet wound in his arm.

Dallas fights hard to shove the gun in my hand, but

his movement's too jerky. The gun bounces off my wrist, crashing to the ground.

I pick it up just as Clementine races at us.

Clementine stops. Her ginger brown eyes lock with my own. She has no idea what I'm thinking. No idea if I'm capable of picking this gun up and shooting her with it. But whatever she sees in my eyes, she knows she has no chance of making it all the way to the front entrance of the cave—all the way down the long well-populated main cavern—without us screaming murder. Switching directions, and not seeming the least bit worried, she tucks the file in the back of her pants and takes off deeper into the cave.

In my lap, Dallas is barely moving. Barely fighting. *"Beecher, why can't I see in my left eye?"* he cries, his voice crashing.

As the blood seeps out beneath him, I know there's only one thing he needs.

A doctor.

"You need to help him," I say, raising my gun and pointing it toward Palmiotti.

But Palmiotti's gone. He's already racing to the back of the cave, chasing after Clementine.

"Palmiotti, do *not* leave him!" I yell.

"She has the file, Beecher! Even you don't want her having that on the President!"

"Get back here . . . !" I insist.

There's a quick drumroll of footsteps.

Palmiotti—and Clementine—are long gone.

108

D allas's head is in my lap. He struggles to sit up. He can't.

"D-Don't you dare sit here and nurse me," he hisses, his breathing quick, but not out of control. "What Palmiotti did to us...you take that, Beecher!" He motions to Palmiotti's gun. "You take that and do what's right!"

Behind me, I still hear the echo of Palmiotti chasing after Clementine. I watch Dallas's chest rise and fall, making sure he's taking full breaths.

"Beecher, y-you need to do what's right," Dallas begs.

But as he fights to get the words out, the only thing I hear is Tot's voice in my head. Two days ago, he said that history is a selection process—that it chooses moments and events, and even people—that it hands them a situation that they shouldn't be able to overcome, and that it's in those moments, in that fight, that people find out who they are. It was a good speech. And for two days now, I've assumed history had chosen me.

I couldn't have been more wrong.

History doesn't choose *individual* people.

History chooses everyone. Every day.

The only question is: How long will you ignore the call?

I've been waiting for Tot…for Dallas…for the Culper Ring…for just about anyone to save me. But there's only one person who can do that.

"I got it," I tell him.

Holding Palmiotti's gun, and still thinking about what Clementine said about my dad, I glance to my right. On the wall, there's a small red fire alarm built into the rock. I hop to my feet and jab my elbow into the glass. The alarm screams, sending a high-pitched howl swirling through the cave.

That should bring Dallas the help he needs far faster than anything I can do. But as I check to make sure he's still conscious…

"I'm fine…" Dallas whispers, drowned out by the alarm. *"I'm fine. Go…"*

Far behind us, there's a low rumble as hundreds of employees follow their protocol and pour into the cave's main artery, ready to evacuate. I barely hear it—especially as my own heartbeat pulses in my ears.

This isn't history.

But it is my life. And my father's. What she said…

I need to know.

Running full speed with a gun in my hand, I turn the corner and head deeper into the cave.

Clementine's out there. So is Palmiotti.

I know they're waiting for me.

But they have no idea what's coming.

109

et back here...!" Beecher's voice bounced off the jagged walls as Palmiotti picked up speed and barreled deeper into the cave.

Using his tie as a makeshift tourniquet, Palmiotti knotted it twice around his forearm. Luckily, it was a through-and-through. The bleeding wasn't bad. Still, he had no intention of waiting. Not when he was this close to Clementine...this close to catching her...and this close to grabbing the hospital file and finally ending this threat to him and the President.

No, this was the benefit of having everyone in one place, Palmiotti thought, ignoring the pulsing in his forearm and being extra careful as he reached another turn in the cave. Unsure of what was waiting around the corner, he stopped and waited. He'd seen what happened earlier. It wasn't just that Clementine had a gun. It was how effortlessly she'd pulled the trigger.

Without a doubt, Wallace was right about her. She was an animal, just like her father. But as Palmiotti now knew, that didn't mean that Wallace was right about everything. Palmiotti tried to tell him—based on what Dallas was reporting—that even though Beecher let Clementine into the Archives, it didn't mean Beecher was also helping her blackmail Wallace and the Plumbers. That's why the President came back and requested Beecher in the SCIF—he had to test Beecher. He had to know. But even so, once Beecher had the book... once he started sniffing down the right path... and the hospital file—and then to bring in Tot and the attention of the *real* Culper Ring... No, at the level that things were happening, there was only one way to protect what he and the President had worked so hard for. Palmiotti knew the risk of coming here himself. But with everyone in one spot, he could put out every last fire. And not leave anything to chance.

Those were the same lessons now, Palmiotti thought as he craned his neck out and found nothing but another empty cavity, slightly longer than a grocery aisle, with another sharp turn to the right. It was the fourth one so far, as if the entire back of the cave ran in an endless step pattern. But as Palmiotti turned the corner, down at the far end of the next aisle, there was a puddle of water along the floor and a red spray-painted sign that leaned against the wall with the words *Car Wash* on it.

Racing down the length of the dark brown cavern—back here, the walls were no longer painted white—Palmiotti felt the cave getting warmer. He also noticed two yellow sponges, still soapy with suds, tucked behind the *Car Wash* sign. Whoever else had been back here, they hadn't been gone long, making Palmiotti wonder for the first time: Clementine was prepared for so much. Maybe there was another cave exit she knew about.

Reaching yet another turn, Palmiotti stopped and slowly leaned forward, peeking around the corner. But this time, instead of another long narrow tunnel, there was a cavern—wide as a suburban cul-de-sac—and a dead end. Straight ahead, the tunnel was blocked and boarded off by tall sheets of plywood. It looked like one of those protective walls that surround a construction site. On the wall was a rusty metal sign that read *Area 6*.

But the only sign that Palmiotti cared about was the glowing one above the red steel door on the far right of the cul-de-sac. *Emergency Exit.*

Sonuvabitch.

Leaping for the door and grabbing the handle, Palmiotti gave it a sharp tug. It didn't open. He tried again.

Locked. It was definitely locked. In fact, as he looked closer at the industrial keyhole, there was an old key broken off and stuck inside. It didn't make sense. Clementine couldn't've got out here. But if she didn't get out here, then she should still be—

Behind him, Palmiotti heard a small chirp. A squeak.

Spinning back, he rechecked the cavern. A mess of muddy wheelbarrows were piled up on his left. Next to that were two enormous wooden spools of thick cable wire and another mound of discarded metal shelving, all of it rusty from the heat and dampness at this end of the cave. Diagonally across was another red metal door. Stenciled letters on the front read: *Treatment Plant.* But before Palmiotti could even run for the door, there was another squeak...

There. On his right.

He didn't see it at first: Cut into the plywood wall, like a human-sized doggie door, was a hinged piece of wood that didn't sway much.

But no question, it was moving. Back and forth.

Like someone had just passed through it.

Rushing to it, but working hard to stay quiet, Palmiotti studied the door. Back and forth...back and forth. It was barely swaying now, letting out a few final squeaks as it settled to a stop. A crush of rocks crackled below his feet. A bead of sweat ran down his cheek, into the tie that wrapped his forearm.

Either Clementine was standing on the other side of this door, waiting to put a bullet in his face, or she was still running, following wherever the tunnel led.

Only one way to find out.

Pressing his open palm against the plywood, Palmiotti gave it a push. Inside, unlike the rest of the cave, there were no lights. Total black. Nothing but silence.

Out of nowhere, the shrill scream of a fire alarm echoed from every direction. Palmiotti jumped at the noise, nearly bashing his head into the top threshold of the doggie door. No doubt, the alarm was pulled by Beecher, who was probably still panicking back where Palmiotti left him.

But a distraction was a distraction. Seizing the moment, Palmiotti shoved the plywood forward, lifted his left leg, and took a full step through the giant swinging door. His foot landed with a squish. His socks...his dress shoes...his entire foot was submerged in water.

Ducking inside, he hopped wildly to his right foot, trying to get to dry ground. Again, he landed with a wet squish as he—

Fttt.

He slapped his neck like he was swatting a mosquito bite. On impact, a wet splash sprayed through the spaces between his fingers. It was too dark for him to see the blood. Like before, he didn't even feel it. As he stood there in the knee-high water, it was the smell that hit him first: the charred smell of burnt skin. His skin.

She shot me. Again. The nutty bitch shot me again!

But before the words traveled the synaptic pathway from his brain to his mouth, Palmiotti was hit again— tackled actually—his attacker ramming him from the right, purposely grabbing at the hole in his forearm as momentum and the electric jolt of pain knocked him sideways, into the shallow water that fed the water treatment area.

Before Palmiotti could get a single word out, two hands gripped his throat, sharp thumbnails digging into his voicebox.

Tumbling backward, he fell like a cleaved tree. The shallow water parted at the impact, then knitted back together over his face. Under the water, Palmiotti tried to scream as his lungs filled with the inky brown lake water. She clawed her way on top, sitting on his chest.

Palmiotti never got to see her.

But he knew Clementine wasn't letting go.

110

*A*nybody there...?" I call out, holding tight to the gun as I turn yet another corner in yet another poorly lit stretch of cave. *"Clementine...?"*

The only answer comes from the fire alarm, whose howl rings hard at the base of my skull.

A minute ago, I thought I heard the muffled thuds of Palmiotti running, but now...

Nothing but alarm.

Racing forward and holding the gun out in front of me, I lick the salty bits of sweat from my lips. At first, I told myself it was nerves. It's not. The deeper I go, the hotter it gets.

This isn't just the maintenance area of the cave. By the hum that rumbles just below the fire alarm, this is where all the HVAC and mechanical equipment is.

Picking up speed, I rush past a dusty spray-painted *Car Wash* sign and some still-soapy sponges, yet as I turn the next corner, there's a sudden dead end.

On my right, there's a door for an *Emergency Exit*.

But straight ahead, built into the construction wall, there's a swinging panel that... *huh*...is still swinging.

My fingers tighten around the trigger. There's no question where they are. I can wait here for help. I can play it absolutely safe. But if either of them gets away...

I take my first step toward the wooden wall, and the fire alarm stops, leaving me in a sudden vacuum of silence that's so severe, the only sound that exists is that phantom hum that follows you home when you leave a loud rock concert.

Straight ahead, the doggie door continues to swing, squeaking off-key.

Below my feet, with every step, bits of rock pop like glass.

In the distance, there's a chirp I can't place.

But what hits me like an axe in the stomach—as I approach the swinging panel and use the barrel of the gun to shove it open—is that there's not a single noise coming from inside.

111

Palmiotti knew what to do.

Even now...with his head underwater...with her hands around his throat...Palmiotti knew what to do if he wanted to breathe again.

Thrashing wildly, he clapped his arms together so his fists collided with Clementine's ears.

He couldn't hear her scream. But he did feel her let go. His head broke the surface of the water. Gasping for fresh air, he heard the fire alarm still ringing. Water dripped from his nose, from his ears, from his chin. His neck—where he'd been shot—was burning now. From the amount of blood that soaked his right shoulder, he knew his internal jugular vein was lacerated. It was bad. Much worse than his forearm. But at least he could breathe.

Still coughing uncontrollably, he rolled sideways in the shallow water. He couldn't see much, but there were small cracks of light in the plywood wall. His eyes adjusted fast.

Clementine rushed at him, raising her gun to—

Krkkk.

Palmiotti kicked hard—it was nothing but instinct—as his heel rammed Clementine's unbent knee.

The crack was audible. Clementine's leg nearly hyperextended as muscles and tendons were pulled like piano wire. Tumbling forward, she nosedived into the water.

She fought hard to get up, quickly climbing to her good knee. She knew what was coming.

She wasn't nearly fast enough.

The first kick slammed into her stomach, lifting her off the ground and taking all the wind out of her.

"D'you even realize how stupid you are!?" Palmiotti growled, spit flying with every syllable. "Even before the hospital file—just on the threat of you knowing what we did to Eightball—we were willing to give you everything! *You had us!* You'd actually *won*!"

Clementine's head was still down. Palmiotti gripped the back of her hair, twisting her head until she faced him and...

Pmmmp.

He rammed his knee in her face, sending her tumbling backward, splashing into the water. As fast as she could, she crabwalked back, trying to get away. She had no chance.

"Instead, when you heard about the file, you had to come here and be greedy...!" Palmiotti added, standing over her and grabbing her by the shirt. With a sharp tug, he lifted her up until the water reached her waist, then he punched her square in the face.

This time, though, it was Palmiotti who wasn't letting go. He felt the throbbing at the wound in his neck. He could feel himself getting light-headed. He didn't care. Cocking his arm back, he hit her again. And...

There was a loud *click* behind him.

"That's enough," a familiar voice announced.

Palmiotti turned, glancing over his shoulder. "Go away. This isn't your problem anymore."

"You are so incredibly wrong about that," Beecher warned, aiming his gun straight at Palmiotti. "Let go of her now, and put your hands in the air."

112

Y ou're done—you're both done," I warn Palmiotti.
"She still has her gun!" he insists, pointing back at Clementine.

I look down to check for myself. The brown water is almost to my knees, though it looks like it gets deeper as it snakes down the length of the cavern and winds into the darkness like the River Styx. This isn't some small puddle. It's a man-made lake.

In the darkness, it's near impossible to see anything but a glassy reflection off the surface. But there's no missing Clementine. Or the way, as she wipes her mouth and backs away from us on her knees, she keeps her other hand conspicuously below the water.

"He hit me, Beecher," she pleads, still slowly moving backward. "I swallowed my tooth—he knocked it down my—"

I point my gun at her and pull the trigger.

The barrel booms with a thunderclap that reverberates through the cavern. From the back of the cave, a speedy red bird—the chirping I heard before—zips out, flies in a few wild circles, and disappears again.

"Gah!" Clementine screams as the bullet slices her thigh, sending bits of skin and flesh flicking across the water. Palmiotti's already injured. Whatever else happens, I'm not letting either of them—and especially her—get away.

At first she looks mad, but as she falls back on her ass and tucks her knee toward her chin, her eyebrows quickly unknot and her eyes go round and weepy. "H-How could you...? You shot me..." she moans.

"What you said about my father—is it true?" I ask.

"Beecher...the documents they're hiding—there's even more in that file. And if we have that, it's not just our word against theirs—"

"*IS IT TRUE!?*" I explode.

The cave is silent, except for the red bird cheeping in the distance. "Th-That's what my mother told me. I swear to you—on her dead body. But if I don't get out of here—"

"No. Do *not* do that," I warn her. "Do *not* manipulate me. Do not try to get away. I've seen that show already—I know how it ends."

"Make her raise her hands!" Palmiotti shouts, stumbling back a few steps and leaning against the cave wall. I didn't notice it until now—all that red on his shoulder...the way he's holding his neck. He's been shot again.

"Don't let Palmiotti twist you," Clementine warns, ignoring her own pain and fighting to stay calm. I can see the wet file folder sticking up from behind her back, where she tucked it in her pants. "Even with everything I did—you know I'd never hurt you. And before...I-I saved you."

"You need to shoot her!" Palmiotti insists. "She's got her gun under the water!"

"Clementine, raise your hands," I insist.

She shifts her weight, raising both hands, then lowering them back in the water, which, from the way she's sitting, comes just above her waist.

"She kept the gun *in her lap*!" Palmiotti adds. "She still has it!"

"I don't have anything!" she shouts.

I don't believe either of them. And even if her gun is still in her lap, I don't know if a gun can work once it's underwater. But the one thing I do know is I need to see for myself.

"Clementine, *get up*! Stand up," I tell her.

"I can't."

"Whattya mean *you can't*?"

"You shot me, Beecher. In the *leg*. I can't *stand*," she explains, pointing to her leg that's bent.

"The bullshit is just never-ending!" Palmiotti says. "If you don't shoot her, she's going to—!"

"Dr. Palmiotti, *stop talking*!" I yell.

"Then use your brain for once instead of thinking with your scrotum!" Palmiotti begs, reaching my way. "If you want, give me the gun and I'll—"

"Do *not* come near this gun," I say, aiming the barrel at his chest. "I know who you are, Doctor. I know you tricked Dallas into thinking he was fighting for the good of the

Culper Ring. And since I know you're the top plumber in the Plumbers, I know where your loyalty lies."

Palmiotti doesn't move.

Across from us, Clementine doesn't either.

"Beecher, listen to me," Palmiotti says. "Whatever you think our mission is, we can fight about this later. But if you don't shoot her—if you don't protect us—she's gonna kill both of us."

"I know you don't believe that," Clementine jumps in, her eyes flicking back and forth between me and Palmiotti. "Of course he wants you to shoot me, Beecher. Think of why he put that bullet in Dallas's chest! He's cleaning up one by one...and once I'm gone, you're the only witness that's left. And then...and then..." She slows herself down as the pain takes hold. "Guess how quickly you'll be dead after that?"

"So now *we're* the bad guys?" Palmiotti asks, forcing a laugh. "For what? For trying to protect the leader of the free world from a blackmailer and her crazy father?"

"No—for helping your boss bury a baseball bat in the side of someone's head! I saw Eightball's medical chart. Puncture wounds in the face! Shattered eye socket; broken cheekbones! And brain damage from an in-driven fragment of his skull! Lemme guess: You held Eightball down while Wallace wound up with a hammer. Did it feel good when you heard that boy's eye socket shatter? What about all these years when you helped the President of the United States keep him in storage like a piece of old furniture—and then used all the real Culper Ring's methods to hide it!? How'd that one feel?" Turning to me, she adds, "Pay attention, Beecher. Palmiotti wants you to think *I'm* the bad guy. But remember, he didn't need you and Dallas to get the file. Once you found it, he could've had Dallas take you home, and he could've grabbed it himself. So what's the benefit to Palmiotti of having all of us in an underground cave in the middle of nowhere...?"

"Jesus, Beecher—even if you think she's telling the truth—make her stand up!" Palmiotti pleads.

"...because even if they smoke that hospital file, the last thing Palmiotti and the President need is you running around, bearing witness to the world," Clementine says, as serious as I've ever seen her. "That's the only reason you're here, Beecher—that's the big ending. Whether you shoot me now or not, you're gonna die here. *I'm* gonna die here. Both of us...with what's in our blood...don't you see...we're history."

Behind her, the bird isn't chirping. There's only silence.

"That's not true," I say, still pointing my gun at her.

"You lie. And worst of all, you lie to yourself," she tells me. "Think of everything you've seen: You saw him shoot Dallas. You've already seen what they'll do to protect what they have in that White House. You pull that trigger on me, and I guarantee you you'll be dead in ten minutes—and you wanna know why? Because that's your role, Beecher. You get to play Lee Harvey Oswald...or John Hinckley...or even Nico. That's your big part in the opera. Think of any presidential attack in history—you can't have one without a patsy."

"Beecher, make her stand the hell up!" Palmiotti begs, his voice cracking. His face should be a red rage. Instead, it's bone white. The way he's gripping his neck and using his free hand to steady himself against the wall, he's losing blood fast.

I look back at Clementine sitting in the water. Both of her legs are straight out, like she's coming down a waterslide. The water's above her waist. I still can't see if she has her gun.

"You know I'm right," she says as she starts to breathe heavily. The pain in her leg is definitely getting worse. But as she sits there, she starts using her good leg to slowly push herself backward in the water. "This is your chance, Beecher. If we leave together…with this file…Forget making them pay—we can finally get the truth."

"Beecher, whatever you're thinking right now," Palmiotti pleads, "she has the file tucked in her pants and her gun in one of her hands. Do not assume—*for one second*—that the moment you lower your gun, she's not going to raise hers and kill the both of us."

"Help me up, Beecher. Help me up and we can get out of here," Clementine says, reaching out with her left hand. Her right is still underwater as she stops maneuvering back.

"S-She's the one who killed Orlando!" Palmiotti says, coughing wildly.

"Clementine, what you told me before…about being sick," I say. "Are you really dying?"

She doesn't say a word. But she also doesn't look away. "I can't be lying about everything."

"*She can . . . she admitted it, Beecher . . . She killed your friend!*"

From the back of the cave, the trapped red bird again swoops through the darkness, and just as quickly disappears with a high-pitched chirp.

I look over at Palmiotti, who's got no fight left in him, then back to Clementine, who's still holding one hand out to me—and hiding her other beneath the water.

The answer is easy.

There's only one real threat left.

I aim my gun at Clementine and cock the hammer. "Clementine, pick your hands up and stand up now, or I swear to God I'll shoot you again," I tell her.

Two minutes ago, Clementine said we were history. She knows nothing about history. History is simply what's behind us.

"*Thank you!*" Palmiotti calls out, still coughing behind me. "Now we can—"

Palmiotti doesn't finish the thought.

As Clementine is about to get up, there's a loud splash behind me.

I turn to my right just as Palmiotti hits the water. He lands face-first, arms at his side, like he's frozen solid. For half a second, I stand there, waiting for him to get up. But the way he lies there, facedown . . .

His body jerks. Then jerks again, wildly. Within seconds, his upper body is twitching, making him buck like a fish on land. I have no idea what that gunshot to the neck did. But I know a seizure when I see one.

"*Palmiotti . . . !*" I call out even though he can't hear me.

I'm about to run at him, when I remember...

Clementine.

"He's gonna die," she says matter-of-factly, fighting to climb to her good leg. Her one hand is still hidden below the water. "You may hate him, but he needs your help."

"If you run, I'll shoot you again," I warn her.

"No. You won't. Not after that," she says, pointing me back to Palmiotti, whose convulsions are starting to slow down. He doesn't have long.

If the situation were reversed, Palmiotti would leave me. Gladly. Clementine might too. But to turn your back and just leave someone to die...

Right there, I see the choice. I can grab Clementine. Or I can race to help Palmiotti.

Life. Or death. There's no time for both.

I think of everything Palmiotti did. How he shot Dallas. And how, if I save him, President Wallace will pull every string in existence to make sure Palmiotti walks away without a scar, mark, or paper cut.

I think of what Clementine knows about my father.

But when it comes to making the final choice...

...there's really no choice at all.

Sprinting toward the facedown Palmiotti and tucking my gun into my pants, I grab him by the shoulders and lift him, bending him backward, out from the water. He's deadweight, his arms sagging forward as his fingertips skate along the top of the water. A waterfall of fluid and vomit drains from his mouth.

I know what to do. I spent two summers lifeguarding

at the local pool. But as I drop to my knees and twist Palmiotti onto his back, I can't help but look over my shoulder.

With her back to me, Clementine climbs to her feet. She tries to steady herself, her right hand still down in the water.

As Palmiotti's head hits my lap, his face isn't pale anymore. It's ashen and gray. His half-open eyes are waxy as he gazes through me. He's not in there.

I open his mouth. I clear his airway. I look over my shoulder...

My eyes seize on Clementine as she finally pulls her hand from the water...

...and reveals the soaking-wet gun that she's been gripping the entire time.

Oh, jeez.

Palmiotti was right.

She lifts the gun. All she has to do is turn and fire. It's an easy shot.

But she never takes it.

Scrambling and limping, Clementine heads deeper into the cave, leaving a wake in the water that fans out behind her. The gun is dangling by her side. I wait for her to look back at me.

She doesn't.

Not once.

I tilt Palmiotti's head back. I pinch his nose. He hasn't taken a breath in a full minute. His gray skin is starting to turn blue.

"Help...!" I call out even though no one's there.

Palmiotti's only movement comes from a rare gasp that sends his chest heaving. *Huuuh.* It's not a breath. He's not breathing at all.

He's dying.

"We need help . . . !" I call out.

I look over my shoulder.

Clementine's gone.

In my lap, Palmiotti doesn't move. No gasping. No heaving. His eyes stare through me. His skin is bluer than ever. I feel for a pulse, but there's nothing there.

"Please, someone . . . I need help . . . !"

113

Clementine is gone.
   I know they won't find her.
   Dallas is dead. So is Palmiotti.
I know both are my fault.

And on top of all that, when it comes to my father, I've got nothing but questions.

In the back part of the cave, the first ones to reach us are Copper Mountain's internal volunteer firefighters, which are made up of a group of beefy-looking managers and maintenance guys who check me for cuts and scrapes. I don't have a scratch on me. No punches thrown, no black eyes to heal, no lame sling to make it look like I learned a lesson as I went through the wringer.

I did everything Clementine and Tot and even Dallas had been pushing me to do. For those few minutes, as I held that gun, and squeezed that trigger, I was no longer the spectator who was avoiding the future and watching the action from the safety of a well-worn history book. For those few minutes, I was absolutely, supremely *in the present*.

But as the paramedics buzz back and forth and I stand there alone in the cave, staring down at my cell phone, the very worst part of my new reality is simply...I have no idea who to call.

"There. I see 'em..." a female voice announces.

I look up just as a woman paramedic with short brown hair climbs out of a golf cart that's painted red and white like an ambulance. She starts talking to the other paramedic—the guy who told me that the water treatment area has a waste exit on the far side of the cave. Clementine was prepared for that one too.

But as the woman paramedic gets closer, I realize she's not here for me. She heads to the corner of the cave, where Dallas's and Palmiotti's stiff bodies are covered by red-and-white-checkered plastic tablecloths from the cafeteria.

I could've shot Clementine. Maybe I should've. But as I stare at Dallas's and Palmiotti's covered bodies, the thought that's doing far more damage is a simple one: After everything that happened, I helped *nobody*.

The thought continues to carve into my brain as a third paramedic motions my way.

"So you're the lucky one, huh?" a paramedic with a twinge of Texas in his voice asks, putting a hand on my shoulder and pulling me back. "If you need a lift, you can ride with us," he adds, pointing me to the white car that sits just behind the golf cart.

I nod him a thanks as he opens the back door of the car and I slide inside. But it's not until the door slams shut and I see the metal police car–type partition that divides the front seat from the back, that I realize he's dressed in a suit.

Paramedics don't wear suits.

The locks thunk. The driver—a man with thin blond hair that's combed straight back and curls into a duck's butt at his neck—is also in a suit.

Never facing me, the man with the Texas twang drops into the passenger seat and whispers into his wrist:

"We're in route Crown. Notify B-4."

I have no idea what B-4 is. But during all those reading visits, I've been around enough Secret Service agents to know what *Crown* is the code word for.

They're taking me to the White House.

Good.

That's exactly where I want to go.

114

I try to sleep on the ride.

I don't have a chance.

For the first few hours, my body won't shut off. I'm too wired and rattled and awake. I keep checking my phone, annoyed I can't get a signal. But as we pass into Maryland, I realize it's not my phone.

"You're blocking it, aren't you?" I call out to the driver. "You've got one of those devices—for blocking my cell signal."

He doesn't answer. Too bad for him, I've seen the CIA files on interrogation. I know the game.

The longer they let the silence sink in and make this car seem like a cage, the more likely I am to calm down.

It usually works.

But after everything that's happened—to Orlando...to Dallas...and even to Palmiotti—I don't care how many hours I sit back here, there's no damn way I'm just calming down...

Until.

The car makes a sharp right, bouncing and bumping

its way to the security shed at the southeast gate. Of the White House.

"Emily . . ." the driver of our car says, miming a tip of the hat to the female uniformed guard.

"Jim . . ." the guard replies, nodding back.

It's nearly ten at night. They know we're coming.

With a click, the black metal gate swings open, and we ride up the slight incline toward the familiar giant white columns and the perfectly lit Truman Balcony. Just the sight of it unties the knots of my rage and, to my surprise, makes the world float in time, like I'm hovering in my own body.

It's not the President that does it to me. It's this place.

Last year, I took my sisters here to see the enormous Christmas tree they always have on the South Lawn. Like every other tourist, we took photos from the street, squeezing the camera through the bars of the metal gate and snapping shots of the world's most famous white mansion.

Regardless of who lives inside, the White House— and the Presidency—still deserve respect.

Even if Wallace doesn't.

The car jolts to a stop just under the awning of the South Portico.

I know this entrance. This isn't the public entrance. Or the staff entrance.

The is the entrance that Nixon walked out when he boarded the helicopter for the last time and popped the double fingers. The entrance where Obama and his daughters played with their dog.

The private entrance.

Wallace's entrance.

Before I can even reach for the door, two men in suits appear on my right from inside the mansion. As they approach the car, I see their earpieces. More Secret Service.

The car locks thunk. The taller one opens the door.

"He's ready for you," he says, motioning for me to walk ahead of them. They both fall in right behind me, making it clear that they're the ones steering.

We don't go far.

As we step through an oval room that I recognize as the room where FDR used to give his fireside chats, they motion me to the left, down a long pale-red-carpeted hallway.

There's another agent on my left, who whispers into his wrist as we pass.

In the White House, every stranger is a threat.

They don't know the half of it.

"Here you go…" one of them says as we reach the end of the hall, and he points me to the only open door on the hallway.

The sign out front tells me where we are. But even without that, as I step inside—past the unusually small reception area and unusually clean bathroom—there's an exam table that's covered by a sterile roll of white paper.

Even in the White House, there's no mistaking a doctor's office.

"Please. Have a seat," he announces, dressed in a sharp pinstriped suit despite the late hour. As he waves me into the private office, his gray eyes look different than the last time I saw him, with the kind of dark puffiness under them that only comes from stress. "I was worried about you, Beecher," the President of the United States adds, extending a hand. "I wasn't sure you were going to make it."

115

You look like you have something on your mind, Beecher," the President offers, sounding almost concerned.

"Excuse me?" I ask.

"On your face. I can see it. Say what you're thinking, son."

"You don't wanna hear what I'm thinking," I shoot back.

"Watch yourself," one of the Secret Service agents blurts behind me. I didn't even realize they were still there.

"Victor," the President says. It's just one word. He's not even annoyed as he says it. But in those two syllables, it's clear what the President wants. *Leave us alone. Get out.*

"Sir, this isn't—"

"*Victor.*" That's the end. Argument over.

Without another word, the two agents leave the doctor's office, shutting the door behind them. But it's Wallace who rounds the desk, crosses behind me, and locks the office door with a hushed *clunk*.

At first, I thought he brought me here because of what happened to Palmiotti. But I'm now realizing it's one of the only places in the White House where he can guarantee complete privacy.

With him behind me, I keep my eyes on Palmiotti's desk, where there's a small box that looks like a toaster. A little screen lists the following names in green digital letters:

> POTUS: *Ground Floor Doctor's Office*
> FLOTUS: *Second Floor Residence*
> VPOTUS: *West Wing*
> MINNIE: *Traveling*

Doesn't take a medical degree to know those're the current locations of the President, First Lady, Vice President, and Minnie. I'd read that Wallace made the Secret Service take his kids' names off the search grid. There was no reason for staff to know where they were at any minute. But he clearly left Minnie on. It's been twenty-six years since the President's sister tried to kill herself. He's not taking his eyes off her.

Otherwise, the office is sparse, and the walls—to my surprise—aren't filled with photos of Palmiotti and the President. Palmiotti had just one, on the desk, in a tasteful silver frame. It's not from the Oval or Inauguration Day. No, this is a grainy shot from when Palmiotti and Wallace were back in...from the early-eighties hair and the white caps and gowns, it has to be high school graduation.

They can't be more than eighteen: young Palmiotti on

the left; young Wallace on the right. In between, they've both got their arms around the real star of the photo: Wallace's mother, who has her head tilted just slightly toward her son, and is beaming the kind of toothy smile that only a mom at graduation can possibly beam. But as Mom stretches her own arms around their waists, pulling them in close, one thing's clear: This isn't a presidential photo. It's a family one.

With the door now locked, the President moves slowly behind me, heading back toward the desk. He's silent and unreadable. I know he's trying to intimidate me. And I know it's working.

But as he brushes past me, I spot...in his hand...He's holding one of those black oval bulbs from the end of a blood pressure kit.

As he slides back into his chair, I don't care how cool he's trying to play it. This man still lost his oldest—and perhaps *only*—real friend today. He lowers his hands behind the desk and I know he's squeezing that bulb.

"If it makes you feel better, we'll find her," he finally offers.

"Pardon?"

"The girl. The one who took the file..."

"Clementine. But whattya mean we'll find—?" I stop myself, looking carefully at Wallace. Until just this moment, he had no idea that Clementine was the one who had the file.

His gray eyes lock on me, and I realize, in this depth of the ocean, just how sharp the shark's teeth can be.

"Is that why you brought me here? To see if I was the one who still had the file?"

"Beecher, you keep thinking I'm trying to fight you. But you need to know—all this time—we thought *you* were the one who was blackmailing *us*."

"I wasn't."

"I know that. And that's the only reason I brought you here, Beecher: to thank you. I appreciate what you did. The way you came through and worked so hard to protect Dallas and Dr. Palmiotti. And even when you found the rest...you could've taken advantage and asked for something for yourself. But you never did."

I stare at the President, who knits his fingers together and gently lowers them in prayer style on the desk. He's not holding the blood pressure bulb anymore.

"Can I ask you a question, sir?"

"Of course."

"Is that the same speech you gave to Dallas?"

"What're you talking about?" the President asks.

"The polite flattery...the moral back-pat...even the subtle hint you dropped about the advantages you can offer and how much you can do for me, without ever directly saying it. Is that the way you made Dallas feel special when you invited him into the Plumbers, and he thought he was joining the Culper Ring?"

The President shifts his weight, his eyes still locked on me. "Be very careful of what you're accusing me of."

"I'm not accusing you of anything, sir. But it is a fair calculation, isn't it? Why risk a head-on collision when you can bring me inside? I mean, now that I think about it—is that the real reason you brought me here? To keep me quiet by inviting me to be the newest member of your Plumbers?"

The President's hands stay frozen in prayer style on the desk. If his voice was any colder, I'd be able to see it in the air. "No. That *isn't* why I brought you here. At all."

He takes another breath, all set to hide his emotions just like he does on every other day of his life. But I see his tongue as it rolls inside his mouth. As good as Wallace is, his friend is still dead. You don't just bury that away.

"I brought you to say thank you," he insists for the second time. "Without you, we wouldn't know who killed that security guard."

"His name's Orlando," I interrupt.

Wallace nods with a nearly invisible grin, letting me know he's well aware of Orlando's name. He's anxious to be back in control—and I just gave it back to him. "Though you'll be happy to hear, Beecher—from what I understand, the D.C. police already have Clementine's picture up on their website. They were able to link her chemotherapy prescription to the drugs they found in Orlando's bloodwork."

"What're you talking about?"

"I'm just telling you what's online. And when you think about it, that young archivist—Beecher whatshisname—who tracked her down, and looped in the President's doctor, and even followed her all the way out to those caves—that guy's a hero," he adds, his eyes growing darker as they tighten on me. "Of course, some say

Beecher had a hand in it—that he violated every security protocol and was the one who let Clementine inside that SCIF—and that together they planned all this, and were after the President, and they even went to visit her father, who—can you believe it?—is Nico Hadrian, who may be trying to kill again."

He pauses a moment, looking over at the office's only window. It has a perfect view of the South Lawn—except for the iron bars that cover it. I get the point. All he has to do is say the words and that's my permanent view. His voice is back to the exact strength he started with. "But I don't want to believe that about him. Beecher's a good guy. I don't want to see him lose everything like that."

It's an overdramatic speech—especially with the glance at the iron bars—and exactly the one I thought he'd give. "I still know about the two Culper Rings," I say. "I know about your Plumbers. And for you especially . . . I know your personal stake in this."

He knows I mean Minnie.

"Beecher, I think we all have a personal stake in this. Right, son?" he asks, putting all the emphasis on the word *son*.

I know he means my father.

It's an empty threat. If he wanted to trade, he would've already offered it. But he's done debating.

"Go tell the world, Beecher. And you find me one person who wouldn't protect their sister in the *exact same way* if they saw her in trouble. If you think my poll numbers are good now, just wait until you turn me into a hero."

"Maybe," I say.

"Not *maybe*," he says as if he's already seen the future. He leans into the desk, his fingers still crossed in prayer. This man takes on entire countries. And wins. "The press'll dig for a little while into what the doctor was up to, but they'll move on to the next well—especially when they don't strike oil. *The President's doctor* is very different than the *President*."

"But we all know this isn't about *the President*. Even for *you*, it's never been about you. It's about *her*, isn't it, sir? Forget the press…the public…forget everyone. We wouldn't still be talking if you weren't worried about something. And to me, that only thing you're worried about is—if I start doing the cable show rounds and say your sister's accident was actually an attempted suicide out of guilt for what she did to Eightball—"

"Beecher, I will only say this once. Don't threaten me. You have no idea what happened that night."

"The barber told me. He told me about the vacuum hose—and the tailpipe of the Honda Civic."

"You have no idea what happened that night."

"I know it took you four hours before you found her. I know how it still haunts you that you couldn't stop it."

"You're not hearing me, Beecher," he says, lowering his voice so that I listen to every syllable. "I was there—I'm the one who found her. You. Have. No. Idea. What. Happened. That. Night."

His burning intensity knocks me back in my seat. I look at the President.

He doesn't look away. His baggy eyes narrow.

I replay the events...The barber...Laurent said it took four hours before they found Minnie that night. That Palmiotti was the one who pulled her from the car. But now...if Wallace says he's the one who found her first...

You have no idea what happened that night.

My skin goes cold. I replay it again. Wallace was there first...he was the first one to see her unconscious in the car...But if Palmiotti is the one who eventually pulled her out...Both things can be true. Unless...

Unless Wallace got there first, saw Minnie unconscious, and decided that the best action...

...was not to take any action at all.

You have no idea what happened that night.

"When you saw her lying there...you didn't pull her out of the car, did you...?" I blurt.

The President doesn't answer.

The bitter taste of bile bursts in my throat as I glance back at the silver picture frame. The family photo.

The one with two kids in the family.

Not three.

"You tried to leave her in that smoke-filled car. You tried to let your own sister die," I say.

"Everyone knows I love my sister."

"But in that moment, after all the heartache she caused...If Palmiotti hadn't come in, you would've stood there and watched her suffocate."

Wallace juts out his lower lip and huffs a puff of air up his own nose. But he doesn't answer. He'll never answer. Not for what they did to Eightball. Not for hiding him all these years. Not for any of this.

I was wrong before.

All this time, I thought I was fighting men.

I'm fighting monsters.

"That's how you knew you could trust Palmiotti with anything, including the Plumbers. He was there for your lowest moment—and the truly sick part is, he decided to stay even though he knew you would've let your sister die," I say. "You belong together. You ditched your souls for each other."

There's a flash on the digital screen that lists the First Family's location. In a blink, Minnie's status goes from:

MINNIE: Traveling

to

MINNIE: Second Floor Residence

Now she's upstairs.

"No place like home," Wallace says, never once raising his voice. He turns directly at me, finally undoing the prayer grip of his hands. "So. We're done now, yes?"

"We're not."

"We are. We very much are."

"I can still find proof."

"You can *try*. But we're done, Beecher. And y'know why we're done? Because when it comes to conspiracy theories—think of the best ones out there—think of the ones that even have some semblance of proof...like JFK. For over fifty years now, after all the Jack Ruby and

Lee Harvey Oswald stories... after all the witnesses who came forward, and the books, and the speculation, and the Oliver Stones, and the annual conventions that still happen to this very day, you know what the number one theory most people believe? *The Warren Commission*," he says dryly. "*That's* who the public believes—the commission authored by the U.S. government. We make a great bad guy, and they all say they hate us. But at the end of every day, people *want* to trust us. Because we're their *government*. And people trust their government."

"I bet you practiced that monologue."

"Just remember where you are: This is a prizefight, Beecher. And when you're in a prizefight for a long time—take my word on this—you keep swinging that hard and you're only gonna knock yourself out."

"Actually, the knockout already happened."

"Pardon?"

"Just remember where *you* are, Mr. President. Look around. By the end of the week, this office will be empty. The photo in the silver frame will be, I'm guessing, slipped inside Palmiotti's coffin. Your doctor's gone, sir. So's your barber. Your Plumbers are finished. Goodbye. All your work did was get two loyal men killed. So you can try to pretend you've got everything exactly where you want it, but I'm the one who gets to go home for the rest of my week—while you're the one at the funerals, delivering the eulogies."

"You have nothing. You have less than nothing."

"You may be right. But then I keep thinking... the whole purpose of the Plumbers was to take people you trust and use them to build a wall around you. That wall protected you and insulated you. And now that wall is gone," I say. "So what're you gonna do now, sir?" Standing from my seat and heading for the door, I add, "You have a good night, Mr. President."

116

Nico didn't like card games.

It didn't matter.

Every few months, the doctors would still have a new pack of playing cards delivered to his room. Usually, they were cards from defunct airlines—both TWA and Piedmont Air apparently gave out a lot of free playing cards back in the day. But Nico didn't know what the doctors' therapeutic goal was. He didn't much care.

To Nico, a card game—especially one like solitaire—could never be enjoyable. Not when it left so much to chance. No, in Nico's world, the universe was far more organized. Gravity…temperature…even the repetition of history…Those were part of God's rules. The universe definitely had rules. It *had* to have rules. And purpose.

So, every few months, when Nico would receive his

playing cards, he'd wait a day or two and then hand them back to the orderlies, or leave them in the day room, or, if they found their way back to him, tuck them into the cushions of the couch that smelled like urine and soup.

But tonight, at nearly 10 p.m. in the now quiet main room, Nico sat at one of the Plexiglas tables near the nurses' station and quietly played a game of solitaire.

"Thanks for being so patient, baby," the heavy nurse with the big hoop earrings said. "You know how Mr. Jasper gets if we let him sit in his diaper too long."

"Oooh, and you're playing cards so nice," the nurse crooned, making a mental note and clearly excited for what she'd inevitably be telling the doctors tomorrow.

It wasn't much. But Nico knew it mattered. The hospital was no different than the universe. Everything had rules. And the number one rule here was: If you don't please the nurses, you're not getting your privileges.

It was why he didn't complain when they let someone else feed the cats tonight. Or when Rupert brought him apple juice instead of orange.

Nico had been lucky earlier today. When he approached that car—the one with the barber and the blasphemous wrists—he was worried the blame would be put on him.

It wasn't. And he knew why.

Whoever had burned Beecher—whoever had caused all that pain—the last thing they wanted was Nico's name all over this. If that had happened, a real investigation would've been started.

The ones who did this...They didn't want that.

In the end, it didn't surprise Nico. But it did surprise him that, when it came to that investigation, they had the power to stop it.

Right there, Nico knew what was coming next.

"I see you put Randall's Sprite cans in the recycling—cleaned up his crackers too," the nurse added. "I know you're sucking up, Nico—but I appreciate it. Now remind me what you're waiting for again? Your mail?"

"Not mail," Nico said. "My phone. Any new phone messages?"

The nurse with the hoop earrings gripped a blue three-ring binder from the shelf above her desk and quickly flipped to the last pages.

Nico could've snuck a look at the book when she wasn't there.

But there were rules.

There were always rules.

And consequences.

"Lemme see…according to this…" she said as her chubby finger skated down the page. "Nope. Sorry, baby. No calls." Snapping the book shut, she added, "Maybe tomorrow."

Nico nodded. It was a good thought. Maybe it'd be tomorrow. Or the day after that. Or even the day after.

But it was going to happen. Soon.

Nico knew the rules.

He knew his purpose.

Beecher would be coming back. He definitely would.

It might take him a month. Or even longer. But eventually, Beecher would want help. He'd want help, and he'd want answers. And most of all, he'd want to know how to track down Clementine—which, if Nico was right about what was in her, was the only thing Nico wanted too.

Shoving his way back through the swinging doors and still thinking of how his daughter had misled him, Nico headed back to his room.

Soon, he and Beecher—George Washington and Benedict Arnold—would again be working together.

Just like the universe had always planned.

117

W here's he, upstairs?" Minnie asked a passing aide who was carrying the newest stack of autographed items, from personal letters to a red, white, and blue golf ball, that the President had just finished signing.

"Solarium," the aide said, pointing up as Minnie headed for the back staircase that would take her the rest of the way.

Minnie always loved the Solarium, which sat above the Truman Balcony on the top floor of the White House and had the best view of the Mall and the Washington Monument.

But Minnie didn't love it for the view. Or because it was the one casual room in the entire Residence. She loved it because it reminded her of home. Literally.

Lined with old family photos from when she and the President were kids, the narrow hallway that led up and out to the Solarium rose at a surprisingly steep incline. Even with her pink flamingo cane, it was tough for Minnie to navigate. But she still stared as she passed each old photograph—the one when she and ten-year-old Orson are smiling with all the chocolate in their teeth...the one with Orson proudly holding his first cross-country running trophy...and of course, the one right after she was born, with her mother placing baby Minnie for the first time in her brother's arms. Back then, the side of her face was covered with skin lesions. But little Orson is smiling down, so proud to be the new big brother. Wallace had personally made sure that picture made the list.

"Don't you dare do that," Minnie called out to her brother, rapping her cane against the floor. As she entered the room, which was decorated with casual sofas, she saw the problem.

With his back to her, the President stood there, hands in his pockets as he stared out the tall glass windows at the bright glow of the Washington Monument.

"Don't do that," she warned again, knowing him all too well.

"You know this was the room Nancy Reagan was in when they told her the President had been shot?" her brother announced.

"Yeah, and I know from the last time you were all upset and moody, it's also the room where Nixon told his family he was going to step down. We get it. Whenever you start staring out at the monuments or talking about other Presidents, you're in a piss mood. So just tell me: What's it this time? What's in your craw?"

He thought about telling her that Palmiotti was dead. It'd be on the news soon enough—complete with the story of how the doctor was blackmailed and lured down to the caves by the criminal Clementine. But Wallace knew that his sister was still riding the high of the morning's charity event.

"Actually, I was just thinking about you," Wallace replied, still keeping his back to her as Minnie hobbled with her cane toward him. "Today was really nice."

"It was, wasn't it?" Minnie said, smiling the half-smile that the stroke allowed. "Thanks again for coming and doing the speech. It made the event..." She paused a moment, trying to think of the right word. Her brother had heard all of them.

"It felt good to have you there," she finally said.

The President nodded, still standing there, staring out at the snow-covered Mall. From behind, Minnie playfully tapped his leg with the head of the flamingo cane. "Make room," she added, forcing him aside. With a sisterly shove, Minnie stepped close to him so they were standing shoulder to shoulder, two siblings staring out at the stunning view.

"It was fun being there. I mean, for me too," the President admitted.

"You should do it more often then. We have a fundraiser next month out in Virginia," Minnie said.

Wallace didn't reply.

"Orson, I'm *kidding*," Minnie added. "But I did mean what I said before: Having you there...I probably don't say this enough, but—"

"Minnie, you don't have to say anything."

"I do. And you need to hear it. I just want you to know...my whole life...I appreciate everything you've given me," she said, motioning out at the monuments and the Mall. "You're a good brother."

The President nodded. "You're right. I am."

Minnie rapped him with her pink cane, laughing. But as she followed her brother's gaze, she realized Wallace wasn't staring out at the Washington Monument. He was staring *down*, at the paved path of the South Lawn, where two Secret Service agents were walking a blond staffer— he looked like all the other young aides—down toward the southeast security gate.

"Who's that?" Minnie asked.

The President of the United States stared and lied again. "Nobody important."

118

I know they want to throw me out.

They want to grab me by the nape of my neck and heave me into the trash, like they do in old comic strips.

But as the two Secret Service agents walk me down the paved path that borders the South Lawn, I stay two steps ahead of them. Still, I feel how close they are behind me.

"Taxis won't stop here," the agent with the round nose says as we reach the black metal pedestrian gate and wait for it to open. "Go down a block. You'll be better off."

"Thanks," I say without looking back at them.

From the security shed on my right, the female uniformed agent never takes her eyes off me. She pushes a button and a magnetic lock pops.

"Have a safe night," the agent with the round nose adds, patting me on the back and nearly knocking me through the metal gate as it swings open. Even for the Secret Service, he's far too physical. "Hope you enjoyed your visit to the White House."

As I rush outside, the gate bites shut, and I fight the cold by stuffing my hands in my pockets. To my surprise, my right pocket's not empty. There's a sheet of paper—feels like a business card—waiting for me.

I pull it out. It's not a business card. It's blank. Except for the handwritten note that says:

> *15th and F.*
> *Taxi will be waiting.*

I glance over my shoulder at the agent with the round nose. His back is already turned to me as he follows his partner back to the mansion. He doesn't turn around.

But I know he wrote that note.

I look down, rereading it again: 15th and F Street. Just around the corner.

Confused, but also curious, I start with a walk, which quickly becomes a speedwalk, which—the closer I get to 15th Street—quickly becomes a full-out run.

As I turn the corner, I'm shoved hard by the wind tunnel that runs along the long side of the Treasury building. At this hour, the street is empty. Except for the one car that's parked illegally, waiting for me.

It doesn't look like a cab.

In fact, as I count the four bright headlights instead of the usual two, I know who it is—even without noticing the car's front grille, where the chrome horse is in mid-gallop.

It's definitely not a cab.

It's a Mustang.

I take a few steps toward the pale blue car. The passenger window is already rolled down, giving me a clear view of Tot, who has to be freezing as he sits so calmly inside. He ducks down to see me better. Even his bad eye is filled with fatherly concern.

Just the sight of him makes it hard for me to stand. I shake my head, shooting him a silent plea and begging him not to say *I told you so*.

Of course, he listens. From the start, he's been the only one.

"It'll be okay," he finally offers.

"You sure?" I ask him.

He doesn't answer. He just leans across the passenger seat and opens the door. "C'mon, let's get you home."

119

Fourteen years ago
Sagamore, Wisconsin

*B*eecher...*customer at buyback!*" Mr. Farris shouted from the back office of the secondhand bookshop.

At sixteen years old, Beecher had no problem darting up the aisles, past the overstuffed shelves that were packed with old paperbacks. The only thing that slowed him down was when he saw who was waiting for him at the register.

He knew her from behind—from just the sight of her long black hair.

He'd know her anywhere.

Clementine.

Ducking underneath the drawbridge counter and sliding to a stop behind the register, Beecher worked hard to keep it cool. "Clementine...Hey."

"I didn't know you worked here," she offered.

"Yeah. I'm Beecher," he said, pointing to himself.

"I know your name, Beecher."

"Yeah...no...that's great," he replied, praying better words would come. "So you got stuff for us?" he added, motioning to the blue milk crate that she had lugged inside and that now sat by her feet.

"I heard you guys pay fifty cents for old records and CDs."

"Fifty cents for records. Fifty cents for paperbacks. And a full dollar if it's a new hardcover—though he'll pay a lot if you've got the '69 Bee Gees *Odessa* album with the original foldout artwork."

"I don't have the Bee Gees," she said. "I just have these..."

From the milk crate, she pulled out half a dozen copies of the CD with her mom's photo on it: *Penny Maxwell's Greatest Hits.*

Beecher knew the rules. He could buy back anything he wanted—as long as the store didn't already have too many copies.

Two hours ago, Clementine's mom came in and told Mr. Farris that her family was moving to Detroit for her singing career and could they please buy back a few dozen of her CDs to raise some much-needed cash. Of course, Mr. Farris obliged. Farris always obliged, which was why the store's front window still had a crack in it and the air conditioning would never be fixed. So as Beecher looked across the counter at Clementine's exact same offerings...

"We can definitely use a few extra copies," he finally said.

"Really? You sure?"

"Absolutely. I've listened to them. Your mom's got a real voice. Like early Dinah Washington, but softer and with better range—and of course without the horrendous drug overdose."

Clementine couldn't help but grin. "I know you already bought my mom's copies—and you're stuck with those."

"And we have thirty copies of *To Kill a Mockingbird*. But each new school year, we sell every damn one."

Cocking her head, Clementine took a long silent look across the counter. It was the kind of look that came with its own internal calculation. "You're not a jackass like everyone else."

"Not true," Beecher said, motioning to the milk crate. "I'm just buttering you up so I can lowball you on that *Frankenstein* paperback you've got there. That's a British edition. I can get big bucks for it. Now what else you got?"

Lifting the crate, Clementine dumped and filled the counter with at least twenty other paperbacks, a few hardbacks, and a pile of used CDs including Boyz II Men, Wilson Phillips, and Color Me Badd.

"I also got this..." Clementine said, pulling out a frayed blue leather book with a heavily worn spine, torn, soiled pages, and a shredded silk ribbon bookmark. "It's not in good shape, but... it's for sure old—1970."

Tilting his head, Beecher read the gold lettering on the spine. *One Hundred Years of Solitude* by Gabriel García Márquez. "Good book. This your mom's?"

"My mom hates to read. I think it's my grandmother's. Oh, and there's one other problem...the cover is..." She flipped the leather book over, revealing that it was missing its front cover.

"Y'know the pages still stay together," Beecher pointed out.

"Huh?"

"The pages...*look*..." he said, lifting the book by its remaining cover and dangling it in the air so all the pages spread out like a fan. "If the binding's good, all the pages stay in place."

"That some sorta used bookstore trick?"

"Actually, it's from my mom. When my dad...when he passed...Reverend Lurie told her that even when one cover gets torn away from a book, as long as the other cover's there, it'll still hold the pages together. For me and my sisters...he said my mom was the other cover. And we were the pages."

Clementine stood there silently, staring down at the old blue leather book.

"He was trying to make an analogy about life," Beecher pointed out.

"I get it," Clementine said, still studying the old volume. She was quiet for nearly a minute, resting her left elbow on the counter. Within a decade, that elbow would be covered with deep white scars from an incident she'd never tell the truth about.

"You think this copy could've belonged to my dad?" she finally asked.

Beecher shrugged. "Or it can just be a book."

Clementine looked up and offered another grin at

Beecher. Her widest one yet. "Y'know, my mom and I are moving to Detroit."

"I heard."

"Still...we should really stay in touch."

"Yeah. Great. I'd like that," Beecher said, feeling the excitement tighten his chest—especially as he saw Clementine reach out and slide the leather copy of Márquez's masterpiece back into her milk crate. "Let me give you my email address," he said.

"Email?"

"It's this thing...it's new and— Actually, it's stupid. No one'll use it." Grabbing one of the small squares of paper that Mr. Farris would make by cutting up used, discarded sheets, Beecher quickly scribbled his mailing address and phone number. Clementine did the same.

As they exchanged sheets, Beecher did a quick tallying of her buybacks and paid out a grand total of thirty-two dollars (rounding up the last fifty cents).

"Make sure you look me up if you ever get to Michigan," Clementine called out as she headed for the door.

"You do the same when you come back here and visit," he called back.

And with twin genuine smiles on their faces, Beecher and Clementine waved goodbye, knowing full well they'd never see each other again.

120

One week from now
Chatham, Ontario

Would you like to order, ma'am—or are you waiting for one more?" the waiter asked, leaning in to avoid embarrassment.

"I'm by myself," the woman in the stylish chocolate brown overcoat replied as she again scanned the entrance to the outdoor café, which was overdecorated to look like an old Tudor-style shop from an English village square. Just outside the metal railing, as it'd been for the past twenty minutes, the only people around were the lunchtime pedestrians passing along King Street. Next to her table, the heating lamp was on full blast. It was January. In Canada. Far too cold for anyone to be sitting outside.

But for the woman in the chocolate brown overcoat, that was the point.

She could've come somewhere private.

A nearby hotel.

St. Andrew's Church.

Instead, she came to the café.

Outside. In public. Where everyone could see her.

"How're the fish cakes?" she asked, making prolonged eye contact with the waiter just to see if he'd recognize her.

He didn't.

Of course he didn't.

Her hair was long now. And blonde. But to anyone who knew her, there was no mistaking that grin.

Just like her father's.

"Unless you have something even better than that," Clementine Kaye said, pulling a breadstick from the basket and turning her head just enough so the pedestrians could see her.

"I think you'll like the fish cakes," the waiter replied, scribbling down the order.

As another wave of locals strolled past the café, Clementine threw a quick smile to a five-year-old girl who was walking with her mom.

Even in a week, it had gotten easier. Sure, her leg still hurt from the shooting, and her wanted-for-questioning photo was still posted across the Internet, but it was still the Internet. The world was already moving on.

Which meant she could get back to what really mattered.

Lifting her menu off the table and handing it back to the waiter, Clementine looked down at the thick manila envelope. As the waiter left, she pulled out a water-stained file folder with a familiar name typed in the upper corner. *Wallace, Orson.*

This was it: the unprocessed file that Beecher had tracked to the cave's underground storage area—the original records from the night twenty-six years ago when they brought Eightball into the hospital, and the future President of the United States was treated for his broken finger. As best as Clementine could figure, this was the only proof that the future President was there that night.

But it paled next to the one priceless detail that Clementine never anticipated finding. Indeed, even with what she now knew about the Plumbers, none of it compared to the two-hundred-year-old spy network that'd been operating since the birth of the United States:

The Culper Ring.

Clementine knew all about the Culper Ring.

Including at least one person who was in it.

Above her, the heat lamp sizzled with a fresh burst of warmth. Clementine barely noticed as she looked out at the Chatham police car that pulled up along King Street.

At the traffic light, the car slowed down. The officer in the passenger seat didn't look at her. Didn't even see her.

But as the light blinked green and the car took off, Clementine reminded herself that there were hazards in rushing blindly.

Sure, she could go public now. She could put Tot and the Culper Ring on the front page of every newspaper and website, and then sit back and watch the world take President Wallace and Tot and toss them all in the shredder.

But that wouldn't get Clementine what she was really after.

For so long now, she had told herself this was about her father. And it was. It always was.

But it was also about her.

And so, after nearly three decades of wondering, years of searching, six months of planning, and the next few months of healing, Clementine Kaye sat back in her seat and—in a small town in Canada, under a baking heat lamp—started thinking exactly how she'd finally get the answers she wanted.

Beecher had taught her the benefits of patience.

The Culper Ring had taught her the benefits of secrecy.

But from here on in, it was no different than when she grabbed that jump rope and leapt onto Vincent Paglinni's back in the schoolyard all those years ago.

Even the hardest fights in life become easy when you have the element of surprise.

121

Washington, D.C.

There's a double tap of a car horn, honking from outside.

Every morning for the past week, I've ignored it. Just like I ignored the calls and the texts and the knocks on the door. Instead, I stared at my computer, searching through the lack of press and trying to lose myself in a few cutthroat eBay battles over photo postcards of a 1902 pub in Dublin as well as a rare collection of World War I battleships.

It doesn't help like it used to.

Grabbing my dad's soft leather briefcase and threading my arms into my winter coat, I head through the living room and pull open the front door.

Of course, he's still waiting. He knew I'd eventually wear down.

To his credit, as I tug open the door of the powder blue Mustang and crawl inside, he doesn't ask me how I am. Tot already knows.

He's seen the President's rising poll numbers. In fact, as the car takes off up the block, Tot doesn't try to cheer me up, or put on the radio, or try to distract me. It's not until we get all the way to Rock Creek Park that he says the only thing he needs to...

"I was worried about you, Beecher."

When I don't reply, he adds, "I heard they finally released Dallas's and Palmiotti's bodies."

I nod from the passenger seat, staring straight ahead.

"And the barber's," he says, turning the steering wheel with just his wrists. The car rumbles its usual rumble as we veer onto Constitution Avenue. "Though there's still no sign of Clementine."

I nod again.

"Which I guess means you still have no proof," Tot says.

"I'm well aware."

"And with no proof, you got nothin'."

"Tot, who taught you how to give a welcome-back talk? The Great Santini?"

"If it makes you feel better, while you've been playing hermit and answering all the FBI and Secret Service questions, I spoke to Orlando's wife. I know it doesn't help much...or bring him back...but—" His voice goes quiet. "They did get some closure from knowing who did this to him."

I try to tell myself that's true. But it's not.

"The only thing I don't understand is: On that night you came back from the caves, why'd he bring you to the White House, Beecher? I know you said it was to ask you to join the Plumbers, but think about it: What was the real point of that meeting with the President that night?"

"You mean besides reminding me what'll happen to my life if I open my mouth? I gave this great macho-y speech, but the truth is, he knew how it'd play out. He was just rubbing it in."

"Not a chance," Tot says, asking it again. "Why'd he bring you to the White House?"

"You do realize we lost, right? So if this is you being rhetorical—"

"Ask yourself, Beecher. Why'd he bring you to the White House?"

"I have no idea! To scare me?"

"Damn right to scare you! That's why he wanted to invite you in—that's all it was about: to scare you," Tot confirms, his beard swaying as he cocks his head. "And y'know the only reason why someone tries to scare you? Because he's *worried* about you. *He's* the one scared of *you*!"

"Then he's a bigger moron than we thought. Because for the past week, I've been racking my brain, trying to think of other places we can find proof, or a witness, or anything else about what happened that night. And believe me, I'll keep trying. I'll dig as long as it takes. But when it comes to being the Ghost of Christmas Past, it's not as easy as you think."

"That's not the ghost he's worried about."

"Come again?"

"Think of what you just said. When that first ghost comes to visit Ebenezer Scrooge...the Ghost of Christmas Past is the one that *fails*. The Ghost of Christmas Present—he fails too. But the ghost that actually gets the job done—the one that does the most damage—that's the Ghost from what's Yet to Come."

"Are you trying to make a really nice metaphor about history or the future? Because if you are—"

"Life isn't metaphor, Beecher. History isn't metaphor. It's just life."

I stare out the front of the car, looking down Constitution Avenue. The Washington Monument is all the way down, but from the angle we're at, thanks to the trees and the lightposts on our right, it's a completely obscured view. A horrible view. Just like that night at the Jefferson Memorial.

It's not metaphor. It's just a fact.

"Beecher, you've spent all this time fighting alone. You don't have to. If you want, we can help you find Clementine."

"It's not just her, Tot. What she said…about my father…She said he didn't die, and that maybe I have cancer. But if he's alive…"

"What she said was complete manure designed to manipulate and take advantage of an emotionally vulnerable moment. But we can find the truth. If he's alive, we'll find him. Same with the cancer. We can help you find all of it. And if we do it together—and we do it right—I promise you, you'll have the chance to make sure that every loathsome bastard—including the one in that big White House—pays for every ounce of pain they caused," Tot says, his voice finding speed. "You thought finding that old dictionary was when history chose you. That wasn't the moment. *This* is. The only question is— and it's a simple question: They think they won the war with you. Are you ready to declare war back?"

"I thought your Culper Ring worked *for* the President?"

"We work for the *Presidency*. And that Presidency has now been corrupted. So. Are you ready to declare war back?"

He called it a simple question. It's not simple. But it is easy. I look right at him. "Tot, are you asking me to join the Culper Ring?"

I wait for him to turn away and stare out the front window. He looks me right in the eye. "It's not for everyone."

"You're serious? This is real?"

"Some days you get peanuts; some days you get shells. This is a peanut day."

"And that Secret Service guy who walked me out of the White House and slipped me that note that you were waiting for me...He's a peanut too?"

"Some people are with us. Some people owe us a favor. We're a small group. Smaller than you think. And we've survived for only one reason: We pick our own replacements. I'm seventy-two years old, and...what you went through these past weeks...They know you're ready. Though if it makes any difference, I thought you've been ready for years."

With a twist of a knob, the radio hiccups to life and the car is filled with the sounds of Kenny Rogers singing "The Gambler."

"'The Gambler'?" I ask. "That's what you had cued up? You were trying to make this a little moment, weren't you?"

"Beecher, it's a moment even without the music."

I let the country twang of Kenny Rogers flow over me as a small grin lifts my cheeks. He may be right.

With a hard punch of the gas, the engine clears its throat and we cruise past the White House on our left.

"I won't let you down, Tot."

"I know, Beecher," he says without looking at me. "I'm just glad you finally know too."

Straight ahead, the morning sun is so bright I can't see a thing in front of me. It feels fantastic.

"So where are we going?" I ask as we reach 9th Street and Tot blows through the turn. He keeps heading straight on Constitution. On most mornings, he makes a left.

"Where do you think I'm going?" Tot asks as the car picks up speed and we leave the White House behind. "Now that we finally got you in the Culper Ring, well…don't you want to meet the others?"

When Beecher White makes a shocking discovery on the White House grounds, he unearths a deadly conspiracy that may shatter his own past—and the country's future…

Please see the next page
for a preview of

The President's Shadow.

PROLOGUE

Every President has secrets. So does every First Lady.

Today, Shona Wallace was deep into her favorite secret as she knelt in the damp dirt, hiding behind the crabapple trees in the White House Rose Garden. On this cold March morning, she didn't have to look for the cameras. She knew where they were. For now at least, no one was watching.

During the day, just a few steps outside the Oval Office, the garden was used for presidential press conferences and greeting visiting dignitaries. But now—at 5:30 a.m.—the outdoor garden was dark. Desolate. As if the First Lady were the last person left on the planet.

And really, wasn't that the point?

Plunging her fingers into the dirt, Shona took a deep breath, letting the smell of fresh mulch transport her back to those days right after college when she and the President lived in that little yellow rental house in

Michigan with the bad toilets and the narrow garden that flooded with every rain. Two weeks after moving in, she got the news that her mother had died. The garden saved her then. She cared for it, and it blossomed: Her matchless burgundy dahlias, which she used to wear in her hair. Three kinds of tomatoes. When they were running for governor, she dug up two hundred tulip bulbs from her mother's garden and planted them in her own.

Even when your mother's gone, and your husband's working so hard he only comes home to sleep, you can count on your garden. You plant it; it sprouts; life blooms. That's not some cheap metaphor for life; it's a basis for sanity. Everyone needs something they can count on, a world they can own all themselves.

"*Dammit!*" the First Lady muttered, down on her knees and tugging with her bare hands on a buried tree root. The root was heading toward her precious bed of English bluebells, set to bloom this spring and perfect for cutting.

Even before Orson's Presidency started, Shona had known she'd need a garden. During the campaign she'd felt the burn that came with the spotlight of public life. And she'd had it all planned. On her very first night in the White House, she had sought out a little patch of land among the flowerbeds of the Rose Garden. It would be her ground. Her sanity.

Telling only the Secret Service, she'd slipped outside at five in the morning, knelt down in the dark, and planted the seeds of coral bells and morning glories. Many of the seeds came from her grandparents' flowerbed by way of her mother's. Shona had even grown early spring flowers in college, in an inconspicuous patch of ground she commandeered behind the dorm. She'd planted more flowers, even some vegetables, when she and Orson lived in that old rental house, and even later when they were in the governor's mansion. Would she stop now, when she needed it most?

Please.

She never told reporters she was a gardener or tried to use it for political gain. Somehow that would ruin the purpose. No matter where life took her, or what her critics said (they had ripped her apart for gaining weight during the first year of her husband's Presidency: "the freshman-fifteen First Lady"), here was the one patch on the entire planet where Shona Wallace, wife of the President, could run things just the way she wanted to.

"*Gotcha...!*" the First Lady whispered, gripping the buried tree root and pulling hard. God, the cold March dirt felt good. And it smelled so fresh, full of promise. Winter had put so much on hold; she loved getting back to work in the earth. With a sharp tug, the root began to yield, though not by much.

Leaning on her left elbow and probing blindly into the dirt, the First Lady felt—

Tunk.

Something solid. Not a rock. The root felt weird—almost soft. Spongy. She turned and pulled a penlight from her tool kit, shining it into the hole and squinting down to see what was in there. Under the dirt it looked light gray, but as she pulled it closer, it was greenish blue, with a tint of pink. Like skin.

A hiccup erupted from her throat. The spongy root had—Those weren't branches. It had fingers. Four fingers. Squeezed in a fist...An arm...*Oh God!* Someone was buried in—

Stifling a scream, the First Lady dropped the penlight, which fell into the hole. She jumped back, scrambling, crabwalking away from the pit. The press and early staff would be here any minute. Her body was shaking. *Just don't scream.*

"Orson..." she whispered, stumbling toward the West Colonnade of the pristine white mansion. She was gagging and sobbing uncontrollably.

In the Rose Garden, the penlight still rested in the open hole, shining its little spotlight on a dirt-encrusted hand.

1

Each morning the nurses watched him.

At 5:45 a.m. they'd see him step through the hospital's sliding doors. By 5:50 a.m. he'd be up among the mechanical beeps and hisses of the ICU. And by 5:55 a.m. the young man with the boyish looks and sandy hair would approach the nurses' station, dropping off that day's breakfast: doughnuts, bagels, sometimes a dozen muffins.

The nurses never made requests for food, but over time the young man had learned that Nurse Tammy liked a pumpernickel bagel with a thin slice of tomato, and that Nurse Steven preferred Asiago cheese. Over these past three weeks of hospital visits, they'd gotten to know him too. Beecher White.

"How's he doing?" Beecher would ask as he presented his breakfast offering to the hospital gods.

"Same," the nurses would say on most days, offering kindly smiles and pointing him to Room 355.

The dim room was sealed by sliding glass doors, frosted at the bottom and transparent at the top. For an instant Beecher paused. The nurses saw it all the time, family and friends picking out which brave face they'd wear that day.

Through the glass was a seventy-two-year-old man with an uneven beard lying unconscious in bed, an accordion breathing tube in his windpipe, a feeding tube snaking through his nose and down into his belly.

"Okay, who's ready for some easy-listening country music from the seventies, eighties, and today?" Beecher announced, sliding the door open and stepping into the room.

Aristotle "Tot" Westman lay there, eyes closed. His skin was so gray he looked like a corpse. His palms faced upward, as if he were pleading for death.

"Rise and shine, old man! It's me! It's *Beecher*! Can you hear me!?" he added.

Tot didn't move. His mouth sagged open like an ashtray.

"TOT, BLINK IF YOU HEAR ME!" Beecher said, circling to the far side of the hospital bed and eyeing the pale purple scar that curved down the side of Tot's head like a parenthesis. When Tot was first wounded and fragments of the bullet plowed through the frontal region of his brain, the doctors said it was a miracle he was alive. Whether he was lucky to be alive was another question.

Three weeks ago, during surgery, they shaved off half of Tot's long silver hair, leaving him looking like a baseball with yarn sprouting from it. To even it out, Beecher had asked the nurses to do a full buzz cut. Now the hair was slowly growing back. A sign of life.

"You're still mad about the hair, aren't you?" Beecher

said, pulling an old black iPod from his pocket and switching it with the silver iPod in the sound dock on the nearby rolling cart.

"Wait till you hear this one," he went on, clicking the iPod into place.

Tot's only response was the heavy in-and-out hiss from his ventilator. In truth, Tot should've been in a rehab facility instead of the hospital, but according to the nurses, someone from the White House had made a special request.

"I brought the Gambler himself," Beecher added, hitting *play* on the iPod as a crowd started to cheer and guitars began to strum. "Kenny Rogers, live from Manchester, Tennessee, then another from the Hollywood Bowl, and a 1984 private corporate concert that cost me a good part of this month's rent," Beecher said, taking his usual seat next to Tot's bed. One of the doctors had said that familiar music could be helpful to patients with brain injuries.

"Tot, I need you to squeeze my hand," Beecher added, pressing his hand into Tot's open palm.

Tot didn't squeeze back. His ventilator coughed out another heavy in-and-out hiss.

"C'mon, Tot, you know what today is. It's a big one for me. Just give me a little something… *anything*," Beecher pleaded as Kenny Rogers began belting out the first verse of "Islands in the Stream."

"By the way, Verona from Human Resources? She said if you wake up and come back to work, she'll wear that tight black sweater she wore to the Christmas party. In fact, she's here right now. In the sweater. You don't want to miss this."

Huh-hssss.

"Okay, Tot, you're leaving me no choice," Beecher said. From his pocket he pulled out a ballpoint pen, then turned Tot's hand palm-down and pressed the tip of the pen into Tot's nail bed.

At the sharp pain, Tot pulled his hand back.

In neurological terms it was called *withdrawal*. According to the neurologist, as long as Tot responded to painful stimuli—like a sharp pinch or a poke with a pen—his brain was still working.

"It's good news," the doctor had promised. "It means your friend's still in there somewhere."

Somewhere.

"C'mon, you chatty bastard—don't ruin my big day. I'm not celebrating alone," Beecher said, again pressing the pen into his mentor's nail bed. As the skin below the nail turned white, Tot again pulled away, but this time... A nurse saw it from the hallway. Tot's head moved sideways, as if he was about to say something.

Beecher shot up in his chair. "*Tot...?* Tot, are you—?"

Tot's head sagged down, a string of drool falling from his bottom lip into his beard as Kenny Rogers—accompanied by Dolly Parton—continued to sing.

Slumping back in his seat, Beecher let go of Tot's cold hand. A swell of tears took his eyes.

"It'll happen. Give him time," a female voice said softly.

Beecher glanced toward the sliding glass door. It

was the nurse with the crooked teeth, the one who liked pumpernickel.

"It's a brain injury. It doesn't heal overnight," she added.

"I know. I just wish he could—" Beecher stopped himself and swallowed hard.

"He's fortunate to have you," the nurse said.

"*I'm* fortunate to have *him*," Beecher replied, standing up from his seat and wiping his eyes. He turned to the body in the bed. "Tot, you get some rest. I know you're tired," he added, leaning in and giving his mentor a gentle kiss on the forehead. "By the way," he whispered into Tot's ear, "if you're good, I'll bring you a photo of Verona in the black sweater."

"If it helps, happy birthday," the nurse called out as Beecher headed for the door.

"How'd you know?"

The nurse shrugged. "I've been doing this for fifteen years. Heard you say it was a big day."

Nodding a thank-you and heading out to the hallway, Beecher glanced over at what bagels were still uneaten at the nurses' station.

Each morning the nurses watched Beecher.

Each morning Beecher watched Tot.

But each morning, Beecher and the nurses weren't the only ones keeping tabs.

Diagonally across the hallway, peering through the open door of the visitors' lounge, the bald man known as Ezra eyed Beecher as he trudged down the hallway toward the elevators.

Ten days ago Ezra had come to the hospital searching for the old man known as Tot. He knew Tot's history. He knew what Tot had done all those years ago. And he knew that with a bit of patience and a side order of good luck, he'd find out everything else he needed just by sitting in this waiting room and studying who else came to Tot's bedside.

A few of Tot's coworkers had visited. There was an old lady who came every few nights and stroked Tot's arm. But more than anyone else, there was the archivist. Beecher.

At the National Archives, Beecher was Tot's protégé and best friend. In a way he was also Tot's family. And based on what Ezra had heard thanks to the nightlight-shaped microphone that he had plugged into the wall socket next to Tot's bed, Beecher was most certainly a member of the Culper Ring.

"Want a bagel?" one of the nurses called out as she passed the visitors' room. "We've got plenty."

"I shouldn't," Ezra said, his slitted eyes curving into a grin. "I've got a big day ahead of me."

2

There are stories no one knows. Hidden stories.

I love those stories. And since I work in the National Archives, I find them for a living. Most of them are family stories. This one is too. But as I once learned in a novel, it's time for me to admit that when you say you're looking for your family, what you're really searching for is yourself.

"I see it on your face, Beecher. This is bad news, isn't it?" Franklin Oeming asks, trying hard to look unnerved. In his mid-forties, Oeming's got a thin face that's made even thinner by narrow wire-rimmed glasses and a long Civil War–style goatee. He's a smart guy whose specialty is declassification. That means he spends every day combing through redacted, top-secret documents and reading beneath the black tape. It also means he specializes in people's secrets. He thinks he knows mine. But he has no idea why I'm really here.

"Just tell me how he's doing," Oeming adds.

"Same as before," I say as I slide both hands into the front pockets of the dark blue lab coat that all of us archivists wear.

He studies every syllable, smelling a rat. Even though he's in a suit, Oeming's wearing an awful Texas-shaped belt buckle that displays the words *Planet Texas* in block letters. I have a matching one at home. They were old Christmas gifts from the mentor we share, Tot Westman, who gave them to us as an homage to Kenny Rogers. We thought they were gag gifts. To Tot they weren't. "Planet Texas" is Tot's favorite underrated Kenny Rogers song.

Needless to say, neither of us ever wore the belt buckles…until three weeks ago, when Tot was shot in the head and left in a coma. For luck or superstition, Oeming's been wearing his since. I've been carrying mine in my briefcase.

"Beecher, I know you're at the hospital every day. If the doctors say he's getting worse—"

"He's not getting worse. He's the same. Last week a nurse said he moved two fingers on his left hand. His right pinky too."

Oeming watches me carefully. For three weeks now, I've sent him daily updates by email. So for me to suddenly show up on the fifth floor and see him in person…

"This isn't about Tot, is it?" he asks.

I run my hand over the back of my recently buzzed hair, but I don't answer.

"Why're you really here, Beecher?"

He puts enough emphasis on my name that just outside his office, I can hear a few employees in cubicles start closing files and covering papers on their desks. Oeming takes a step back toward his own desk and does the same.

Five floors below us, the National Archives is home to original copies of the Declaration of Independence, the U.S. Constitution, and twelve billion other pages of history, including Lincoln's preliminary drafts of the Emancipation Proclamation, the actual check that we used to purchase Alaska, and even a letter written by a twelve-year-old Fidel Castro to FDR, asking for ten dollars. If the government had a hand in it, we collect it, including the downed weather balloon that people thought was a wrecked flying saucer outside of Roswell, New Mexico. But as with that weather balloon, which was classified for decades, when you store America's *history*, you also get America's *secrets*.

And as I said, secrets are Franklin Oeming's specialty.

"I actually need your help with something," I tell him, offering a grin.

He doesn't grin back. "What kind of help?"

"I need a file."

Oeming is a second-generation archivist. His mom used to work in the LBJ Library in Austin, and he grew up playing in the stacks and pulling rusty staples from important documents. That makes him more of a stickler than most, which around here is saying something. "You mind taking a walk?" he says, tilting his head toward the door.

Before I can answer, he's out of his office, weaving around the cubicles and heading out to the Archives' marble(?)-lined hallway. Every person in a nearby cubicle is now staring my way. By the time I join him in the hallway, Oeming's on my left, swiping a security card at a set of locked double doors. As I follow him farther down the hallway, he points to a set of square metal lockers, each one the size of a small safe-deposit box.

I know the rules. Taking my cell phone from my pocket, I slide it inside one of the lockers, slap the small door shut, and take the orange key. He's not talking until he's sure no one's listening. I don't blame him. But if he's taking me *here*—to the true inner sanctum of fifth-floor secrecy—either things are looking up, or I've got a bigger problem than I thought.

Let's go, he motions, pointing me to the end of the hallway and stopping at our destination: Room 509. It looks like any other room, except for the thick steel door that resembles a bank vault's.

Oeming swipes his ID through an even more high-tech scanner, then punches in a push-button PIN code, which lets out a low *wunk* as the lock unclenches and the door to this giant safe pops open. In the Archives we have SCIFs—secure areas to read classified files—all over the building. We also have Treasure Vaults on nearly every floor. None of them hold what we keep in here.

Inside, it looks like any other fancy conference room: long oval mahogany table surrounded by two dozen black-and-tan leather chairs. On the walls are original posters from World War II, including a navy poster that reads *Button Your Lip* and another that reads *Silence Means Security*. It's not just décor. They mean it.

"Watch your hands," Oeming snaps, sounding annoyed as the automatic door with nonremovable hinges locks us inside. As the door slams, my ears pop. This room isn't just soundproof; it's airtight. The concrete walls are double the normal thickness and lined with foil and steel to stop eavesdropping, while the ductwork, telephone, and electrical systems are all on their own dedicated grids to do the same.

Around the Archives, this is the home of Ice Cap. The official acronym is ISCAP, which stands for Interagency Security Classification Appeals Panel, which means every other Tuesday, in this fifth-floor vault, some of the highest-level thinkers in the U.S. government come together and take a biweekly vote on which classified documents will get released to the public.

Set in motion by Richard Nixon of all people, Ice Cap has released thousands of blacked-out files, from Cold War presidential briefings to My Lai massacre details to top-secret reports of Soviet nukes. For the American people, it adds trust and transparency. But for the archivists who wade though the documents and read what's below the black tape, it adds a whole office of people who have access to what's otherwise top secret and off-limits.

"Beecher, how could you put me in that position?" Oeming asks, circling around to the far side of the table.

"Listen, before you lose your cool—"

"My cool is *lost*! Are you even listening to what you're doing? You're asking me to break the law."

"That's not true."

"It most certainly *is* true. If you had a high enough security clearance, you'd get the file yourself. But if you're asking me to get it for you—"

"Will you just stop? I'm not asking for myself. This isn't for *me*. It's for the Archivist."

He stops when I mention the boss. Our big boss. The Archivist of the United States. "You're telling me Ferriero asked for this?"

"He did. Call him," I challenge. "I told him I was coming up here. He asked me to do him a favor."

Back when I first met Oeming, I remember him telling me that when it came to classified information, the only files that had ever haunted him were the ones about the government secretly abducting people who wouldn't be missed—the elderly and homeless—and the human radiation tests that they were subjected to. Oeming said he was sick to his stomach that day. He looks about the same now.

"Beecher, y'know whose chair you're touching?" he asks, pointing to the high-backed chair near the head of the table. "When we vote, that's where the CIA sits. The chair next to that belongs to DoD, representing our entire military and the Pentagon. On the other side, you've got the State Department. Then the NSA. Then the Director of National Intelligence," he adds, pointing out each chair one by one. "The only bad seat in the room belongs to the Justice Department," he adds, motioning to a chair by the door. "And y'know why that's the bad seat?"

"Because it's closest to the door," I say.

"That's exactly right. You have to move every time someone wants to go in or out. And y'know why the Justice Department gets that bad seat?"

"I understand you're trying to make this analogy work—"

"It's because they always want personal favors," Oeming says coldly, pressing his fingertips down on the table. "Everyone else—CIA, DoD, NSA—they all understand how the process works. But Justice, with all its lawyers, always wants to know if we can make a special exception. So once again, Beecher, what's the real story behind this file? And don't tell me it's for the Archivist, because I was in Ferriero's office this morning, and if there was anything he needed, he would've asked me himself."

I take my hands off the back of the chair. "I wouldn't ask if this wasn't an important one."

"So it's work-related?"

I shake my head. "It's personal."

"Is it for Tot?" he adds with enough concern that I start to wonder if he knows our real secret: that three months ago, Tot recruited me to become a member of the secret society known as the Culper Ring. The Ring dates back over two hundred years and was originally founded by George Washington.

I know. It still sounds insane to me too.

Back during the Revolutionary War, Washington created his own private spy ring to help him move information among his troops and beat the British. It worked so well that after he won the war, Washington kept the Ring around to protect the Presidency. To this day the Ring still exists, and now I'm a part of it. Sounds sexy, right? I thought so too—until Tot was shot in the head and I figured out that the Culper Ring has been whittled down to barely half a dozen members. Tot chose me to help rebuild it. But right now that's the least of my worries.

"This isn't about Tot," I tell Oeming.

"So if it's not Tot, how much more personal can you—?"

"It's about my father," I blurt.

Oeming's eyes narrow, but not by much. "That's still about Tot, though, isn't it? With him in the hospital, and you all alone, well…looking for some info about your father would—"

"It's not about being alone," I tell him, finally realizing that the tone I hear in his voice isn't anger. It's concern. Franklin may be a second-generation archivist, but he's a first-class good person. He doesn't have a ruthless bone in him, which probably explains why Tot never picked him for the Culper Ring. "Listen," I tell him, "I'm sorry for lying to you."

"I don't blame you, Beecher. I'd lie for *my* dad. Hell, I might even lie for Tot."

"No, you wouldn't."

"You're right. I wouldn't," he says, forcing an awkward laugh and looking down.

I pretend to laugh along with him.

"Y'know, Beecher, when you first started at the Archives and Tot started mentoring you, I was so jealous. Those first years he mentored me were some of the best of my life."

"That's funny, because every time I see him talking with you, I feel like you're that firstborn child I can never measure up to."

We both stand there a moment, the giant table between us. He finally looks up.

"Franklin, my entire life... going back to my very first memories...I was told my dad was a mechanic in the army—that he died when I was a baby, in a car crash on a bridge," I offer, my voice hitching on the words. "Last month, someone gave me proof that there was no bridge... and no car accident. They showed me a hand-written letter that he wrote a week after his supposed death. Now I don't know which story is true."

Anyone else would cock an eyebrow or ask how that's possible, but Oeming spends every day reading the secrets that people keep from each other, including their families.

"You think your dad's still alive?"

"No. I actually don't. But what keeps me turning at night is this one thought: You don't cover up someone's death unless there's a reason to cover it up," I explain. "Pretend it was your own dead father. Before he died, this is the story he couldn't tell you. The bosses at his job said he tripped and took a bad tumble. Then you find out he might've been pushed."

"I assume you've searched through everything at Archives II?" he asks, referring to our facility out in College Park, which holds most of our modern military records.

"There, St. Louis, even out in the Boyers caves. I've spent the last month looking for anything that would give me the full story. Then, a few weeks back, I found *this*," I say, pulling a folded sheet of paper from the front pocket of my lab coat. As I unfold it, there's no mistaking the handwritten file citation at the center of the page.

Oeming reads it for himself. "You said your dad was in the army."

"I did."

"This file, though…the record group…it's from a navy file."

I nod. "Didn't make sense to me either. So you tell me: Still think my dad was just a lowly mechanic in the army?"

Oeming doesn't answer. "How'd you even *find* this file?"

"A friend," I say quickly enough that he knows not to ask any more questions. "The person who gave it to me, her dad was in my dad's unit. She was the one who found their real unit name. Apparently they used to call themselves the Plankholders."

Oeming frowns.

"You know this group?"

He looks down at the file number, his hand starting to shake.

"Franklin, if you know something—"

"This is really your father's unit?" he says. "He was a member of the *Plankholders*?"

"Tell me what's going on," I demand. "You've heard of them?"

"Not until yesterday."

"*Yesterday?* What're you—?"

"That's what I'm trying to tell you. This group…the *Plankholders*…When I got into the office yesterday, someone had just asked for this exact same file."

I cock my head, totally lost. "If you—If someone—I

don't understand. Who would possibly want my dad's files?"

At that, Franklin takes a half-step back. He's standing right in front of the World War II poster that reads *Button Your Lip*.

"Beecher...you're not gonna believe it."

3

So your office said today's your birthday," a Greek fiftysomething archivist named Helena says as she angles our navy blue van onto Pennsylvania Avenue.

I nod from the passenger seat, staring out the front window and squinting toward our destination. I could walk if I wanted. But if I plan on pulling this off, the van's my best way in.

"So no big birthday plans?" Helena asks, with no clue as to why I'm tagging along.

"Just the usual," I tell her. "Birthday cake shaped like a book. Strippers dressed like naughty librarians."

"The sad part is, you just described the fantasy of every Archives employee."

"And some women," I add.

"Speaking of, you ever reach out to—"

"I did. I'm going to," I say, knowing who she's talking about. Mina. A fellow archivist I'm friendly with. Helena thinks I should get friendlier, but until Tot's health starts to—

"Please don't tell me you're waiting for Tot to get better. He'd hate that more than anyone," she says, making me wonder if there's anyone in the Archives who doesn't know my business. It's the occupational hazard of working in a building full of researchers. "Beecher, let me pass you the proverbial folded-up note in class…"

"No one passes notes anymore. They text."

"Then I'm texting you," she says, pantomiming a fake phone in her hand. "Mina likes you. Ask her out."

"We went out. We had a good time. It's just her brother was sick and—"

Before I can finish, my phone vibrates in my pocket.

"*You there yet?*" a text asks, popping up on the screen. It says it's coming from our old hometown church in Wisconsin. That tells me who it really is. Marshall Lusk. Also known as a penetration tester who spends his days breaking into buildings and security systems. Also known as one of my oldest childhood friends and the kid who always had nudie magazines in his treehouse. Also known as the one person I'm hoping will help me rebuild the Culper Ring.

Marshall wants no part of it—or pretty much anything. Years ago he was burned and disfigured, leaving his face looking like a melted candle. It also left him with an understandable bitterness and a ruthless streak that means I'm still not sure he's 100 percent trustworthy. But since Marshall's dad apparently served in the same Plankholder unit as mine, he's willing to help. For now. As a result he's the only one who knows where I'm currently going. And who I'm trying to see.

"*Almost there,*" I text back.

Marshall knows what it means. My phone vibrates again, this time with a phone call. It's from a different ten-digit number. I pick it up but never say a word. On the other end of the call, neither does Marshall. But now he's listening. If anything happens, at least there'll be a record of it.

"Y'know, Beecher, even putting Mina aside, I'm just glad you're getting out of the building," Helena adds from the driver's seat, tucking a thick ringlet of graying black hair behind her ear. "I know how hard it's been. I say a prayer for Tot every night."

"I appreciate that. And I appreciate you letting me ride along with—"

The van hits a pothole, sending our cargo in back—half a dozen red plastic collection bins—bouncing through the van. Right now every one of the bins is empty. Not for long.

"See? Even *he* has pothole problems," Helena says with a laugh. In Washington, D.C., there's only one *he* who gets talked about like that, and it's not God.

Helena makes a sharp right, sending the old van bumping and climbing through a set of black metal gates, stopping at a small security shed.

I lean forward in my seat, looking out through the front windshield and finally seeing it: the world's most famous mansion—and the home of the one person who, yesterday, requested the military files that hold information about my dead father.

"Welcome to the White House," a uniformed Secret Service agent says. "Who're you here to see?"

VISIT US ONLINE AT

WWW.HACHETTEBOOKGROUP.COM

FEATURES:

OPENBOOK BROWSE AND
SEARCH EXCERPTS
•
AUDIOBOOK EXCERPTS AND PODCASTS
•
AUTHOR ARTICLES AND INTERVIEWS
•
BESTSELLER AND PUBLISHING
GROUP NEWS
•
SIGN UP FOR E-NEWSLETTERS
•
AUTHOR APPEARANCES AND TOUR
INFORMATION
•
SOCIAL MEDIA FEEDS AND WIDGETS
•
DOWNLOAD FREE APPS

BOOKMARK HACHETTE BOOK GROUP
@ WWW.HACHETTEBOOKGROUP.COM